THE SEVERED TOWER

ALSO BY J. BARTON MITCHELL

Midnight City

THE SEVERED TOWER

A CONQUERED EARTH NOVEL

J. BARTON MITCHELL

THOMAS DUNNE BOOKS
ST. MARTIN'S GRIFFIN
NEW YORK

THOMAS DUNNE BOOKS.
An imprint of St. Martin's Press.

THE SEVERED TOWER. Copyright © 2013 by J. Barton Mitchell. All rights reserved. Printed in the United States of America. For information, address St. Martin's Press, 175 Fifth Avenue, New York, N.Y. 10010.

www.thomasdunnebooks.com
www.stmartins.com

Library of Congress Cataloging-in-Publication Data

Mitchell, J. Barton.
    The Severed Tower : a Conquered Earth novel / J. Barton Mitchell.— First Edition.
        p. cm.—(The Conquered Earth series ; 2)
    ISBN 978-1-250-00947-0 (hardcover)
    ISBN 978-1-250-02070-3 (e-book)
    1. Fantasy fiction.   I.   Title.
  PS3613.I8548S48 2013
  813'.6—dc23

                                                                    2013028724

St. Martin's Griffin books may be purchased for educational, business, or promotional use. For information on bulk purchases, please contact Macmillan Corporate and Premium Sales Department at 1-800-221-7945, extension 5442, or write specialmarkets@macmillan.com.

First Edition: November 2013

10 9 8 7 6 5 4 3 2 1

For Jeff, wherever you are, you are missed.

Our doubts are traitors,
And make us lose the good we oft might win
By fearing to attempt.

—WILLIAM SHAKESPEARE

SHE CROUCHED ON TOP of what was left of the old granary, staring at the strange contradictions of the landscape, everything dark and light at the same time.

The sky was full of thick storm clouds, but it would have been dark without them. This far in, what Freebooters called the Core, midafternoon looked like night, and the only illumination was a sickly shade of yellow that came from the strangely wavering, prismatic sky.

Lightning flashed from the clouds. Bright streaks of red, blue, or green, and whenever it struck, there was a flash of color. Shards of glowing crystals erupted from the ground and froze in place, and the earth was covered with their remnants, a maze of jagged, sharp walls that glowed in various colors.

They filled the remains of what was once a small rural town below, consuming the streets and roads that once ran through its center. The old buildings had fallen in on themselves for the most part, or had been blown to bits by the lightning strikes, but she could see it had been a nice place once. Quaint and quiet.

It was neither of those things now.

More lightning, red this time, illuminated a figure next to her. He was dressed in the same style of black-and-gray. Rugged-looking pants, light boots, tucked-in shirt, a vest with pockets, utility belts crisscrossing his torso. Around both their necks hung woven cloths that could be lifted up to cover nose and mouth. Also on their necks were identical pendants. Two strands of white metallic cord wrapping around each other, with bars in between them, making small spirals—or a double "helix."

On their left hands, each finger wore a ring made of glowing crystal, exactly like the ones that filled the ground, and strapped to their backs were strange weapons. Long, double-tipped spears, almost as tall as the figures themselves, with a glowing crystal at either end, only these had been polished and shaped into razor-sharp spear points and set into rounded, brass casings that snapped into the shaft. Clearly, it was a double-pronged striking weapon, but looking closer revealed other aspects. The base was rounded into mirrored hand grips on each side, with separate gun triggers, as if the weapon could fire the crystal points from either orientation. It was a strange weapon. Ornate and well crafted, elegant even, but dangerous, too.

The man was Asian, older, probably past sixty years old. His eyes, while clear and free of the Tone, were strange. Something was off about them. They were unfocused and clouded white, and never seemed to look anywhere in particular; but there were volumes of wisdom and experience in their depths.

Next to him, the girl was much younger, sixteen or so. Black, somewhat small, but clearly agile and quick, her unkempt hair tied behind her head without any thought to appearance. Her eyes were clear of the Tone as well, but, unlike the old man, she wasn't blind, and she wore one thing he didn't—a pair of pure black goggles on her forehead that could be dropped over her eyes, though it seemed unlikely she could see with them on. Wearing them, she would be just as sightless as the old man.

He stared blindly toward the north. The storm clouds and the darkness obscured the horizon, but, for him, it made no difference. He could *see* neither.

"What are we doing *here?*" she asked. "I thought the point was to attack Polestar."

"Why are you always so eager for violence?" The old man's dead gaze didn't waver. His voice was quiet. As much as she loved him, Gideon had an annoying habit of answering questions with questions.

"I'm not interested in violence," the girl said tightly. "Just action."

"Change comes through patience as much as action," he said. "Stand by the river long enough, and the bodies of your enemies will float past."

"It's no secret I'm not very good at patience, Master."

Gideon smiled. "You are more your father than you care to admit."

The girl felt an angry heat rise within her, but she said nothing. He was right, most likely. Gideon always seemed to be right—but that didn't mean she had to like it.

More lightning flashed nearby, green this time, and strange thunder rolled around them like waves breaking on a beach. The girl rubbed the hair on her arms, flattening it where it stood up. The Charge felt different today. "Feels like another storm."

The old man said nothing. He only nodded.

The girl studied the horizon, but all she could see was the current storm, its thick clouds surrounding them on all sides. The lightning flashed red and blue in the air. "Ion or Antimatter?"

"Neither."

The girl looked at the old man oddly. What other kind of storms were there in the Strange Lands? "Should I pull my Arc back to Sanctum?"

The old man was silent a long time, staring at what lay hidden in the distance. "No," he finally said. "This storm . . . we cannot weather. And it's why I brought you here."

He looked at her now, or at least as much as he could. Gideon's stare always seemed to float just a few inches in the wrong direction. "I have two tasks for you, Avril," he said. "One you will like, and one you will not."

Far away, the storm swirled and parted like a giant curtain, allowing the horizon to burst into view. In the far distance, what was left of the broken buildings of a city rose into the sky, tiny slivers of brightness in all the black. Beyond them, distorted through a churning haze of fog or dust, was a massive shape that hovered over the ruins.

It looked like a giant keep or tower, yet, somehow, suspended in the air. She could see where it was broken near the middle, the top half tearing away from the bottom, detached and falling, yet *frozen* in the sky. The sight chilled her the same as it always did; pure power and fate combined into one, but, still, she couldn't look away from it. She was grateful when the clouds massed again and blocked the dark thing from view, wiping it away behind them as they bellowed inward.

In the air above her, the strange lightning flashed again, distorted thunder rolled. It sounded closer now. As though it was building.

PART ONE

THE STRANGE LANDS

1. RUDE AWAKENING

"MIRA . . ."

The voice was far away. A girl's voice, she could tell. A little girl. And it sounded worried.

"Mira . . ."

She heard other things in her hazy delirium—dull, booming thumps that might have been explosions. Something shattering. And other sounds—strange, distorted and electronic, but familiar enough to stir fear in her.

"*Mira!*"

The cry yanked her painfully out of the dark. Light poured in as her eyes blinked open.

The sky was directly above. It was midafternoon, bright and sunny. Pieces of buildings and other things drifted past—windows, gutters, old billboards she couldn't read, the top of a rusted school bus. It was as though she were floating underneath them all.

Then she figured it out. She was being *carried*. Through some kind of city ruins.

The world shifted again as someone set her down and rested her against something hard and rough. It felt like a wall, brick maybe.

More sensations came back. Pain in her head, a searing burn on her left leg, just above the knee. Her vision sharpened. Sounds took on clarity—and they were all terrifying.

An explosion flared up and rocked the ground from the other side of the wall. Yellow bolts of light sizzled through the air around her, ripping into other buildings she was just now noticing. A drugstore, a gas station, a post office, all of them crumbling and falling apart where they stood.

As Mira Toombs's memory returned, she remembered where she was and why.

She'd stashed an emergency kit in these ruins years ago, inside an old school. Supplies for the Strange Lands, if she ever needed to go there on her own or in a hurry, and she'd convinced Holt and Zoey to help her find it before heading to the Crossroads.

The good news was that they'd found the pack. A black canvas bag with a strap that fit around her waist. It was still there, she could see the red δ symbol embroidered on its front flap. The bad news was that, right as she'd found it, *they* had shown up.

Assembly walkers. The frontline troops of the alien armada that had conquered the planet almost a decade ago, and who had been obsessively pursuing them for more than a month.

She hadn't had time to see what kind or how many before the plasma bolts sent her to the floor and everything went dark, but judging by all the heated death flying through the air right now, there were a lot of them.

"Mira!" The voice was masculine this time. One she recognized and depended on. She felt hands on her, one of them turned her head to the left, and when it did Holt Hawkins came into view.

Mira smiled, still groggy. He looked the same as always.

His thick, wavy hair messed up and unkempt, but somehow still intentional in its look. Tall and well built, with brown eyes that never seemed anything but confident, no matter how crazy the world got. Even now, in the middle of this chaos, there was a calculated awareness of everything going on around them that somehow made her feel safe. He was one of the few that ever had.

"Mira! Can you hear me?" More plasma bolts flew by.

Mira made herself focus, quickly brushed the red hair out of her eyes. "How'd you get us out of there?"

"Wasn't easy," Holt replied. "You're a lot heavier than Zoey."

"Thanks a lot," she said tartly.

"Mira!" It was the little girl's voice from before. Mira felt tiny arms wrap around her from the other side, and she looked down.

Zoey's head was buried under Mira's arm, the little girl's eyes peeking out through her blond hair. It always felt wrong seeing Zoey in a place like this, in the middle of something life threatening. A little girl, barely eight years old, didn't belong here. Yet here she was.

Next to Zoey sat something else, its chin and paws across the little girl's legs, its beady eyes staring right at Mira. She felt her usual loathing at the sight of it.

"You . . ." she said.

Max, Holt's stinking cattle dog, growled back at her, but that was nothing new. The dog still saw her as Holt's prisoner. But as long as Mira didn't have to touch the thing, she was fine having it around. Holt had trained Max well, and he had his uses.

Zoey flinched as another explosion rocked the ground.

"We have to get out of here," Holt said. "Can you move?"

"I think so." She felt the wound on her leg and grimaced. It wasn't bad, the plasma bolt had only singed her, but it stung nonetheless. "What are you thinking?"

"I have . . . kind of a plan." He wasn't entirely convincing. "We gotta find a residential neighborhood."

The corner of the wall exploded in shards of plaster. There was a series of loud thuds on the roof above them, and Mira craned her neck to look up.

Staring down at them, a silhouette against the bright sky, was a powerful and terrifying machine. As she'd guessed, it was an Assembly walker—but of a type, up until a month ago, she'd never seen before.

Green and orange, like the ones that had chased them into the Drowning Plains; three legs, a tripod, lithe and agile—but it was different, too. It looked more heavily armed, with blocky equipment on its back. Also, it looked newer. Its armor and colors were unscratched.

LEDs flashed on its body, and its red, blue and green–triangular, three-optic "eye," the same one all Assembly walkers had, whirred as it focused down on her.

Mira stared back at it, frozen in fear.

"Come on!" she heard Holt shout as he yanked them up.

A mass of metallic netting fired from the walker above and slammed into the ground, barely missing. It was clearly meant to snare them.

"At least they're not trying to *kill* us," Holt yelled—and then ducked as a stream of plasma bolts sparked into the ground all around him.

"You were saying?" Mira shouted back.

As they ran, strange noises filled the air. Trumpet-like sounds almost, but electronic and distorted. They seemed to echo from everywhere, answering each other back and forth.

Max raced past, charging after Holt as he dodged another blast of plasma.

"Mira!" Zoey shouted behind her. The little girl was falling behind, her little legs unable to keep up. Mira lifted Zoey onto her back and ran after Holt.

Holt headed for a row of crumbling houses nearby, but the walkers were everywhere. She could see them in the streets, leaping between old buildings or cars. They were surrounded.

As they ran, Mira saw Holt's hand slip into his jacket pocket. A second later, a sphere of yellow energy crackled around him briefly, then disappeared.

Mira's eyes widened. Had she just seen what she—

Mira ducked as plasma fire whizzed harmlessly by and sparked against what was left of a delivery van. They were out in the open, the walkers shouldn't have missed. But somehow they had.

Mira kept running, following after Holt and Max.

Zoey screamed as a tripod leaped into view behind them and gave chase, its cannons beginning to hum; but before it could get close, an errant stream of plasma bolts slammed into it, sending it spinning and crashing to the ground in flaming debris, a victim of friendly fire.

Another improbability.

Mira kept running with Zoey, weaving in and out of old cars, headed for the houses just ahead. She caught Holt, and together they rounded the side of an old, badly leaning billboard—and came skidding to a jarring stop.

In front of them stood another Hunter.

The thing sprung toward them . . . and the decrepit billboard chose that moment to come crashing down. Holt shoved Mira and Zoey out of the way as the structure collapsed in a shower of wood and steel, and buried the tripod where it stood.

When the dust cleared, Mira checked Zoey. She was fine. So were Holt and Max. Mira looked at Holt with suspicion.

"How are you—?" Mira began.

Holt grabbed Zoey before she could finish, pulling her onto his back as they all started running again. Another flash of color, orange, flared around him, and Mira's heart sank as she saw it.

There was no denying it now. The colors. The improbable outcomes that kept saving them. The Chance Generator was in Holt's pocket, and he was using it.

Ahead of them she saw what Holt was running for. The exterior garage of a ruined house; a small, barely standing building that still covered what remained of an old, rusting pickup truck.

Holt ran for it as fast as he could, carrying Zoey with him, and Mira followed. Max must have figured it out, too, because the dog dashed ahead and bounded into the back of the truck.

Mira felt the heat of plasma fire as she ducked inside the garage.

The truck was in bad shape, a hulking piece of metal with broken windows, but, miraculously, it had four working tires.

"Zoey, get inside," Holt told the little girl as he sat her down. She climbed into the old truck, over to the passenger side.

"*This* is the plan?" Mira asked skeptically.

"If Zoey can get it running, yeah," Holt replied. "Might outrun those walkers."

"This thing couldn't outrun a beached whale!" Mira yelled.

"Do you have a *better* idea?" he asked.

Mira frowned at him. She didn't.

"You're driving." Holt headed for the truck's rear.

Mira moved for the door, jumped inside. "And what are *you* going to do?"

"Whatever I can." Holt jumped into the rear with Max. More of the trumpet sounds outside, coming closer. "Zoey, do it!"

Zoey looked at Mira from the dirty passenger seat. Mira nodded back. "Hurry, honey. If you can."

Zoey smiled. She closed her eyes and concentrated. "I can."

Nothing happened at first. The little girl just sat motionless on the torn seat, breathing in and out. Then something flickered around her hands, faint at first, then it grew. A layer of wavering, golden . . . *energy*. There was no other word for it. It moved and throbbed, almost in slow motion, like frozen fire, spreading from Zoey's hands, up her arms and toward her shoulders.

Mira stared in shock, feeling her pulse quicken.

Holt had mentioned this, the light, but it was all new to Mira. She'd missed Zoey doing her thing at Midnight City. She had been lost at the time, and the little girl had saved her. Another of her powers, the most important one. Zoey could stop the Tone. Block it somehow, make you immune to it. It was still mind-boggling to think about.

Mira watched the energy slowly envelop the girl, knowing they were running out of time. If Zoey couldn't get this thing going, they were as good as—

Mira jumped as the truck suddenly shook. Golden energy bubbled up from underneath the hood, as the engine, impossibly, came back to life and rumbled loudly. The dashboard sparked once, twice—and then the old analog gauges all floated into place. Static hissed from the aging radio.

Mira looked at the controls, stunned. She remembered riding on her father's lap as a kid, steering the family wagon in a parking lot. It had been all the driving experience she'd gotten before the Assembly came. She hoped it was enough.

Mira yanked the driveshaft down and stepped on the gas. The truck jumped forward . . . then jolted to a stop.

"Parking brake!" Holt yelled behind her.

"Where is it?" Mira frantically studied the interior of the truck.

"Where the parking brake usually is!"

"It's been awhile for me, *okay!?*"

The garage shuddered as the entire rear wall was ripped away by one of the alien machines. It trumpeted angrily, a horrible mix of electronic tones and static.

"Mira!" Holt shouted, pushing back as far as he could. Max barked wildly.

Mira found the brake, a hand lever on the floor, and shoved it down. The old truck lurched forward violently, roaring out of the garage.

The Hunter behind them let out a sharp, surprised sound and jumped after them.

As the truck bolted forward, it plowed through the garage's door frame—which was enough to bring the entire thing down like a house of cards. Mira watched in the dusty mirrors as the tripod was buried underneath a massive pile of wood and refuse. Another one down, but there were plenty more.

Nearby, new walkers gave chase, their three spiked legs pushing them forward with dizzying speed.

Next to Mira, Zoey sat, eyes closed, the golden energy pulsing all around her.

The truck shook badly as it caught a curb, slammed back down, and skidded onto the road. Ahead of them, coming fast, was an obstacle course of old cars and other debris . . . and the Hunters were still closing.

Mira gripped the steering wheel so hard her knuckles turned white.

HOLT HELD ON AS the battered truck lurched forward. All around him the street began to whiz by. A street full of hazards.

The vehicle reeled left suddenly, barely avoiding an old burned-out car. Then it yanked back to the right, around a pile of debris. Holt went rolling, crashed into the side of the bed and grabbed Max as he flew past, barely keeping him inside.

"What the hell are you *doing!?*" he yelled, holding on.

"Would you rather I hit everything in front of us?" Mira yelled back. "Because that would be easier!"

Distorted trumpets sounded from behind them as the two Hunters chased after them. Holt ducked as they opened fire, yellow plasma bolts spitting from their cannons. Mira screamed as the rear windshield exploded.

Holt looked around the truck bed. It was full of junk, pieces of trash, about a dozen old cans of paint . . . and two large crumbling, wooden crates. He gave them an experimental push. They were full of something heavy and metallic. It would have to do.

"Try to keep us moving straight!" Holt shouted as he moved for the tailgate.

He grabbed it, but it was rusted shut. He'd have to kick it open if he—

Holt lunged backward as a gleaming silver spear point punched straight through the tailgate, almost impaling him.

Eyes wide, he looked up and saw a metallic cable running from the harpoon back to one of the Hunters. When he'd spotted the green-and-orange walkers, he'd thought they looked different. Now there was no doubt. They'd upgraded, and Holt had no desire to find out what other new tricks they had.

The walker drew back the cable with a powerful yank, and ripped the tailgate completely off. It slammed onto the street and skittered backward on the asphalt in a shower of sparks.

The tripod jettisoned the cable, leaped over the tailgate and kept running.

"Thanks for the help," Holt said. He reached in his pocket, and when his hand closed around what was there, he felt the same sense of comfort he always did.

The Chance Generator was an old abacus, an ancient counting device, but it was so much more: a major artifact from the Strange Lands, with the ability to increase the luck of anyone who used it. It had saved their asses in Midnight City, and it was saving their asses right now.

Holt pushed more beads up to the top, and a sphere of red flashed around him. Every time he pushed more of them up, the effect intensified. Which meant he had to be careful. He'd already used it a few times, and the artifact only had so much power per day. If it ran out of juice before they escaped, they'd be in a lot of trouble.

He got behind the crates, shoving them toward the edge of the truck bed. They were falling apart, but somehow stayed together just long enough to tip off the back. They exploded on the street and sprayed their contents everywhere, most of it scrap metal—springs, nails, bolts, aluminum shavings, broken tools, exploding all over the road.

The walkers ran right into it.

For one brief moment, they lost their footing on the metal bits and pieces, their legs splaying wildly. That was all it took. They tipped over and crashed into an old water truck, plowing right through it in a shower of metal, dust, and black liquid. They didn't get up.

"Yeah!" Holt yelled in triumph—but it was short lived.

More tripods vaulted down from nearby buildings, charging after them on the street.

Plasma bolts sliced the air and slammed into the truck, tearing the rear end to shreds. The vehicle listed dangerously as Mira tried to stay in control. "Holt!"

It was a short, unsuccessful battle.

They skidded left, twisting and grinding toward a pile of old cars, and crashed straight into them. Mira screamed. Holt grabbed Max as the impact tossed them forward along the bed and into the back of the cabin.

Holt hit hard. The world went fuzzy. Somehow he found the edge of the truck bed, pulled himself up and out of the wreckage, and slumped down on the ground.

"Holt!" Mira yelled as she scrambled out with Zoey.

"Having fun yet?" Holt groaned as tried to get to his feet. Mira frowned, helped him move. More plasma fire seared the air, and they pressed their backs against the ruined truck. The Hunters would be on them in seconds.

Holt looked around, trying to find a way out, and saw something down the street, a block or so away. It looked like a large concrete drainage ditch that vanished into a dark tunnel, probably an old runoff exit. If they could reach it, the entrance might be cramped enough to keep the tripods from following.

Reaching it was the problem. It was open territory between here and there, and there was no other cover. They had to run for it. They didn't have any—

On either side of them tripods burst into view, lunging into firing positions.

Holt instinctively focused on one in front of the others. It was marked differently. Its green-and-orange color pattern was bolder, more commanding. New armor or not, Holt had seen that walker before. Twice. And it was even more frightening now.

From the Hunter came a flash. A mass of metallic netting flung forward, hissing through the air toward them. Mira screamed. Holt tried to cover them.

Something big, bright, and powerful landed between them and the walkers with a thunderous crash.

The net slammed into it and bounced off.

Holt and Mira stared at it in shock. Another walker—but different.

It was big, much larger than the Hunters, and it had five massive legs arranged around a blocky body. There was no discernible weaponry, but a shimmering field of clear energy circled it, like some kind of protective barrier.

There was something else.

This walker, unlike every other Assembly machine Holt had ever seen, *had no colors.*

It was just bare metal, as if its paint had been stripped away. The machine gleamed in the afternoon sunlight.

Its three-optic eye shifted and focused, bore into them. Then it emitted a strange, deep rumbling sound, and leaped powerfully into the air, soaring over them. It shook the ground when it hit. Three more Hunters skidded to a stop in front of it. The boldly marked one trumpeted in anger, missiles and plasma bolts flashing out.

The ordnance sizzled and exploded as the machine's flickering energy field absorbed them, protecting them but each impact sent it reeling back a step or two.

The silver walker charged forward, slamming into the tripods like a battering ram, sending them crashing through the wall of a grocery store.

Whatever the thing was, it had drawn attention away from Holt and the others.

"Um, if there's more to this 'plan,' we should probably make it happen right now," Mira said.

She was right. This was their chance. Holt whistled two short notes and Max darted forward. He got Zoey up and moving, and they all raced after the dog. Behind them came more explosions, thuds, and distorted electronic sounds.

Max barreled into the concrete structure and Holt rounded the corner right after him. Then his eyes widened at what was there. It was a tunnel, alright, just like he'd guessed—but it was *huge*, about twenty feet in diameter, disappearing into the darkness beyond.

"Damn it," he said under his breath. The tripods could *easily* follow them through this. It wasn't an escape at all.

The huge silver walker landed with a bone-jarring thud on the ground right outside, its multicolored eye instantly finding them.

Zoey grabbed Max's collar, stopping him from charging the machine. Holt instinctively pulled everyone behind him, pushing them farther inside the tunnel.

More plasma bolts slammed into the walker's shield. It was flickering now. It looked weaker. The thing hesitated a second more, studying them intently—then it rumbled and rushed right at them.

"Back! *Get back!*" Holt shouted, pushing everyone down, trying to get away from it.

The silver walker slammed with incredible power into the concrete overhang of the tunnel. The whole thing cracked and sprayed dust, then fell apart in a fury of fractured sound.

Holt shoved the others to the ground as the entrance collapsed in on itself, sealing away the daylight and the battle raging outside—and leaving them trapped in a thick cocoon of darkness.

2. RED FLAGS

THE TUNNEL WAS A BLACK SQUARE of nothingness that stretched endlessly ahead. Only what Holt's and Mira's flashlights illuminated was visible, and it was all so repetitive—gray concrete, clumps of dirt, water trickling by—if it wasn't for the decades-old graffiti here and there, it would have seemed as if they weren't moving at all.

Max walked ahead of them, tail wagging enthusiastically, and Holt had to keep calling him back before he disappeared ahead and got into trouble. Behind him, Holt heard the plodding sounds of Mira and Zoey as they followed through the water of the tunnel floor.

He kept thinking back to that strange silver walker, stripped of its colors, how it had seemingly blocked the nets that were about to ensnare all four of them, and then crushed the sewer entrance, sealing them inside. Even for Assembly, it was odd behavior, though when it came to Zoey, Holt had given up trying to understand their motives. Their interest in the little girl was as mysterious as her powers.

"Holt, what's in your pocket?" Mira's voice startled him from his thoughts, and he looked back. She was studying him with a strange look. A suspicious one. It was only then that Holt noticed his hand was stuck in his coat pocket, his fingers clutched protectively around the Chance Generator. He couldn't remember exactly when he'd reached in for it.

"My head hurts," Zoey said before Holt could answer.

"Hurts *how*, kiddo?" Holt asked.

"On the sides mainly, comes and goes." Zoey stopped moving and rubbed her temples.

"From the truck maybe?" Mira asked. It was a good question. Holt couldn't imagine what kind of strain came with Zoey's abilities, and to be honest, a headache would be the least of what he'd expect.

"Everyone gets headaches now and then," Holt said, gently rubbing the little girl's head. "Rest a sec, there's no rush."

The little girl leaned against the wall and Max whined gently, pushing his nose into the girl's hand. "The Max . . ." she said softly, petting the dog's head.

Holt looked back up at Mira. Her eyes were already on him. "You're using the abacus." There was a note of accusation in her voice.

Unexpectedly, Holt felt a swell of anger. Who was she to ask? She wasn't his boss, or in charge of him. Hadn't he saved them back in Midnight City, saved *her,* all with the artifact? Hadn't he and it just saved them a few minutes ago?

The anger grew so intense, it startled him a little. It wasn't like him to feel that way. He was probably just jumpy, he told himself, on edge from the previous experience.

When he thought about it . . . why *wouldn't* Mira question him? She'd already said she thought the Chance Generator was dangerous. She was an expert, wasn't she? She'd warned him.

Besides, signs that suggested she cared had been rare the last few days. There were moments where he thought he detected it again. Glances. Smiles. Incidental touching that lasted longer than it should, but they had only been glimpses, a dim reflection of what had passed between them at the dam when they'd kissed.

Holt wasn't positive where her hesitation came from, but he had an idea.

The other one, the Freebooter she'd been close to, the one they were probably going to run into sooner or later. *Ben.* It wasn't something Holt was looking forward to.

It didn't really matter, though. Mira wasn't the real reason he was here. Zoey was.

As much as he didn't like it, the kid had pulled one hell of a rabbit out of her hat at Midnight City. She'd saved them all, and at the same time done something even more impossible. She'd gotten Holt to believe that things could change—maybe even that the Assembly could be beaten— and Holt had promised to help her, whatever it took. He'd promised. . . .

"Holt?" Mira asked again.

"Yeah, I was using it," he answered, trying to keep the anger out of his voice. "And if I hadn't we'd all be dead. We wouldn't have made it to that truck, and we definitely wouldn't have outrun the tripods."

"That doesn't make it right!" Mira exclaimed. "We can't start depending on something unpredictable. We have to rely on our own skills or we're going to wind up in trouble, especially where we're going."

Where they were going, of course, was the Strange Lands. A dangerous place to the north, where, for whatever reason, time and space no longer worked right. Mira was a Freebooter, someone who specialized in traversing that landscape and bringing back the artifacts that lay there—common, everyday objects that had been imbued with otherworldly powers. The abacus in his hand, the subject of their argument right now, was one such artifact, one Holt had unwillingly become the owner of in Midnight City. Since then, it had proved to be more valuable than he could have imagined.

Holt frowned. "I don't see what's wrong with having a little luck on our side."

"What's 'wrong' is that, in order to increase your luck, that thing drains someone *else's* nearby. Did you forget that?" Her eyes burned into his. "What happens when you use it in the Strange Lands, and there *is* no one else nearby? Who do you think it'll take the luck away from? Max? Me? *Zoey?*"

Holt shook his head. "If we stay in its influence sphere, we should be—"

"You don't know that! It could kill *everyone* in order to profit, you—me, and Zoey included." She held her hand out toward him. "I'm sorry, Holt, but I need you to give it to me. It's just too dangerous. I shouldn't have asked you to carry it in the first place."

Holt stared at her and felt the anger begin to rise again. Now she was giving him *orders?* She just expected him to do as he was told?

Holt pushed it back down. Again, it wasn't like him . . . and maybe there was something to that.

He pulled the Chance Generator out of his pocket. It looked harmless—an ornate antique piece of wood with chipped, colorful beads running its length. As he looked at it he felt the need to slide a few of them upward. Just to be safe.

Just a few of them . . .

Holt's eyes narrowed. He pushed all the beads down, shutting the abacus's power off. He showed it to Mira. "Look, it's off, see? If it'll make you feel better, I won't use it anymore."

"Holt—"

"I *promise*. If you think it's dangerous, then I'll leave it alone. You know more than me, and nothing's more important than you and Zoey. I'll shut it off, and I'll keep it. You said it shouldn't be near your other artifacts, that they might react to each other."

Mira stared at him, unsure, thinking things through. In the end she nodded. "It *would* be best if you could hold it, but I'd feel better if it was in your pack, not your pocket."

"Done," Holt said, though he felt a slight twinge of worry. All the same, he shoved it in his pack and sealed it away. "Okay?"

Mira smiled and reached out, touching his hand. "Thank you." It had been a day or more since Holt had felt her hand. It felt good.

The two stared at each other, then Zoey spoke up beneath them. "I feel better now," she said. "The Max helped, I think."

They looked down at her. The little girl had an arm around the dog's neck while she scratched his ears.

Mira frowned. "I doubt that. Unless his smell overpowered the pain."

"The Max doesn't smell!" Zoey insisted.

"You know, if her powers are causing the headaches, it's just another reason she shouldn't use them," Holt said. "The Assembly come running every time she does."

"Once we get to the Strange Lands, that won't be a problem." Mira smoothed the little girl's hair. "The Assembly never go in there."

"I can't even imagine that," Holt said. "Not having to look over our shoulder every five minutes."

"We might lose the Assembly," Mira replied, "but there'll be plenty of other things to watch out for. You might end up *missing* our alien friends."

Holt doubted that was true, but then again, he had very little idea what was ahead of him. He'd never been farther north than Midnight City, and certainly never stepped foot in the Strange Lands. Yet, their plan was to go farther than even that.

In the Midnight City artifact vault, Zoey had interacted with the Oracle, a major artifact that functioned something like a fortune-teller. Holt didn't completely understand all that it had revealed to the little girl, but it had been clear about one thing: To get the answers Zoey needed, there was a place she needed to go—an infamous landmark in the center of the Strange Lands called the Severed Tower. Supposedly, so the stories went, if you could survive the Strange Lands and make it to the Tower, it would grant you one wish.

It always sounded like a fairy tale to Holt, but lately he'd been witness to some fairly amazing things he wouldn't have believed a few months ago. He really didn't know what to think anymore. All he knew was that Zoey said she needed to get to this Tower, and he had promised to help her.

"Is that a way out, Holt?" Zoey asked. Holt followed her gaze upward with his flashlight.

A steel ladder ascended the concrete wall to what looked like the bottom of a manhole. "Good eye, kid." Holt tested the ladder. It was rusted, but it seemed sturdy enough.

He quickly scaled it and pushed the heavy cover out of the way. Daylight poured in and Holt winced at the brightness before crawling up and out.

They were near the edge of the old city now, just a few wrecked houses and buildings, most of them burned-out husks. He looked south, where they had come from. There were no sounds of explosions, no flashes, but there were several columns of smoke a few miles away, probably from the battle they'd escaped.

While there was no sign of anything now, those green-and-orange ones could cloak themselves, Holt reminded himself, so you never really knew.

He looked north, saw the plains widening and advancing again, back toward where they needed to go. Toward the Strange Lands.

He hoped Mira was right about the Assembly not following them inside. That would be a blessing, even in spite of her insistence that the place itself could be much worse. It was a chance he was happy to take.

"Look safe?" It was Mira, underneath him.

"Safe as it's gonna be, ladies," he said. "Come on."

In a few minutes they were all up, moving northward, Holt making sure to take advantage of whatever limited cover the remains of the urban environment offered. All too soon they'd be back in the plains, where everything was open.

The giant Antimatter storm they'd witnessed a few days ago was gone now. They could no longer see its strange, multicolored lightning, but there was another indication they were headed the right way: the eerie aurora effect, wavering and fluctuating like the pictures he'd seen of the northern lights as a kid. Only these were visible in the middle of the day, and they were coming closer.

Instinctively, Holt's hand slid into his pocket—and found it empty.

There was a brief flash of panic before he remembered he'd shoved the abacus inside his pack. He relaxed. He could get to it if he needed to, he told himself.

Regardless of what he'd said, Holt knew if they got into something really dangerous—if Mira's or Zoey's lives were in danger—he'd do the same thing he did in Midnight City. He'd use the Chance Generator again . . . but only in an emergency, he told himself. Only in an emergency. He'd promised, after all.

SUNRISE LIT A HUGE rolling landscape of hills covered in overgrown prairie grass. Holt had never been this far north, and he couldn't believe how open and empty it seemed. He understood why in the World Before it had been called Big Sky Country. The blue above them was the dominant feature, so big it felt like walking in a snow globe. In the distance, the aurora continued to waver.

Mira was re-sorting her gear underneath the overgrown water tower they'd made camp next to. It stood at the top of a crest overlooking the Missouri river, as it cut a path through the hills to the north.

Zoey and Max were playing "Keepaway Fetch," an invention of their own making. The game began like regular Fetch, in that Max gleefully raced after a thrown ball, but after that it took a hard turn in a different direction. The dog was much more interested in someone chasing *him* to get the ball back, than in returning it and starting over.

Zoey screamed gleefully as she ran after Max, in and out of the rusted support columns of the tower, but the dog was too quick, and kept slipping away.

"Zoey, watch out for sharp things, please," Mira intoned without looking up. If the little girl heard, she didn't show any sign. She just kept laughing and spinning after Max.

Holt looked at Mira. Artifact components littered the ground in front of her—pencils, magnets, vials of all kinds of dust, batteries, paper clips, coins of different denominations wrapped in plastic. They looked like everyday objects, but they were anything but. Each was imbued with unique, otherworldly properties, and they could be combined into stronger and stronger ones that did incredible things.

Holt had hated artifacts even before he met Mira, but they had their uses, he had to admit now, and Mira was amazingly skilled with them. She was studying one in particular, a complicated combination made up of over a dozen different objects, all tied together with linked silver chain and purple leather twine. Its main aspect was an antique gold pocket watch that rested on the exterior, with a silver δ ornately etched into the metallic cover.

Holt had only seen the artifact twice since they'd left Midnight City. Mira kept it deep in her pack, as far away from her as possible. She hated it. It repulsed her, and for good reason.

It was the ugly result of an obsession with forging a combination that could slow down the Tone but it had all gone wrong. The combination didn't slow down the Tone, it *accelerated* it. Made it so that anyone, Heedless or otherwise, would Succumb in a matter of seconds. Making it had cost her everything—her life in Midnight City, her freedom, whatever future she might have had.

She was bringing it into the Strange Lands to destroy it, and Holt didn't blame her.

"You okay?" Holt asked.

Mira stared at it a moment more, then stuffed it down into her pack. "Yeah."

"You can destroy it at this Crossroads place?"

"It's not that easy." Mira's voice was bitter. "To destroy an artifact, you have to be in the ring where it was created. If it's a combination, you have to be in the ring of its most powerful component."

"So what ring is that, then?" Holt asked.

"The fourth." There was a look in her eyes suddenly that Holt had never seen there. To see it in Mira was startling. It looked like . . . fear.

"You *sure* you're okay?" he asked.

Mira blinked and looked up, but not at him. She looked at Zoey, running back and forth after Max. "I'm . . . worried."

"About what?"

"The Strange Lands."

"You're a Freebooter. You've been there a million times."

"Never on my own." Her voice was so low he almost couldn't hear it. "Except once. A long time ago."

Holt studied her in confusion. He had never seen Mira rattled, never seen her doubt herself. She was always so confident, so capable.

"Mira, if anyone can get us to where we need to go, it's *you*," he said, trying to reassure her. "Zoey knows that, too."

She looked back at him. The fear was still there, he could see it even more clearly now and it felt like Mira wanted to tell him something. To reveal whatever weight she was carrying—but Zoey's voice stopped her before she could.

"How do we know when we're *in* the Strange Lands?" The little girl and Max were wrestling on the ground now. The foreign look vanished from Mira's eyes. Whatever it was, she had pushed it back down.

"We'll *feel* it, for one thing," Mira replied. "It's called the Charge. Makes the hair on your arms stand up. Gets stronger the farther you go in. But there's only so many ways into the Strange Lands. The Crossroads, where we're headed, is one of them. Once you leave there . . . you're inside."

"Why can you only go in from certain places?" Zoey asked.

"Because of the Stable Anomalies."

"What's a . . . 'stablonamy'?"

Mira smiled. "Anomalies are the dangerous parts of the Strange Lands, honey. Stable ones are permanent, they stay in place for the most part, and they're usually invisible. Unstable Anomalies can move around, but the good thing is you can see them."

"Like the storms a few days ago?"

Mira nodded. "Exactly. All the rings are circled by Stable Anomalies, including the first. You can only enter the first ring in a few places, where there's a gap. The Crossroads is one of those places. It's the main entrance for Freebooters from Midnight City, so it gets a lot of traffic."

Something flashed and caught Holt's eye to the northeast. He looked and saw the Missouri river, and on the river he saw the source. In the distance, powering north, were two large river craft painted solid black. Each flew the same flag.

Red, with a white, eight-pointed star.

Holt felt his heart skip. He hit the ground, pulling Zoey and Mira down with him. They studied him questioningly, until he nodded toward the river.

Mira's eyes widened when she saw it. "*Menagerie*. What the hell are they doing here?"

"Raider ships," Holt replied. It was a nice way of saying pirate ships. They attacked merchant vessels and River Rat crews up and down the larger streams, and it was a fairly new phenomenon. The Menagerie was a pirates and thieves guild, and until a few years ago they kept mainly to a place called the Barren, the desert wastelands of the old American Southwest. Then, the first Menagerie pirate ships appeared up and down the Mississippi and Missouri rivers, as far south as the Low Marshes. It meant they were expanding, and for a group as dangerous as the Menagerie, that wasn't a good thing.

"Never heard of them coming this far north, have you?" Mira asked.

The answer was no. There was no profit in it. Few ships worth plundering ran this stretch of the river.

"Why'd we drop down?" Mira turned back to him.

"Just playing it safe. If those ships are having a bad week, there's nothing stopping them from unloading a shore party and coming after *us*."

Of course there was a lot more to it than that. The Menagerie had put a death mark on Holt's head almost a year ago. A death mark from the highest ranks, and he'd been on the run from them ever since. The bounty on Mira's head was supposed to finance his trip east to escape, but, well . . . complications had ensued, as always.

Mira knew he had a death mark, but Holt had never told her from whom, if only because it would beg other questions. Questions he wasn't eager to answer. What would Mira think if she knew the truth? The half-finished tattoo under Holt's glove itched. . . .

"The Missouri goes almost right to the Crossroads," Mira said, watching the ships fade away. "But why head there?"

"Trading for artifacts?" Holt guessed.

"Midnight City's much better for that. And the Menagerie don't mount Strange Lands expeditions. Doesn't make sense."

"Add it to the ever-growing list," Holt replied glibly.

Mira turned and smiled, and as she did the thought occurred to Holt that he was keeping a lot from her. More than he'd kept from anyone else. What he wasn't sure about was if that was a sign of his feelings for her— or a sign of something changing within him.

He honestly didn't know.

They all watched, hunkered down near the water tower, until the boats finally disappeared in the distance.

Everyone finished packing quickly and moved out, pushing through the tall grass and climbing down the soft, rolling rise. As they walked, Holt kept checking the length of the river. He would have thought running into the Menagerie was the least of his worries. Yet here they were. And he was walking right toward them.

He had a sudden intense desire to have the Chance Generator in his hands.

3. CROSSROADS

HOLT, ZOEY AND MIRA WALKED north along an old dirt road dotted with abandoned cars and crumbling farmhouses. Max trotted ahead of them, bouncing back and forth between the roadsides, always finding something exciting to smell or look at. Eventually they passed a barn that sat off to the the right. A big two-story one, with its giant doors open, and the broadside of its faded red wood wall facing them. Huge letters stood out on its side in a white-painted notice, peeking out above the overgrown corn stalks.

STRANGE LANDS BEGIN 1 MILE
STAY ON ROAD
WELCOME TO THE CROSSROADS
SOUTHERN ENTRY FOR RING 1

The δ symbol was there, too, filling the barn's wall. The aurora effect ahead of them seemed bigger now, shimmering in giant waves that ebbed and flowed in the sky. They were almost there . . . but where was "there"?

The barn welcomed them to the Crossroads, but as far as Holt could see it was nothing but empty, overgrown farmland. The only thing he *did* notice was that the road continued ahead of them and passed through the remains of a chain-link fence and gate, with an old, crumbling guard shack. Other than that, there was no indication of what was beyond. The road just abruptly ended a couple of hundred feet beyond the gate. Vanished from sight, as though it had fallen into a hole. It made him nervous.

Next to him, Zoey rubbed her head.

"More headaches?" It was becoming a trend, and he was worried. Zoey had come to mean a lot to him, and at the thought, he noticed he didn't feel the same discomfort he would have only a few months ago. The little girl had really changed him, as ironic as that was.

She nodded. "It's okay, it doesn't hurt too much. I can be tough." Zoey held one of Max's ears in her hand as they walked. "But Mira's nervous."

Holt looked ahead at Mira, walking several lengths in front of them. "Why?"

"It's this place, I think. She's never been in charge here, not really. It bothers her."

It was strange, how used to Zoey's ability to read other people's emotions he'd gotten. It was another sign of all that had changed. "Having responsibility for people *can* be scary. But she'll be fine. She has it in her."

"I know that," Zoey said sadly, "but I don't think *she* does."

Holt stared at Mira as they walked. She *had* to see it—how good she was, how skilled. Why wouldn't she? It was obvious to him; it had been since he first met her, and it was obvious to Zoey as well.

"Heads up," Mira yelled back at them. They were almost to the chain-link fence. The road still vanished just past it, but something was different now.

There was a crowd of people there. Dozens of them, all kids.

As they got closer, Holt noticed they wore bulging packs, and most had duffel bags or boxes in their hands, too. If he had to guess, he'd say they'd been displaced and had as much of their personal items with them as they could carry.

Max growled low, and Holt put a reassuring hand on the dog. All the same, he removed the safety buckle on his Beretta.

"Occurs to me way too late that we should have gotten you a pair of sunglasses," Holt observed. Mira sighed in exasperation and looked back at him. It was an obvious thing they had both overlooked. Her eyes were clear now, the black tendrils of the Tone were no longer present. Anyone who knew her would eventually notice the change, and the questions that would follow were going to be tough ones to answer.

"Are they Freebooters?" Zoey asked.

"No. They live at the Crossroads," Mira said. "And they're *leaving*."

"Is that unusual?" Holt inquired.

"Yes."

They walked through the old gate, passing the empty guard station, toward the crowd. Old U.S. Air Force warning signs still hung on the fence, but Holt barely noticed them. He was studying the approaching crowd warily, but no one seemed to be paying attention to them. They were too busy yelling and fighting. Whatever was happening, it wasn't being well received.

Holt saw a boy—short, probably nineteen, with blond hair and a long scar across the left side of his face that crossed his brow, jumped over his eye socket, and continued down his cheek. It was an old scar, Holt could tell. Even from this distance, Holt could see the kid's eyes were almost colored in with black.

"This isn't a debate," the boy shouted at the crowd. Four other kids stood on either side of him. They were armed. Two with slings, the others with old hunting rifles. They must be enforcers. They were the only things keeping the crowd at bay.

"Deckard didn't approve this!" someone shouted.

"Deckard isn't here," the boy shot back. "And no one's heard from Polestar in a week. You can leave whatever you want, there won't be anyone left to steal it. When it's safe, I'll send word to—"

The crowd erupted into more yells, cutting him off. Some of the kids moved forward—then backed up immediately as the boy's armed guard raised their weapons.

"Go, or stay outside, but you're not coming back down! Get used to it!" The boy turned and moved off, leaving the four guards. Some of the residents conceded defeat, heading south down the road, lugging their gear and items. The rest kept yelling.

"Echo!" Mira shouted next to Holt, trying to get the attention of the boy over all the angry voices. "*Echo!*"

The boy stopped and turned around in surprise. His eyes found Mira, and the one the scar passed over twitched a little.

Echo hesitated, staring at Mira. Then he shouted to the four guards. "Her!" Echo pointed at Mira. "Let *her* through!"

"And my friends!" Mira yelled back.

Echo frowned. "Fine. Sure. Why not."

The crowd watched as Holt and the others were escorted past the guards and into the clear, and then they yelled even louder, angrier than before.

When they reached him, Echo shook his head in frustration. "Picked a hell of a day to show up."

"Echo . . ." Mira said and moved for him. He hugged her back with warmth, then pulled away. Something passed between them, something that hinted at a past, but Holt had no way to know what. He just nervously watched the short kid study Mira up close. If he noticed her eyes, he gave no indication. It was a subtle thing, and in a tense situation like this, he might not notice at all. Holt hoped their luck held.

"What's going on?" Mira asked.

"Evacuation is what's going on."

"Clearly a popular decision," Holt observed.

"Clearly." Echo studied Holt and Zoey a moment. "But it is what it is. Things are getting out of control. The Strange Lands are changing, Mira. And no one has the first clue why."

"Changing?" Mira asked. "Changing *how?*"

"Stable Anomalies are in place, they're still where they were. The Mix Master, the Compactor, all of them. Though some people say they're stronger. It's the unstable ones that are the problem. They're moving *outside* their normal rings. Been getting reports of everything from Ion Storms in the second to Quark Spheres in the third."

Mira was stunned. Clearly this was serious news. "The Strange Lands have been the same for almost a decade, they don't *change.*"

"Well, they do now," Echo answered darkly.

"What about farther in? What about Polestar?"

"Deckard's not evacuating, but that's no surprise. Polestar's his life. He'll hold on as long as he can, maybe longer. I just hope he doesn't get everyone there dead." He looked at Mira squarely. "I lied to them back there, you know. He ordered the Crossroads to stay open."

"But you're not doing it," Mira said.

Echo shook his head wearily. "I'm moving everyone the hell out until it's safe. If Anomalies are showing up in different rings, who's to say they won't cross outside the border altogether? If Deckard has a problem with it, he can come tell me himself."

Mira's gaze intensified. "We need to get into the Strange Lands, Echo. It's important."

Echo shook his head. "I closed Northlift two days ago. No one's going in. If it makes you feel better, Ben wasn't happy about it either."

At the name, Holt stiffened.

"Ben's *here?*" Mira asked in surprise.

"Yeah," Echo replied. "Figured that's why *you* were here."

"Not exactly."

"He got here right after I closed the lift. Another hour and he could have gotten in. Been trying to get him to leave with everyone else, but he's got a whole expedition of Gray Devils down there, and they're probably more than my guards can handle. He's refusing to leave. If he keeps it up, I'll have to push the issue, and that's not something I'm looking forward to."

"Can I see him?" she asked.

Echo thought it through. "I guess. Maybe you can talk some sense into him. You were the only one who ever could. But that's *all* you're going down for. *No one's* using Northlift."

They started walking, the shouts of the crowd fading behind them, and Holt finally saw why the road seemed to end so abruptly.

Ahead of them, the ground disappeared into a sheer drop off the edge of a cliff. Yet it was more than that. A giant, jagged hole stretched in a roughly circular shape outward, two lines of plummeting rock that met back together in the far distance. It was an old rock quarry, Holt saw, and it had been repurposed long ago as something else entirely. A junkyard, a very specific kind. Hundreds of old military planes—bombers, transports and fighters—from all eras and ages, most rusting and falling apart, sat at the bottom of the quarry and stretched into the distance.

The road didn't just end, either. It took a sharp left and then banked steeply in a wide path that carved through the wall of the quarry. A big trail, but it would have to be to get these planes in here.

Near where the road turned away, a framework of steel and old railroad timber held a giant series of chains that ran through a complicated system of pulleys and cables, and several refurbished tractor engines that were loudly cranking something upward from below.

It was a huge box-shaped elevator, big enough to hold several dozen kids and their belongings. It was made of wood and sheet metal and plastic siding all hammered and blended together, with the chains running through the pulleys in the supports attached to each of its four corners.

What looked like the steering column from some old boat sat in the middle, with thick cables running from it up the walls, through the pulleys and over to the tractor engines.

An operator inside yanked a lever downward and the engines gurgled and shut off. The lift rocked badly, slamming into the edge of the cliff, but the kids inside seemed to expect it. They piled out just as angry as the others, all yelling and clamoring for Echo's attention; but the lift also brought with it three more guards, and they shoved the group away toward the rest.

"When did you start evacuating?" Mira asked.

"About a day ago, but it's been slow going," Echo said. He seemed tired, Holt noted. "No one leaves until the guards force them to. Plus, using Southlift is taking forever. Going to have to make people use the old road."

They got inside and Echo slammed a lever upward on the old controls. The lift jolted as the engines outside grumbled back to life and began to indelicately lower them down. Southlift, Echo had called it. Northlift, Holt guessed, was most likely a similar elevator at the other end of the junkyard that people used to enter the Strange Lands. With the cliffs all around them and the only road exiting to the south, if Echo shut it down he could definitely keep people from going in. They'd have to scale the quarry walls, otherwise.

Southlift rocked and swayed as it lowered, and Holt grabbed a strap from the ceiling for good measure. He felt Zoey cling to his leg, trying to balance. She didn't seem scared, though.

"What's up with you and Lenore?" Echo asked Mira. "Heard there was some kind of dustup? You in trouble?"

Mira and Holt looked at each other. Mira had basically killed Lenore Rowe, the leader of the Gray Devils, in their escape out of Midnight City. It wasn't technically death, but using an artifact to spontaneously Succumb someone to the Tone was about as close as you could get.

"It's . . . all okay now," Mira said. It wasn't entirely a lie, it was "okay" as far as Mira was concerned. But Holt doubted any Gray Devils they ran into would agree. "It's one of the reasons I'm here, actually."

"Well, like I said," Echo replied testily, "if that reason involves going into the Strange Lands, you're not doing it from the Crossroads."

Before Mira could argue, the lift touched down with a jolt. Echo yanked another lever, silencing the engines up top, and stepped out the opposite side.

Holt and the others followed, and when they did the full breadth of the Crossroads came into view.

Airplanes of all kinds and types, in various states of disrepair, stretched into the distance, most of them laboriously repurposed into houses, stores, workshops, eateries, and warehouses, arranged all the way to the other side of the crater, parked and lined up next to each other long ago.

Bridges made of rope and wooden planks stretched between the tops of the old aircraft, making the place a city of two levels, the ground and the open air above. Ramshackle structures made of wood and fiberglass were attached to the tops of some of the bigger planes, and Holt saw what looked like a food court hanging onto an old green C-130 transport.

And there were people. Lots of people. Mostly teens, Holt noticed. There were fewer children here than in Midnight City or Faust, probably because this was a fringe location. It was more dangerous living here at the border of the Strange Lands.

They moved in and out of the planes and buildings, most packing and filling bags, getting ready to leave. More armed guards, Echo's men, moved in between, making sure progress was being made, and Holt saw a line of kids a hundred strong stretching back and waiting to ride Southlift up to the top. Echo was right, it would take forever that way.

They kept walking, pushing through the crowds and the strange, converted city of crumbling airplanes, and as they did Holt saw something else. Every once in awhile, he spotted a flag flying above a plane or a ramshackle structure. Colorful ones, ones he recognized with a sinking feeling.

Auburn red, with a huge white wolf's head. Black, with a white Celtic cross. Green, with a sharp yellow sword.

Midnight City factions. Their outposts in the Crossroads. They'd have to be careful. It wasn't just Mira they might recognize. Holt still felt a chill when he thought about seeing his name on the Scorewall.

"You come from Midnight?" Echo asked as they walked.

Mira nodded.

"Are the rumors true? The Assembly actually attacked it?"

Mira hesitated. "Yeah."

"Wow." Echo seemed stunned. "Still can't imagine that. I mean, they've left it alone for so long, why attack it now, you know?"

This was a dangerous conversation, given that the answer to Echo's question was walking along with them, holding Holt's hand. He quickly changed the subject. "We saw Menagerie boats on the way here."

Echo's demeanor darkened. "Heard about that, too. Scouts said they anchored about a mile away; been pulling equipment and gear off. Looks like they're heading into the Strange Lands, crazy as that is. Never met a Menagerie Freebooter, and I wouldn't want to either. But so far they haven't made it here, if that's what they're intending."

"Will you turn them back, too?" Holt asked. He hoped the answer was yes.

"Plan to, yeah," Echo answered tightly. "If I have my way, they won't get past Southlift. But Menagerie are always armed. And they don't like the word 'no' very much." He sighed and rubbed his eyes. "Sometimes I'm not sure it's worth all the headache. Maybe I just oughta leave, let Ben and the Menagerie and Deckard and everyone else do what they want."

"You're not Deckard," Mira said. "But you do keep your promises. You've been the Overseer here longer than anyone. No one said it would be easy."

"Yeah," Echo replied, "you got that right."

Someone shouted from ahead of them, a boy's voice, somewhat soft, but it carried regardless. "Mira!"

Holt looked up at the sound.

The Crossroads was a ghost town this far in, but sitting under a thick, gray canopy was a group of about twenty kids. The canopy was made of tough fabric, strung back and forth between three old fighter jets, marking off a pretty large area of ground. Holt could see sleeping cots, a cooking area, a pool table and showers—and he saw something else, too. From the top of the fabric structure a flag flew, outstretched in the wind. Deep gray and white, with a laughing devil's face, a forked tongue snaking out of its mouth, horns on its head.

It was the Gray Devils outpost, Holt realized, but, did that mean . . . ?

Someone appeared out of nowhere and grabbed Mira. Holt's first thought was that the Gray Devils were attacking, but it only took one look to know that wasn't the case. A boy lifted Mira off the ground and spun her.

He was about her age, with lean muscles under a gray utility shirt. His eyes were full of the Tone, and his hair was razored close to his scalp, leaving a dark outline of color over the top. He had a pair of black-rimmed eyeglasses on his nose, and he smiled up at Mira as he spun her around once, twice . . . and then kissed her.

It was a short kiss. That was Holt's only consolation. But still, Mira didn't push him away. When it was done she just stared down at the boy with a mixture of emotions.

"Hi, Ben," she said in a low, conflicted voice.

It felt like somebody had just stepped on Holt's heart.

4. BEN

BENJAMIN AUBERTINE had never been classically good-looking. He was lean and agile, in good shape, but most Freebooters were. He had sharp features set in an angular face, and a detached self-confidence behind his eyes. His hair was something he didn't have an interest in maintaining, so he kept it shaved close, leaving a thin layer of black over his head that gave him a hard-edged look that belied his true nature.

In reality, Mira had never seen Ben fight anyone, never seen him lift a hand in anger, never seen him mad at all. Maybe that was because he had no reason to be. Ben could talk himself out of anything. Mira once watched him convince some Crossmen Freebooters who'd lost their supplies in the third ring that choosing *not* to rob Mira and himself would ultimately result in two hundred and thirty Points for each of them on the Scorewall. They'd believed him, and he'd been right. That exact amount was figured into their totals when they got back, due to their navigation of the third ring without food or equipment.

Moments like that were reasons why Mira had been pulled to Ben. She rarely found herself attracted to conventional sorts. She was drawn to different qualities, like intellect or creativity or some unique personality quirk. Even with Holt, for all his obvious physicality, her feelings for him mostly stemmed from his wits, his ability to improvise, his calm under pressure.

It was the same with Ben.

Ben was brilliant. He was brilliant everywhere, but most of all in the Strange Lands. He was made for it. His ability to quickly solve complex problems was why he was the best Freebooter in the world. He could study an Anomaly once and have it mastered, could always pass through it from then on, faster than anyone else. His brain was like a sponge for details and patterns, and once something was learned, he never forgot it.

Looking at him beaming up at her, his eyes sparkling in spite of the Tone, she saw the other reason she'd been attracted to him. Ben relied on facts and logic and numbers, and it made him almost emotionless. If he wasn't, he wouldn't be who he was, someone who went the direction his mind pointed him, not his heart.

But it had always been different with Mira.

With her, he smiled. His masks dropped. He shared secrets and dreams, he was a whole person, not an automaton. She was the only one who brought that out in him. And she liked it, she liked that he had opened for her, and for her alone.

Not unlike how Holt had very recently opened for her, too, she thought.

Holt.

The world came flooding back, and she remembered that he and Zoey were right behind her. Watching.

She squirmed in Ben's grasp until he set her on the ground. Behind him, his team of Gray Devils Freebooters stood up as they slowly recognized who she was.

Mira recognized most of them, too. A redheaded kid named Scott Norwood, the third-highest-rated Freebooter in the Gray Devils and the fifth overall. He'd always had a competitive streak with Ben, though Ben never seemed to notice. Twin sisters, both fourteen, Tara and Ranee Enright, had only been Freebooters a few months before Mira had been exiled, but she remembered they'd shown impressive pathfinding skills. Joseph Pisano, a tall, lanky kid, who had always had a crush on Mira, she thought, though he was too shy to act on it. And others, about twenty in all.

She used to be one of them, someone they looked up to. But now they stared at her with hostility. In their minds, she had betrayed their faction, she was a Point fabricator, and things were very different now. It was another reminder of just how much she'd lost.

The Gray Devils moved toward her.

Behind her, Mira sensed Holt step forward, saw his hands slide toward his pistol. She opened her mouth to speak—

"No." Another voice beat her to it. Ben's. Calm, soft and low. But somehow it always carried, everyone always heard it. He slowly held up a hand as he spoke.

The Gray Devils froze in their tracks, staring between Ben and Mira.

"Everything's fine," Ben said. "It adds up. If Mira's here, then things are resolved. Right, Mira?" Whether he was covering for her or believed what he'd said, Mira couldn't tell.

"Yes," was all she said. She'd tell Ben the truth later, but not with the other Gray Devils nearby. She quickly moved on before anyone else spoke. "Ben, I want you to meet my friends."

Mira was surprised by the effort it took to say that. It was a moment, like many others, she'd been dreading. A part of her hoped it would never come, but it had. And there was nothing to do about it now. "This is . . . Holt." She forced herself to look at him. Her throat felt dry. "He's the one who got me here. And he helped me in Midnight City, too. I wouldn't be alive without him."

Ben looked at Holt. And Holt looked back.

Ben had an amazing ability to deduce things from simple observations. He could put seemingly random and unconnected pieces of a puzzle together with very little effort, and right now his gaze moved up and down Holt with intensity.

"He was also the bounty hunter who captured you," Ben said. Holt's eyebrows raised. He looked at Mira questioningly. "It's your shoes, mainly," Ben continued. "You don't wear boots like most people. And yours are new, probably salvaged a month ago, maybe less. That makes it a conscious choice. Shoes over boots. Only reason you do that—so you can *run*. Which means you run a lot."

Holt's stare hardened, but Ben didn't seem to notice.

"You're clearly not timid, I can see it in your eyes, so you're not running *from* anyone. You're running *after* them. Chasing people . . . and you do it a lot. That, combined with the handcuffs on your belt, suggests you're a bounty hunter. Someone who chases people for a living. You must be good, too. Catching Mira couldn't have been easy." Ben's voice shifted slightly. The barest hint of darkness. But for him, it said a lot.

Holt smiled slightly. "She definitely made me work for it."

Mira felt a shudder, almost smiled herself, but stopped. This wasn't the place. This was a charged situation.

Ben nodded. "I'm sure." He looked away and down at Zoey, who was holding on to Holt with one arm and Max with the other. Ben's eyes moved over her in the same laborious way.

"This is Zoey," Mira said. Zoey just looked back up at him silently. "She's a very good friend of mine."

Ben studied her curiously. "There's something different about you. Something familiar, too. I can't put my finger on it, which is . . . unusual for me."

Zoey's voice was almost as soft as Ben's. "There's something different about you, too. Your emotions are hard to see. Like the Librarian. But he did it on purpose. That was how he tried to be. With you . . . I think it's just who you are. Like you just don't feel much."

As she spoke, Ben's gaze magnetically locked on the little girl.

"Sometimes it worries you," Zoey said. "But not for long. There's always something new to take your mind off it, something new to figure out. Your thoughts come one after the other, but they're not all jumbled up. They're . . . together. They make sense to you." Zoey seemed surprised. "You must think about things a whole lot."

Mira had rarely ever seen a look of surprise on Ben's face, but he wore one now. "Yes," he said. "I do."

Ben was the one used to figuring people out, and the fact that Zoey had just done the same thing virtually ensured he would try and deduce why. The problem was, Zoey's deductions weren't based on physical evidence or deduction. They were based on amazing and dangerous powers that no one here needed to know about. If Mira let him, Ben would figure it out eventually. Ben figured *everything* out.

"I didn't know you would be here," Mira pressed on, trying to distract him. And she knew there was one thing she could say that would guarantee it. "But I'm glad you are. I was hoping we could go with you."

Ben pulled his gaze from Zoey in genuine confusion. "Go with us where?"

Mira swallowed. "The Severed Tower."

Ben raised an eyebrow. A second later, the entire collection of Gray Devils behind him laughed out loud.

"You wanna take a little girl and a dog into the *Core?*" one of them asked in disbelief.

Her name was Faye. Mira knew because she used to tutor her on artifact creation, and Faye had been so grateful she'd gotten Mira a box of
hot chocolate mix in thanks. Now Faye looked at Mira with scorn.

Mira just kept her eyes on Ben. His opinion was the only one that mattered. Ben looked back curiously. Who knew what pieces he was putting
together, but it was too late now to stop it.

"Go back inside," Ben told his team. "Double-check your gear. We're
going to make Polestar in two days, make up for lost time, and that means
passing through the Mine Field and the Compactor without rest." Ben's
Gray Devil team reluctantly disappeared back under the canopy.

"No one's going anywhere *near* Northlift," Echo piped up from the
other side of Holt. He'd been watching everything in the background,
but he was just as firm in his opinions now as he had been earlier. "You
won't be seeing either of those Anomalies anytime soon."

"I'm not convinced of that," Ben said absently. "You're evacuating.
The Crossroads will be empty soon, and you won't have enough people
to stop us. I know how to work Northlift, I've watched the operators do
it, and it only takes once for me to see how something works."

Echo stiffened, but Holt spoke up. "I think these two have a lot to talk
about," he said. "Is there someplace Zoey and I could rest? Been moving
pretty much nonstop for three days."

Echo looked at Zoey's weary eyes and frowned. "Yeah. Sure. Come
on." He turned and headed back the way they'd come, and Holt pushed
Zoey and Max after him.

Mira tried to catch Holt's eye as he did, but he wouldn't look at her.
There was a hollowness in her stomach as she watched him walk away.

When they were gone, Ben moved closer.

It made her uncomfortable, she realized with surprise. Somehow it felt
wrong, and, at the same time, natural and comfortable, too. Ben's mouth
opened to speak, but then abruptly shut as he noticed something. His
features contorted in a way Mira had rarely seen. He was shocked, and it
took a lot to shock Ben Aubertine.

"Your . . . eyes . . ." he said in a stunned whisper. Ben had noticed the
one thing Echo hadn't, that her eyes no longer held the telltale traces of
the Tone. "That's . . . how did . . . ?"

"Ben," she said firmly, stopping him before he got going. "It is *exactly* what it looks like. And I know you want to know, I know it's almost impossible for you to sideline something you're curious about, and I know 'curious' probably doesn't even begin to describe it, but I *can't* tell you about my eyes right now. I will, I promise, but I need you to be patient. Okay?"

Ben just kept staring into her eyes, searching the pupils for evidence or clues, and she wasn't even sure he'd heard her.

"*Ben.*"

He blinked, refocusing—and then smiled.

A smile from Ben was unusual, and it filled her with emotion like it always did. "I'm . . . so *happy* for you." It was genuine, the sentiment, devoid of any envy or bitterness, and it only complicated things in Mira's mind. He leaned in toward her. Mira didn't move, a thousand thoughts swirling through her head. "I missed you. You're the only one I ever miss."

Mira pulled away from him at the last second.

Ben studied her curiously. He hadn't predicted that reaction. But, as always, he quickly surmised where it came from. "I see." He didn't look hurt or worried, just resolved. "Lenore's dead, isn't she?"

The question hit like a lightning bolt. "Yes . . ." Mira said, her voice shaking. "I mean *no*. She's not . . . dead. She's . . ."

"Succumbed," Ben finished for her. Mira's eyes widened. Sometimes his ability to deduce things was staggering. But he just shrugged. "You said 'yes,' at first, which means she might as well be dead, but if she's not, the closest thing is Succumbed. There's only one thing I know of that could Succumb a Heedless." He was right. Even now she was aware of the horrible artifact that sat in her pack. "When you were getting your artifact . . . Lenore said I was the one who told her about it," Ben said slowly. "You feel betrayed."

When she spoke her voice wasn't shaky anymore. It was stern and cold. "Did you?"

Ben looked back at her but said nothing. He just turned and started walking down a path between half a dozen rusting helicopters. "You'll need your Lexicon," he said.

Her Lexicon was one of the last things on her mind, but he was right. She would need it if they were going into the Strange Lands.

Mira stared after Ben a moment, then followed him. A small brass dice cube appeared from one of his pockets, the same die he always carried. He juggled it on his hand, floating it between his knuckles, back and forth. It was a habit for him, something he did when he was deep in thought.

"I *was* the one who told Lenore," he finally said.

A wave of heat rushed through Mira. She was surprised by how tangible the anger and pain was. Even after Lenore had told her, even after she'd seen Ben's name on the Scorewall outside the Unmentionables column, a part of her hadn't believed it. Or at least, hadn't wanted to. But now it was real.

Mira stopped and stared at him. "How the hell could you *do* that to me? You were the one person I could *trust!* Do you have *any* idea what I've been through because of what you did!?"

Ben turned and studied her calmly. He seemed introspective, not ashamed or hurt. It only made Mira angrier.

"No," he said. "I won't pretend I do. But what I do know is that whatever it was, you could handle it. And that's the reason I did what I did. It wasn't an easy choice for me, Mira."

Mira spoke slowly in a voice laced with so much venom she barely recognized herself. "Please try to explain it in a way that makes sense to those of us without your ability to intellectually rationalize every goddamn thing you think and want."

Ben sighed, as if summoning patience. She wanted to hit him. "It was my opportunity to get a Severed Tower expedition. You know how important that is."

"More important than *me*, apparently," Mira shot back.

"Like I said, I *knew* you'd be fine. You're always fine, you always get out of whatever mess you're in. It was mathematically certain you'd escape, and then either come back with a plan to get your artifact—or accept Lenore's offer, which, by the way, wasn't a bad one."

"Ben . . ."

"If it was certain, *really* certain, that you would be okay, if I knew you would make it—then why shouldn't I take Lenore's offer? Everyone wins. It's easy math."

"Because people are *dead* because of what you did," Mira replied. "There's more than just you and me in the world, Ben."

"Not as far as I'm concerned." Finally there was a hint of emotion in his voice.

Mira sighed and looked away. She felt tired all of a sudden. It was the kind of answer she should have expected from Ben, and in its own way it actually did make sense. But that didn't make it feel any better.

"I . . . know you're mad at me," he said. She looked back up at him. "But you have to believe I knew we would be together again. It's the only thing other than the Tower that matters to me. I wouldn't risk either. I *promise* I'll make it up to you. You're back now. Everything's over. You and I can go to the Tower like we always—"

"I told you, I have to go with my *friends* to the Tower." She walked past him, back down the path through the old helicopters.

Ben followed silently. The die reappeared, dancing on his knuckles. "Hauling a non-Freebooter, a little girl, and a dog through the Core is suicide. And why the Tower anyway? If not with me, why with *them?* You don't need to reach the Tower to destroy your artifact. The fourth ring Anvil is far enough for that."

He was figuring things out, Mira knew, about to be lost in a stream of thoughts that would lead to one inevitable conclusion.

"The bounty hunter is a means to an end. He helps you survive, I get that, but there's no reason for him to go to the Tower either. It must be because of the girl. She's the only unknown."

"Ben . . ." Mira said.

"Then there's your and the bounty hunter's eyes, clear of the Tone. He could be Heedless, there's no way to know, but you definitely *aren't.*"

"Ben, stop—"

"The girl probably factors into that, too . . . but *how?*"

"Ben . . ."

"There have been rumors, even here, of someone who destroyed the Assembly army at Midnight. Someone who stood on the dam and unleashed the waters. I hadn't put much credence in it, it didn't add up. But maybe—"

"*Stop!*" Mira yelled and quit walking. "Just . . . *stop.*"

Ben looked at her oddly. Studied her like she was new to him all over again, like she was a mystery. Ben liked mysteries. "What have you gotten yourself into, Mira?"

"Like I said . . ." She stared back at him, feeling the anger starting to build. "You don't know what I've been through."

They started walking again.

It was weird moving through the Crossroads in its abandoned state. Buildings and planes and structures she'd been in countless times before, for various reasons, now all stood empty and quiet. It was unsettling.

Ahead was the wingless fuselage of a colorfully painted old bomber. A B-17 Flying Fortress. She knew that because her grandfather had served on one in the Pacific.

Mira and Ben moved toward it. One of its doors hung open, a red δ spray-painted next to it, and they stepped inside. The walls had been rigged with old lockers from a ruined school or gymnasium, probably. Each was padlocked and decorated with different ornaments and pictures, making the room an arc of color all around the inside of the old airplane.

Mira moved to hers, a dull yellow one with M.T. written on the side in white paint. There were no pictures, just the writing. She'd never gotten around to properly decorating it, because there had always been other things to do. Now she wondered if this was the last time she would ever see it.

Ben watched as Mira dialed in the combination and opened her locker. There was only one thing inside, hanging from a rusted coat hook.

At first glance it looked like a big leather-bound book with a long shoulder strap woven into the binding, but it was actually much more than that. It was Mira's Strange Lands Lexicon, a vital tool for any Freebooter. In fact, the possession of a Lexicon is what *made* you a Freebooter. Only those who completed the Librarian's training and survived their final trial received one.

Lexicons were handed down from Freebooter to Freebooter, either collected after they were killed in the Strange Lands, or turned in before the Tone took them. As such, they represented the collective knowledge of every Freebooter who had owned it in the past. The loss of a Lexicon in the Strange Lands was nothing short of a tragedy.

Mira's was bound in thick, faded red leather with frayed edges, worn smooth from years of use. Etched into the cover was a gray δ, and she ran her fingers around the outline of the symbol. Straps passed though tarnished brass buckles, keeping it sealed, and two metal locks on either side ensured that only she could open it. Inside were detailed maps of the Strange Lands' rings and the Core—if any of its owners had made it that far—as well as writings, drawings, sketches and diagrams for the Anomalies that inhabited the different rings. No Freebooter went into the Strange Lands without their Lexicon, and being without one inside meant certain death.

Mira slid the thick padded strap over her head and let it rest on her shoulder and cross down her chest. The Lexicon rested comfortably against her hip. It felt good having it back. Without it, she'd always felt like a piece of her was missing.

"Are you serious about getting the bounty hunter and the little girl to the Tower?" Ben asked.

"Don't forget the dog," Mira said wryly. "He's coming, too."

Ben didn't laugh, just waited for her answer.

"Yes."

"Why?"

"I can't tell you that."

Ben's eyes thinned. "Just like you can't explain your eyes." He didn't seem hurt so much as intrigued. "There's never been anything you couldn't tell me."

"I'm sorry." Mira meant it.

"If I knew the answer, would I risk it?"

She looked up at him. It was a good question. She guessed the answer was yes. Rationally, getting Zoey to the Tower might be the most important thing anyone had ever done in the Strange Lands, but she still couldn't risk telling him. Not yet. Or maybe she was still angry with him.

"I think so," Mira finally answered.

Ben nodded. "Then you can all come with the expedition as far as Polestar, but after that it's too dangerous. I can't risk the lives of my team."

Mira was surprised at the amount of relief she felt, even if Ben had only agreed to take them as far as Polestar. It meant *he* would lead, *he* would navigate the Anomalies, *he* would get them through. It wouldn't fall to *her*.

The moment Mira promised Zoey she would get them all to the Severed Tower, the faintest embers of an emotion had formed inside her. As they left Midnight City, the emotion began to build, growing like a cancer. It was fear, she knew. Fear of having to lead people through the Strange Lands. Like she told Holt, it was something she had done only once, and the memory of what happened still haunted her. The thought of failing Holt or Zoey in that place was petrifying.

"Thank you, Ben," she said.

He just studied her intently. "Do you remember the first time we reached the edge of the Core? And you had to pull me back from going right in."

"Yeah. It scared me."

"I know. I don't really feel fear. Everything to me is just . . . patterns and probabilities. Not much else. I see risk, but only enough to factor it into how I act. I don't *feel* it." He gently stroked her cheek with his fingers. "It's one of the reasons I need you. You're my . . . emotional side, Mira. You keep the other parts in check, you balance them. I know now, that's why the Librarian decided what he did, why he made it so we could only go into the Strange Lands together."

She was so accustomed to Ben's touch, she almost didn't notice it. In spite of everything, a part of her liked being close to him. It was familiar and comfortable. And that was something she hadn't felt in awhile.

"Once we get to Polestar, you'll come with me," he continued. "To the Tower. Like we always talked about. You and I against the Core. We can beat it, Mira. I *know* it."

He was right. They were a great team; they always had been. The Librarian had seen that. And she would be lying if she said she didn't want to go with him, that the idea of casting off her burdens and promises wasn't very attractive.

Why were things never simple?

5. LINES

HOLT SAT ON TOP the thick wing of a ruined C-17 Globemaster, staring at the Crossroads around him as it emptied out, its residents all circling the drain of an uncertain future. As he did, he threw a handful of rocks, one at a time, at the back of an old air tanker, absently listening to the dull sound each made as it dented the rusted metal.

Zoey was asleep in the plane under him, Max lying next to her. The plane had been retrofitted into a visitors dorm, with three or four sleeping areas. Echo had stayed only long enough to point them to the beds, before he got pulled away into some new conflict. When Zoey fell asleep, Holt climbed up through an opening onto the roof.

The Crossroads was one of the more unique places he'd been, but it was still familiar. In a way, it was like every other place in the world now. Built on the crumbling remains of the World Before. Nothing was ever new anymore, everything was just repurposed. In its own way, it was inspiring . . . and sad.

Southlift had been rising and falling steadily. Full going up, empty coming down. If he turned around, he could just barely see Northlift at the opposite end of the quarry, over the tops of hundreds of rusting, forgotten aircraft carcasses. It sat silent and unmoving, underneath a horizon that just looked wrong. Darker, thinner, and wavering. More colorful, maybe, but not more cheery.

Foreboding was the word that came to mind.

Holt threw the last of the rocks, then pulled something else from a pocket. A polished black stone, something he had carried for weeks. It meant something to him. It was more than just a relic of a dance around a campfire. It represented something stronger, something that spoke of his change from isolationist to someone willing to trust.

But where had any of it gotten him?

He thought of Mira and Ben, back near the city's center, alone. He could still see her kissing him. He saw it no matter how hard he tried to block it out. His hand gripped the stone tightly. His arm tensed. He should throw it like the others, toss it away, get rid of it. But he didn't. He couldn't.

Holt stuck the stone back in his pocket and grabbed something next to him. The Chance Generator felt warm in his hands. Pulling it from his pack had been automatic, like reaching out for an old friend.

Maybe he should just leave now, while he could. While Mira was gone and Zoey was asleep. He could just ride Southlift back up and disappear, head southeast like he'd always planned, toward the Low Marshes.

Of course, it wasn't that simple, was it? He'd made promises. He'd told Zoey he believed in her, said he would help her however he could, and he'd meant it at the time.

But she didn't need him. Not really. The truth was this Ben was who she needed now. Both Zoey *and* Mira. They needed someone to get them through the Strange Lands, and that definitely wasn't Holt.

And then there was the Menagerie, less than a mile away, two full ships. Every time Southlift lowered down, Holt expected to see it full of pirates, all wanting to drag him back to Faust to pay for what he'd done, even if what he'd done had been the right thing.

Holt's thoughts stopped as a bright flash to the southwest caught his eye, away from Southlift but near the edge of the quarry. It was like the sun flashing off metal.

It was gone just as quick as—

Two more flashes to the Southeast, visible near the edge again.

Holt's eyes narrowed. Two more made three. Three of anything made a pattern. And a pattern meant something was real.

But what? What was up there? Whatever it was, it seemed to be slowly moving to either side of the city. He looked down at the beads, thought of sliding one up . . . just one. What would be the problem with—

"What are you doing?" It was Mira's voice.

He looked behind him and saw her above the same opening that had let him up, standing still and looking at him.

"There's something along the edge of the quarry," he told her. "Something flashing."

But Mira's eyes were on the abacus in his hands. "I meant what are you doing with *that?*"

He felt a stirring of guilt at the question. "I . . . I just wanted to make sure it still worked, that's all."

"It's a major artifact, Holt, why wouldn't it still work?" Mira asked with forced patience. "And you aren't supposed to be using it, even if it does."

Holt felt the anger fill him again. Everything from the last few hours combined with the tone in her voice boiled over in him. He saw Ben lift Mira up, saw him kiss her. . . .

"Why shouldn't I use it?" he snapped.

"Because you promised me you wouldn't."

Holt froze. She was right. Something about the dishonesty, or the casual way he had forgotten his own oath, stopped him. He looked down at the Chance Generator.

"The abacus makes you paranoid," Mira continued. "It becomes an addiction, and you're being *affected* by it. If you keep using it, you won't be able to do anything without having it turned on. That's what it *does*." Mira looked at him with sad concern. "I want you to shut the artifact off—and hand it to me."

Holt looked up at her.

"It'll be tough," she continued, "there's no doubt, but after a week or so without it . . . you should be okay. You should be yourself again."

Holt was silent. He looked back at the abacus. Was she right? Was this thing really affecting him? If it was, shouldn't he be able to tell?

"Think about how you were before the artifact," Mira said. "You were strong, self-sufficient. It's what meant the most to you, your ability to survive. And you *hated* artifacts. Can you honestly tell me you would rely on something like the Chance Generator instead of yourself?"

Holt was silent. What she said, it made sense. Didn't it?

"I need you where we're going, Holt." Mira's voice sounded raw. He wasn't sure what had happened with Ben, but it had been emotional. "The *real* you. I rely on you, don't you see? I don't know if I can make it with you like this."

Words that were meant to placate him cut like a knife. He looked up at her with a new look, a heated one. "You don't need me, you've got *him* now. I'm a liability here, you and I both know it. That's what you really want to say, isn't it?"

Mira sighed and looked away. "What happened between us at the dam . . . happened because I wanted it to, but it wasn't fair to you. I had things that weren't resolved, things that—"

"You told me," he said, cutting her off. "Not in so many words, but you did. I just didn't listen, like an idiot. I stuck around when I shouldn't have, when everything pointed for me to leave. Survival dictated it—but I stayed anyway. I keep doing it over and over again with you."

Mira looked up at him, and her eyes were glistening. "I wanted you to stay," she whispered.

"Why?" If she would just answer that, he would be there for her as long as she needed, whether he was any use or not, whether he died or not. If she would just tell him, he would stay.

She didn't answer. She held his gaze a second—and then looked away.

Holt got to his feet, the anger building. "Can't even answer me that, after everything we've been through." He clutched the abacus in his hand, and it felt good there. The anger felt good, too. Why *shouldn't* he be angry? After all he'd been through and done for *her?* What had he ever gotten for his trouble?

Mira looked back at him. "Holt, you're not yourself right now. Please give me the artifact. Give it to me and then we can talk. We can talk about anything you want."

She offered her hand out, but it only made him more angry. "No," he said firmly.

Mira frowned. "Holt, I *have* to have it. You're not thinking clearly. It should be *obvious* to you!"

He felt more heat build inside him at the arrogant way she barked her orders, at how she thought she knew him. The Chance Generator throbbed in his hand.

"This artifact is the best thing that's ever happened to me." His voice held nothing but scorn, and Mira's eyes widened. He didn't care, just felt the anger flow through him, the abacus burning in his grip. He liked it. "You can have your Ben and your Strange Lands, and all of it—but I'll keep this. I'll keep it and leave."

She stared at Holt a second more—then stepped toward him. "I can't let you do that."

"It's not up to you."

She reached for the artifact, tried to grab it from his hand. Holt resisted, and pushed her away from him.

"Holt, *stop!*" Mira shouted and moved forward again, grabbing at the artifact, trying to yank it away.

More anger flared inside Holt, hot and powerful. His reaction was fueled by it, drove everything that happened next, and it was all virtually automatic and mindless.

Holt shoved Mira hard, watched as she fell and slammed down on the old wing. He rushed forward, full of fury. His hand raised, curling into a fist, readying to strike downward and—

Mira's scream snapped him from the action.

He froze in place, one hand poised to hit her, the other hand holding the Chance Generator.

He had never seen the look on Mira's face directed at him. A look of shock and fear, of confusion and pain. She stared at him like she had no idea who he was. He could hear her frightened breathing.

With wide, horrified eyes, Holt stepped back.

There was a hollow thump as the abacus fell from his hand and clanged against the metal wing. He didn't look at it. He just stared down at Mira with a blank, stunned look.

"Take it," Holt said, his voice a ragged whisper, barely audible. "Take it."

Slowly, Mira reached out and grabbed the artifact, keeping her eyes on Holt. He could see the pain there, the damage. He hadn't hit her, but he'd hurt her all the same, crossed an invisible line. He had a sick feeling in his stomach.

"Mira . . . I'm . . ." he started to say.

A shower of sparks exploded into the air at the northern end of the city, where the cliffs rose upward.

Holt and Mira both looked toward the sight, trying to find the source. Another plume of sparks, and something else.

A single point of light, bright enough to be visible in the afternoon sun, hovered in the air. Holt watched it sink slowly down, pulled by some unseen force toward one of the old planes. When it touched it, another shower of sparks plumed upward.

"Oh my God." Mira said next to him. There was genuine dismay in her voice, like she was looking at something that made no sense.

"What is it?" Holt asked. Screams echoed in the distance. More sparks shot into the air.

But Mira didn't answer. She just jumped to her feet and moved for the opening in the plane's roof.

ZOEY STOOD AT THE EDGE of Midnight City's massive dam, staring at the breadth of the flood plain that fanned outward from the sheer drop at her feet.

It wasn't like before.

There was no battle this time—no explosions, no shrapnel or plasma bolts burning the air, no screams and no dying.

Everything was silent and still. The world seemed frozen, like she was standing in a photograph. Except far beneath her, in the water, there were shadows, and the shadows writhed and moved in disturbing ways.

Zoey felt sensations pouring up at her from them. The same suggestions, over and over, and she tried to stop them, but she couldn't. They filled her mind and there was nothing she could do.

If she had to put the sensations into words or into a thought, it would simply be: "Why?"

Again and again. The same question.

Then a voice. From no source she could discern. It was loud. So loud it overpowered the suggestions from the squirming, unsettling shadows below.

"Wake up, Zoey," it said. "Balance must be restored."

The voice, Zoey noticed with some alarm, sounded exactly like her own. *"Wake up!"*

WITH A START, ZOEY woke and found her head full of pain.

She grimaced and held her temples, curling into a ball on the cot the Echo person told her she could sleep on. The Max whined next to her, and his cold nose pushed under her hand. He had a worried look, Zoey could tell. She had come to know the dog's feelings strictly from his expressions, and it was a source of endearment and relief. He was the only one in her life she couldn't read with her powers, whose emotions and thoughts didn't come involuntarily streaming into her mind. With him everything was quiet; she felt only her *own* feelings. It was one of the reasons she loved him so much.

"The Max," Zoey said softly, scratching his nose. "I'm okay, I promise. I can be tough, too."

Something pushed through the pain. More sensations, but not like those from the dream. These were real, and different. It was like the air was vibrating outside, at specific points. As the points moved, whatever they were, the pain in Zoey's head shifted to match. She could feel them, could tell where they were. She could tell something else, too. They were multiplying. Seconds ago there had been two of them. Now there were four.

Zoey had never felt anything like it. It was another sign things were changing—and it frightened her.

Something stirred in the back of her mind—a pleasing sensation, as if its source was trying to comfort her. The Feelings, the ones she'd been carrying as long as she could remember, like some sort of strange, disconnected hitchhiker. Her powers all stemmed from them, Zoey knew. Whatever they were, they were real and something apart from herself, something no one else had.

The Oracle at Midnight City had shown her many things, but it hadn't explained what the Feelings were. How did she come to have them? What connection did they have with the Assembly?

The Oracle didn't tell her, but it had shown her where to get the answers. The place Mira called the Severed Tower. Whatever it was, however it worked, Zoey knew it would reveal the truth to her. The Feelings knew it, too. They swirled warmly whenever she thought of it.

Yet, she had to get there first.

Zoey heard screams outside, strange popping sounds, and she sat up. Max growled low, staring out past the exit of the old airplane as Holt and Mira swung down from a hole in the ceiling and into the cabin.

"Zoey, we have to leave," Mira said.

"What is it?" Zoey asked, but no one one answered her.

As Holt and Mira quickly geared up, Zoey sensed strange emotions from them. Distrust and anger, shame and a little fear. Nothing unusual in themselves—but it was the first time she'd ever felt those emotions directed from Mira and Holt *at each other.*

Something had happened while she was asleep. Did it have to do with that Ben person from before? Zoey wasn't sure how she felt about Ben. His emotions were too faint. But, as he'd said, they had things in common.

An explosion echoed in from outside, the concussion wave rocking their plane.

"What's happening?" Zoey asked again. This time Mira responded.

"Tesla Cubes. Unstable Anomalies." The shock was still evident in her voice, and Zoey could sense the fear drifting off her. Whatever Tesla Cubes were, they were bad.

"I thought we weren't in the Strange Lands yet?" Holt asked, just as confused.

"We're *not!* They shouldn't be here, it's impossible," she answered back.

A violent rumbling sound outside. More screams.

"Maybe someone should tell *them* that," Holt said as he shouldered his pack. "What's our plan?"

"Ben will try to get to Northlift now. We need to be there when he does. Assuming you're still coming." Mira had yet to look at Holt, Zoey noticed.

"I'm coming," he said tightly. "Made a promise, didn't I?"

"More than one."

Holt stiffened. Something had definitely happened up top. Zoey wished they could see each other the way she saw them. If they did, they would understand everything, but people, she'd found, rarely saw the truth about each other or themselves. They always saw something else instead, and it made her sad.

An explosion suddenly, more crashes, more screams.

"That's it, let's go." Holt strapped his guns to their usual spots. "Whatever you didn't pack, leave it." He whistled at Max and moved for the exit. Zoey followed them, peering into the Crossroads.

When she had last seen the city, it had a strange beauty. Built on ruins, on top of things that had been lost and forgotten, and yet it had been remade with imagination into something new. It had been cared for and loved.

Now it was burning.

Flames spread quickly between some of the old planes at the northern end, blackening and consuming them where they stood. What was left of the populace ran in a panicked surge toward Southlift and the old roads that wound up the sides of the cliffs.

In the distance, sparks shot into the air. Zoey couldn't tell how, but the pain in her head throbbed in ways that told her the things she'd sensed before had grown again. There were almost a hundred now—and she had a feeling there would be more soon. But what *were* they?

Holt turned and lifted Zoey onto his shoulders. "Which way?" he shouted at Mira.

Mira pointed north, down a path of hulking, rusted planes, and Holt ran down it, shoving his way through the frothing crowd of kids.

The good news was, the more they went in this direction, the thinner the crowd got. The bad news, of course, was that they were headed straight for whatever everyone was running from.

Mira dashed past, taking the lead, and Holt whistled for Max. The dog bounded gleefully after them.

"What do these things look like?" Holt yelled after Mira.

"You'll know them when you see them!"

Zoey held on to Holt's neck as they kept running, heading north toward the cliff wall and Northlift, at the far end of the city. Then she screamed as a massive, old plane fell to pieces in front of them, collapsing to the ground.

"Holy crap!" Holt shouted, barely keeping his footing as debris sprayed everywhere.

The top of the collapsed plane was covered in a mass of strange, glowing objects. Small, each about the size of a softball, except they were perfect cubes. Cubes of pure energy that glowed in different colors, and they seemed almost magnetically drawn to the old planes and helicopters. Whenever they touched one, plumes of colored sparks shot everywhere, and Zoey could see they were *burrowing through* the rusted metal, dissolving it.

As the glowing cubes pushed down and in, their colors changed, starting at a cool blue, rising to purple, red, orange, becoming brighter and brighter, until they were nothing but white-hot light. Then there was a flash, and another, identical cube formed out of the first one.

Every time they did, the pain in Zoey's head grew slightly worse. She moaned and struggled to keep her arms around Holt.

"They're attracted to metal," Mira shouted as they ran. "They break it down and absorb it, until they have enough energy to create a clone of themselves. They replicate *exponentially*, and with all the junk in this place, there's going to be millions of them." Sparks shot into the air everywhere, and Zoey could see hundreds of cubes, floating toward and absorbing into the planes and helicopters, one after the other, spreading and growing like a virus.

"What's the big deal, if they're just attracted to metal?" Holt yelled.

"See what those things are doing to the planes? Touch one and they'll do the same thing to you. In a few minutes, this whole place is going to be flooded with them."

Zoey felt Holt groan under her. "Forget I asked."

Mira skidded to a harsh stop, almost falling over. Ahead of her the air was full of the lethal glowing cubes—a thick mass of hundreds of them drifting between the various wrecks, igniting into sparks when they made contact.

"Back!" she shouted, then turned—and stopped again. When Holt spun around, Zoey saw why. The air behind them was full of the same cubes, sparking violently as they began to cover and bore into a cargo helicopter.

The air was filling with them, and Zoey moaned as the pain in her head kept rising. There was nowhere to—

Someone grabbed Mira and Holt and yanked them off the path and underneath a rusting fighter jet. Zoey climbed off Holt as they ducked under the old plane, and saw a group of five other kids. Max darted underneath with them, barking, until Holt silenced him.

More sparks, and another plane collapsed inward on itself under hundreds of the glowing cubes. There were thousands now, Zoey guessed.

"Mira!" Echo shouted, pushing toward them. His voice was shaky, and Zoey could feel the shock and fear coming off him. "Been pinned here five minutes. Lost four of my guys already. They're Tesla Cubes! *Outside* the—"

"Yeah, I have eyes!" Mira yelled back, just as shocked. "How can this be happening?"

"I don't know! I . . . I should have evacuated sooner. I felt it, I *knew* something like this—" More plumes of sparks sprayed into the air as a helicopter disintegrated loudly.

"No one could ever predict this, Echo, it's insane!" Mira tried to console him, but Zoey felt no change in the emotion coming from him. "Listen to me, we need to get to Northlift! Before the Crossroads are completely over—"

"I said *no!*" he retorted angrily. "I'm not losing anyone else! Besides, it's at the other end of the city, where the cubes are the densest. You'll never make it."

"Hate to break it to you," Holt told him, "but those cube things are behind us now, too, and with the way they're multiplying, in another ten minutes they're going to be pretty much everywhere. The northern side's closer, it's less of a run. That lift's our best chance."

Echo snapped to the sound of screams, watched as a giant B-1B bomber fell to pieces in a shower of rust, covered with cubes. Zoey could sense the emotions drifting off him. Frustration, disdain, and anger. He had lost a lot of friends to the Strange Lands, but he had always seen the Crossroads as safe. The realization that it wasn't hit him hard.

"Echo," Mira said. "It's important. If we can get inside the Strange Lands . . . we can maybe change *everything*."

His eyes slimmed. "I don't even know what that *means*, Mira. Change everything? How?"

"I can't tell you," she said, and Echo frowned. "But I think I've earned your trust. After everything we've been through."

Echo's gaze visibly softened. Zoey felt new emotions from him. Guilt mainly, and sadness. "Cashing that chip in, huh? It's that important?"

"It is," Mira said simply.

Echo and Mira stared intently at one another, then he seemed to relent. "Fine. But then you and I are even. And I can stop feeling guilty every damn time I see you."

Mira nodded. "Deal."

"We can't use the main paths," Echo stated, "they're too open, and the air's gonna be full of cubes, especially up high. Only shot is to stay low, move under the planes."

The glass from a ruined Apache helicopter next to them burst into shards.

Holt nodded encouragingly. "How about we get going with that?"

Echo spun and told his men what was happening: They were moving for Northlift; they would try to get out of the city that way. No one argued.

Mira grabbed Zoey's hand and pulled her forward, dashing out from the cover of the fighter plane and running toward another one. Zoey's head throbbed and pulsed, and she could sense the cube things all around her, growing, filling the air and decimating the city. Thousands upon thousands of them now.

They rushed toward a cluster of helicopters.

Behind them two of Echo's boys screamed, and Mira clamped a hand over Zoey's eyes, stopping her from looking. The cubes must have touched them. And that had been that.

Behind them came more explosions. A blossom of flame shot out from the side of the cliff at the far end of the city. There were screams as something big and dark fell loose from the wall, plummeting downward and crashing to the ground in a cloud of dust and fire.

Southlift, Zoey realized. And right before it fell out of sight, she could see it was completely covered in the glowing cubes.

"Damn it!" Echo cursed as they slid under another plane. Zoey felt his frustration. His city was being eaten alive and there was nothing he could do to stop it.

More cubes burst to life in bright flashes around them. Tens of thousands. The number growing every second. Everywhere, the old planes and helicopters, and the city buildings they had been turned into, were covered by the cubes, and they shook and rocked as sparks sprayed from them.

They kept moving, running between and under the planes, dodging the cubes above.

Ahead of them, not more than a hundred feet away, Zoey saw the cliff face rising straight upward, and climbing up along it were the tracks of Northlift, the elevator which would get them into the Strange Lands. So far, it hadn't attracted the cubes—but it wasn't on the ground either, it was hanging in the open air at the top.

"Damn," Echo said, staring at the lift. "Have to lower it."

"Did Ben use it?" Mira asked.

"Who the hell knows. We gotta do this fast." Echo rushed out from under the plane toward a bank of controls near the lift's platform, and started shoving levers and pulleys in different directions.

From up top came a stuttering sound, as the engines began to turn. Zoey saw Northlift shudder and start to descend, crawling at a glacial pace down the cliffside.

Holt groaned in frustration. "You have got to be *kidding* me!"

The last kid with Echo screamed violently, and this time, Mira wasn't close enough to shield Zoey's eyes.

"Danny!" Echo shouted, but it was too late.

The kid's right arm touched one of the cubes in the air. His body flashed once—and then dissolved into a thick cloud of black particles, amid a mass of orange sparks that burst outward and fell to the ground.

Zoey shut her eyes, her head throbbing powerfully. The cubes were everywhere, multiplying, burrowing into and decimating the nearby planes, filling the air like a glowing swarm of insects.

Mira grabbed Zoey and pulled her back. Holt held onto Max as he howled at another explosion nearby. The elevator was lowering too slowly. The cubes were pushing in.

Zoey stared up at Mira fearfully. "What do we do?"

Mira didn't say anything, just clutched Zoey tightly, staring at the cubes that were growing and filling the air.

"Mira!" Holt shouted.

Zoey felt desperation and fear pour off of Mira in great torrents. She was frozen, unable to move. The cubes closed in. . . .

Then there was a sound like a powerful, punctuated blast of static and noise. In a flash of light, something big materialized out of thin air about twenty feet away. An Assembly walker, big and powerful, with five legs. The one from before, the one stripped of its colors. One second it hadn't been there, and then the next . . . it had. The machine gleamed brightly in the afternoon sun. Its three-optic eye whirred as it focused on Zoey.

"Assembly!" Echo stumbled back, his eyes wide with shock, but the machine ignored him.

"Zoey!" Mira screamed, the sight of the walker breaking her spell. Holt ripped his shotgun free.

Then the cubes in the air all pulled away and drifted faster and faster toward the walker, drawn by its thick metallic fuselage.

The machine's shield flashed to life around it, a glowing sphere of energy—and then sparked violently as the cubes made contact. The energy barrier flickered, but it held. The cubes couldn't punch through.

But they kept trying. Dozens. Hundreds. All magnetically pulled toward the walker. In seconds, it was covered in them, and Zoey could barely see inside the flickering shield.

Even so, she could feel the thing's triangular eye bore into her. And then it lunged away, leaping farther into the city, trailing hundreds more cubes with it, and clearing the air around the lift.

If only for a second.

"Would someone like to tell me what the hell's going on?" Echo yelled.

"When we're *out* of here!" Mira shouted. Northlift sat down with a thud, and everyone ran for the platform nearby.

Max growled as, feet away, an old jet detonated and lifted straight up into the air.

Holt sat Zoey inside the lift, and she noticed something unique about Northlift. It had no controls inside it. It was just an empty, polished wooden box. Probably so that its use could be more strictly controlled, she figured.

Holt pressed her protectively into a corner as more glowing cubes moved in to fill the vacuum outside. There wasn't much time.

"Echo, get in here!" Mira yelled as she jumped in.

The little kid didn't answer, just shoved the control levers back into place. Northlift rocked and groaned as it started to climb back up the cliff wall.

"Echo!" Mira screamed, and Holt pulled her back before she leaped off after him.

"Someone's gotta run this thing," Echo said. "You know that. Besides . . ." Echo finally looked up her. "I owe you one."

Mira screamed Echo's name again, trying to break free of Holt's grip, but she couldn't, he was too strong. The air filled with cubes, and Echo was surrounded. There was nowhere for him to go, and he knew it. So did everyone inside the lift.

He stared at Mira a second more . . . then he stepped directly into the swarm, touching three cubes at once. He didn't even have time to cry out, his body flashed into black dust and red sparks almost instantaneously.

Mira cried in pain. She ripped free of Holt's grasp, and pushed to the edge of the lift. Holt stared after her but left her alone.

As the lift rose, Zoey stared down at what was left of the Crossroads. From higher up, they could see everything—and it was all horrible.

There were hundreds of thousands of cubes now filling the air, covering the old planes, dissolving them. What was left of the buildings and wrecks sparked violently and fell in on themselves in bursts of flames. The city was done for, it was imploding in a torrent of sparks and fire.

At the opposite end, dozens of kids raced up the road that wound around the walls of the quarry, fleeing to the south. Thanks to Echo, most of the city had probably escaped. Images of the Librarian flinging himself into the pit of the Artifact Vault filled Zoey's head. Echo was another person who had died so that she could continue on.

What if she wasn't worth it? It made her ashamed.

Northlift shuddered as it came to a halt at the top of the cliff.

Max darted outside, and Holt followed, grabbing Zoey. Mira was the last to leave, staring out over the destruction a moment longer before finally rushing after them. Zoey could feel the anger and the grief and the shock swelling off of her like ocean waves.

Holt seemed to recognize it, too. "Mira, are you—?"

"We need to get to the river," she said tightly. "It's the main path north, at least for awhile."

Zoey looked ahead of them. There was nothing but open country there, more rolling grassland, with the occasional old road crossing through it, and sporadic groves of trees. The Missouri wound northward less than a mile away.

A sudden surge of sensations pushed through the pain in the little girl's head. She felt presences. Nine of them. Anger and disdain and obsession poured out from one in particular, stronger than the others. Something about it was familiar . . . and frightening.

She figured out what it was too late.

"Holt!" Zoey screamed as the metallic netting flashed toward her. It hit her hard, sent her crashing to the ground and rolling through the grass, wrapping her tighter as she did.

Pain flared in her head again. Everything went hazy and slow motion.

Zoey heard Mira scream her name, saw her run desperately forward.

She heard the electronic trumpetings of the Hunters as their cloaking fields dropped, and then the scary one, the differently marked one, charged into Mira and sent her flying.

Anger and fear flowed from Holt as he pulled loose his shotgun—then nothing but pain as the plasma bolts spun him to the ground.

She heard Max's howl. Then it, too, went abruptly silent.

So did everything else. There was only her throbbing head.

She felt the green-and-orange walkers lift and tuck her underneath one of their bodies. Then they were moving, rushing through the grass and leaving the Crossroads behind.

Zoey tried to fight the growing numbness in her head, but she was too weak. The last thing she remembered was the flash of cloaking fields activating around the Hunters as they carried her away from everything she had come here for.

Then the world faded to nothing.

7. TIME SHIFT

LIGHT FROM STAINED GLASS WINDOWS hung in the dusty air, lighting everything in the antique shop with beams of pastel color. Suits of armor, old typewriters, paintings, vases, and crystal, a crossbow, an Apache headdress, books—all of it disused and forgotten in what was left of the old store.

Mira Toombs, no older than seventeen, clung to the shelves that ran from floor to ceiling, wall to wall, and were just strong enough to hold her weight. She slowly slid her way along the side of it, easing toward a specific glass-covered shelf at the very top, painfully passing by the multitude of items stored there.

It was hard ignoring them. Each gave off a unique, distinct hum—the mark of all major artifacts in the Strange Lands—and this far into the fourth ring, it wasn't a surprise that everything in the store gave off that hum. It was a treasure trove, and if Mira could bag it all up and bring it home, she would have more Points on the Scorewall than she could ever spend.

But that wasn't why they were here. They'd come for something specific. And there wasn't time for anything else.

"How we looking?" she asked, tentatively taking another step. The dirty floor was maybe six feet below her. A fall from this height would hurt.

"Between four and five minutes," Benjamin Aubertine stated, about the same age as Mira, one eye watching her, the other on a ticking stopwatch. If he was worried, his face didn't show it. But then again, he rarely betrayed any emotion.

Mira frowned. "That's a pretty big gap."

"I told you, there's no exact math for Time Shifts. All you can do is estimate."

"Easy for you to say," Mira retorted, taking another step. "You're not climbing a shelf like it's Yosemite."

"Well, of the two of us, you're the lighter one."

Ahead of her the shelves where Mira had been placing her feet vanished, an empty space for a collection of large brass telescopes, each humming in a unique tone. What would a telescope do as a major artifact, Mira wondered. What would you see if you looked through it? The thought excited her as much as it chilled her. You might never recover from what you saw through one of those lenses.

Unfortunately, the shelf they needed was just above the gap, and she had no way to reach it. Mira studied the shelves and, near the one she needed to get to, saw an old coat hanger screwed into the frame.

Quickly, she unslung the Lexicon from her shoulders and carefully leaned toward the hanger, circling its thick strap around it. When it was done, she shifted her weight to the right, leaning outward and holding onto the strap to keep her from falling. It held her weight, which meant she could reach the top shelf now.

"The odds are good I'm gonna end up breaking your fall," Ben observed.

"Do you want what's up here or not?" Mira used her free hand to rub off the dust that had caked the shelf's glass cabinet. It was filled with exactly what Ben predicted: timekeeping devices from a variety of eras—water clocks, hourglasses, pendulums, wrist watches, even an old armillary sphere made of gold, silver, and topaz. Of all the items, it hummed the loudest, and Mira stared at it greedily. She could only imagine what *that* would do if activated.

"Three minutes, give or take," Ben announced from below, studying his stopwatch. "You see them?"

She made herself focus. Near the back of the shelf rested six chronographs, complicated kinds of stopwatches that could record individual times for comparison. Of course, Mira only knew that because Ben had told her. It was what he'd brought them this deep into the Strange Lands for: a chronograph of a certain era that had become a major artifact. He had his own theories about what it would do, but the truth was he never intended to use it. It was a bargaining chip, a valuable one. Something he would give Lenore Rowe, the leader of the Gray Devils back at Midnight City, in exchange for what he truly wanted: a fully funded expedition to the Severed Tower.

It would probably work, too, if the artifact did what Ben thought. It was something someone as ambitious as Lenore Rowe would trade anything for.

But they had to get it first.

"What am I looking for again?" Mira asked, gingerly opening the glass cabinet.

"An older one, early twentieth, late nineteenth century. No Seikos or Timexes."

"What about Gallet?" she asked, studying two of the older looking ones.

"Gallet works," Ben said. "But it can't be a wristwatch."

"One is," Mira told him, her eyes finding the oldest one. "But the other looks like a pocket watch. An old one."

"Grab it. Hurry," Ben instructed her.

No one knew why, but major artifacts didn't fuse to whatever they were touching like the minor ones did. It was a good thing in time-sensitive situations like this, it meant you didn't need to use Paste to get them loose. All Mira had to do was reach in and pull the old chronograph out of the shelf—and when she did it vibrated slightly in her hand, which was a good sign. Whatever it did, it was powerful. She smiled and looked down at Ben and saw what she hoped. The barest, most subtle glimpse of excitement in his expression. It wasn't often you saw it, and Mira relished times like these.

"This the one you want?" she asked, letting it dangle by the silver chain.

"Yes," Ben said, reaching up.

Mira held it out of his grasp. "You're *sure?*"

"Mira . . ."

"I'm just checking," she told him innocently. "We only get one shot at this. Scale of one to ten, how certain are you that, of all the chronographs in this place, this is—"

"*Mira,*" Ben said with intensity. There was a new emotion on his face now. Annoyance. And it was even cuter than the first.

"Okay, here, take the—"

The coat hanger her Lexicon strap hung from broke loose from the old cabinet in a shower of splinters.

Ben rushed forward, valiantly trying to catch Mira, but her momentum was too much. They both went crashing to the floor, Mira on top of him.

When the dust cleared, he stared up at her with the same, dim annoyance. "As predicted . . ."

She stared back down at him—and then was overcome with laughter. Ben didn't join in, he rarely laughed, but he did smile, and that was worth just as much. They stared at each other, close, inches away, the chronograph and the Time Shift and the major artifacts all around them forgotten.

Then Mira saw it in his eyes. Something that flickered to life in moments like these, and it stirred the same tension as always. Her smile vanished. She rolled off him and sat up on the floor, dusting herself off.

Ben did the same. He didn't say anything, but she could still feel his eyes on her, knew what he was thinking.

"Don't," she said.

"You never want to talk about it."

Mira sighed. "Because we've *already* talked about it, Ben. And we agreed."

"*You* agreed," Ben replied.

She frowned and looked back at him. "We *both* agreed. And you know it."

Mira and Ben had been tied together since their trial to become Freebooters. Initially it had been because of the Librarian's decree, a unique stipulation that neither could enter the Strange Lands without the other. Agreeing to the Librarian's condition was the only way they could become Freebooters, and they had taken it.

They both knew, however, that even if the requirement was suddenly removed nothing would change. They had a connection now, a stronger one than either had felt for anyone since the invasion, and it had only grown.

They had given into it only once. And as nice as it had been, they both agreed it could never happen again. What was the point, after all? They had three, maybe four years left before the Tone took them. Developing feelings like those made no sense in the world as it was now. It only made the inevitable that much harder to deal with.

But still there were moments—like just now—where Mira wondered how much sense it really made.

When she looked back at him, the old chronograph was clutched in his hand, but his eyes were on her.

Mira sighed. "Ben—"

She cut off as a rumbling grew around them, deep and powerful, but somehow it couldn't be felt. The items on the shelves or the floor didn't shake. It was as if the air itself was vibrating. And there was something else. It was growing brighter, too. Steadily.

Mira's eyes widened. "You said *three* minutes, give or take!"

"I also said there's no exact math!" Ben lunged forward and yanked her up, dragging her forward through the store.

Mira tried to balance, to turn forward so she could—

Something occurred to her. Something bad.

"My *Lexicon!*" she shouted, turning back around, spotting the big, precious tome on the floor where it had fallen.

"There isn't time!" Ben kept pushing her forward.

"Wait! You don't understand!" She squirmed desperately in his grip, trying to get free, but he was just too strong. "*Ben!*"

The rumbling and the brightness continued to grow. Everything around them—the pieces and parts of the old shop, the shelves, the items—flickered like lights, and then one by one began vanishing into thin air . . . only to be replaced with other pieces and parts that had nothing to do with an antique shop: drill presses, router saws and lathes. The Time Shift was engaging, morphing the local area into a completely different point in time, one that appeared to be when this same building had been a *machine shop*.

If they didn't get out now they would be wiped away with the antiques.

Mira felt physical pain as she realized the truth. They had to run. She had to leave the Lexicon, and everything inside it, behind. With a scowl, she turned and ran with Ben toward the front door, as the air continued to rumble and flash, the world morphing around her.

8. COMPASS

THE DARKNESS RECEDED IN SLOW MOTION as Mira opened her eyes. When she did, she wasn't where she expected to be. She could hear water rushing by fairly close, and there was a strand of spruce trees towering over her against the wavering aurora that filled the sky.

Mira wasn't in an antique shop, and she wasn't where she'd fallen earlier. She was lying on a sleeping bag on the perimeter of a camp, and she could hear voices around her. Ones she recognized. There were about twenty kids, all dressed in some shade of gray and white, some around camp fires, others checking gear or sleeping under the shade from the trees.

It was a Gray Devils camp. Which meant . . .

"You're safe," a voice assured her, and Mira spun around. Ben sat next to her, working in his green-and-blue Lexicon on the ground, a pencil behind his ear. His brass dice cube was absently moving over the knuckles of his left hand, back and forth. "We're away from the Crossroads."

Her shoulder hurt. She remembered where she had been before. With Holt and Zoey. And the Hunters.

"Where are . . . ?" she started, but couldn't finish. Her throat was sore and her mouth was dry. Ben handed her a canteen and she drank from it greedily.

"My guys found you outside Northlift," he said. "Sent them to look for you, figured you might follow us. They watched until your friends were taken away, then they brought you here."

Mira sat up angrily. "Why didn't they *help?*"

"Because then they'd be dead, too. Fighting Assembly is suicide, you know that."

"Holt and Zoey aren't *dead*," Mira said pointedly. "The Assembly took them, it's not the same thing."

"Might as well be. Either way, you'll never see them again."

She glared at him—but a part of her knew he was right. If the Assembly had them, then . . .

"No," she said and stood up, fighting through a wave of dizziness. "They're *alive*. We can get them back. It's like you say, there's always a solution."

"There's always exceptions, too. This isn't a problem you can solve."

"Damn it, Ben—"

"*Think*, Mira," he cut her off softly. "Even if you weren't talking about going after a pack of Assembly walkers, the Strange Lands are different now. The old routes might not work anymore. Everything might be new. Everything might need to be solved—all over again." Mira could hear the faint traces of excitement in his voice as he contemplated the possibilities. "Besides, I finally have what I need to get to the Tower. I can't risk that, it's too important."

"More important than people's lives?"

"Yes," he replied without hesitation. "The Tower represents infinite possibilities. If I can get there I can make everything right. Isn't that worth two lives? Or four? Or a hundred?"

Mira closed her eyes. "Ben . . ."

"I understand why you're torn, Mira," he said. "You've always had problems detaching yourself emotionally when you needed to, especially here. But you know I'm right. Going after them makes no sense. It doesn't add up."

What he said rang true in the same cold, logical way that everything he said did. The odds of her finding Holt and Zoey were beyond small. And even if she did, what would she do? Fight the Hunters by herself? But that wasn't what really bothered her, was it? She was in the Strange Lands, and it meant she would have to navigate it by herself, without Ben. On her own she would fail. Eventually. She wouldn't be good enough. And whoever was with her would pay a price for that. Just like they had so long ago.

Instinctively, Mira thought back to the Crossroads. How she froze when the Tesla Cubes were almost on them. How she couldn't move, couldn't even think. How could she hope to make it on her own?

"Your things are over there," Ben said. "Your Lexicon, your packs." Mira saw her stuff piled neatly on the other side of the campfire. "I saw your plutonium. Good quality. Couldn't have been easy to get."

The plutonium was the batch from Clinton Station. That had been a month ago, but it seemed like forever. It had been in her pack ever since, a glass cylinder wrapped with a Dampener, an artifact that absorbed the heat that naturally poured off the contained element inside, making it safe to transport. For the most part, anyway.

"I got it to trade for your life," Mira said. "But turned out that wasn't necessary. Didn't it?"

It was true. She had hoped to use the plutonium to bargain her way out of Midnight City after she rescued Ben. But Ben had been long gone by the time she'd gotten there. It would have worked, too, the bargain. Plutonium was one of the most valuable substances on the planet because of what it supposedly granted you entrance to. The Severed Tower.

It was ironic, in a way. Everything she had gone through to get the plutonium—avoiding bounty hunters, scouring different cities for clues, eluding Holt, surviving Clinton Station—had seemed pointless once she'd learned that Ben had been the one who told Lenore about her artifact. And yet it turned out to be critical in a different way. If she hadn't gotten it, how would they possibly get Zoey to the Tower, where she claimed she needed to go? It all felt like . . . fate.

Ben moved closer to her, took her hand. "I know it must have been difficult," he told her. "But you're safe now. And you'll go with me. We'll go to the Tower together, like we always said. We'll make the loss of your friends worth it. I promise."

Mira looked up at him. Ben had a singular belief, one that had driven him his entire life. It led him to become a Freebooter, it pushed him deeper and deeper into the Strange Lands, it dictated everything he did. The belief wasn't a simple one. Ben believed that the Severed Tower, the mysterious center of the Strange Lands, was a fusing of all possibilities and realities. If you could reach it and enter it, then you could do *anything*. Ben's intention was and always had been to change the world.

Literally. To make a new reality, one where the Assembly had never invaded, where none of the horror had ever occurred. And he believed that he was the only one who could do it.

Maybe he was right. Maybe he wasn't. Mira wasn't sure if she believed in his theory or not. It sounded too easy. But it had never been a pressing concern, really. After all, they could never reach the Tower, they didn't have the resources. No one reached it without an expensive expedition, funded by a Midnight City faction. It was just too difficult. But now it was within Ben's reach. He could find out the truth for himself. And she could go with him, if she wanted. It was something she always *had* wanted. But things had changed a lot in the last few months.

"No." Mira spoke with a finality that made Ben move away.

She didn't have a lot of faith in herself, it was true. And going with Ben would be a much easier decision—but she knew she couldn't. She had responsibilities to Zoey and to Holt. She had brought them here, which meant in a way they were lost *because* of her. If they were dead, it would be one thing, but they weren't. They were *alive*. And not going after them . . . was betraying them. Even if going after them was futile.

"You asked me about my eyes earlier—about the Tone," Mira said. "Zoey was the one who did that. Zoey can *stop* the Tone. She can do other things, too. Amazing things. And the Assembly is chasing her. She's . . . the key, I think, to whatever it is they're doing here."

As Mira spoke, Ben's brow wrinkled inquisitively. This was unexpected, and for Ben unexpected things were the most interesting. "So she *is* the one from the rumors? The one who saved Midnight City, brought the dam back to life?"

Mira nodded. "They're hunting her. Different groups from all over. She has to reach the Severed Tower, Ben."

"Why?"

"I . . . don't know," Mira admitted. "The Oracle told her, it said she would learn the truth there. And the Librarian said Zoey was the Apex. He died to save her."

For one of the only times since Mira had known him, Ben's eyes widened in astonishment. "The Librarian is . . . *dead?*" She didn't blame him. It didn't seem real to her either. The Librarian was more a force of nature than human. She would have bet on him living forever.

Ben looked away, thinking. "The Apex. That crazy equation he was always working on. The only person to ever come out of the Strange Lands."

Ben had never put much stock in the Librarian's private research, but Mira figured that was because the old man's equations were one of the few things Ben couldn't wrap his mind around.

"That's . . . fascinating," he admitted. "But it doesn't change anything. Apex or not, the Assembly have her now. They went farther *into* the Strange Lands, Mira, not back. I've never heard of the Assembly doing that. But these did."

"I have to try," Mira said.

"Mira." There was a subtle hint of desperation in his voice. "If you do this . . . you do it *alone*. You know that." Mira felt a chill run through her. "It's simple math. You won't make it."

At his words, Mira felt two things: trepidation, because a part of her believed him. She had the proof, didn't she? But she felt something else, too: anger. What he was saying wasn't intended to hurt her, she knew. Everything he said was based on facts and data, but they still amounted to one thing.

"You don't believe in me." She stared back at him. "You never have."

"I'm just telling you the truth. Because you mean the world to me. And I . . . *can't* lose you." Mira sighed at the faint edge of emotion in his voice. He did care. He was just blunt. "You don't have it in you to make the tough decisions that surviving here requires."

Mira nodded. "It would be easier if I were more like you. But I'm not. I have to go after them. Because I owe them. Both of them."

"I need you," Ben said, his voice wavering the slightest bit.

"No," Mira told him. She touched his face. "You don't need anyone, not in here."

She could see in his eyes that he was torn. Which was unusual for him. He would come if he could, but, in his way of thinking, he simply couldn't. Ben sighed and nodded to where her packs and Lexicon sat. "I had them loaded with water and food. And I gave you some of our reagents for the waist pack."

Mira stared at him curiously. Ben just shrugged.

"Figured this is what you'd choose," he said. "It's what the math pointed to."

Ben knew her better than anyone, and even now it was a comfort.

"This will be the first time we've gone into the Strange Lands without each other," he said. "It feels wrong." His hands gently pulled the necklaces from her shirt. Among them there was the old brass dice necklace. He held it in his hand. "You still wear it."

"Every day. Even though you don't believe in luck."

"Only with you," he said, looking back up at her. "Only with you."

Ben leaned forward and gently kissed her. She kissed him back. It felt natural. Familiar. It was comforting. It pulled her. But she couldn't stay here.

Mira backed away, tears beginning to form. Then she grabbed her things. "Can you . . . do something for me?"

"Anything."

Mira opened her pack and pulled out the Chance Generator. Instantly she saw Holt on top of the plane, his hand hovering to strike. It wasn't him, she told herself. But it was hard to remember that, hard not to see that image.

She hated the artifact, it made her sick just holding it.

"Is that . . . ?" Ben's voice was curious.

Mira nodded. "Holt used it in Midnight City to get us out. We brought it here to destroy it, but . . . it started affecting him."

"The compulsion," Ben said.

"He finally gave it up, but I don't like carrying it. Would you . . . ?"

Ben held out his hand for the artifact. "The fourth ring Anvil's on the way to the Core. I'll destroy it when we get there."

At his promise, she felt like a weight had lifted off her. She handed it to Ben and he studied it inquisitively. For a moment, Mira felt a twinge of concern as she watched him with the artifact. But she pushed it away. Ben was too smart—he knew the risks, knew the price that came with it. He would never use it.

They stared at one another a moment more. Ben's eyes had more emotion in them than she had ever seen. "Be careful," he told her. "For *me*."

Mira smiled a little. "Have you seen the scorpion yet?" she asked. It was a personal question, a private one, just between them. She wasn't sure, but it looked like he was smiling a little, too.

"No," he said. "Not yet."

"Keep looking." And then she turned and started moving, heading south, following the river. It was amazing, how hard it was. Not just leaving Ben, but also the safety and familiarity he represented. She was moving into unchartered territory in more ways than one.

Mira walked for about a mile, following the river, before she noticed something odd. The overgrowth around the trees that flanked the water stirred as she moved. Like something was pushing through it, following her.

Mira frowned when she figured it out. "You can come out now."

A shiny black nose pushed through the grass, followed by a fuzzy head with pointed ears. Max stared at her over the distance, and she heard a low growl.

Mira almost laughed. At least *something* was still familiar. "I'm going after them, what more do you want?"

Max didn't move.

"Don't guess you have any ideas on how to find them?" If he did, the dog didn't say.

Mira saw the necklaces were still hanging outside her shirt. She grabbed them to stuff them back inside, then noticed one of them. It had a tiny compass for a pendant. And the strange thing about it was that the needle didn't point north. It pointed northwest. Mira smiled. She had given Zoey an identical necklace weeks ago in the Drowning Plains. They were both Strange Lands artifacts, and they were linked. They always pointed directly to each other.

"What do you know," she said. It didn't solve everything, but it was a much better position to be in than a few seconds ago. Now she just needed a way to deal with the Assembly. An idea occurred to her. A desperate one—but those were the only kind she had now.

Mira looked back to Max, still hovering in the grass near the trees. "You coming or what?"

9. LASER LIGHT

ZOEY TRIED NOT TO CRY, but it wasn't easy. She'd been hanging underneath the green-and-orange tripod for hours as it darted over the ground. The netting that held her was some kind of thin superstrong metal, and it was sharp, too. It cut into her skin, and the worst part was, the more she moved, the tighter it got.

It was night now, and what she could see of the landscape raced past—but it made no sense.

It wasn't trees or grass or farmland. It was cars. Thousands of them, all different kinds and sizes, stretching ahead unendingly, along some desiccated highway. Where was she? Still in the Strange Lands? She'd lost track of how long they'd been moving, and she had no idea how fast the walkers could go.

How would anyone find her now, she wondered. This far away, lost in the dark. She felt more alone than she ever had. The first thing she could remember was Holt finding her in the wreckage of that ship, and since then she'd always been with him and Mira and the Max. No matter how scary things got, they were always there, and now they weren't. She felt tears welling up and pushed them back.

The world ceased its rhythmic bobbing as the walker slowed. When it stopped, the net released. Zoey came down hard on her elbow, but before she could cry out, there was an intense flash of blinding blue light. She felt the netting that held her dissolve away.

For the first time in hours, her limbs stretched out, and Zoey's eyes teared at the relief of it.

Then she sensed movement around her. There were nine of them. She couldn't see them yet because of the blue light, but she knew all the same. This close to her, each of their presences glowed separately in her mind, like colors. Not specific colors, but *all* colors at once, each blending and swirling in a unique way all its own.

Ironically, it was pretty.

The machines stared down at her, their sharp legs puncturing the soil, their armor gleaming in the moonlight. One of them pushed forward and the others gave it room. It was differently marked, its patterns of green and orange were bolder.

Its triangular multicolored eye focused on her, and as it did Zoey felt sensations from it. Pride, arrogance, lust, a heavy mixture that drifted off it like heat from a radiator, and all of it directed at her. Zoey tried to shrink into the ground, but there was nowhere to go.

The walker trumpeted a single, distorted note. The others echoed it, as if agreeing.

Zoey flinched as laser light streamed from two walkers. Triangular shaped beams of purple and red energy that seemed both solid and intangible at the same time. She shut her eyes at the brightness, and these she could feel. They gave off a muted heat as they moved over her slowly, like hands examining a patient.

Then the beams flashed off, and Zoey sensed satisfaction from the walkers.

Something else dropped to the ground near her. Something heavy and big, and she turned to see what it was.

It was another body. Blue laser light seared outward and dissolved away the netting which constrained it. The figure groaned and unwrapped itself, but otherwise didn't move. Zoey recognized him instantly.

"Holt!" she shouted. The Assembly had brought him, too!

She felt a burst of relief—then regretted it. Holt was hurt, a prisoner like she was. It wasn't right to be glad he was here. But she was. She wasn't alone anymore, and it mattered.

Zoey tried to move for him, but one of the walkers stepped in front of her.

The same walkers that scanned her a moment ago did the same thing now for Holt, running their lasers over his still form. Zoey could see the blood soaking his clothes. He must have been shot, she realized.

Zoey looked at the differently colored walker. Its eye looked back, whirring indifferently.

"Please," she told it. "I know you can help him. It's why you were scanning me a second ago, to see if I was hurt."

The walker's three-optic eye stared into her. Did it understand her? She had no way of knowing.

"Please . . ." she begged it. "Please don't let him die." Tears started to form in her eyes, but she stopped them. She wouldn't cry in front of the Hunter, no matter how much she wanted to.

The machine studied her a moment—then it trumpeted an almost disdainful sound, and looked toward the walkers near Holt.

As if by command, the tripods there turned and faced his crumpled form on the ground, and a different set of beams, green this time, emitted from diodes on their bodies. Slowly they moved over Holt, hovering above his different wounds, where the most blood was.

As they did, Zoey reached out to Holt with her mind. There was nothing there at first. He was blank. It scared her, the idea that he might already be dead, but as the laser light moved over him, she started to sense glimmers of emotion and thought. Faint at first, but gradually building strength.

He was coming back, she realized. Zoey felt more relief. The walkers were *healing* him.

Zoey looked back at the differently marked tripod. "Thank you," she said.

She felt sensations wash out from it. Disappointment and confusion mainly, it didn't seem to understand her concern. But Zoey didn't care. Holt would *live*. She wouldn't be alone. If he was alive and with her, then there was a chance, however slim, for things to all be okay.

Zoey watched as another tripod turned its back toward her. There was a series of clicking sounds as slots opened in its rear armor. Four of them. Two near the bottom, two more at the top. To Zoey's eye, they looked like . . . hand grips and foot rungs.

The differently marked walker's targeting laser streamed to life in red and purple. Zoey watched as the beam moved to the back of the other walker, splitting into distinct streams, each lighting up one of the four slots.

Zoey understood. She was to put her feet in the rungs, use the others like handholds, and ride the tripod like some kind of mechanical horse.

At first she felt fear and revulsion—but the more she thought about it, the better a deal it seemed. What choice did she really have? She couldn't run, the walkers would be on her in seconds, and anything was preferable to being wrapped up in that net again.

Zoey moved for the back of the machine, climbing on top of it, placing her feet and hands in its back.

It wasn't a perfect fit, but it worked well enough, and the height was such that she could just peer over the top of the machine and look straight ahead.

One of the walkers shot out a new mass of netting that wrapped around Holt. He moaned but didn't awaken as it scooped him under its body.

The world rocked up and down as Zoey's walker moved with the others and formed into a line. Laser light streamed from each of them, red and purple triangular beams lighting up the night and the endless length of dead, ruined vehicles.

Zoey followed the lasers into the distance . . . and gasped.

Things hovered in the air ahead of them, hundreds of them. They looked like perfect spheres of crackling energy. Some were absorbed into the old vehicles or buried in the ground, but most floated heavily in the air. If she watched them long enough, Zoey almost felt like she could see them moving, slowly drifting one way or another.

They were invisible, Zoey figured out, only appearing when the lasers touched them, and when they did, they flared to life in brilliant color. The walkers were using the beams to *find* them.

They were beautiful, but something about them was also menacing. She had little doubt that touching any one of them would be very bad. They must be more Anomalies, like the cubes back at the Crossroads, and the realization made her remember Echo. A chill went down her back.

The bold walker trumpeted again—and Zoey held on as the line of tripods burst forward into sprints, their lasers streaming ahead, finding the Anomalies as they ran faster and faster.

Zoey, eyes wide, watched as her walker leaped on top of cars, jumping back and forth, dodging in and out of the floating spheres of crackling energy. The wind whipped through her hair. Bright waves of red and purple and white light streamed all around her as the strange spheres lit up and then went dark, over and over, as the walkers dashed through them.

Zoey felt the machine's legs under her, pushing it powerfully forward. Sensations reached her from the walkers. More elation, more joy, but this wasn't about her. It was because they loved to run, to move fast. It was a love of something foreign to them, she somehow knew. A love of something not of their own nature, and it accentuated the experience.

In spite of herself, Zoey smiled, watching the flickering spheres of energy whip past as the walkers jumped and dashed nimbly forward through the night. It was . . . exhilarating.

It wasn't until much, much later that Zoey realized that right then she had no longer been scared.

10. SOLID

MIRA LAY OUT OF SIGHT at the edge of the tree line, staring at two black boats moored on the riverbank. They were big, and looked like they'd been river ferries at one time, before being extensively modified. Extra decks and levels had been constructed, and they held huts and shacks, probably crew quarters and cargo holds, and the hulls were lined with gun ports.

Each boat flew the same flag, red with a white, eight-pointed star in its center. It was what Mira had been looking for.

Menagerie boats, the ones Holt had seen on the way to the Cross-roads. The Menagerie were bad sorts to deal with normally, and Mira hated having to approach them. It wasn't smart, but she'd been doing a lot of not so smart things lately.

Gear and equipment sat on the riverbank where it had been unloaded—packs and supplies, guns and ammo. It looked like a military operation, and it meant one thing: The Menagerie were going into the Strange Lands. But why? Mira had never heard of them doing that before.

Max whined at the sight of the ships, not liking it. She didn't blame him.

"Yes, I have a plan," she told him. Max looked up at her skeptically. "And you're not gonna like it."

On the riverbank beside the boats, a crowd had formed in a tight cir-cle, watching something happening in the middle, amid cheers and yells. Mira couldn't see what it was, but she'd bet it wasn't a friendly game of horseshoes.

She took a deep breath, grabbed her pack, and stood up. None of the pirates noticed, the crowd was too busy. Even when she and Max started walking toward them, no one sounded an alarm or even glanced in their direction.

More than three dozen kids, none of them older than twenty, had made a ring around two others in the center who were circling each other warily. Both held knives. One was a boy sporting a goatee and a wicked looking scar down one side of his face. He had a tattoo on his right wrist, like all Menagerie members, his a blue shark. He also had several cuts across his arms and a larger one on his chest, presumably recently acquired from the person he was facing.

And that person was not what Mira expected.

A very fit, lithe girl, about Mira's age, with olive skin and obsidian-black hair that trailed down her back, tied into a tight braid. She was beautiful, but in a hard-edged way. She wore black cargo pants, a T-shirt, and a single utility belt across her waist. A black crow or raven was tattooed on her right wrist, and on the left was an eight-pointed star, just like on the flag above, with four of its points colored in. It marked her as a Captain, Mira knew, the fourth leadership rank of the Menagerie, and it entitled her to run her own ship.

It meant she was in charge here. It meant she was who Mira needed to talk to.

The girl moved with quick, controlled steps. Her eyes never blinked, only watched and calculated.

The boy lunged for her like a charging bull—and the girl sidestepped and kicked him in the rear with a disappointed frown. The crowd cheered and laughed and the boy whirled around with hatred in his eyes. The girl didn't seem to care.

"This is already boring me, Leone," she said.

He moved for her again, slashing wildly with his knife.

The girl dodged the strike, then another, then kicked out with a knee, caught the boy in the stomach and sent him reeling backward. As he did, she twirled the knife in her hand and threw it.

The boy howled in pain when it stuck in his leg. He fell to one knee.

The girl was a blur as she closed the distance. Her momentum fueled a kick that sent her opponent crashing on his back, and then she stomped down on the kid's stomach with her boot. The air burst from his lungs. He shuddered, tried to move, but couldn't.

Slowly, the girl kneeled down, yanked the knife out of his leg. The boy screamed again—and then went silent as he felt the cold blade on the scruff of his goatee, near his throat.

"So tell me if I'm wrong, Leone," the girl spoke with a hint of amusement, "but I'm sensing a formal removal of your challenge to my leadership."

The boy nodded. Quickly. Agreeably. There were laughs from the crowd.

"Good," the girl said—and then rammed down the knife. Leone flinched as it punctured the sand just inches from his head. "Now get your ass back to your post."

The boy leaped up and hobbled toward the boats as fast as he could, jeers from the crowd following him. They didn't last long, however.

"And would someone—*any* of you idiots really," the girl yelled, a new hint of menace in her voice, "like to tell me who *that* is." She looked right at Mira on the outskirts of the circle. Mira swallowed nervously as the pirates all whipped around toward her. "I posted lookouts for a reason. Or at least I thought I did."

The looks of surprise on their faces were quickly replaced with anger. They started moving for Mira. They were all armed, she noticed, all about her age. Mira took a step back, but Max growled next to her. He didn't budge. The advancing boys stopped in their tracks, eyeing the dog warily.

"Oh, don't bother," the Captain said in annoyance, standing up, wiping the blood from her knife before sheathing it. "If she was trouble, we'd know by now."

The black-haired girl pushed past her crew, studying Mira a moment, before looking down at Max.

"Looks like you brought us dinner," she said. "Been a long time since we've had dog." The pirates all around her laughed.

"You're welcome to try eating him," Mira said evenly, "but I wouldn't recommend it. His bite's a lot worse than his bark."

"I might eat you both, you don't tell me who you are and why you're here."

Mira had to play this right, the Captain wasn't like the others. She was smarter, and dangerous, it was obvious. If Mira seemed too eager, the girl would sense weakness. If Mira dragged it out too long . . . she'd grow impatient. Neither was a good thing.

"What was all that in the circle?" Mira asked, ignoring her question, trying to seem unintimidated. "Somebody slip too many notes in the complaint box?"

The pirate girl's demeanor was anything but warm. "Leone was trying to get his third star point," she said. "One of the more fun ways you can do that is to challenge and kill your Captain. It's how *I* did it. He miscalculated, though. Just like you are by playing games with me, little girl. I like your red hair. Maybe I'll take some for a trophy."

"I wouldn't recommend that either." Mira casually opened her pack, reached inside it.

The Menagerie all raised their weapons, but the Captain didn't move. She just studied Mira with growing impatience. Mira pulled out a square piece of metal about the size of a dog tag. On it was stamped the same symbol as on the flag, the eight-pointed star.

Mira tossed it on the ground in front of them. When the pirates saw it, they slowly lowered their weapons. Even the Captain raised an eyebrow.

"A Solid," she said with genuine curiosity, "and where did you get that, little one?"

Her repeated use of the word "little" irked Mira. "You know, you and I are pretty much the same size, right?"

"If there's one thing Leone just learned, it's that size is a relative thing. Where'd you get the Solid? Steal it from someone—or stumble across it on a corpse?"

"Look closer," Mira said. The Captain frowned, then knelt down and picked up the small piece of metal. When she saw what was on it her eyes widened. She looked back at Mira in a different way. It was the reaction Mira had hoped for. That was no ordinary Solid. On it, the eight-pointed star had been colored in with metallic red paint. Only one person in the entire Menagerie gave Solids like that.

"I'm a Freebooter," Mira said, holding the girl's gaze. "Did a job for your boss, found something he was looking for a few years ago. Wasn't easy. He was grateful. Next time you see Tiberius, tell him Mira Toombs says hi."

"And what if I say you don't look like the kind that'd be palling around with Tiberius Marseilles? What if I say I don't buy it?"

"Then you can come find out for yourself," Mira said, trying to sound confident. "But I guarantee you won't have as good luck as you did with that dimwit a second ago."

The Captain studied Mira intently, weighing things, calculating. Then a slight smile formed on her lips. "Well . . ." she said as she stood back up and the Solid disappeared into a pocket, "color me convinced. How exactly were you hoping to cash this in?"

A Solid was a token given out by high-ranking Menagerie leaders to non-Menagerie who did them important favors. They could be presented to any other Menagerie leader, and that leader was obligated to help them in some task as repayment. It was never that simple of course, but Solids were rarely given out, and it was assumed anyone possessing one must be in the good graces of someone important. At a minimum, a Solid would usually ensure your safety.

"Two of my friends have been taken by the Assembly," Mira said. "They're headed northwest, and I need help rescuing them."

The pirates all stared at her a moment—then burst into laughter, the sounds filling the air. Even the black-haired girl chuckled.

"Well why didn't you just say so?" she asked. "I was expecting something difficult or out of the question."

"What's so funny?" Mira asked in a low voice. She had to stay firm, had to be strong.

"What's funny is that getting killed isn't part of honoring a Solid, no matter who it's from. Even the Menagerie don't tangle with Assembly unless we can't avoid it, and you're talking about chasing down a group of them. Trust me, if the aliens have your friends, they're good and gone. So drink to their memories, and spend this Solid on something nice for yourself."

Mira sighed. It had been too much to hope that the Solid alone would get their participation, but there was another approach.

"You're going into the Strange Lands," Mira observed, studying all the gear that had been offloaded nearby. "Why?"

"What, we're best friends all of a sudden? It's nothing you need to stress about," the Captain replied. "We're here for something special. It's another reason I can't just go off looking for your friends. Of course . . . the way it's looking now, we might be experiencing something of a delay."

Mira smiled. It was as she'd hoped. "You need a guide. And all the Freebooters you would have hired at the Crossroads are gone now. There's nothing left of that place."

The girl spat. "That's about the long and short of it, yeah."

"You hoping to get to Polestar?"

"Among . . . other places."

Any other time Mira would be incredibly curious what the Menagerie's goals might be here, but right now she had other things to worry about.

"The Assembly took my friends *inside* the Strange Lands," Mira said carefully. "It's not totally the direction you need to go, but it's close. You help me find them, I'll help you get to Polestar, and you get to turn in one of Tiberius's Solids when you get back to Faust."

There were murmurings from the pirates around her. The Captain stared at Mira intently. "You any good?"

"I'm not the best, but I can get you where you need to be. Either way, looks like I'm the only chance you've got."

The Captain's stare hovered on Mira a few seconds more, then she smiled again. It was disturbing. "My name's Ravan. If I agree to this it means three things. I'm in charge, you're a hired hand; you do what I say, when I say it. Fighting Assembly's a deadly game, and I can't have you running around on your own."

Mira nodded.

"Two: If we don't find your friends—if the Assembly makes it to a Presidium or a processing center or an Osprey den—it's *over* . . . and I keep the Solid for my trouble, and you're still taking us to Polestar. Agreed?"

Mira nodded again. She didn't like it, but it was what she expected.

"And three . . . if at the end of this you start thinking of ways to get off honoring our bargain . . ." The smile again. "Well. I've known lots of people who've tried very similar things, and they aren't members of the living anymore. Need I be any clearer?"

Mira forced herself to muster as much calmness as she could. "No, I think I get the gist of it." The two held each other's stare a moment longer. Then Ravan nodded.

"Assume you got some way of tracking these friends?"

"I do," Mira said.

"What is it, an artifact?"

"Yes."

"How far away are they?" Ravan asked, starting to think and plan.

"I can't tell distance, but they've had about half a day's head start."

"You said northwest?"

Mira nodded. Ravan's eyes slimmed, thinking it through. She turned to one of the boys next to her.

"Get everyone ready, we head out in thirty. Tell them to pack light, we're moving fast."

"What about the boats?" the kid asked.

"Tell Steans and Riddick to take them downstream and wait at the Gillespie Interchange. We'll meet you there when this is all said and done. Give it . . . five weeks. You haven't seen us, we ain't coming back."

The kid nodded, moved briskly toward the boats, shouting orders, yelling at other kids. They all started scrambling, making ready to leave.

Ravan looked back to Mira, and when she did Mira noticed something she had overlooked in the tension of the past few moments. Ravan's eyes were a perfectly clear, sapphire blue. The black, fingerlike veins of the Tone weren't there. She was Heedless. Whether Ravan had noticed the same thing about Mira, or she just didn't care, Mira wasn't sure.

"Looks like you got exactly what you wanted, Red," Ravan said, her blue eyes flashing, "and you know what they say about that." She turned and moved back for the boats to collect her gear.

Yeah, Mira thought, staring after the Menagerie Captain. She knew exactly what they said about that.

Beneath her, Max whined and looked up questioningly.

"Told you you wouldn't like it."

11. MAS'ERINHAH

ZOEY PUSHED BACK into the wall of the dark building, staring at everything around her. It was a big scary place, with shadows clinging everywhere, and she didn't like it. Her head hurt, too. It seemed to be getting worse, the more the walkers took her in to the Strange Lands, and she didn't know why.

Night had fallen outside, and Zoey could see the half moon through a giant crack in the building's far wall that ran floor to ceiling. It was a large structure, with brick walls and heavy frames, and it seemed to consist of just one huge room. What remained of rows of long wooden benches stretched all the way to the other side.

There was something else. Something almost impossible to wrap her mind around.

The far wall from where she sat was bursting open inward. Bricks and mortar and debris hung in the air, spraying outward. The benches and chairs there were thrust forward, shattering into splinters and flying forward, and the beginning of some kind of huge truck exploded through the wall, its headlights still shining like glowing eyes, flooding the interior of the old building.

But it was all somehow amazingly *frozen in place*.

Like you were watching it on TV and someone had hit PAUSE. Zoey kept staring at it as her mind tried to make sense of it all.

While the truck was the most dramatic example, Zoey could look around and see others.

On the desk near her, a stack of papers had fallen off a desk, fanning outwards toward the floor—but they never reached it. They hung in the air, frozen in place just like the truck and the debris at the other end of the room.

Curiously, Zoey slowly reached out and touched one of the papers.

There was a sizzling sound, then a flash of light—and the paper unstuck like someone had hit PLAY. It floated downward, and as it did it hit other papers, and they too sizzled and flashed and unstuck, settling along the floor like fallen leaves.

Zoey watched in fascination. She wished Mira was there to explain it.

An annoyed electronic sound echoed behind her, and Zoey turned around.

There were four green-and-orange Hunters in the building, watching her intently. Since the others had left, these four had kept their glowing triangular eyes locked onto her, never moving, just watching her like some prized possession.

They didn't want Zoey touching things in here, and she understood why. If just touching the frozen things unstuck them, what would happen if she touched that truck bursting through the wall?

It made her shiver thinking about it.

The other tripods, including the differently marked one, were outside. She could feel each of them, could point to them if she had to. They were circling the city ruins they'd found, but it was probably less for pursuers, Zoey guessed, than for the Anomalies.

It was odd, but she found comfort in the closeness of the Hunters, of relying on their senses and technology. Every time she thought of them, she thought back to riding as they raced through the dark. The walkers had run all night. Zoey had held on as they leaped and dodged through the invisible Anomalies, moving with agility and power, until she forgot she was holding on at all, and for a moment it felt like she was one of them. The Feelings stirred inside her pleasantly at the memory. . . .

But she *wasn't* one of them, she told herself, pushing the Feelings away. The walkers were bad, and they had hurt her friends.

Before they left, the machines had hung Holt from the thick wooden rafters that spanned the length of the old building. He was still unconscious, recovering from his injuries, hanging limply about five feet off the floor, legs dangling underneath him.

Zoey swallowed and got to her feet, took a few tentative steps toward Holt. The walkers watched, but made no move to stop her.

"Holt," she whispered. He didn't respond, just hung silently. She said his name again, louder. On her tiptoes she couldn't even reach his dangling feet. Zoey jumped upward, swatted at them, but she was still too short. She frowned, made ready to jump again . . .

. . . and then shrieked as the cloaking shields of more walkers flashed and dropped away, revealing three green-and-orange machines right beside her.

One was the leader, the scary one. It trumpeted angrily, stomped forward, and Zoey scampered back. The other two walkers just watched. So did the four at the other end of the room. The machine's three powerful legs impaled the floor on all sides of her. It towered over her, its three-optic eye spinning and staring into her.

Zoey shut her eyes.

Then her mind was suddenly full of imagery and sound. It all came lightning quick, an impossible blend of sensation and impressions, and it was all too fast to make sense of. It flowed through her mind's eye faster and faster, consuming all her thought.

And then it stopped.

Zoey exhaled violently. Her head was full of pain now. She moaned and clutched it between her hands. It was worse than it had ever been.

"Please . . ." Zoey said. "It hurts."

The sensations came again, pouring into her head in a thick stream of suggestion. Zoey cried out, crumpled to the floor. "Please . . ."

The sensations ended. Above her, the walker trumpeted again. There was a note of frustration to it.

Green laser light flashed from two of the Hunters, and bathed Zoey in their glow, moving and focusing on her head. The pain *lessened*. Zoey looked up at the walkers. Somehow, they were stopping the pain.

The four tripods from the other end of the room joined the rest and added their own streams of warm, green laser light to Zoey's head.

The pain vanished almost completely. More pain than she even knew she had been feeling. She slumped against the wall in relief, breathing in and out. It felt so amazing, a world without pain.

The lasers shut off. The differently marked walker stepped back, and stood unmoving like a statue. A humming emanated from it, so deep and low it vibrated the crumbling floorboards underneath Zoey's legs. The sound began to grow louder and louder, building in power.

Zoey had no idea what was about to—

She shielded her eyes as bright, powerful light flooded the interior of the building.

The illumination bled up and out of the three-legged walker, drifting into the air, filling more and more of the interior with its radiance. When it was clear of the machine, it almost instantly formed into a brilliant, huge crystalline shape, made of pure energy, that hovered over Zoey.

The tripod that the field pulled itself out of suddenly became lifeless. Its lights died, there was a slow, descending hum as its mechanics shut down and it slumped downward. It was as if without the strange pulsing field of energy the walker was dead.

Zoey stared up at the bright, fluctuating crystalline shape. She had seen those shapes before, of course. They floated up and out of any destroyed Assembly craft. But those weren't like this one. The glowing, geometric shape above her was not golden like all the others she had ever seen.

This one . . . was a brilliant *green and orange*—just like the colors of the walkers around it.

The two colors mixed together so perfectly it was impossible to tell where one began and the other ended. At the same time, both were distinct and prominent, and they lit everything in a combination of emerald and rusted light.

The sight was so beautiful, Zoey almost smiled.

An intense burst of static exploded to life in her mind. It overtook everything, roaring through her consciousness, and Zoey grabbed her ears, futilely trying to block it out.

But the static hiss pushed in regardless. The bright green-and-orange, light-filled shape pulsated above her. She wanted to cry out in fear—but stopped when the first "suggestion" came.

It was the best word Zoey had to describe it.

It was almost the same as the Feelings. Only these were much, much more powerful—forceful, insistent, and aggressive. They were loud and scary. And the pain was coming back. Building inside her head again, threatening to rip it apart.

Zoey screamed as the suggestions came in a powerful steady stream, filling her mind. They were like words or thoughts translated directly into pure perception, and they flashed by too fast for Zoey to make sense of.

"Stop!" the little girl cried out on the floor. "*Please . . .*" The crystalline shape hovered over her. The stream of suggestion continued. Zoey wanted to weep, but she forced herself not to. She had to be strong. Like Mira and Holt. Like Max. But, the pain . . .

Green laser light flared outward from the walkers around her.

Zoey breathed out as the pain diminished. Even with the combined laser light of all the Hunters together, it wasn't enough to stop it completely, but it was enough that she could think.

The sensations continued, one after the other, racing past like a flooded river.

Zoey reached out for the Feelings, the ones deep down in that other part of herself, and they rose, flooding her with comfort, giving her strength. She let their ideas wash over her, feeling what they intended. If she could just slow down the suggestions somehow, they seemed to say. If she could give herself time to *read* them, maybe it would be bearable then.

Instinctively, Zoey did the only thing she could think of. She pushed back with her own thoughts against the pure sensory information being force-fed into her mind.

And the stream shuddered. It *slowed*. For a brief moment she could almost make sense of the suggestions. The Feelings swirled in encouragement. Zoey pushed back even harder, projecting her own thoughts directly at the crystalline shape with all the strength she had.

The suggestions slowed again—and this time they stayed that way.

Zoey felt elated. As long as Zoey pushed back against the stream of sensations, she could force them into a more tolerable speed. She could understand them.

They were just impressions, just suggestions and senses. It was simple and concise, the same idea over and over, and if she had to put it into words, it would be:

Can you hear us?

The shock of the question's simplicity made Zoey's concentration slip.

The stream overwhelmed her again and she grimaced, feeling the pain rising. She concentrated, pushing back once more.

The suggestion was still the same. *Can you hear us?*

Yes, Zoey thought in response, *I can.*

As she did, the crystalline shape above her flashed brightly, its fluctuating shades of green and orange blending together into pure white light. The walkers on either side trumpeted electronically in surprise.

A new sensation bombarded Zoey then.

There was no way she could translate it into words, it was just simple emotion, uncomplicated and pure, nothing else, and it felt like . . . *pride.* Zoey knew it came directly from the hovering energy field above her, and the realization troubled her.

If that green-and-orange shape was transmitting feelings into her mind, did that mean . . . it was *alive?*

Another suggestion came more powerful than the first.

Do you remember?

Remember what? Zoey thought back.

The suggestion shifted and morphed almost instantly, different streams of consciousness and ideas merging together into something new.

Us, the crystalline shape seemed to imply. *You are of us.*

Zoey stared up at the shape in fear and confusion. A part of her wanted to recoil at the thing's thoughts, but another part felt a familiarity with communicating this way. It was almost like hearing your native language for the first time after living in a foreign country. Part of her felt drawn to the shape now—and that made her even more frightened.

We are Mas'Erinhah. We have waited long.

The feelings of satisfaction and joy bloomed—and then cut off completely.

The stream ended. The glowing field of green and orange floated back toward the machine it had left earlier, burying itself into the walker until it disappeared.

When it did, the tripod reactivated. Lights flashed, mechanics hummed to life, its triangular eye burned red, green and blue. The tripod stood up powerfully and glared down at Zoey.

The suggestions came once more, only they were muted and focused, as if filtered somehow, but now Zoey found she could read them as easily as before.

You are honored, they implied. *You are the* Scion.

Zoey stared back in confusion—and then the walkers moved for her as one.

12. RAVAN

IT ONLY TOOK TEN MILES into the Strange Lands for Mira to see that everything was wrong.

Impossibly huge storm clouds massed on the horizon, flashing lightning of different colors. Antimatter Storms in the third ring, judging by the distance, and that should have been impossible. They were fourth ring Anomalies, but that wasn't all. The landscape was darkening. The sky, the light around them, everything was fading and becoming dimmer.

In itself that was nothing new. The farther you went into the Strange Lands, the darker it got. Midafternoon in the fourth ring felt like midnight. The problem was, it was getting dark much too soon. They were still in the first ring, and Mira wouldn't have expected to see the light begin to fade until halfway through the second.

None of it added up, and it only served to increase her nervousness.

What if the Strange Lands were completely changed? What if everything in her Lexicon, everything she'd ever learned, no longer mattered? She felt a sinking feeling in her stomach. If that was the case, then she was in big trouble.

But what choice did she have except to try?

Max walked next to her at the front of the line, traversing a wide, ever-stretching remnant of the world before—a huge highway that stretched forward over the rolling hills of what used to be the South Dakota plains.

When whatever created the Strange Lands occurred, it wiped away every single person inside, ripping them completely out of existence. Evidence of the abrupt snuffing out of hundreds of thousands of lives was everywhere you looked, this road especially. Rusting and crumpled signs identified it as Interstate 12, but no one called it that anymore.

Now it was known as the Forlorn Passage, a key safe-route into the the northwestern Strange Lands. Once a major road artery between Bismarck and Sioux Falls, it had been packed with cars when the Strange Lands formed. The vehicles sat where they careened and crashed, driverless and out of control, years ago, their remains stretching all the way to the horizon.

It was always eerie looking at the cars, knowing that people had been driving inside them one moment . . . then simply erased, like chalk on the Scorewall, the next.

Mira glanced behind her at the line of people there. Ravan had brought the majority of her men, almost thirty Menagerie, and they followed after her and Max in a tight single file line, as Mira had instructed. There was still no indication of what the pirates were doing here, but in the course of the trek Mira had noticed one odd thing.

Two kids near the middle of the line were carrying a large wooden crate between them. It looked heavy, whatever it was. It would have been a major hindrance, carrying it on foot. Which meant it must be important, but Mira knew better than to ask.

The group moved between the ruined vehicles, following the Passage northwest, which just happened to coincide with the needle of Mira's compass. It meant the Assembly had gone this way, too. They were heading in the right direction, at least.

Mira's opinion of the Menagerie had always been low—degenerate disorganized thugs who preyed on the weak. While this trip hadn't done anything to change the "degenerate" part of that opinion, she came to see they had as much discipline and work ethic as any survivor group out there. They were all in good shape, used to quickly obeying Ravan's orders, and the pirates had made good time since leaving the boats. But . . . they were still Menagerie.

"You sure we have to stay single file like this?" Ravan's voice asked behind her. "I'd feel better if I could group my men, at least in threes. Makes us more defensible."

"You expecting to be attacked?" Mira asked.

"Expecting the worst's the best way to be prepared for it."

"Guess it's hard to become a Menagerie Captain without being a little paranoid."

She thought she heard a smile in Ravan's voice. "You have no idea."

"Well, sorry, but bunching up here is a bad idea."

"Why? Just hills and old cars, I don't see anything to be scared of."

As they walked past a pickup truck, Mira reached inside its bed and grabbed an old grimy bottle. She turned and threw it into the grasslands just outside the freeway.

It flew about ten feet—and began to spin, accelerate, and rise upward, as though something was pulling it into the air. Then it exploded in a bright shower of splintered light.

As it did, things became visible.

Walls of rippling energy that moved at various angles in the air, shimmering with color like curtains of light, stacked one after the other. Even in the daylight they stood out. There were hundreds of them out there. A few seconds later they disappeared again, leaving no trace behind.

Ravan's eyes widened in surprise. Behind her, her men stared nervously at the air outside the highway. Even Max whined a little bit. But Mira took no satisfaction from it. She was stunned by what she'd seen.

"Holy God," she said under her breath.

Ravan turned to her. "What? You weren't expecting them?"

"Not that *many*," Mira said. "There should be a dozen at any given spot; but that was . . ."

"A lot more than a dozen. What are they?"

"Vector Fields. Two-dimensional walls of charged particles. The first ring in this direction is full of them."

"What happens if you touch one?"

"Every atom in your body explodes," Mira answered simply. Ravan unconsciously took a step toward the middle of the highway. "They're repelled by metal. Which makes this old road the only safe passable route to the northwest. The cars repel the Fields. There's a Stable Anomaly coming up. Once we're past it, we shouldn't have to worry about Vector Fields anymore."

At least Mira hoped so. For all she knew, the Grindhouse was gone and the Vector Fields were replaced with something much worse.

"Why's it different now?" Ravan asked.

"I don't know," Mira admitted. "Something's wrong with the Strange Lands. They're changing. It's why the Crossroads was evacuated."

There was a commotion behind them, back near the middle of the line. One of the pirates had collapsed next to an old station wagon and was on the ground.

"It's Keller," one of Ravan's men said. The name was enough to grow a scowl on the girl's face. Whatever was happening, it wasn't unexpected. Ravan moved down the line toward the boy.

"Come on, stinky," Mira said to Max, following after the girl.

The boy lay shuddering on the ground, spasming and breathing heavy. Two of the pirates were holding him down, while the others stood in an ever-tightening circle, trying to get a glimpse.

"Get back, give him room," Ravan yelled, pushing through them.

The boy was tall and big, older than Mira, probably about twenty, easily the most muscular of the group, and he was missing a finger on his left hand. One look and Mira knew what was wrong. His eyes were full of black. He was fighting the Tone—and he was losing. He had a tremendous will to stay himself, she could tell, but it wasn't going to be enough.

"Keller. You hear me?" Ravan knelt down and put her hand on the boy's chest. He didn't respond, he was lost in his struggle. "I know it's tough, you're a fighter. I get that. But there's always something stronger than us. Nothing to be ashamed of, just the way of the world. You listening, Keller?"

Keller just kept shaking on the ground, groaning.

"You remember that Landship we took in the Barren, the fast one, the one with the train engine grill on its front?" Ravan asked with a soft voice, smiling slightly. There was a surprising touch of tenderness in her tone. "It was your idea to jump off a Gyro onto the masts, rip the sails with knives, and ride them down onto the deck, strand the ship. Said you saw it in some stupid pirate movie. Most insane idea I'd ever heard for robbing a Landship—but hell if it didn't work."

The pirates around her laughed softly, remembering the moment themselves. Keller's body slowly calmed as Ravan spoke, until he was lying peacefully on the ground, staring up at the sky with his black eyes.

"No one else would have been crazy enough to try that," Ravan said. "It's what I'll remember about you."

A barely audible, cracked voice answered her, and it took a moment for Mira to realize it was Keller. "Just . . . give me a moment, boss," he said hoarsely. "Be back on my feet. Keep going. You . . . know I can."

Ravan nodded. "Yeah. I know. You're one tough bastard, Keller."

Keller's chest rose as he inhaled a long, last breath—and then the air hissed slowly out of his mouth. His body went limp as he Succumbed, sinking peacefully into the asphalt of the old highway.

Mira closed her eyes as he faded. She felt guilty. Guilty at the relief that came, knowing this was a fate Zoey had spared her from. Even though he was Menagerie, she still felt sorry for him. He became a pirate because of the very thing that had just taken him. Who knew what Keller would have been if the Assembly hadn't come? Peace activist? Philosopher? Poet? In this world he became a brigand. And that was how it was.

The pirates were all silent now. Ravan stared down at Keller another moment and then stood back up. She nodded to one of her men, and the boy unstrapped a rifle from his back and threw it to her. Ravan cocked it and aimed down at the boy who had been Keller. The group of pirates backed up.

"Wait!" Mira shouted, horrified. "What are you doing?"

Ravan slowly turned to Mira with a look that suggested she wasn't used to being questioned.

"You can't just . . . shoot him," Mira continued, aghast. Surely even *they* could see that.

"He's worse than dead, little darling," Ravan replied with an icy tone. "Killing him's a charity."

Mira's fists clenched. She'd had enough. "My name is *Mira*. It's not 'little one' or Red or Freebooter. It's *Mira*."

"You haven't earned me using your name, Red." Ravan took a step toward Mira, and the others backed up farther. "Until you do, I'll stick with 'little girl' or 'dear heart', or any other name I feel like calling you. And you sure as hell haven't earned the right to tell me what to do with my men. What is it you'd like to see happen here? Let him become some mindless drone for the Assembly? That what you do with your friends when they Succumb?"

Mira glared back. "It's not that simple."

"Isn't it? How about we take a poll?" Ravan looked around at her crew. "Anyone here who'd rather be put down when your time comes than become some vegetable for the Assembly, raise your hand."

The arm of every single Menagerie pirate raised without hesitation. They stared at Mira with fire in their eyes.

"Any other objections?" Ravan asked.

Mira sighed and looked away. What was there to say? Everyone made their own choices. Just because they were ones she wouldn't make herself, that didn't invalidate them. "At least do it with some compassion."

Beneath them, what used to be Keller stirred and slowly pushed himself to his feet. When he was up, he stared sightlessly behind them, unaware of anything anymore. He began to walk, trudging step after step, back the way they'd come.

Ravan kept her back to him, still staring at Mira. "What, everyone should gather around and sing hymns before we do it? What's the point of that? I already gave him my compassion. That story I told a second ago wasn't just to calm him. It's what I'll carry *forward* for him, just like I carry forward something from every one of my boys who Succumbs. Because just like you, I'm Heedless. It's the only thing I can offer them. The fact that they won't be forgotten."

Ravan spun on her heel and raised the rifle in a blur. She pulled the trigger and Mira flinched as the gun flashed. What used to be Keller, about twenty feet away, fell to the ground and went still.

Ravan tossed the rifle back to the same boy, and looked again at Mira.

"Compassion comes in all kinds of flavors," Ravan said tightly. There was pain in her voice. "But they don't all taste like pumpkin pie."

The two girls held each other's gaze. Mira forced herself not to look away.

"Get moving, Freebooter," Ravan told her. "You got a lot of ground to cover."

Mira stared back a second more, then spun and headed back to the northwest, down the ruined highway, pulling Max along with her. She could hear the others gathering their things behind her, readying to move again.

As she walked, thunder rolled around them, a strange anamorphic kind that was unique to the Strange Lands, and it always seemed to echo longer than it should. Mira looked to the black Antimatter clouds in the darkening sky to the north and saw flashes of green and red lightning.

The storm was growing. It looked ominous. Just like everything else.

13. GRINDHOUSE

MIRA'S FLASHLIGHT FINALLY FOUND what she was looking for. A school bus, an old one, crashed into what was left of a pair of military Jeeps. A giant message was spray-painted across its length, next to a large painted version of the δ symbol.

STABLE ANOMALY BEGINS 100 FEET
ANOMALY R1-3, THE GRINDHOUSE

The sun had set an hour ago and everything was dark except for the flashes of purple lightning in the distance and the beams from two huge, razor-straight pillars of light that shot up into the sky fifty or so miles away. They were Gravity Wells, Mira knew, and one of them was a place she didn't have very fond memories of.

The Mix Master. The place where she had failed. The source of all her fear and self-doubt. But that was the last thing she wanted to think about now.

Mira's light shone across the bus, and she felt a chill looking at it. There was no way to know if it had been full of kids when the Strange Lands formed, but still, the black windows that stared lifelessly outward were haunting.

"What's that supposed to mean?" Ravan studied the crude writing on the bus. The line of Menagerie stretched back behind her into the dark, and Max watched them warily from the hood of an old Mercedes. One thing about having the pirates with them, they drew the dog's suspicions more than Mira. She was kind of getting used to having the mutt around. And he didn't smell all *that* bad, she guessed.

"It's an Anomaly warning." Mira pulled her Lexicon off her shoulder and set it down on the hood of the Mercedes next to Max. "Catalogued so Freebooters can look it up." The large book was sealed shut by two metal locks on either end, and she used a tiny key hanging from one of her necklaces to unlock it. Inside the front cover, three different names were scrawled along with Mira's. The book's previous owners. Other Lexicons had more names, only because Mira had managed to survive the Strange Lands much longer than most.

The book had three bindings that unfolded into separate parts, each with its own collection of papers, notes, drawings, and diagrams. The first section held artifact combination schematics, instructions for building them. It was the largest section in Mira's Lexicon, but that wasn't a surprise. Artifact creation was her specialty.

The second section contained maps of the Strange Lands. Illustrations for each ring and for the Core, as well as detailed maps for important areas of each one. But it was the third section Mira turned to now, a catalog of Strange Lands Anomalies. Mira's was complete, for the most part, with the exception of a few inside the Core.

The Anomalies were organized by type (stable or unstable) and the ring they existed in. Mira shuffled through the pages for ring one until she found *R1-3, Grindhouse.* She folded out the section and studied it. She knew how the Anomaly worked, but Ben had always led her through it. If she was going to have to take point, she wanted to cover her bases.

There were drawings and notes, information on what she should expect, and Mira tried to ignore the queasiness she felt as she studied the pages. Her fingers moved over a specific diagram that showed a crude representation of a sphere, with writing underneath it:

Sub-Anomaly: Condenser Spheres.
Effect: Violent compaction of mass.
Catalyst: Touch only, no draw effect.
Movement: Very slow drift, random direction, direction is constant.
Natural Visibility: Invisible.

Incidental Visibility: Visible after direct contact, three to five seconds.
Suggestions: Reveal location from distance, map locations, determine route through Anomaly, move fast.

That last part was what bothered her. "Move fast." That was going to be a real problem, with all the people behind her. It was ironic, actually. This would have been worth a lot of Points back at Midnight City.

"What does it do?" Ravan asked, looking ahead of them into the dark. Mira looked up from the Lexicon. "Shoot off a few rounds."

Ravan unslung her rifle, raised it, and fired in an arc. Bullets fanned forward from the muzzle, but they didn't make it very far.

The Menagerie winced as perfect spheres of bright white energy crackled to life and absorbed the slugs. Each was the size of a beach ball, filling the air with intense light. About a half dozen of them, at various distances and heights.

Seconds later the spheres vanished, fading out and plunging everything back to black, leaving no indication they were there at all. Max whined uneasily.

"Condenser Spheres," Mira said, closing and locking her Lexicon. "Touch one and they suck you inside. What's left gets compressed into something about the size of a marble."

Ravan laughed. "That doesn't sound pleasant." Her men didn't laugh, however. They looked at each other nervously. "How do we get through?"

"Tediously." Mira zipped open the black bag with the red δ on her hip. "The Condensers are moving, just really slowly. Means the path through them's always different. I'll have to find them and mark a trail for your men to follow."

"And how long will that take?"

"An hour, probably."

Ravan's eyes thinned in thought. "If these things are moving, how long will the path be safe?"

Mira was surprised. People didn't immediately catch that wrinkle. Menagerie or not, Ravan was smarter than most.

"I don't know," Mira admitted. "All depends on the spheres. Long enough, hopefully. Never tried moving through a group this large." Of course, the reality was, she'd never moved *anyone* through the Grind-house, but she didn't mention that.

Mira forced herself not to think about it. She had to do this. Zoey and Holt were depending on her. This was a first ring Anomaly, it would be no problem as long as she took it slow. The thoughts, however, felt hollow.

Mira pulled out the tools she'd need from the waist pack: a notepad and pencil; a mass of metal pegs strung together with red wire; a small hammer; and a leather pouch full of nuts and washers.

"Hold your men here," Mira told Ravan. "Keep them on the highway."

Mira started to move ahead, but Ravan grabbed her arm. "Make sure you know what you're doing, little one. I lose any of my men because of a mistake you made, you won't like the results."

A stirring of emotion filled Mira. Not because of the implied threat, but because of what it reminded her of. Instinctively, her eyes looked at one of the white pillars of light in the distance, but then she pushed the thoughts away. She had to be strong.

"As I said," Mira told her, "I've never moved a group this big. Far as I know, no one has. The Strange Lands isn't the Barren, it has a million ways to kill you. Frankly, I'd be surprised if you make it to Polestar with half your men, but you should have known that. And if you kill me, the farther in we are, the less chance you have of getting out." Mira ripped her arm free and stepped toward the Anomaly. Ravan didn't say anything more.

Mira opened the leather pouch and grabbed a handful of nuts and washers, staring at the dense field of ruined cars that stretched into the dark.

So it was finally here. What she'd been dreading since leaving Midnight City—facing a Stable Anomaly on her own. Her hands shook, and she clenched them tightly before anyone behind her could see.

Damn it, it's just the *Grindhouse,* she told herself. She'd been through it a hundred times. She was good, she was skilled. So . . . why didn't she *believe* it?

Whatever the answer, it didn't matter. She didn't have a choice.

Mira put the pencil to the notepad and started drawing. A grid, ten-by-ten squares, with a rough map of the freeway and the cars in front of her. She only drew the immediate ones now; anything in front of that, the perspective was distorted. She had to wait until she got closer.

When she was done, she knelt on the ground and pulled something else from her pocket. It was her stopwatch, tarnished and old, but it worked flawlessly. The sight of it was comforting. She and it had been through a lot.

Her hand froze on the watch. It was now or never.

She took a breath . . . and clicked a button. The watch clicked as it began to count time. Mira hung its cord around her neck, then threw one of the washers forward into the air.

It traveled just a few feet before it was yanked hard right and disappeared in a flash of energy as the Condenser Sphere flared to life, lighting up the night.

She marked its location on the pad, then threw another washer. Another sphere flared brightly, this one closer, and she felt the slight tingle of static electricity before it vanished out of sight again.

She marked it, too, then hammered in one of the metal pegs through the asphalt at her feet.

Mira tried to stay calm. She could *do* this. Another breath . . .

. . . and she moved forward into the blank air between the two invisible Condensers just feet on either side of her.

The hair on her arms stood on end from the Spheres' proximity. It was the only indication of the hovering death surrounding her. But she'd routed it correctly. It was only the first step into the Anomaly, but it filled her with relief all the same.

Mira knocked another peg into the asphalt then started the process all over, throwing more nuts and washers, finding the flaring Spheres, marking their locations, moving forward in a zigzag pattern between the Anomalies and the cars, and laying down pegs and red wire to mark the route.

Time seemed to slow, but her heart never stopped beating wildly.

Eventually, she found herself so far ahead that the flashlights from the Menagerie were just pinpricks of light behind her.

Mira threw another washer. This time nothing happened. She threw another. The same result. She threw a handful of nuts in a cloud in front of her. There was nothing but blank air now, no giant crackling spheres of deadly light.

Mira exhaled and looked down at the stopwatch. Fifty-four minutes. Not bad, she thought, even Ben had done it slower a few times. But it wasn't over. Now was the most dangerous part.

She turned and headed back into the Anomaly, following her path of metal pegs and red wire back through. Each step was nerve-racking. What if she laid it wrong? What if she miscalculated? Figuring out the drift of Condenser Spheres required a lot of math. She kept moving, one foot after the other. She could see Ravan ahead, sitting on the hood of an old pickup, her men nearby. Mira concentrated on seeming confident, on looking like she actually wasn't—

The hair on her arms stood up. A Condenser Sphere flared to life right next to her.

Mira gasped but froze in place like she'd been taught. In a Stable Anomaly like this, going still was the best idea if something went wrong. And something was definitely wrong. The gleaming ball of energy was literally only a few inches from her shoulder. She felt her heart thudding in her chest.

Mira swallowed, staying as still as she could, and looked down at her notebook. She could see which Condenser this was, and there was supposed to be another to her right, about five feet away.

Slowly, very slowly, Mira took a step in that direction. The flickering sphere disappeared as she did, fading away to nothing. Nothing materialized on her right. She was back in the safe zone.

She exhaled, knelt, picked up the peg and moved it about a foot over.

Her heart continued to pound, and she felt a surge of doubt and fear that replaced any sense of victory she might have felt before. How did she think she could do this? Mira forced herself to stand and move forward again, following the rest of the path. No other Condensers appeared, the rest of the route was safe. For now.

Ravan hopped off the car as she approached, and Max lazily opened an eye. The damned dog had been napping the whole time.

"Well?" Ravan asked.

"It's ready," Mira said. She was surprised by how little her voice shook. "I just tested it, but we need to hurry. Tell your men to stagger their entry about twenty steps per person, and keep that distance. Walk, don't run, and follow the *path*. Any deviation . . . and they're dead."

"My men can be precise *and* fast," Ravan replied. "We don't have to stagger them that much. Might save us time."

Mira shrugged. "Your call. I'll go last, follow behind and collect the pegs. If things go bad in there, that's where I need to be."

Ravan gave her an unreadable look, then shouted for her men to line up, yelling instructions.

In moments, the Menagerie were moving, filing past Mira and Ravan. Just like the Captain had said, they were making good time, following the path precisely. Ravan joined the line in the middle, walking into the Anomaly and disappearing into the dark.

Mira looked at Max. "Come on, it's our turn."

The dog looked back but didn't move.

Mira sighed. "Look, mutt, this is dangerous," she told him. "I have to hold your collar. You go running off course, you'll get us both killed. If you want to see Holt again, you have to trust me."

Max stared back with a noncommittal look. Then he hopped off the Mercedes and stood next to Mira. She slowly reached down for his collar. He stared up at her, but didn't object when she grabbed it.

Mira smiled. *How about that.* She moved forward after the pirates, and started down the path, stepping into the Anomaly after the others. The hair on her arms stood up again, and the effect felt stronger. But there was no way to know if it was just her imagination or if the Spheres really were closer.

As she moved, she gathered the pegs from the ground, wrapping them up. Max walked next to her without complaint, and the Menagerie kept moving ahead, even faster than they had before. They were about three quarters of the way through, and, to her surprise, they hadn't triggered a single sphere. Mira smiled, maybe they were going to make it out of this in one—

The old mirror of a crashed motorcycle reflected bright light behind her.

Mira turned and saw the Condenser Spheres flashing to life at the far end of the Anomaly, where they'd started. Had they left someone behind? No, she'd checked. The spheres were exploding to life, though, one after the other, and moving forward, which meant something was approaching and triggering them, as it did.

A second later she saw what it was.

A group of dark figures, maybe a dozen, rushing through the Anomaly at full speed. Flashes of different colored light glowed around them as they moved, and they weren't just running, they were leaping and flipping through the air like gymnasts.

"What the hell . . ." Ravan mumbled from ahead. The pirates froze and turned, staring behind them as the spheres continued to flare to life and the figures darted between them with almost superhuman agility. It implied a perception of the Anomalies that was like a sixth sense. And it could mean only one thing. A chill ran down Mira's spine.

"Ready weapons!" Ravan yelled, and the pirates instantly unstrapped and cocked their rifles.

"No!" Mira shouted back desperately. "No guns!" If what was coming saw a threat, they would all be dead. But the pirates were raising their rifles anyway.

The figures kept flipping forward, tumbling through the Anomalies in rapid-fire progression. They made it look easy. They made it look like a dance.

It was breathtaking to watch.

The Condensers continued to flash, lighting up the figures, and Mira made out the details she expected. They were dressed in black and gray— boots, pants, tucked-in shirts, vests with pockets, utility belts on their chests.

Black masks were pulled up over their mouths and noses, and their eyes were covered by black goggles, so dark their wearers surely couldn't see. It made the way they flipped through the Anomaly even more impressive. They were doing it *blind*.

On their left hands, Mira could see the glowing colors of the rings they wore on their three middle fingers. Each wielded a long, spearlike weapon, with glowing crystals of different colors on either end shaped into points. The colorful marks of light streaked through the air as they quickly leaped closer.

They were White Helix.

Mira ducked instinctively as the first one used her weapon as a pole-vaulter would, to flip over Mira's head. A sphere roared to life next to her. Max howled and Mira tightened her grip, trying to stop him from leaping forward.

Two Menagerie weren't so lucky. They stumbled backward. A sphere flashed to life; their screams were ripped away as they were yanked inside. They vanished, but not so fast that you couldn't make out their bodies being crushed into unrecognizable things the size of thimbles.

That was all it took. Mira saw it coming. *"No!"* she shouted.

But it was too late. The Menagerie opened fire, their guns flashing and lighting up the night.

The Helix adjusted instantly, spun in different directions, some in midair, in flashes of orange and purple light.

The rings they wore were made from Antimatter Crystals, the remnants of the colorful lightning that flashed deeper inside the Strange Lands, and they had very unique properties. Touching them in different combinations could manipulate gravity, inertia, or momentum. It let their owners do death-defying things.

The black-clad figures dodged the gunfire easily, as if everything but them was moving in slow motion, weaving through the flaring Condensers as they did.

Another Menagerie lost his balance and stumbled forward. He screamed as a Condenser Sphere flashed to life—and Mira shut her eyes tight as it sucked him inside.

Ravan yelled for her men to cease fire. The guns flashed off.

As they did, the strange figures landed on the ruined cars and trucks and buses all around them. Their weapons, the strange double-pronged spears, lowered and leveled at the Menagerie. Mira could hear a slight humming fill the air from the weapons' glowing crystals.

"No one do *anything!*" Ravan yelled. She still had her gun raised, though—as did the rest of her men, sighting at the figures that knelt above them on the ruined cars.

It was a standoff. As dangerous as that was by itself, they were still standing *inside* the Grindhouse. Even though they couldn't see them, the Condenser Spheres were drifting, and they were running out of time.

14. WHITE HELIX

THE WHITE HELIX CROUCHED on top of the cars, their strange double-pronged spear weapons pointing downward at the Menagerie.

Mira prayed no one moved. The strange, goggled figures might be outnumbered three to one, but they were White Helix, which meant they could kill every single one of them if things went bad.

Mira saw the pendants on their necks now—white ones, two strands of cord twisting around each other, with thin bars in between them. It made what was called a double helix, a symbol typically associated with DNA, and Mira had never understood why they chose it as their symbol.

The White Helix were a cult, for lack of a better description. They kept to themselves, deep back in the inner rings of the Strange Lands, and they had an almost supernatural sense and understanding of it. They could do amazing things: leap incredibly high; flip through the air; accelerate their movements—all by using the glowing rings on their left hands. Their spears were called Lancets, Mira knew, and their points were made of the same crystals. Supposedly, they could pierce solid steel, but she had never seen it for herself.

No one knew exactly how many Helix there were, but some guessed it could be in the thousands. Hundreds of survivors tried to reach the cult every year, but Mira had a feeling very few made it. To join the White Helix, you had to prove your dedication. And you did it by looking for them. If you could survive the Strange Lands on your own and make it to a certain ruined city in the second ring, the stories said the Helix would find you. What happened after that, Mira could only guess.

They were highly skilled fighters, which implied a great deal of training, and that had never made much sense. Why train to fight in the Strange Lands, where there wasn't much use for it? And how did they get so skilled so quickly? From all accounts, the White Helix fought and did things as though they had been studying and training for a lifetime. But they were a reclusive group, and their secrets were their own.

One of them, between Mira and Ravan, slowly stood up on top of a rusted pickup. A small, black girl, with an easy grip on her Lancet. From this distance, Mira saw what looked like triggers on either end of the shaft, as if for a gun. Could the Helix fire those crystals like projectiles? The thought was unpleasant, especially with them all pointed in her direction.

Ravan's gun tracked to the girl.

"Don't," Mira warned. "They'll kill us all."

The black girl lifted off her goggles and looked at Mira. Like Ravan and herself, the girl's eyes were clear of the Tone. And they sparkled in a way that suggested a smile under her mask.

"You should listen to her," the girl said. "Freebooters don't belong in this place—but at least they understand it." Her eyes focused on Mira in an uncomfortable way. "And yours seems to know enough to *fear* it, too."

Mira instinctively hid her shaking hands behind her back. Was it that obvious?

"But you," the girl said with disdain, looking at Ravan. "Menagerie *scum*. You understand *nothing*."

Ravan's glare intensified. "I understand you killed three of my men." Her voice was harsh. Whatever the girl might be—pirate, thief, or murderer—she valued the lives of her crew. "And you'll pay for that, one way or another."

The Helix shook her head. "Is it my fault if Menagerie lose their balance?"

The pirates' grip on their rifles tightened. The Helix crouched perfectly still, their eyes unreadable behind the black goggles.

"I won't threaten you back," the girl said, "there's no need. This land will kill you all on its own."

For the first time in the exchange, Ravan smiled. "Surviving's kind of my strong suit. I plan on being around a long, long time."

The girl nodded as if she expected the answer. "That's why everyone like you is destroyed here. The only way to survive this place, the only *true* way . . . is to accept that it will eventually kill you."

Mira watched the Helix girl shut her eyes in concentration and calmly reach outward. A Condenser Sphere flared to life in bright, crackling energy right next to her, lighting up the night. Max whined, and Mira held on tight, keeping him in place.

"In this place, you're already dead," the girl said, eyes closed. She ran her hands around the perimeter of the pulsating sphere, almost touching it, keeping it flared and visible, courting death. An inch or two more and that would be it. "Once you accept that, the fear no longer holds any power over you."

If only, Mira thought bitterly. The girl withdrew her hand and the Sphere vanished, blending back into the night.

"You wanna die?" Ravan seemed unimpressed. "I can accommodate that before any of your friends fire their pointy little sticks. I know a rifle when I see it, no matter how silly it looks."

The girl smiled. "Killing us only makes the rest grow *stronger*." At her words, the other White Helix nodded silently in agreement.

Ravan's eyes narrowed. So did Mira's. The Helix were definitely an eccentric bunch. They revered the Strange Lands, saw it and its artifacts as holy. Some thought they even saw the Severed Tower as a manifestation of God, but no one Mira knew had ever asked one. Freebooters and White Helix didn't exactly get along. The Helix saw them as intruders on sacred land, vultures who picked it clean of divine artifacts. It meant, if the cult came across Freebooters, things tended to get violent. There was no way to know how many had died at the hands of White Helix, but Mira guessed it was no small number.

"Why are you so far south?" Mira asked hesitantly. "I didn't think you came farther than the second ring."

The girl looked at Mira. When she spoke, there was a hint of frustration. "We're tracking Assembly. Strange ones. Fast movers. Waste of time probably, but I do as I'm told."

Ravan's stare moved to Mira suspiciously. Mira didn't blame her, that answer was the last thing she'd expected. The White Helix were tracking the Hunters, too? *Why?*

"And you?" the girl asked. "What brings Menagerie filth into the Strange Lands?"

Ravan brushed off the insult, but only because she seemed surprised. "You . . . don't know?"

For the first time, the girl hesitated. "Don't know what?"

"Your boss and mine came to an agreement," Ravan replied. "A trade of sorts. I'm bringing our end of the bargain—then I'll collect yours."

The girl stared at Ravan disbelievingly. Her eyes moved to the large, wooden crate at the center of the line of pirates. "Gideon wouldn't have anything to do with Menagerie," the girl replied darkly.

Ravan was suddenly enjoying herself, Mira could tell. She had the upper hand again. "Maybe you don't know him as well as you think. Or maybe he just doesn't trust you all that much."

The girl's stare moved from the crate back to Ravan. "Menagerie are liars and thieves. Your words mean nothing. And my instructions don't mention you. If Gideon did send for you, he didn't tell me about it, so I have no reason to help you." The girl's voice was ragged and harsh, almost venomous. She was barely holding back some kind of anger. Mira didn't know what was going on in the girl's mind, but whatever it was, it felt personal.

Ravan held the girl's stare easily. "Your name wouldn't be . . . 'Avril,' would it?"

The girl's eyes thinned. "If I see you again, Menagerie, I will end you."

Ravan smiled again. "Now that sounds like all kinds of fun."

The White Helix all stood up, ready to leap away.

"Wait!" Mira shouted. "Do you know what's happening to the Strange Lands? Why it's changing?" If anyone would know, they would.

The black girl turned to Mira and considered her, then pulled her goggles back over her eyes. "Yes."

She touched two fingers together. A sphere of yellow light flashed around her and she launched into the air like a missile, flipping into the distance. The other Helix did, too, in flashes of similar color, and the Condenser Spheres flared as they danced and tumbled gracefully through them. The Menagerie stared after them in awe, watching them disappear into the darkness.

But, for Mira, the sight of the Anomalies brought everything rushing back.

"We have to move," she yelled to Ravan. *"Now."*

Ravan understood. "Everyone, double-time it through—"

"No," Mira stopped her. She handed the pegs she'd been collecting to the nearest pirate and pushed forward down the line, dragging Max with her.

"What?" Ravan asked.

"The Condensers have drifted by now, the path isn't safe." Mira's heart beat heavily in her chest. It was true. They were in a lot of trouble. Mira yelled to both ends of the line. "Everyone watch me. Follow, and step where I step *exactly*. People ahead of me, stay still until I get to you, then follow with the others. And do it all as fast as you can."

Mira let go of Max and the dog stared up at her intently. She wasn't sure if it was Holt's training or the dog's intuition, but he seemed to understand that the situation was serious. Hopefully, he'd follow close behind her. She wouldn't have time to hold on to him.

Mira grabbed a handful of washers and nuts from the pouch. The pirates in front of her quickly knelt down as Mira started throwing them into the air.

The Condenser Spheres flashed to life, lighting up the night with strobic, wavering energy. Some of them were less than a foot from the pirates, and they backed away warily.

"If any of my men—" Ravan began.

"Threaten me later!" Mira snapped. Her eyes were on the spheres, studying them, committing their locations to memory. She was going to have to do this on the fly, there wasn't time to pathfind as she'd done before, not with all of them standing in the middle of the Anomaly. She had to focus.

The spheres flashed away and disappeared, but Mira remembered their placement. Her heart pounded as she took the first step. The fear never went away, it was always there, burning at her heels, but it took a backseat to the immediacy of the situation. There just wasn't time to focus on it.

"Now!" Mira yelled as she pushed down the line, flinging more washers and nuts into the air, forcing the hidden spheres to reveal themselves, storing their locations in her head. Or trying to, anyway. There were more Condenser Spheres in the Grindhouse than she'd ever seen. If she forgot even one of them . . .

She pushed the thoughts away. She had to concentrate. She could do this, she told herself. She had to. Or it wouldn't just be her that died, it would be dozens of people.

Mira kept moving forward, one foot after the other, throwing the bits of metal and finding the Anomalies on the fly. She was dimly aware that she had moved off the path she'd marked before, but she tried not to think about it. As she went, more and more Menagerie began to follow, watching where she stepped, moving as she did.

She pulled the last handful of washers and nuts from the pouch. If she ran out, then finding the Condensers would be impossible.

But it wasn't an issue.

She threw three washers forward, one after the other—and nothing happened. The air ahead of them was blank. She was clear.

Mira stepped forward quickly, getting out of the way of the pirates as they followed after her, one by one, quickly exiting the Grindhouse.

As they did, Mira realized, with the exception of the three that had died earlier because of the White Helix, she hadn't lost any of them. They were all still alive.

But Mira felt a surge of frustration.

How many Freebooters could have done what she'd just done? Navigating the Grindhouse without a marked trail? Not to mention bringing almost thirty people behind her? She should be *proud*. She should have a feeling of confidence now, but she didn't.

You don't have it in you, she heard Ben's voice say in her mind.

"Not bad," Ravan's voice startled Mira. The Captain studied her evenly. "You can handle yourself under pressure."

Mira looked at her. "Is what you told the White Helix true? Are you here to meet with them?" She hadn't had time to really process that revelation until now. It seemed incredibly unlikely. What could two such radically different groups as the Menagerie and the White Helix want with one another?

"Everything I say is true, little dear," Ravan replied. "I wonder if you can say the same? Finding out those pointy sticks are tracking our

Assembly makes me think you haven't been entirely honest. Just who *are* these friends of yours?"

Mira kept her eyes on Ravan's. "No one special. Assembly never come here. It probably got the Helix curious. They're very protective of the Strange Lands."

Ravan studied Mira a long time, and there was no way to know if the black-haired girl believed her or not. Then she turned and looked behind them. They both watched the last of the Condenser Spheres go dark, as what was left of the Menagerie made it through. "Don't know why anyone would be protective of this place."

Mira was coming to agree. The longer she was here, the more she despised it. There was a time when it had seemed magical—but now all it did was frighten her. Just like the Helix leader had said.

"I wanna keep moving," Ravan stated. "Unless you need a break?"

Mira shook her head. She was exhausted, but she wouldn't let Ravan see that. She turned and started walking through the dark, past the eerie unending line of ruined vehicles. As she did she pulled the compass pendant out of her shirt. It still pointed northwest, in the direction of the Forlorn Passage.

They were still headed in the right direction. If you could call it that.

Something moved next to her. Max trotted at her side, sniffing the cars as he went.

Mira smiled. She scratched the spot between his ears as they walked. He didn't seem to care.

15. AWAKENINGS

ZOEY SAT IN A CIRCLE of the Hunters. The one who had revealed itself to her before stood closest in its differently marked tripod, watching. She could feel its intense gaze without looking up. To the others, it wasn't just a leader, it was something else. *Royalty* was the closest word Zoey had to describe it. They would fight and die at its bidding, and for them dying was something much less immediate than it was for humans. That dedication carried tremendous weight.

Arranged in front of Zoey were four mechanical toys: a car, a train, and two helicopters. Their dusty boxes lay forgotten a few feet away. The walkers had brought them to her from somewhere outside.

The "suggestions" she felt from the Royal were insistent and firm, and they filled her mind. She was exhausted from pushing back against them, but it seemed to be getting easier, as if that part of her was growing stronger. It had been the same suggestion for an hour now. If she were to piece them together into words, it would be . . .

Power. Control.

It had taken a while to understand that the Royal wanted her to "power" and "control" the toys that lay beneath her. Just as she had done with the dam at Midnight City, and the old truck. The Royal was testing her, as if that specific ability was important somehow. She could do it instantly, if she wanted, but she made no move to do so.

These things had hurt her friends, scared her, commanded her about like a slave. They had healed the pain in her head, true, but only when it suited them. They were not her friends, they were not Holt or Mira or the Max. So she just stared back up at the Royal, unmoving.

120

Power. Control. The suggestions came again.

"No," she said. Speaking, itself, was a form of defiance. The Mas'Erinhah preferred she communicate with her thoughts. Judging from the sensations that bled from them every time she spoke, they seemed to consider it primitive and disdainful. "Honored" guest or not, she had been repeatedly punished whenever she spoke. The thought of another psychic lashing by the Royal made her cringe, but still she did nothing.

They were *not* her friends.

One of the Hunters lunged toward her. Zoey scooted away in fear . . .

. . . and the Royal rammed into the machine, sending it reeling backward.

The chastised tripod lowered itself, turning away its triangular eye. The menacing sensations that pulsed from the Royal suggested only *it* was "worthy" of disciplining the "Scion."

Zoey still had no clue what that term meant. Any attempt to ask the Royal questions was met with punishment. All she knew was that she was important somehow. If she only knew why.

The Royal turned back to Zoey. *Power. Control.*

"No."

From across the room came an unusual sound. A human moan, weak and groggy. With wide eyes, Zoey looked to where Holt hung from the rafters.

"Holt!" Zoey shouted and stood up—but the Hunters moved in front of her, blocking her.

New suggestions, new feelings, poured from the Royal. It was considering, it had an idea, and Zoey watched as the machine leaped toward the other end of the room where Holt hung, coming to stand underneath his still form, almost tall enough to touch him with its metallic body. Holt moaned again.

Hope sprung inside Zoey. He was waking up.

From a diode on the Royal's fuselage, a bright, tightly focused red beam erupted. It burned into the building's wall, and where it hit, the bricks sparked and dissolved.

Slowly, Zoey noticed, the beam of energy tilted upward, cutting a deep fissure as it moved. She followed its path, and felt a chill as she came to a realization. If it continued to rise, the beam would stop cutting into the wall . . . and instead cut into Holt.

Power. Control. The impressions came again.

The implication was clear. The Royal would hurt Holt unless she moved the toys. Zoey's heart beat frantically.

Power. Control, the Royal projected. The beam continued to rise. Zoey had no doubt the alien would follow through. It would hurt Holt. It would hurt him badly. It had no reason not to.

The walkers around Zoey watched eagerly. The Royal looked up, as the beam was about to cut into Holt's shoulder. When it did, it would slice his arm completely—

"Stop!" Zoey shouted.

The Royal turned back, its red-green-and-blue "eye" buzzing as it focused on Zoey. The beam cut off instantly.

Underneath her, the car and train ran in circles around one another. The blades of the helicopters whirred rapidly, hovering just to the side of Zoey's head.

Zoey could feel the tiny machines—everything about them—their plastic mechanics, the infinitesimal power in their circuits, the turning of their wheels, the spinning of blades.

She moved them effortlessly, feeling them bob and weave and spin. She wasn't just *aware* of the toys. In that moment Zoey *was* the toys. Just as it had been before, and as always, it felt . . . amazing.

There was a rush of emotion from the Royal at the other end of the room. It was satisfaction again. Pride.

Holt moaned, stirred in his bonds, but this time Zoey didn't notice.

THE WORLD SLOWLY BEGAN to focus, and the first thing Holt saw was the burning, three-optic eye of one of the green-and-orange walkers. It was staring curiously up at him, which was odd in itself. Eventually he figured it out. He was *hanging* from something. He craned his neck to look up, and saw he was tied to the thick wooden beams that ran along a very high and long ceiling.

The walker under him emitted a brief, bored, distorted sound, then walked off. Holt quickly checked out the rest of the building.

A single, huge room made of crumbling brick walls. Rows and rows of pew-like seats stretched to an elevated area, where rested benches and high-backed tables, all of it falling apart where it stood.

Holt recognized the building immediately. A courthouse. A small one, probably in the middle of what remained of some little town.

The wall to his right had cracked and split, and through it he could see the remains of a street, the broken glass of store widows just on the other side.

And there was something else, something mind-boggling. The opposite wall was bursting inward, in a frozen explosion, where a huge tractor trailer truck was punching through. Bricks, debris and wood, it all hung suspended in the air.

He suddenly knew why, and he groaned out loud at the realization. He was in the Strange Lands now. Wonderful.

Holt struggled against his bonds, trying to break them loose, but the strands of strange material holding him were too strong. He looked at the other end of the building. The elevated part of the room contained an old judge's bench, and the rest of the walkers were gathered around it, standing in a circle, looking down at something underneath them.

It was Zoey.

She was here, too, he saw with relief. She was okay.

Then Holt looked closer. In front of her were four small toys. A train and a car were doing figure eights around each other, helicopters were zigzagging in between the walkers that circled Zoey. She appeared to be concentrating intensely. The little girl's eyes were shut, and her hands were covered in the same glowing, wavering golden energy Holt had seen at the dam.

She was controlling the toys—but why?

"Zoey?" he asked softly.

The girl's concentration broke. The golden energy vanished. Her eyes ripped open.

"Holt!" Zoey yelled. The car and train slowed to a stop. The small helicopters crashed to the floor.

The group of Hunters watched as Zoey rushed to Holt and stared up at him, beaming. Then the smile vanished. The little girl turned, looked back toward the tripod that had been underneath him—the one with the different markings, the Royal.

Holt watched the little girl and the alien machine stare at each other intently. Though no words passed between them, they held themselves as if speaking to one another. The thought was chilling.

"It says I can talk to you. For a second," Zoey said. "It says it's my reward."

"Reward for what?" Holt asked warily.

Zoey told him everything, and most of it came back to him as she did. The death of the Crossroads, how he was shot, his wounds. These walkers had carried them both a long way, ventured into the Strange Lands to avoid other Assembly clans that were looking for her, had taken up inside this old ruin. They were waiting for a ship to come and pick them up, to take them back across the sea.

"The sea?" Holt asked.

"The one to the east," Zoey said. "Their land's on the other side."

Did she mean the *Atlantic?* Was their "land" Europe? Africa? It implied the Assembly had divided the planet between clans of some sort. If so, it meant these green-and-orange walkers had come a long way to find *her.*

"Zoey," Holt continued. "Did they . . . fix me where I was hurt?"

Zoey nodded.

"Why? Why not just kill me? Why bring me along?"

"You impressed it, the Royal liked the way you did things in the flooded place, and how you escaped it the other times, too. It thinks you're good enough for . . ." Zoey paused as she tried to put words to something, as if translating a foreign language. "The 'Criterion,' I think is right. The Mas'Erinhah are more picky about who they test than the others."

"Mas' what?" Holt stared down at her like a complete stranger.

Zoey looked at the green-and-orange tripod walkers behind her. "It's the name of their clan, or at least the best I can pronounce it. They don't really use words to talk with. I have to make my own up sometimes, to fit what they show me."

Holt felt the same chill at her words.

"It's not really talking; it's hard to explain. But . . . I understand them. And they understand me." She looked back up at him and he could see the fear in her eyes. "They make me . . . remember things, Holt. The things they teach me, it's like I've done them before. Like I forgot how to do them and now I'm remembering again." Her voice had a haunted tone to it. "I remember more and more, the longer I stay near them. I don't understand why, I don't like what they show me. It scares me. They call me the Scion."

The word bothered Holt for all kinds of reasons. It wasn't just that they had a name for Zoey, a label, or that she was something specific to them. It was also that the word itself had a sense of menace to it, somehow.

He had to get them both out of this. Quick—before whatever drop-ship these "Mas'Erinhah" were waiting for showed up.

Holt looked and followed the thin line of cable that held him to the rafter. It looked like the same strange, fibrous material the aliens used to tie Zoey inside that crashed ship so long ago. From what Holt remembered, it was thin and cut easily, but it was also incredibly strong. He wouldn't be able to simply snap it, and he had no way to sever it.

But the rafter the line he was tied to was a different story. Holt could make out the cracks that ran through it. It had been weakened, probably by that truck plowing into the building. If he could use his weight somehow, shake that rafter hard enough—it might break. He'd hit the floor pretty hard, but he should be okay.

Holt could feel his Swiss Army Knife in a pocket of his cargo pants. In fact, he could feel *all* his stuff, minus what had been in his pack, of course. The Assembly hadn't bothered to remove it. They probably didn't consider any of it a threat. If Zoey could get that knife once he hit the floor, she could cut his bonds herself.

The problem was, for the plan to work, they would pretty much have to be alone inside the courthouse, which meant . . . they needed a diversion.

"Did you see the wall, Holt?" Zoey asked. She was looking at the truck with wonder.

Holt frowned, refused to look back at the thing. "Yeah, I saw it."

"If you touch it, it unsticks in time."

Holt shivered. This place was a nightmare. "Then we probably shouldn't do that, wouldn't you say? How far are we into the Strange Lands, anyway?"

Zoey shook her head. "I don't know, but the Mas'Erinhah are very good at finding Anomalies. We're safe with them."

Holt didn't say so, but he wasn't sure he felt the same way.

"Do you think Mira will come after us?" Zoey asked.

Mira.

The mention of her brought pangs of shame. He saw himself standing over her, Chance Generator in one hand, his other poised to strike. He remembered the scared and hurt look in her eyes.

He'd almost *hit* her. It still didn't seem real, but he knew it was.

The Chance Generator. If only he had that now, he could—

No, he told himself sternly.

He had to let that go. Mira was right. It had changed him, made him reliant on it instead of himself. It had made him do things he never would have imagined, and it may also have cost him whatever feelings Mira still had for him. He hoped he never saw that thing again.

"Unfortunately, kiddo, I think she's too smart for that," Holt said. "Don't worry, though. I'll figure something out."

"I know, Holt," Zoey said simply. "You always do."

Behind her, the green-and-orange walkers watched them. Holt sighed, looked back up to the rafter he was hanging from. All he needed now . . . was a miracle.

16. KENMORE

THE ASSEMBLY TRACKS HAD VEERED OFF the Forlorn Passage about ten miles back, and headed down a rural road lined with old barns and farmhouses before ending here. That road hadn't been marked as safe in Mira's Lexicon, and she'd spent a good amount of time steering the pirates through pockets of Vector Fields and Daisy Chains.

The Menagerie were still proving themselves capable; they hadn't slowed their pace at all, and much to Mira's relief, no more had died. Ravan, for her part, seemed unsurprised by her men's performance. She drove them hard and expected their best.

As they approached an old town a rusted welcome sign proclaimed KENMORE. Ravan called a stop. City ruins were a good place for an ambush, and she wasn't going to just walk right into the town square without a little recon.

The ground sloped up on either side of them, and both hills were peppered with trees—cottonwoods and spruce, thick and unkempt. It would give them good cover.

Ravan split the group in two, ordering the divided units to climb separate hills. Mira and Max followed Ravan's group up the larger one. At the top, they crawled to the edge, trying to keep out of sight of whatever might be below. It was a small town, maybe ten square miles all in all, and from here Mira could see old houses, the steeple of a church, gas stations, businesses, and right in the center an old courthouse. Strangely, it all seemed in good shape. Like it hadn't aged for some reason. That would be expected in the deeper rings, where time actually ticked slower, but here in the first ring it was unusual. Mira didn't like it. Anything unusual in the Strange Lands usually meant trouble.

Ravan handed Mira an extra pair of binoculars. They sighted through them, studying the town, looking from building to building. It was a dead zone, silent and eerie, and Mira could see the breeze stir the dirty remains of tattered curtains in some of the buildings' broken windows.

Then Mira saw the answer to the question of the town's near pristine shape. Everywhere, incidents appeared to somehow be *frozen* in time.

At one corner a billboard was falling over, its pieces suspended in the air. Nearby, the beginnings of an explosion flared outward at a gas station, a blooming ball of petrified flame that sat like a sculpture. In a street below, vehicles listed in a three-way collision, their pieces and parts hanging in the air. The most dramatic example was a semitruck, its cargo trailer jackknifing and tearing loose as the engine punched straight through the side of the courthouse.

Mira moaned. "This whole place is a Time Sink."

"Let me guess. Bubble of frozen time?" Ravan asked mildly, still sighting through the optics.

"Pretty much. They're fragile and they're dangerous. Any sort of kinetic movement against an object in a Time Sink frees it from the Anomaly's effect."

"Lovely," Ravan replied.

Mira kept scanning the town. Other than the evidence of the Time Sink, it was unremarkable. It seemed devoid of life and movement.

"I don't think there's anything here," Mira said quietly. "If there was—"

"Town square, northeast corner," Ravan cut her off.

Mira spun her binoculars, saw the remains of a bank, one of the more heavily damaged buildings in the city. On its roof something moved. A green-and-orange Assembly walker.

Mira almost dropped the binoculars, the flood of relief was so strong. She'd *found* them.

She watched as it slowly paced along the edge, scanning the ground and the horizon. A sentry, most likely, and after another few steps it disappeared behind some of the building's ductwork.

"Another one, coming out of the courthouse," Ravan said. Mira spun her binoculars again, found the walker emerging from a huge crack in the building's wall. She watched it take a few slow steps—then leap into a run. As it did, the Menagerie let out a collective gasp. A shimmering field of energy enveloped the walker—and it disappeared from view.

"Son of a gunderson," one of Ravan's lieutenants said next to her. "Did that just happen?"

"That just happened," Ravan said tightly. "Tell the others to report in."

The lieutenant grabbed a small mirror, aimed it so that it caught the sun, and flashed signals to the hill on the other side of town. A few seconds later Mira saw similar flashes from the far tree line.

"Looks like they spotted three more," he said, translating the flashes, "running patterns on the south side."

"Patrols," Ravan said with distaste. "They're dug in. But why? What are they waiting for?"

"More than that," the lieutenant said, "*look* at them. They're *green and orange*. I ain't ever seen any that weren't blue and white."

Ravan lowered her binoculars and looked at Mira darkly. Mira stared back carefully.

"Green-and-orange walkers." Ravan's tone was dangerous. "Three legs. Small, mobile—and *invisible?* I don't know what it is. Maybe it's my naturally distrusting nature, but . . . I'm starting to have a hard time taking what you say at face value."

"I've told you everything I know," Mira lied. "I don't know why these Assembly are different, or what it means. All I know is, these walkers have my friends and you made a deal to help me get them back."

Ravan's crystal-clear eyes stared into Mira's, probing and searching for deception. If she found it, Mira wasn't sure what the girl would do, but she had a feeling it wouldn't be pleasant. Ravan considered her a moment more, then just turned and looked back through her binoculars, as if the issue were settled. "Like I said. Probably just me." Her optics moved over the city, scanning and searching again. "So, if I were a prisoner, where would I be?"

It could be any one of dozens of buildings. Mira couldn't pinpoint it, but she could definitely narrow it down.

She took out the compass pendant and pointed it toward the city. The needle aimed into the heart of the square. Ravan and Mira followed its line to the big, white-bricked courthouse. It was a sturdy building, covered, a good defensible position. The giant crack in its exterior allowed a glimpse inside.

Mira focused her binoculars, and when she saw what was there, barely visible through the hole, her stomach tightened like a fist.

Someone hung in midair, tied to what was left of the building's rafters. Mira couldn't see his face with any detail, but she recognized enough to know who it was.

Holt. Hanging lifeless and unmoving in the shadows of the ruined building.

Mira dropped the binoculars and shut her eyes. He couldn't be gone. Not after how they'd left things.

Ravan turned to Mira. "Don't worry, Red, doesn't mean he's dead. They're Assembly. Everything they do has a purpose," she said with disdain. "If he weren't alive they wouldn't bother stringing him up, would they? Of course, doesn't mean they've kept him in mint condition, either."

She was right, Mira knew. On both counts. He probably was still alive, but there was no guarantee that would last. Holt wasn't the one they really wanted, after all.

"Don't see your other friend," Ravan said. "What are we looking for?"

"A little girl," Mira replied. "Eight or nine, blond hair."

"Probably just out of sight, one side of the gap or the other." Ravan lowered the binoculars, looked at her lieutenant. "We brought a Portal, right?"

The lieutenant nodded. Mira was surprised. A Portal was a pair of linked artifact combinations, complicated, expensive ones. When activated, they each formed a gateway that anyone could pass through no matter how far the distance. Even Mira had only made a dozen or so, and usually only by special request. Ravan was well supplied, obviously.

"Still need a distraction." The pirate Captain stared back into the town, thinking. Mira followed her gaze to the frozen gas station explosion at the opposite end. "Kinetic movement, huh?"

"Yeah," Mira replied. She saw what the girl intended. "Throw something into that—a rock, a bottle, whatever—it'll merge back into real time. In a *major* way."

"What about a bullet? From a distance?" Ravan asked. "Would that work?"

"As long as you hit it."

"We'll hit it." She looked at the lieutenant. "Signal the others. Tell 'em we're gonna run a Deneen Gambit. Reinhold's our best shot, he can do the distraction. You and Sparks are on point for the Portal. We get one go at this, don't mess it up."

The lieutenant nodded grimly, turned and started flashing instructions to the pirates on the other hill. The others who were with them started gearing up to move. Two of them set down the big crate as they did, and Mira looked at it.

"What's in that thing anyway?" she asked.

"Something the White Helix wants, and that's all you need to know," Ravan replied, loading shells into a shotgun. When she spoke next it was in a low whisper, meant for Mira's ears alone. "But if you want something to worry about, then worry about this: If I get in that courthouse and find that you've misled me in any way, Solid or no Solid, I'll kill you myself."

Ravan smiled pleasantly—then started gathering her things, making ready to move. Mira didn't doubt the girl's sincerity.

17. YOU ARE OF US

ZOEY WOKE FROM A DEEP DREAM where planets circled huge red suns and giant moons sank along impossible, purple horizons. Alien worlds . . . or just her imagination? She wasn't sure. Her back hurt from how she'd fallen asleep against the old wall, and she grimaced when she sat up.

Two of the Hunters stood guard over her. The Royal was across the room, powered down, its machine body dark and still. Zoey stared at it warily, regardless.

Her feelings for the aliens were complicated now. Before, there had been only fear. There was still that, but now it was mixed with different things. She didn't like it, but what was forming between her and the Hunters was some kind of twisted closeness.

The Royal had kidnapped her, threatened her friends, but at the same time it seemed to know her in a way no one else did. It had hurt her, but it had also taken her pain away. It was interested in her powers, but unlike many people, including Holt and Mira, who had witnessed what she could do, its instinctual response wasn't to recoil in fear or confusion. Instead, it had been pleased. It had encouraged her, and it had praised her when she succeeded.

It wasn't Holt. She didn't care for it like she did him. But there was something oddly comforting about her interactions with it the last few days. It made no sense, those "lessons" had been laced with fear and pain, but it was there nonetheless.

From the distance came a loud, shuddering sound.

An explosion. A big one. From the north, just past the edge of the small town, probably. At the sound, the walkers inside the courthouse trumpeted to one another, a series of sounds that conveyed both confusion and alarm.

The Royal shook as it powered back up, lights flashing to life all over its body. It instantly broke into a run, its cloaking field enveloping it as it leaped outside and disappeared into the sunlight.

Two guards remained behind, moving back and forth agitatedly, staring after their leader. Zoey felt their frustration. The explosion might mean action, battle. It took a great deal of self-control for them to remain behind.

"Zoey," a voice whispered above her.

She looked up and saw Holt. He was awake, staring at her with that look he had when he'd decided to do something dangerous and altogether not smart.

Zoey could guess what it was, now that only two walkers were left in the courthouse. She shook her head at him, trying to tell him no, but, she knew, once Holt decided something, he carried through with it.

"Be ready," he said. She watched him take a deep breath and look up at the rafters. Whatever he was about to do, it was going to cause big problems.

From nowhere, something landed in the center of the old courthouse, tossed in from outside, through the broken roof.

It was too far away for Zoey to make out what it was, but she saw the two remaining Hunters turn, their triangular laser sights streaming toward the object, moving over the ground where it landed.

Zoey gasped as the thing pulsed in a powerful burst of illumination.

The walkers trumpeted as a hole of light—that was the only way Zoey could describe it—ripped the air apart, forming into a perfect, bright, hovering circle.

Zoey watched, stunned, as kids began pouring out of the hole into the courthouse, as though it were some kind of gateway. One, two, three, four, they just kept coming—and they were all carrying shotguns.

The Hunters reacted with surprised, distorted sounds, their plasma cannons spraying yellow bolts outward in a stream. Zoey felt lustful joy erupt from the machines. This was battle, this was action, and it had found them after all.

One of the kids took a plasma bolt in the chest, spun and fell.

The rest of them, whoever they were, returned fire, their shotguns thundered to life, the shells exploded in sparks as they hit the Hunters. Zoey cringed in terror at the loud, jarring sounds, covering her ears.

Above her, Holt jerked his whole body downward. The rafter above him groaned, but it didn't break.

Zoey watched him jerk again. Again. The rafter weakened with each impact, spraying rotted splinters until it finally came apart.

Holt slammed onto the hard floor with a grunt.

The two remaining walkers didn't notice. They stood protectively between Zoey and the strange gateway, firing at the kids that continued to leap out of it, one after the other.

"Holt!" Zoey rushed toward him, tried untying the strange, fibrous bonds that held his feet and hands together, but they were too tight. She couldn't get them to untangle.

"My knife," Holt said. "On my belt."

Zoey reached for his belt, found the red Swiss Army Knife.

Nearby, more kids poured through the gateway. By now they outnumbered the two green-and-orange walkers ten to one, but the Hunters were significantly more powerful. Raw numbers were no advantage here.

The tripods waded eagerly into the kids, lashing out with their powerful legs. One kid went flying. He crashed to the ground, rolled, but didn't move.

A plasma blast blew another one across what was left of the courthouse. His body almost instantly exploded in flames.

"Smoke!" a voice yelled. A girl's voice, commanding and forceful.

A hissing, as three metallic cylinders hit the ground, rolling toward the Assembly walkers. As they did, they sprayed out clouds of colored smoke that quickly flooded the large building.

The walkers trumpeted in alarm. Zoey felt their sudden trepidation.

They couldn't see now, they were blind. Instinctively, they started firing erratically, spraying yellow bolts of heated death that sparked all around Holt and Zoey—on the walls, the floor and the rafters above. Zoey screamed as two bolts burned past their heads.

"Hurry, kiddo," Holt yelled. She looked back down to the knife. The thing had so many pieces, she wasn't sure which one to open. She looked at Holt desperately. "The blade! *The big blade!*"

Plasma fire streaked everywhere, lighting the smoke like yellow lightning while shotgun blasts shook the building. They were running out of time.

Zoey began to pry the knife open . . . and then stopped as the sensations overtook her.

They were weaker, farther away, but she recognized them. It was the Royal.

Scion. We return.

In the distance, Zoey heard the electronic cries of the missing Hunters. The explosion was a trick to draw them away, while these kids attacked through that strange gateway. It hadn't fooled them long. The Royal was on its way back, rushing as fast as it could. Zoey could feel its emotions. Anger at the humans who dared attack it, shame for falling for their simple ruse, fear of the possibility of losing its prize.

Scion. We return. There was a sense of desperation to its thoughts now, it was something she had never felt from it before. The sensations startled her. She could feel just how much she meant to it.

"Zoey!" Holt shouted frantically. Her fingers moved for the knife again.

More Hunters burst into the courthouse, trumpeting, plasma fire already spraying. Two more kids spun wildly and hit the floor dead.

The Hunters advanced, joining the other two, targeting lasers lighting up the dispersing smoke. The kids, whoever they were, were in a lot of trouble, and more Hunters were on the way. Zoey could feel them. They were about to be overwhelmed.

"Be ready!" The same female voice again. A shotgun blast lighted up the smoke, and sparks burst off the frozen semitruck barreling through the wall. The girl, whoever she was, had shot it intentionally. Zoey's eyes widened. She knew what was coming.

There was a flash—and then the truck and its impact roared to life.

It blew through the wall in a violent explosion that sprayed brick and mortar and fire everywhere, ramming into the batch of new walkers, slamming them into the floor and burying them as it exploded past and crashed to a stop.

"Damn!" Holt exclaimed in shock, eyes wide.

Three kids rushed through the smoke toward them. As they did, they shouldered their shotguns, and Zoey screamed as they grabbed her and started pulling her away.

"Zoey!" Holt yelled behind her, struggling frantically against his bonds.

Zoey screamed again as they dragged her into the smoke. At the same time, she instinctively projected her terror outward. The Royal responded instantly.

Scion! We return!

The gateway of light lit the smoke in dreamlike patterns as she reached it. It was pure white energy, and if there was something on the other side of it, Zoey couldn't tell. She struggled against her captors, trying to break free, but they were much older, and they were too strong.

You are of us, another ferocious projection from the Royal. *We will find you.*

Zoey wasn't sure if she found the thoughts alarming . . . or comforting. Then her mind and vision filled with the color red as she was dragged into the gateway.

18. REUNIONS

HOLT WATCHED AS THEY DRAGGED ZOEY into the smoke. More kids appeared from the haze. A plasma bolt slapped into one and flung him to the ground. He didn't get up.

The remaining kids grabbed Holt, started pulling him away, too.

"Who the hell are——" Holt started.

"Shut up, goon," one of the smoky shadows said. "Lost three of my friends getting you out of here. You better be worth it."

Worth it? To whom?

They dragged him by his feet through the smoke. It was all surreal and dreamlike—sizzling plasma bolts flying through the air, flashes of gunfire. Ahead, the bright white circle was coming closer. The kids were retreating back through it, and Holt was pretty sure now that this entire thing had been arranged to rescue him and Zoey. But *why?*

The kids dragged Holt through the strange gateway, and as they did he was blinded by the color red. It wasn't a light or anything specific, the color red simply flooded his senses in a jarring, violent blast, and he felt a rush of intense cold from head to foot.

It only lasted a second. The red vanished, so did the cold. He could see again.

The afternoon sun shown down on him. Hundreds of strange, light brown reeds brushed against his skin and tore at his clothes as he was dragged through them. Wheat stalks, Holt realized. He was out in the open, away from the ruined city, in some overgrown field, who knew how far away.

Behind him, the remainder of the kids were jumping through the gateway. Some of them were helping their injured fellows pass back over. The last of them made it just as one of the green-and-orange tripods lunged through after them, its plasma cannons spinning and firing.

"Shut the gate!" a girl's commanding voice shouted. "Blow the artifact if you have to!"

Two shotgun blasts rang out, and Holt saw the dark object underneath the portal explode in a shower of sparks. The white circle hovering in the air died and vanished, cutting off the path back to the courthouse.

But they weren't out of the woods yet. The lone walker whirled around, firing sporadically at whoever was closest. Another boy fell to the ground.

There were dozens of kids Holt could see, all around the walker. They raised their shotguns and fired as one, pumping new shells into chambers, firing again, over and over. The sound was deafening, even in the open air of the wheat field.

The walker trumpeted wildly, shuddering from each blast, sparks spraying off it in pulsing flashes, from one blast after another. Fire shot from its exhaust ports. There was a great whine as its internal mechanics failed, and the thing collapsed in a heap. It spasmed once, twice, then went still.

Everyone covered their eyes, they knew what was coming.

Brilliant golden, wavering energy flooded up and out of the destroyed walker, blindingly bright, even in the afternoon sun. As it floated up into the sky, it formed into a complicated crystalline shape. Holt's mind filled with intense static, so powerful and consuming it blotted everything else out. By the way some of the kids dropped to their knees, he could tell it was having the same effect on them.

The mass of pulsing light rose into the air, higher and higher, moving westward, until it finally faded away. And when it disappeared, so did the static.

Holt took a deep breath and opened his eyes. Still bound and lying on his back, he could see very little except the tops of the reeds as they wavered in the breeze. But he could hear the kids all around him, congratulating themselves, reciting stories of the mission and laughing. There were also moans of pain and hurried calls for help.

"Holt!" he heard Zoey shout from somewhere. The wheat parted as she ran to him and kneeled down, her eyes full of fear. "Holt, they took your knife."

"It's okay," he smiled. "We'll get it back. Did they say who—"

The sound of barking cut him off, loud and exuberant. A dog exploded through the reeds, leaped onto Holt's chest, and started licking his face with unlimited enthusiasm.

With shock, Holt realized he knew the mutt.

"The Max!" Zoey shouted, her fear vanishing. Max leaped for her next, and she petted and scratched him and laughed. Holt stared at the dog in astonishment. Everything seemed unreal. How could Max be *here?* Holt had left him behind at the Crossroads. But there he was, jumping all over Zoey.

A realization came to him then. If the dog was here, did that also mean . . . ?

Someone else pushed into view. When Holt saw her, everything suddenly made sense. At least on the surface. He could add the pieces together and see what they pointed to—but it still felt like a dream.

Mira stood above Holt, staring down at him amid the blowing, golden stalks. Her red hair hung loose just past her neck, gently brushing her collar bones. Her eyes were clear and green. She was disheveled, dirty, and clearly exhausted, but to him, right then, she was the most beautiful thing he had ever seen. In spite of the odds of finding him, in spite of all the reasons she had to do otherwise—she had come for him.

Mira smiled at him. It wasn't as warm as it had once been. She was conflicted, unsure. He didn't blame her. Things had changed between them, but still . . . she was smiling. And that was something.

"Goodness. Gracious. Sakes alive," an alarmingly familiar voice said from somewhere nearby. Holt knew that voice. His thoughts worked themselves back together. He placed the voice to a face, and that face to memories—and his blood ran cold.

"And I thought this Solid was going to be a complete waste of time," the voice continued. The other kids began to emerge, pushing through the tall stalks of wheat that surrounded them. Holt could see the colorful tattoos on their wrists, similar to the half-finished one on his. They glared down at him evilly.

They were Menagerie, and he was in very big trouble.

A final figure pushed into view. A girl with long, black hair trailing down her back, and a dark bird on her right wrist. Her perfectly clear eyes held Holt's as she took in the sight of him. Ravan was as beautiful and cold as he remembered, and the sight of her stirred a combination of feelings, not all of them unpleasant. The look between them spoke volumes.

"Holt Hawkins," Ravan said with fervor. "As I live and breathe."

To his right, Mira looked back and forth between Holt and Ravan, and he didn't have to look at her to see her bewilderment. He could guess what happened. She went to the only people she could for help—not knowing they were the very ones who were looking for *him*.

"Holt, I didn't . . ." Mira started, then faded off, confused.

Zoey seemed to sense something was wrong, moved back toward Holt, but the pirates grabbed her. She screamed as they lifted her into the air.

"Zoey!" Mira shouted and moved for the little girl. One of the pirates grabbed her and yanked her off her feet. Mira kicked and clawed, tried to get loose—until someone put a gun to her head. It drove the point home.

Max barked and lunged. The kids kicked him away, knocked him down. It took three of them to pin and hold the squirming, violent, growling dog. The Menagerie pirates laughed. The haze of the previous battle had faded, and they could sense blood in the water now. Their violent, malicious sides were reappearing.

Slowly, Ravan knelt down and reached for Holt. He tried to pull away, but there was nowhere to go. She brushed a few stray hairs out of his eyes. The gesture wasn't just tender, it was familiar.

To his right, out of the corner of his eye, he could see Mira watching.

"It may not seem like it right now." Ravan leaned in close, whispering softly. "But you're lucky it was *me* who found you."

Holt didn't answer. Their stare lasted a moment longer, then Ravan looked back to her men.

"Leave him tied and bring him with us," she ordered. "Take the others, too. We'll figure out what they're worth at Polestar." Ravan stood up and looked at Mira, who stared back with fury. "What? We honored the Solid, we rescued your friends. Not my fault you didn't stipulate anything about us letting them go once we did."

Mira's stare was venomous.

She tried to break free with renewed effort, almost managed to do it, struggling to get to Ravan. Two more kids joined the others, subdued her, carried her off kicking and fighting. Holt wasn't sure what had transpired between the two, but he could tell there was already a lot of history.

"Holt!" Zoey screamed in anguish as she was pulled away, too. Max howled after her.

But there was nothing Holt could do.

Two Menagerie pirates stood over him, smiling wickedly. Then a shotgun butt slammed down onto his head and everything went black.

AVRIL STOOD AT THE crest of a rocky hill, staring down at the valley below. The Menagerie were there, grouped in what remained of an old wheat field. They'd taken the Freebooter prisoner, as well as another boy who seemed injured, and there was the girl as well, the small one.

The one Gideon had sent her to find.

Avril watched as they started marching in a column to the east, through the wheat, leaving a trail behind them, flattening it all as they moved. It was just like them. The Menagerie wilted everything they touched and never looked back.

She felt anger begin to rise as she remembered the black-haired girl and what she'd said. Avril wanted to believe it was a lie, but she knew it wasn't. The girl had used her name. She *knew*. The artifact they were carrying in that crate was just the right size. She could guess what it all meant—but even so, she just couldn't believe Gideon would do this to her.

Then again, in his own way he'd told her, hadn't he? *One task you will like. And one you will* not.

The wind picked up again, blowing from the north, and she casually tied her hair behind her head. It was warm air, and the hair on her arms stood up as it swept over her. The land was changing and it had everything to do with that little girl down there. Even from this distance, Avril could tell the Pattern joined with her just like it would with any Anomaly. It meant Gideon was right. She was the one they had waited for, as hard as it was to believe.

"You feel it, too?" someone asked next to her. His name was Dane, tall and handsome, with wavy hair and lithe muscles, and he balanced his

Lancet on his shoulders, arms hanging from either end. She could feel his closeness, and she liked it. She'd gotten used to it in a way she never believed she could.

Avril nodded. "From the north, coming hard."

"Ion Storms in the second ring. It doesn't feel real," he mused in disbelief. She felt his eyes on her. "The one below, the one who knew your name. You *know* why she's here."

"Yes."

"I won't let them have you," Dane said with conviction. She turned and looked into his eyes—and saw the passion there. "I *won't.*"

Avril felt warmth spread through her. He would fight and die for her, she knew. Not because she was his Doyen, but because of who they were to each other when they were alone. Dane was the only person she'd ever let see her weaker side, the side that was vulnerable, and she wished she could curl up in his arms right then, but she couldn't. The rest of her Arc was behind them, waiting, watching. She had to be strong; they had to see her as fearless.

"Sometimes we don't have the choices we hope we will," she replied.

"Why not just kill them?" one of the others asked before Dane could reply. "Why not just kill the Menagerie and take the little girl and be gone?"

"Know thyself, know thine enemy," Avril simply said. "Right now, the Menagerie and the Freebooter are unknowns. We need to find shelter. We can pick up their trail after the storm."

"Assuming there's anything *left* to follow," Dane said.

"There will be. I doubt it's the Tower's will for the Prime to die here." Avril turned and lowered the black goggles over her eyes, cutting off her sense of sight. She concentrated in the way she'd been taught, felt the Charge all around her, followed it until she could see the Pattern of the land in her mind, the Anomalies that pulsed and moved all through the distance.

Then she and the rest of the White Helix leaped into the air in flashes of yellow and purple light.

19. RIFTS

MIRA AND ZOEY WALKED AT THE HEAD of the line, down an old, narrow country road, flanked on both sides by endlessly stretching fields of wheat and rotted cornstalks. Holt was unconscious, near the middle, carried next to the mysterious crate the Menagerie had been lugging.

Max refused to walk anywhere but underneath him, growling menacingly at the pirates if they got too close. Though they outnumbered the dog, none of them wanted to be the first to challenge him. Mira didn't blame them.

Mira had kept the group moving northeast, hoping to come across one of the landmarks that pointed the path to Polestar. It would be much safer, from then on.

Theoretically.

Her ability to get the Menagerie through the Strange Lands was, at this point, probably the one thing keeping her alive, and she felt Ravan's glare on her back constantly now.

They were still traversing the uncharted areas, and near as she could tell, they'd entered the second ring about fifteen miles back. It had been a casual affair, she hadn't even mentioned it to Ravan. In fact, it was the easiest ring crossing she'd ever done, but that was because of where they were.

The Western Vacuum.

There were only three Vacuums in all the Strange Lands, zones devoid of Stable Anomalies. For whatever reason, they couldn't take hold there. It didn't mean Mira and the Menagerie were completely safe, there were still Unstable Anomalies to worry about, but most of those were visible.

Then again, the Strange Lands were different now. She hoped what Echo had said about the Stable Anomalies not moving proved right.

Echo . . .

The thought of him brought a mix of feelings, most of them sad or guilty. He'd sacrificed everything to get them into the Strange Lands, and she hadn't thought about him once since the Crossroads. There just hadn't been enough time, but that was her reality right now. It seemed like it had been for a long time.

"It's getting darker," Zoey said, next to her. "And it shouldn't be, should it?"

Mira looked down at the little girl. It was one of the few times she'd spoken since they'd found her. Mira wasn't sure what had happened while she was a captive, but it had had an effect. Mira didn't push her. Zoey would tell her when she was ready.

Zoey was right, though. The skies shouldn't have started darkening until almost the third ring.

"How do you know that, Zoey?"

"It just . . . feels like things are different, but I'm not sure how I would know."

The little girl kept looking behind her every few minutes, staring back down the old roadway to where it disappeared into the horizon.

"Are they following us?" Mira kept her voice low as possible.

Zoey shook her head. "No, but it's looking. It won't give up until it finds me."

"It?"

"The Royal one. I can't hear it anymore, it's too far away. But it will come."

The little girl was clearly traumatized. Maybe if she—

"And what are we talking about?" Ravan had walked close, studying them with a calm detachment, her hand on the shoulder strap of her rifle.

"We were just wondering if the Assembly was following us," Mira answered, looking away.

"Doubtful," Ravan said. "The Portal was a long way from town. They'll have to run search patterns just to find our tracks. By the time they sort it all out, we'll be at Polestar."

"If you're lucky," Zoey said offhandedly. "They're Hunters. It's what they do."

Ravan studied the little girl. The pirate Captain was no fool, and the less she figured out the better. If Ravan knew that different Assembly factions were blowing each other up to get to Zoey, she might decide to kill the girl and be done with it.

"What are you going to do with us?" Mira asked.

Ravan moved her gaze back to Mira. "Haven't decided yet. If I see some value in keeping you, then I will."

"And if you don't?"

"I'm sure you can figure that one out all by yourself."

"I have a Solid."

"And I honored it."

"You didn't honor *anything*. You cheated me. That Solid came directly from Tiberius, and when he hears—"

"Whatever debt he may have owed you was rendered null and void the moment you started traveling with Holt Hawkins," Ravan calmly cut her off.

Mira stared back. "Why?"

Ravan just smiled. "If Holt didn't trust you enough to tell you, I don't see why I should."

Mira looked away. The Menagerie was the group looking for Holt, she knew now, the one he'd been running from since she'd met him. Ravan had recognized him, that much was clear. In fact, it seemed liked they *knew* each other. If that was the case, did that mean Holt had been *in* the Menagerie?

Mira wouldn't believe that. Holt was . . . Holt. He wasn't a thug or a thief. He wouldn't have been in the Menagerie.

What did it all mean then?

She remembered the way Ravan had touched him, how she'd whispered into his ear. It implied . . . a familiarity.

Why hadn't he just told her the truth? Then she never would have gone to the Menagerie in the first place. Then again, what would she have done instead? No one else would have helped her. Holt and Zoey would still be in the Assembly's clutches, if not for Ravan.

Mira sighed. Nothing was ever simple.

Zoey groaned next to her, holding her head with both hands.

Mira felt for the little girl. The headaches hadn't lessened any, it seemed. She touched her tenderly. "Sweetie, you okay?"

"It feels like . . ." Zoey whispered. "It feels like something's coming."

"What does *that* mean?" Ravan asked dubiously, but Mira ignored her.

Mira had come to trust Zoey's instincts, as unpredictable and strange as they were. If she said something was coming, Mira took note. "What's coming, sweetie?"

"That." Zoey pointed to the north. When Mira looked icy fear gripped her spine. A mass of swirling darkness was building there, and it seemed to glow faintly with blue light; massive, towering into the sky, out of sight for miles, and it was moving, toward them. *Fast.*

The sight was stunning. Everyone down the line stopped automatically to stare at it.

"Looks like a sandstorm," Ravan said.

"It's no sandstorm," Mira answered in horror. "It's an *Ion Storm.*" Mira couldn't believe it. Ion Storms were *third* ring Anomalies, but there it was, sweeping powerfully down the hillside, tumbling toward them, a wave of darkness that blocked out the dim sunlight as it moved.

"It'll rip everything organic apart, down to the atoms. It won't leave anything. We have to get inside something."

Mira looked around wildly. There were a few abandoned cars nearby and an old tractor, but their windows were broken, they wouldn't be any shelter.

"There," Ravan pointed.

In the distance, half a mile maybe, a dirt road diverged off theirs. It ended in the middle of an overgrown field, where a small clearing was encircled by a large chain-link fence. Inside the clearing rested a group of five or six small, square buildings.

There was no indication of what it used to be, but it didn't really matter. Even from here Mira could tell the buildings were made of concrete. If they were still sealed, they might survive the storm inside. Might.

"Tell your men to run," was all Mira said. She lifted Zoey onto her shoulders and bolted down the road as fast as she could. Behind her Ravan shouted, and the pirates reacted instantly, following in a dash.

The storm swirled powerfully down the hill, and then leveled out and blossomed forward when it reached the valley.

It was coming fast. Too fast.

"Mira!" Zoey shouted. She had almost run past the road leading to the fenced area.

Mira's feet slid as she turned and raced down it. She could hear the frantic footfalls of the Menagerie behind her. The storm was barreling forward. Mira reached the fence, and skidded to a stop in front of it.

There was a gate, but it was padlocked. Next to it, a rusting metal sign hung on, with a message that was barely readable.

PROPERTY OF STATES AIR FORCE
ENTRY STRICTLY AUTHORIZED
USAF PERSONNEL
USE OF DEADLY FORCE
SECURED FACILITY

Mira set Zoey down, ignoring the sign and kicking the fence. It was old, but it was strong. It wouldn't break. "Damn it!" She kicked it again.

"Move!" Ravan shouted behind her. The rest of the Menagerie were coming fast. One of her men had pulled a pair of bolt cutters from his pack. Mira jumped out of the way as he placed its open mouth onto the padlock and squeezed. He groaned with the effort.

"Parker!" Ravan yelled at him. "You wanna die out here?"

"No, skipper," the boy said through gritted teeth, trying harder. The padlock snapped apart. Ravan kicked the fence in and everyone charged forward. The rumbling sound of the Ion Storm filled the air.

"Mira!" Zoey shouted as the pirates ran past and knocked her down.

Then one of them scooped her up as he ran. "Got her!"

Mira didn't argue, she found her footing and ran into the fenced yard. The storm was almost on them now, blooming and rolling forward, blocking out everything as it towered over them, coming fast, darkening the sky.

She could hear it now, too. The strange, voltaic rumble that came from whatever charged particles the storm was made of bouncing off one another. It was growing. Louder and louder as it roared toward them.

Max barked frantically, and Mira turned as she ran, saw him growling and biting at the pirates carrying Holt, disappearing with them inside one of the buildings.

They were little more than shacks, cubes of concrete, maybe twenty square feet each, with heavy metallic doors on the outside. The closest one was ahead of her and to the left. Ravan was running for it, too, and Mira double-timed it.

As she ran, she saw something else in the middle of the field. A giant circle of steel, hundreds of feet across, stretching from one end to the other. Some kind of huge, metallic door set into the earth. What the hell *was* this place?

Mira would be happy never finding out. She kept running for the shack, saw Ravan ram into its door with all her weight and blow it open.

The rumbling static grew and everything went dark as the Ion Storm closed the distance.

Mira lunged inside, hit the ground, and rolled to a stop. She just had time to see two Menagerie behind her scream and shudder as a cloud of blackness washed over them, ripping them off their feet. Their bodies disintegrated into a black, powdery substance that mixed with the rest of the darkness.

Ravan slammed the door shut, holding it sealed with her body.

The two girls looked at each other as the charged rumble built to a fever pitch outside. The building, concrete or not, vibrated as the brunt of the storm washed over it.

"You sure this place will hold?" Ravan asked.

"Ion Storms don't do as much damage against rock or metal. Give it a few days and it'll disintegrate the building, but it won't last that long." At least, so the old logic went. The Strange Lands were changing, for all she knew this storm could last a month. Mira tried not to think about that, though.

"Wouldn't roll over if I were you," Ravan said.

Mira slowly craned her head around slowly. The floor beneath her wasn't concrete, it was wood, and most of it was rotting away. She could hear it groan under her.

Less than a foot away the wood ended, and a gaping hole of blackness began, a sheer drop into darkness. She had almost rolled off it into . . . who knew what. The bottom was nowhere to be seen.

"Told you." Ravan stepped away from the door. The air still rumbled outside.

The floorboards, where they still remained, came to a smooth, orderly stop before the chasm. It meant the hole was intentional, and this shack was built to contain it.

But what *was* it?

The floorboards creaked dangerously as Mira moved to a crouch, peering downward. The hole had concrete walls that dropped into the dark. Along the edge of the wall to her right she could see rusted metal supports bolted into the hard surface.

Mira had seen a lot of desiccated urban environments, and she could put the pieces together. "A stairwell," she said. "Or it used to be."

The floorboards groaned as Ravan stood next to her. Mira could see lines of rotted dust tumbling into the dark as the wood began to loosen and split.

"I don't think we should both be on here," Mira said, starting to rise—but Ravan's boot stepped on her shoulder, pushed her back down.

Mira froze. She was right at the edge of the hole.

"Why not?" Ravan asked in a casual tone. "Nice place, this. Out of the storm. Dangerous, though. Who's to say what might happen in here? Would be easy to just . . . take a wrong step, wouldn't it?"

The floorboards creaked again. Mira swallowed. "Still got a ways to go until Polestar," she said. "Killing me wouldn't be the smartest thing you've ever done."

Ravan had always exhibited powerful self-control, but the look in her eyes right now held more ardor than Mira had ever seen. "Who is Holt to you?" she asked with slow, deliberate words.

It wasn't the question Mira was expecting. "Holt?"

"You followed him into the Strange Lands, all the way from the Cross-roads. Chased after some of the most dangerous Assembly I've ever seen, and burned a Solid from Tiberius himself to get me to help you. Who *is* he to you?"

Mira felt the anger that had been building inside her peak. She'd had enough of Ravan's constant threats and power games. "Who's he to *you*?" She shoved Ravan's foot off her shoulder and sent the girl back a step. "Just another Menagerie deathmark with a price on his head? Another

Star Point on your hand?" Mira advanced on Ravan and the floor swayed and cracked under them. Neither noticed.

"He's much more than a dollar sign." Ravan didn't flinch as Mira stepped closer. "Especially to me."

"I'm supposed to believe you two are buddies, is that it? Holt wouldn't have anything to do with the Menagerie."

"Oh, little angel, that is *precious*." Ravan smiled sardonically, studying Mira with thinly veiled contempt. "Holt had *plenty* to do with the Menagerie. And he and I are a lot more than friends."

The implication wasn't something Mira had considered, and the words hit hard. She was flustered, tried to find something to say, but couldn't. It only made Ravan's smile more intense.

"The Menagerie isn't what most people think, you know. It's more than just a disorganized band of idiots pillaging everything they see. It's a community. For instance, do you know how couples in the Menagerie show their commitment to each other?"

Mira said nothing. She didn't like where this was going.

"We take the same tattoo. It's called a Troth." Ravan held up her right hand. The black raven stood out prominently, wings outstretched to either side. "Has Holt ever shown you *his* right hand?"

Mira's thoughts wavered, remembering the single glove he always wore. "He . . . keeps it covered."

"Does he?" Ravan asked. "Well. I guess you two aren't very close at all, then."

Mira stared into Ravan's clear blue eyes, her emotions reeling back and forth like they were caught in the storm outside. Then the floor disintegrated beneath their feet. Both girls screamed as they plummeted down into the shadows that yawned open beneath them.

20. CHRONOGRAPH

MIRA TOOMBS WAS SEVENTEEN AGAIN, running for her life through the old antique shop with Ben as it violently transformed around them.

The air kept rumbling and brightening. The front door was just twenty feet ahead, but getting there wasn't as simple as it looked. Mira flinched as a whining table saw materialized in front of her, its blade spinning wildly.

Everywhere around her, time was shifting everything into a machine shop that must have existed in the same space at some different time.

Normally, it would have been a fascinating thing to watch, but the fact that she only had about twenty seconds to get out of the Time Shift's perimeter before she was wiped out of existence sort of killed her curiosity.

And then there was Mira's Lexicon. Left behind. Lost. Mira forced herself not to think about it.

She dodged out of the way of the table saw, but raked the side of it as she ran by. The impact sent her reeling and crashing to the floor. Mira tried to push up—then cried out as a shelf of books became a shelf of screws, nails, and bolts that poured down and flattened her.

"Mira!" It was Ben's voice. In a daze, she felt him lift her off the floor and drag her toward the exit, barely dodging a welding station as it formed out of nothing, its blowtorch flaming and sparking.

Somehow they reached the door, burst through it and out into the street. The small town was dark, with an ominous sky full of swirling black clouds and colored lightning. Mira could hear the air crackling around them. The Shift was about to solidify, and they ran as hard and as fast as they could.

The rumbling silenced. The air returned to its normal shade of dark. Mira and Ben spun around, staring back behind them at the antique store. It was surrounded in a sphere of flickering light, the edge of which was just a few feet in front of them.

The perimeter of the Anomaly. They'd made it out. Barely.

Streaks of lightning-like fingers flashed all over the building, and where they touched it the structure transformed. The signage and framing and paint of McKelvey's Lost Treasures antique store shifted into the equivalent version of Miller and Sons Machine Works.

Mira watched it morph into its new form, watched it all being wiped away. Tears glistened in her eyes. Slowly, pointedly, Mira began to count. "One, two, three . . ." Out of the corner of her eye, she saw Ben studying her, but she didn't look back. "Four, five, six . . ."

"Mira?"

"Seven, eight, nine . . ."

"What are you doing?"

"Counting how many extra seconds we had before the Time Shift finished." When she spoke, the bitterness and anger in her voice surprised even her. "Seconds we could have used to get my Lexicon."

"Calculating the time it takes a Time Shift's energy to expend is even more difficult than calculating how long between the events," he told her, and his dispassionate voice only made her angrier. "You saw how off we were in there."

"How off *you* were," she said, still not looking at him. "I would have taken the chance, Ben. I would—"

The shimmering and the flickering lightning all vanished in a heartbeat, sucked away into the air. The Time Shift was gone. So was the antique shop, and so was her Lexicon and all it contained. Everything was still and quiet.

The tears that had been threatening to form now fell from Mira's eyes.

Ben seemed confused. "A Lexicon can be replaced, Mira."

"It wasn't just a Lexicon, Ben, it's . . ." Mira shook her head, feeling the anger rising. "Never mind. You wouldn't understand. You don't *feel* anything."

"Mira . . ."

"Nothing means anything to you, except the Tower and your Points, though I'm not sure you feel anything for *them*, either. But, hey, I'm glad you got your artifact. That's what matters, right?"

Ben stared down at her. His face was blank, but there was a slight impression of sadness there. Mira had hurt him. Or at least as much as someone *could* hurt Ben. It was irrational of her, she knew. Feeling the anger toward him. It was selfish and silly, but what was in that Lexicon meant everything to her. It was all she had left, and now it was gone.

Ben looked down at the tarnished chronograph in his hand, its silver chain dripping through his fingers. He stared at it for a long moment in silence.

Then he clicked the button at its top.

Mira could just hear the second hand began ticking clockwise around the colored dial inside the glass, moving from one number to the next, counting up. As it did, the chronograph began to glow. A slight hum formed around Ben, growing louder as the artifact powered up and its second hand kept ticking to higher and higher numbers.

Mira's eyes widened. She knew, just as well as Ben, that a major artifact of that orientation could only be used once. It was what made it so valuable.

"Ben . . ."

"I *do* feel things," he said quietly. The hum kept building. "Not anywhere near as much as you, but I do."

"Ben, what are you doing?" she asked nervously. She could feel her heartbeat quicken.

"Showing you that I understand." He let the second hand move a few more clicks, then clicked the button once more.

Mira gasped as a violent sound ripped the air. The world flashed blindingly.

When her eyes adjusted, Ben was gone, and everything in front of her was *moving*.

Reversing was a better word, actually. It was as if someone had hit REWIND on a VCR, and Mira watched as time somehow rolled itself backward in front of her. The glowing perimeter of the Time Shift flashed back to life. The machine shop began to painstakingly undo its former transformation, shifting back, piece by piece, into the old antique store.

As it did, the sound of roaring static filled everything. Mira covered her ears with her hands, trying to drown out the building wall of—

The sound and the light vanished. Time advanced forward—just like it had before. Whatever Ben's chronograph had done, it was spent now.

The streaks of lightning-like fingers arced against the building again, transforming it back to the machine shop. As it did, a frightening realization occurred to Mira. The chronograph could rewind time, just as Ben thought. Which meant that Ben was now *inside* the shop again. He *must* be.

"*Ben!*" Mira shouted starting to move for the Anomaly.

But he exploded out the door just then, running hard toward her. Her heart skipped at the sight of him. Tucked under his arm was her Lexicon, undamaged and whole.

The light gleamed everywhere. The Time Shift was almost done. Ben had seconds only.

He lunged past the Time Shift's perimeter . . .

. . . just as it flashed and faded, plunging everything back to darkness.

Mira stared at him as he stopped in front of her, breathing hard, sweating. There were two new cuts on his arm, where he'd hit something sharp this time. His eyes found hers, and then he looked down at her Lexicon and opened the red leather cover. She watched him flip the pages over and reveal the inside binding. Tucked into a fold was a picture.

Ben lifted it out.

It was a black-and-white photograph of a man, leaning against an old station wagon, holding a tiny girl on his shoulders. Behind them the ocean stretched to the horizon. The girl was Mira, years ago, and the man was her father. It had been taken by her mother during one of their summer visits to Portland. It was the one thing still left from that time, the thing she'd had the longest of any of her possessions. The relief she felt at the sight of it was overwhelming.

"I know what this means to you," Ben said softly.

The chronograph in his hand was no longer silver. Now it was blackened and crumbling. It fell to pieces through his fingers like burnt paper, and then the full realization of what Ben had done hit her. He'd used the chronograph, sacrificed his chance to get what he what he wanted most in the world. He'd risked his life, and he'd done it for *her*.

Mira's eyes glistened again.

"You're right, I don't feel much," he said, staring at her with more emotion than she had ever seen. "There's logical and illogical choices, that's how I see things, but . . . it's always been different with you. Logic goes out the door." His hand gently stroked her cheek. "I *do* feel things, Mira. For whatever reason, I just . . . only really feel them for *you*."

Mira stared back at him a moment longer. She didn't care anymore what made sense and what didn't in the world now. She grabbed his shirt and pulled him to her. Their lips found each other, their bodies pressed tight, and they didn't need any artifact to make it feel like time had frozen.

21. FALLOUT

MIRA AWOKE FROM PLEASANT MEMORIES to pitch blackness and instantly felt sharp pain in her knee and left side. There was no way to know how long she'd been out, but she didn't really care right then. She just grimaced and waited for the pain to pass.

A shadow shaped like Ravan sat next to her, her back against what must have been the wall of the concrete shaft they'd fallen into. Her rifle lay just to her side. She was shaking, and her right fist was clenched so tightly the knuckles were white.

Even in the dark, she could see the pain in Ravan's eyes.

Mira had been lucky, it was obvious. She'd gotten scraped and banged, but as far as she could tell, she didn't have any major injuries. Judging from the way Ravan was shaking and breathing, the pirate hadn't been as lucky.

Mira could hear her sharp, painful intakes of air. The girl was tough as nails. If she was showing this much discomfort, she must be hurting bad. "Your shoulder?" Mira asked.

"Dislocated," Ravan said through clenched teeth, breathing as shallowly as possible. Mira could see the girl's left shoulder jutted upward, far behind where the ball normally would be. It made Mira wince.

Ravan groaned as she sat up against the wall. She braced her feet on the dirty floor, squared her shoulders, took a deep breath—and pushed backward.

The move was clearly designed to flatten her protruding shoulder blade and shove the ball back into the socket. It didn't work. Ravan screamed,

156

pushing as long as she could, and then collapsing to the floor on her right side, breathing heavy and moaning.

"Well," Mira said. "That didn't look fun."

"Screw you," Ravan said between ragged breaths. Through sheer force of will, she started driving herself back up against the wall. She made it about halfway before collapsing back down.

Mira watched the girl start to try again, then rolled her eyes. "Oh God, hang on . . ." She pushed herself toward Ravan.

With her good arm Ravan grabbed her rifle. She may have been injured, but she wasn't helpless. "What do you think you're doing?"

Mira froze. "I was thinking about helping you."

"You think I'm stupid? You think I'd let you get close to me?"

Mira frowned. "You know, the problem with being so tough and self-reliant is that, once you get in trouble, you're all on your own. Sit there in pain if that's what you want, it doesn't matter to me."

Ravan gave her a skeptical look. "*Why* would you help me?"

Mira stared back. It was a good question. "You saw that big steel door in the ground up there. You and I both know that's the only way out of whatever this place is, and it's going to take both of us to figure it out." Mira held Ravan's stare, a half smile forming on her face. "Besides, me pulling your shoulder back into place? That's going to really, really hurt."

Ravan returned Mira's look—then she laughed out loud. It was loud, full of irony, and in its own way contagious. Mira started laughing, too. Their voices echoed up and down the small, dark, concrete hole.

Ravan grimaced and stopped herself. "Okay—okay, stop, that hurts. Come over here, sit down on my left."

Mira did as Ravan said. From this close, the shoulder was even more clearly out of alignment. Mira noticed something else. On Ravan's right forearm, above the dark bird on her wrist, there were three long horizontal scars. They looked like they had been cut there intentionally.

"You like my badges?" Ravan asked, her voice laced with pain.

"Did that to yourself?"

"Oh, yeah." Ravan slowly eased down onto the floor, lying on her back. "When a Menagerie leader fails in a raid without being wounded, they wound *themselves*. A punishment. A reminder. It's not something that happens to me very often."

Mira shivered at the brutality of it. "You've failed three times?"

"Two were raids. One was . . . personal." Ravan looked at Mira squarely. "You're gonna put your foot in my armpit, then grab my left hand."

Mira nodded, took the girl's hand and wedged her foot into place.

"You have to use your foot to brace the shoulder. Then you pull as sharp and hard as—"

Ravan wailed as Mira yanked the girl's arm toward her.

There was a horrible crunching sound as her shoulder snapped down and forward, back into its socket. Ravan groaned through a clamped jaw, rolling over onto her side. Every breath was a moan of pain. Mira smiled. She couldn't help it.

"Better?" she asked.

"You . . . bitch . . ." Ravan growled.

"What? Was I supposed to count to three or something?" Ravan looked up at her, her eyes full of pain and fury. Mira grabbed her pack and Lexicon from the floor, pulled out two flashlights and tossed one to Ravan. Bright white light streamed outward, illuminating the environment around them.

The "hole" was really a square concrete shaft dug maybe fifty feet into the ground. When Mira lighted what was left of the floor above, she realized just how lucky she and Ravan had been. As far as they fell, they should both probably be dead.

What remained of a rusted metallic staircase wound its way up the walls of the pit. It stopped about halfway up, the remainder hanging loosely where it had ripped from its supports long ago. It groaned eerily in the shaft, bending and shifting dangerously.

Mira guessed what was left of those stairs had broken her fall and saved her life. They touched down just a few feet away, opposite a thick, metallic door set into one of the shaft's walls.

Mira watched Ravan slowly pull herself up into a seated position, grimacing as she moved. She was sore, obviously, but she wasn't shaking anymore.

Mira helped her slowly stand, and Ravan winced as she came to her feet. Once she was up, Mira shined her light onto the heavy door set into the wall. It was rusted, still in one piece, and it was cracked open. There was only pitch dark on the other side.

Mira pulled on it experimentally. It didn't budge. She tried again. It groaned, the bottom of its frame cutting into the floor, but it only moved a few inches.

"Gonna take both of us," Ravan said. She grabbed the door with her good arm and nodded to Mira.

Together, they yanked it backward—and the door scraped open with a sound like nails on a chalkboard. The echo reverberated into the chamber beyond, bouncing mournfully back and forth in the darkness there.

The two girls looked at each other, neither eager to step through.

From above came a sudden, horrible groaning sound. They looked up in time to see what remained of the rusted staircase begin to crumple in on itself. The supports ripped free from the walls, spraying great plumes of concrete and mortar.

With a shuddering lurch, it all came crashing down with a howl of bending metal.

22. THE UNDERNEATH

MIRA FELT RAVAN GRAB AND SHOVE HER forward through the dark doorway. They hit the floor hard on the other side, as the stairs crashed down, burying everything in a flood of metal and concrete where they had just been. Dust poured through in a huge wave.

When it was over Mira sat up and coughed raggedly, swatting away the dust and mortar and staring back at the doorway. Her light showed it had been replaced by a bulging mass of metal from the collapsed staircase.

"Just perfect," Ravan said next to her, covered in dust, gingerly rubbing her shoulder.

"Well, you couldn't have climbed out of there anyway," Mira replied.

"I still would have liked the option."

Mira looked at Ravan. She knew what she was about to say was probably going to hurt. "Thanks." She wasn't wrong.

Ravan watched Mira squirm. "Don't make too much out of it, you were just in my way."

The dark around them was thick and weighted, and the girls' flashlights painted the interior with circular globes of brightness. It was another concrete square, like the shaft they were just in, but bigger, thirty feet across at least. In the dusty air, Mira could see strange, hulking shadows on the floor. The closest one was a large rectangular shape covered in a thick layer of gray dust, but there were still patches of soft green that showed through. Small pockets sat along its edges, three on each side, evenly spaced, and several wooden rods lay haphazardly on its top.

Ravan recognized it before Mira. "A pool table."

All around them more and more shadows were revealed. Two arcade games, an old television set, a refrigerator, movie posters—all of it dust-covered and falling apart where it stood.

"It's a rec room," Mira realized out loud.

Ravan grabbed one of the old pool balls on the table . . . but it didn't budge. She pulled harder. Nothing. It was as if it was seared in place.

"Those won't move," Mira told her. "They're artifacts now."

Ravan looked at her. "These pool balls are artifacts?"

"Everything in here is. When the Strange Lands formed, it fused them to whatever they were touching. Takes work getting artifacts back to the world."

Mira studied the room closer. It only had one other exit, straight ahead of them. This door, unlike the first, already yawned open, framing more of the heavy darkness that lay beyond.

The dust was getting thicker. Mira took the pullover she was wearing off her T-shirt, and wrapped it around her nose and mouth. Ravan did the same. It seemed to help, though Mira's eyes still stung. There was nothing to do about that.

"You know, eighty percent of dust is human skin," Ravan observed.

"I could have done without knowing—" Mira cut off as the arcade machines suddenly flickered to life, their dust-covered screens lighting the room in pale, crackling, blue light. The girls jumped in fright as the television behind them lit up in a burst of static.

Mira's heart beat frantically. "Damn."

Ravan looked around them at the flickering screens and machines. "This place still has power."

"Yeah, but how? Generator?"

"One hell of a generator, to still be working after a decade."

Mira moved for one of the arcade games and brushed off handfuls of grime. Underneath the screen flashed and flickered; the image was scattered and fragmented, but she could still make it out. A list of high scores scrolled up and down.

"If we're trapped, at least we'll have something to do," Ravan said.

Mira almost smiled. It was easy to forget the girl had been a razor's edge away from killing her a few minutes ago. And Mira remembered why. "I don't believe you, you know. Holt wasn't in the Menagerie."

Ravan shook her head in contempt. "You certainly are naïve about how things work, aren't you? Must come from living in this crazy, fantasy world." She touched more pool balls, all of them melded to the table. "I live in the *real* world—where survival is everything and nothing is pretty or fair. If you know Holt at all, you know he lives there, too."

Ravan was partly right, of course. That was exactly who Holt had been when Mira met him, but he'd become much more than that. Hadn't he?

"Holt was *not* in the Menagerie," she insisted.

"You're right. He wasn't," Ravan admitted, "but, he *almost* was."

Mira hesitated, staring at the black-haired girl, unsure. "What does that mean?"

"It means that things, as they often do, got complicated. And when they did, Holt ran. He left everything . . . and everyone." Mira wasn't sure, but she thought she detected a slight note of bitterness in the girl's voice. "And that, as they say, was that."

Something moved in the hallway outside, past the room's other door.

Both girls spun, aiming their lights—but now there was nothing, only shadows.

Mira felt her pulse quicken. "You heard that, right?"

Ravan nodded and unslung the rifle from her shoulder.

"Don't bother," Mira said. "There's not much in the Strange Lands a gun's good for."

"I'll hold onto it all the same, thanks."

Slowly, carefully, they moved for the hallway, Mira wielding her flashlight, Ravan her rifle. One step. Two. And then Mira stopped as a sudden wave of dizziness filled her head. It was so sudden, she almost lost her footing. It lasted a few seconds—and then receded.

When Mira looked at Ravan, she was clutching one of the old arcade games for support. "You, too?" Ravan asked.

Mira nodded. Whatever had just happened, it had made both her and Ravan dizzy at the same time, which meant it was environmental. A thought tried to rise in her mind, an important one, but she lost it. As though she knew exactly what had happened, but couldn't remember.

Mira and Ravan moved into a hallway of more concrete, that held only dust and shadows. The girls' flashlights scanned around it. It had a few more doors on the sides, another one at the far end that looked like thick, reinforced metal, and that was it. The hall was empty.

"No. There was something here," Ravan said. "I *know* there was."

There was movement in the corner of their eyes, like a black, floating ooziness.

They both spun, lights raising—and realized they were looking *back* into the rec room. Like before, it was empty; just the old pool table and the dim light from the same screens.

"That's impossible," Ravan said tightly. "We were just *in* there. It was empty."

More sounds from behind them. They spun again, their lights illuminating the inside of an old shower room. Something globulous and dark disappeared as their light found it. Or was it a trick of the eye?

"What's going on?" Ravan asked.

The dizziness swept over Mira again. She didn't lose her balance this time, she just shut her eyes and tried to think. Making her mind concentrate was difficult all of a sudden. Her thoughts came at a glacial pace or not at all, dissolving away before they materialized. She knew what this was, she was sure of it, but it was so hard to remember . . .

Mira unslung her Lexicon and set it on the floor. She unlocked the big book with her necklace and ripped it open, flashlight in her mouth. She turned to the binder of Unstable Anomalies, flipping through them almost in a panic. *Corkscrew. Corporeal Flux. Corporeal Ice. Dark Energy. Dark Matter Tornado. Dark—*

Dark Energy! She ripped open the section, studying it, fingers tracing the pages of notes and equations, and as she did everything she remembered about the Anomaly came back to her, and it was all very, very bad. "Oh, God . . ."

"What?" Ravan demanded.

Mira shut the Lexicon and slipped the strap over her head. "Turn off your light."

Ravan stared at her like she was insane.

"Do it!" Mira told her sternly. "I'm going to turn mine off, too. For just a second. When I turn it back on, you do the same."

"Why?" Ravan flipped off her light. The illumination diminished by half.

"There's something I need to see. Just pray I'm wrong."

Mira took a deep breath—and then flipped off her own light. Everything went completely, utterly dark.

And in that darkness, shapes were revealed.

Floating bubbles of blackness in all shapes and sizes, all throughout the air, bouncing in slow motion into each other. So dark they somehow stood out.

And other things. Worse things. Things roughly *humanoid*—but not.

Devoid of any features, with eyeless faces of smooth, oily darkness. Strange hands rose up, reaching for the girls with impossibly long fingers of putrid—

Mira screamed. Both girls flipped their lights back on.

The hallway again. Dirty and crumbling, but *empty*. There was nothing there now.

"What the hell was *that?*" Ravan shouted, aiming her rifle all around.

"We're in trouble," Mira said, icy terror beginning to form in her stomach. "Put the gun away, it's useless. Get behind me. Back to back. We have to keep shining our lights at everything in our field of view. We're going to move down the hall for the door at the end."

"What for?" Ravan planted her back against Mira's.

"Because we need to find a way out of here right now."

They started moving, shining their lights all around.

"Those things—they looked like *people*," Ravan said.

"This place is flooded with Dark Energy," Mira said, shining her light everywhere in front of her. The floor, the ceiling, the walls where each met. "It's an Anomaly. A bad one. It's why we're dizzy, why it's getting hard to think. It's changing our molecular structure, which means it's messing with our brains."

"That doesn't tell me what those things were!"

"They're called Void Walkers. They're . . . impressions, sort of, all that's left of the consciousness of whoever came in here before us."

"You're saying that's what's going to happen to *us?*" Ravan almost turned around, but Mira shoved her back in place. They had to keep moving, had to keep *thinking*.

"Yes," Mira said. "Just keep looking everywhere with your light. They can't do anything if you're looking at them."

"Why?"

"There's something in chaos theory that says things don't actually exist until you *look* at them."

"That's crazy," Ravan said tightly.

"It is what it is! I don't understand it, I'm not a scientist, all I know is Dark Energy works the *opposite*. It only exists when you're *not* looking at it."

It took a while for Ravan to process that concept. "So—we just, what? Keep looking at everything and we'll be fine?"

"Until we can't think straight anymore," Mira replied, "and we're just two vegetables sitting on the floor. Then they'll come for us."

"I am *not* ending up like *that*. How much time?"

"Funny thing. Technically, we should already be gone."

"Why?"

"Dark Energy works fast. It's created by any preexisting source of radiation. I don't know why, but if you bring an *outside* source of radiation into a field of it, it acts like a dampener. It slows down the effect."

"You're carrying something *radioactive!*" Ravan fumed.

"It's a long story. I need it for something important. And don't complain. We'd already be like those things if we didn't have it. At least now we've got a shot."

"*How much time?*" Ravan asked again.

"Half an hour, maybe less." It was true. The plutonium's radiation wouldn't hold off the Dark Energy for long. Mira just hoped the exit was on the other side of this door. If it wasn't . . .

They reached it, and it was as she thought, reinforced steel. A card reader rested to the side of it, probably for allowing entry, but they wouldn't have to worry about that. It was already yawning open.

Mira opened it the rest of the way and moved in, shining her light everywhere, with Ravan at her back.

While the first rooms had been interesting, they were more or less mundane, and they provided no clues to the underground structure's function. This new room changed all that.

The walls were lined with old computer consoles covered in dust. Half the monitors were dark and dead; the rest were either flashing on and off or showing frozen images of error messages. Three chairs sat at different places at the computers, designating individual work stations. On the wall, just visible under a coating of grime, was a huge electronic map of the United States, with small, pinprick lights embedded all through it. Most of them were dark and lifeless now, like the cities and places they used to represent, but the occasional one still flickered weakly under the dust. All of it bathed the room in an eerie, flashing, and pulsing hue of dim color.

The wall across from them held something even more unexpected. Windows. A whole row of them. It was too dark to see what was on the other side, but a door was inset next to them.

Mira was having a hard time processing it all. Was the dizziness back? Honestly, she couldn't tell now. She wasn't sure what "normal" was anymore. She shook her head, tried to think as they moved.

"It's some kind of control room," Mira managed, "but for what?" Keep reasoning, she told herself. Keep *thinking*. She moved to the nearest computer bank and wiped away years of dust with her hand.

Ravan eyed it all strangely. "Where are we?"

Mira's head swam. She lowered the light to rub her temples.

Something moved on the other side of the glass and she instantly raised the light back up. There was nothing now.

Mira swallowed. "Ravan. Keep your light up, we have to concentrate."

There was nothing near to help them, which meant only one place left to go. They stepped through the door in the wall of windows. The room beyond was circular—its walls curving outward, well beyond the reach of their lights. Wherever they were, it was huge.

"This . . . Dark Energy," Ravan began, her light shining up. "You said radiation creates it?"

Mira tried to think, to push through the fog in her head. "Any source of radiation that was here before the Strange Lands would create a fountain of the stuff. A generator, scientific instruments, even a microwave would—"

"I think it might be a little bigger than that."

Mira followed Ravan's light upward. Something massive filled the center of the chamber. At first she only saw dusty metal, painted white and black. Whatever it was stretched up to what must be the giant, circular door in the ground they had seen earlier, more than a hundred feet above them.

Mira eventually recognized it. "Great," she said in a whisper. "It's a missile silo."

And they were in its launch tube. What was in front of them was very unmistakably a giant missile, resting stoically where it had been placed who knew how long ago, towering upward toward the door in the ceiling. Ravan's light found the USAF logo on its side, and it became clear that what they were looking at was just the top of the missile, only its warhead. The rest of the thing's girth lay below them, in some deeper chamber.

"Okay. We know what it is. Now how do we get *out?*" Ravan asked, shining her light all around. There were no stairs, no ladders, nothing that would allow them to reach that huge door. Climbing the missile wasn't an option either. It was sheer and smooth, and there were no handholds.

Mira tried to think, but it was getting harder. Her thoughts formed like ice in a—

Something moved back where they had been. They shined their lights inside.

Nothing.

"Jesus . . ." Ravan said through clenched teeth. "We gotta think quick, I'm starting to fade here."

So was Mira. She forced herself to concentrate. An idea occurred to her. An unlikely one, but it was something. She moved back into the control room and Ravan followed. Together they brushed off the computers and knobs and dials, revealing the different controls: FUEL PRIME; TARGET ACQUISITION OVERRIDE; WARMUP PROCEDURE; LAUNCH CYCLES; ENGINE A, B, C. GO/NO GO. All archaic, lost terms from a technological world that no longer existed. Mira's attention moved over them as she looked for something that stood out to her. Eventually she found it.

LAUNCH DOOR OVERRIDE

"Bingo," Mira said. It was a big, blue rubber button, and Ravan dug out as much of the dirt and grime as she could. The button clicked as she pressed it in. Mira looked back out to the launch tube hopefully.

Nothing happened. "Damn."

"Wait," Ravan said, blowing more dust off the control board, revealing two different colored lines running from the launch door switch down through the maze of buttons and knobs. She brushed more dirt away, following the lines to where they ended—at two key slots.

The keys still stood in their holes. The girls looked at each other.

A sound came from behind, like something dragging itself toward them.

They spun, shining their lights. It was gone. There was nothing.

"Shine behind me," Mira told Ravan. "I'll shine in front. I turn my key, then you turn yours."

"We have to turn them at the same time, idiot," Ravan said, watching the darkness behind them warily.

"How do you know that?"

"Didn't you watch any movies growing up? They always turn the keys at the same time. Do it on three."

Mira frowned but didn't argue. "One . . . two . . . *three*."

They turned their keys. The panel sparked violently. Then it lit up in bright colors underneath all the dust.

Ravan and Mira looked at each other triumphantly. Ravan hit the launch door button again. From the huge room beyond came a crash, then a massive shuddering and the rumbling of hydraulics. Dirt fell in a torrent from the ceiling as a sliver of sunlight lit up the top of the old silo.

"It's working!" Mira shouted.

"What if the Ion Storm's still up there?" Ravan asked.

"I'll take an Ion Storm over Dark Energy any day."

Then an explosion of sparks erupted from a corner of the huge ceiling, spraying outward in a vicious arc. As it did, the sounds of the opening door cut off, the whine of hydraulics faded. The door shuddered . . . and then collapsed back down. The daylight disappeared.

Ravan screamed in frustration and punched one of the windows.

Mira looked back up at the ceiling through the control room windows. It was just as dark as before, with the exception of the sparks shooting out from up top now.

She stepped back into the launch tube and shined her light up. The sparks were coming from a large metallic box at the edge of the door, with large cables running out of it.

"It's a junction box," Ravan said behind her. "Big one. Runs that door, I bet."

"Can you fix it?" Mira asked.

"Sure. Probably just needs a few cables resoldered, but how am I supposed to get *up* there?"

"I think I have an answer for that." Mira turned to Ravan. "You're probably not gonna be a fan."

"Well, isn't that a big shock," Ravan said wryly.

Both girls noticed something then. Ravan's flashlight was dimmer. It was starting to die.

"That's the opposite of good, isn't it?" Ravan asked.

Movement from behind them—back in the control room. The girls spun.

Mira had a fleeting image of two featureless, smooth black figures reaching for them . . . then they vanished under the fading flashlights.

"Polar opposite," Mira said.

23. AMPLIFIER

MIRA AND RAVAN BURST THROUGH A DOOR and slammed it shut, then lit it with their flashlights, staring as if they expected something to explode in after them. Nothing did.

"Keep your—" Mira began.

"Eyes on the door. Got it." Ravan put her back to the wall. "What are you going to do?"

"Make an artifact combination," Mira said. "If I can find what I need."

She flashed her light around the room. It was what she'd hoped—a storage closet full of all sorts of things—bottles, tools, nuts and bolts, chains, brooms, cleaning supplies, spare linen, rubber bands, office supplies, brushes, and disused furniture.

And it was all artifacts.

Mira stared at the stocked shelves lustfully. If she had more time to spend here, this place would be profitable, but time was something she was running out of fast.

The closet had its own sink. That meant they could do what they had to right here, which was good news. Assuming, of course, she could find the right components.

"What does this artifact do?"

"It's called an Amplifier," Mira replied. "Magnifies any element it touches. In our case, it's going to be *water*."

"Magnifies it by how *much?*" Ravan asked suspiciously.

"A lot. We're going to flood the silo and ride the water up to the top. Then you fix the junction box. Doors open. We swim out." Even to Mira it sounded crazy. "Easy."

"What if we can't get the doors open?" Ravan asked angrily.

"Then we're both in a lot of trouble. Look, it's this or nothing. I can't think of any other—"

The door to the room rattled and Ravan spun her light back to it. It stopped instantly.

"Ravan, you have to keep your—"

"I know!"

Mira looked back to the shelves and shook her head. It was getting harder and harder to think. In about fifteen minutes they'd be lucky to remember their names. She tried to remember what she needed, and it was like trying to think while half-awake.

Mira unslung her Lexicon and set it on the floor. When she unlocked it she opened it to the artifact combination section and flipped through the pages there. They were alphabetical. *Aleve. Ambient. Amplifier. Android. Anr—*

Amplifier. She open the pages and studied them, and at the top was a summary.

Name: Amplifier.

Effect: Amplification of element: air, water, heat, cold, electricity, possibly others.

Effect Time: Immediate.

Area of Effect: Must physically touch element.

Power Effect: Power source dependent; larger coins = more amplification. See Note 2.

Duration: Power source dependent; larger coins = longer duration. See Note 1.

Multitier?: Yes. Two tiers.

Underneath the summary were diagrams and charts, notes Mira had made about the combination's use with different elements. But she ignored all that, looking down to the list of ingredients at the bottom, and then compared it to what she had in her pack.

She still needed a Focuser for the first tier, as well as a vial of water, and, ideally, a nine-volt battery.

Mira quickly scanned the stuff on the shelves. There was a box of drywall screws. One of those would be fine for the first-tier Focuser. She was hoping for something spherical, and she remembered the pool balls in the rec room, but that meant going back into the hall with those things.

No, a screw would have to work. She also saw a box of Duracell D batteries.

D batteries could work in a pinch. They produced almost the same effect—but the phasing would be off, which meant it would be more powerful. That wasn't going to matter, either—more power in this case was probably better.

But what about the vial of water? That was going to be tougher.

Mira studied each shelf but saw nothing. She looked to the floor piled with boxes of different things, and shone her light on them, flipping through each one.

After the fourth one she found something. A case of tonic water, all in separate glass bottles. Would tonic work, Mira wondered? Did it have to be plain water? She'd never researched it, she didn't know.

What other choice was there?

Mira sat her pack down and started rummaging through it. She pulled out a toothbrush and a tube of some kind of paste, as well as the other components she would need for the combination. She opened and squeezed the tube, and a thick, gray substance squirted out onto the brush. She quickly started spreading it on the drywall screws in the box.

"What's that stuff?" Ravan asked.

"Ever get bubble gum in your hair as a kid?" Mira asked back. "What did your mom do?"

"My mom was too drunk most the time to do much of anything, but I think you mean peanut butter. Spreading it in the hair loosens the gum."

Mira nodded. "This works the same way. We call it Paste, it's a mix of silicone, magnet shavings, and mercury. It separates artifacts from each other, loosens the molecular bonds between them and whatever they're fused to. It's how we get artifacts loose."

As Mira spread the paste over the screws they sparked and sizzled, vibrating, pulling loose. She reached in with her fingers and worked one of them free. She smiled. They might get out of this yet.

The door rattled behind Mira. She spun, saw the handle turning and raised her light at it.

The rattling stopped.

Ravan was slouched against the wall, staring off in a daze.

"Ravan!" Mira shouted. It snapped the girl out of it, and she raised her flashlight again. Mira glared at her. "You have to stay *awake* or we're both dead! The only reason we have a shot is because there's two of us—we can watch both directions."

"It's so hard . . ." Ravan said, blinking her eyes, trying to focus.

"Talk to me, then," Mira said. "It'll help."

"About what? I don't got any gossip to share."

"I don't know. Tell me your story." It was the only thing Mira could think of. "Tell me who you were before the invasion."

Ravan shook her head angrily. "Screw that. Everyone has stories. I'm tired of hearing them. It doesn't matter who you used to be."

"Fine. You pick the topic. But *talk*."

"Fear," Ravan answered. "Nothing keeps you more focused than fear. It's the most useful emotion. More than pain, even."

"You must be a blast at parties." Mira turned back to the artifacts on the shelf—but for the life of her, she couldn't remember which one she needed to—

The battery! Right.

She started working on one inside its box with the Paste, loosening it, watching the sparks as she did, using them to guide her. "So tell me what you're afraid of then."

"Dying alone," Ravan simply said.

Mira laughed at the answer. "Well, you beat that one. If we're going to die, it'll be together." Mira burned loose one of the D batteries and grabbed it, set it on the floor with the screw. Then she turned to the case of tonic water, started working on it next. "Is that it? Just dying alone?"

"No. Dying and not . . . earning it."

Mira's eyes narrowed. "What does that mean?"

"Means . . ." Ravan didn't finish; just sat blinking, trying to think.

"*Ravan*," Mira said louder. "What does that *mean?*"

"It means . . . I've seen the Tone take kids worth ten of me. But, I'm still here, and I don't know why. I don't know why *me* and not *them*. All I know is, whatever the reason, I don't want to waste the extra time I got. And I'm scared I might." Mira felt the girl's attention shift to her for just a moment. "I mean, doesn't that bother *you*?"

The truth was, Mira hadn't always been Heedless. Her answer would be a lot different. But before she could reply, her head filled with dizziness and the components spilled from her hands. She tried to reach for . . .

What was she reaching for again? Something. Something important . . .

"*Hey!*" Ravan yelled at her.

Mira focused, remembering what she was doing. She grabbed the components, arranged them on the ground. God, it would feel so much better to just shut her eyes—but she couldn't. She had to keep going.

"Make the stupid artifact," Ravan told her. "Talk. Tell me yours. Tell me what you're afraid of."

Even in spite of the dizziness, the answer came to Mira's mind easily, but was it really something she wanted to share with *Ravan?* She hadn't talked about it with anyone, not even Holt; she'd kept it bottled up inside, and it was starting to ache there. But maybe Ravan was the perfect person to confide in. She didn't care about Mira one way or another. Plus, they were probably going to die, anyway.

"I'm scared of failing," Mira said. It was strange to hear the words. A simple sentence that broke down a host of complicated emotions into its most basic idea. It hurt to hear them.

Ravan, however, scoffed. "That's a softball answer. Everybody's scared of that."

"No. I mean failing people I care about. That scares me more than anything."

Mira finished the first tier, wrapped it in duct tape from her pack, then broke the bottle of water against the concrete floor.

When she did, there was a bright spark and a hum, like something electrical powering up.

A rippling sphere of some kind of blue substance formed over and wrapped around the artifact. It was like a shell of water, only petrified and hard. Mira picked it up. It was cold in her hand.

"Failing who?" Ravan asked her.

Mira tried to focus, to think . . . "Holt and Zoey. I promised them I'd get them to the Severed Tower. They're relying on me, but I know I'm not good enough. I'm going to fail, and when I do, they're going to die. They're going to die and it will be my fault." There it was: the truth. Spoken out loud.

Ravan was silent a moment. "The quickest way to screw something up is to believe that's what you're going to do," she said. "You don't believe in yourself, you might as well quit."

"It's not that simple. I know my limits."

"Limits are bullshit," Ravan said. "They don't exist except in your head. Something bad happened to you. Whatever it was, someone should have kicked your ass and got you back out there, but they didn't. They did the opposite. They told you this stuff and filled your head with it, made you doubt yourself. Whoever that is, they ain't your friend. I've had people like that around me my whole life: bastard father; pathetic mother; brothers in juvenile for stupid, senseless crap. I would have got out of there as soon as I could pass for eighteen, but the Assembly took care of that for me. I meet those kinds of people now—I shoot them."

Mira laughed. "I'm not really sure that's an option for me."

The door to the room creaked open.

Ravan tried to kick it shut, but she was too weak now. She lost her balance and fell over, weakly raising her light back up. Shadows, horrible ones, massing and pulsing around the door, disappeared.

But her light was dimming, it was running out . . .

"Hurry," Ravan whispered.

Mira put together the second tier, using the blue-shelled one as the Essence. Her hands shook as she did. It wasn't just becoming impossible to think, it was getting hard to *move*.

She wrapped the combination in duct tape. Another flash, another hum. It was ready.

Mira tried to stand—but failed. She fell to the ground, her head full of fog. She was losing herself.

"Mira . . ." Ravan's voice was weak. Her light was dying. The door rattled.

Mira forced herself to move, crawling toward the sink. Above them the air vent into the closet shook as something tried to rip it off. Mira aimed her flashlight up at the vent. The shaking stopped.

There was a soft exhale from Ravan at the other end of the room, and Mira saw her slump to the floor, the flashlight fading away.

"Move." Mira tried to yell, but the words came out feeble. "Move. Move! *Move!*" Each separate word was louder, carried more force, filled her with partial strength. "*Move!*"

The door creaked open. Things squirmed in the dark outside.

She grabbed the edge of the sink and pulled herself up until she was looking down into the grimy basin. She dropped the artifact inside and reached for the handle. If there was no water, then they were—

The faucet shook and groaned—and then dumped out a stream of blackish liquid.

The Amplifier flashed and water erupted from the basin like a volcano, surging powerfully into the air.

The pipes under the sink burst apart as the liquid was amplified by a factor of around a thousand. Mira was ripped off her feet and blown backward as the closet flooded in seconds.

The chill of it made her gasp, refocusing her dimming mind, and she heard Ravan do the same, as they were flung violently into the hallway, carried in a tidal wave of amplified murk that thrust them forward.

They burst into the control room. Ravan slammed into the reinforced windows, pinned there by the current. Mira was almost shot through the door into the launch tube, but she managed to grab on to the frame and hold on.

Ravan tried to push off the windows, but the wall of water was too strong.

"Grab my hand!" Mira shouted, reaching for Ravan. The pirate reached back, but the distance was too much. "Push *toward* me!"

Ravan groaned as she slowly slid across the windows, the water pressing into her. She reached Mira's hand. Mira pulled Ravan loose. Together they flew into the huge launch tube, rolling end over end.

Mira broke the surface of the frothing water, gulped air. Ravan appeared next to her, doing the same.

Because the tube had so much more area to fill, the water level was rising slower. Underneath them, the rest of the facility was already submerged. They watched as the door to the control room disappeared. Slowly the two girls began to rise up, following the curving body of the giant missile toward the door in the ceiling.

They could see the still-sparking junction box in the corner, and Ravan started paddling to put herself directly under it. From her belt she removed a pair of long-nose pliers.

"We only get one shot at this before we're underwater," Ravan yelled. "What about those things? They gone, or are they in here with us?"

Mira shook her head. "I have no idea." It was true, she didn't. She'd never heard what water did to Void Walkers, probably because no one had ever flooded a missile silo to find out. Above them the light peeking through the crack of the giant door was growing brighter. They had light. That was something.

"If I were you, I'd stay on the far side of the tube," Ravan announced. "Water and high-voltage electricity don't mix very well."

If the water kept rising they'd be pushed up to the box in moments—which also meant they would quickly be pushed into the ceiling. When that happened there would be nowhere else to go. Their air would be gone.

Mira swam to the opposite end from Ravan. It was difficult to stay in one spot, with the water churning. She watched the nose of the giant missile sink and disappear. There was only about ten feet of air left between them and the thick door now.

The water carried Ravan high enough to reach the junction box, and she yanked it open, staring inside. More sparks exploded into the air, and Ravan grimaced. "It's stripped wires!" Ravan shouted.

"Is that good or bad?" Mira yelled back.

Ravan ignored her, just rammed her hands inside the box as more sparks blew out, then yelled in pain and yanked back. "Dammit!"

"Can you fix it?" Mira yelled desperately. The current was becoming impossible to swim against, not just because it was growing stronger, but because Mira was growing weaker. The chill of the water had given her some of her senses back, but she could feel her mind going numb again.

Ravan kept twisting and turning things inside the box.

Then, above, came the groaning of the massive door as its hydraulics reactivated. A speck of daylight shot in from a crack near the center of the room. Mira yelled for joy—and then cringed as the sound died and the door stopped. More sparks shot from the box, and Ravan stared at her.

"I can get it working, but I have to hold the connection," Ravan shouted. "The cables are falling apart."

Mira stared back. "I don't understand! What does that mean?"

Ravan looked at Mira, as if thinking things through. Then, with a scowl, she reached back into the box with one hand. The door started opening again, groaning horribly as its massive hinges jerked to life for the first time in decades.

But this time, Mira just stared at Ravan, the girl's hand holding the cables together. The first silky strands of the top of the flood seeped into the junction box as the door continued to open, allowing light to burst in.

"Ravan—" Mira said.

The junction box exploded in a massive, violent torrent of sparks that blew in every direction. Ravan screamed, then disappeared behind a wall of smoke.

The huge door stopped again, but it stayed open this time. Daylight flooded in through a crack in the center large enough for her to slip through. But Mira didn't notice. Her eyes were glued to where Ravan used to be. Now there was just the churning water.

"Ravan!" Mira yelled, but she was gone, and there was nothing Mira could do.

Mira felt her head smack into the ceiling. Her air was running out fast. She should get out, start crawling through the hole made by the rusted door, but she didn't.

Ravan had held the wires, even though she knew she would be electrocuted, and she had done it to help Mira escape.

In the back of her mind Mira heard Ben's words. *To survive here, you have to think only of yourself.* It was logical, Mira knew, it made sense—but there was something about owing her life to Ravan that bugged her. Something about living with the idea of the pirate's sacrifice that steeled Mira's conviction to a place far beyond the safety of the burning daylight above.

"Damn it." Mira took a deep breath—and dived *downward*.

The current was strong below. She had to swim against it, and it wasn't easy. Her flashlight shined ahead of her as she did. The hulking shape of the giant missile appeared from the murk, and Mira slipped around it. Her best chance of finding Ravan was on the other side.

The water was becoming darker, and her flashlight provided less and less help, but she kept diving down, looking for any sign of—

Shapes wavered in the current, blacker than the shadows around them. Humanoid and deformed and reaching for her with impossibly long fingers.

They vanished when she looked at them.

More appeared in the corners of her vision, disappearing when she turned, only to reappear in her periphery, coming closer.

Mira kicked away frantically, backed through the water, watching the hideous things disappear and reform just out of sight, closer, closer . . .

Something hit her from behind. She let loose a distorted, underwater scream.

Mira spun—and saw an unconscious Ravan floating near the wall.

Mira dropped the flashlight and grabbed the girl, didn't waste time, kicked for the surface as hard as she could. The darkness grew brighter, the daylight coming closer. Mira's lungs were burning, spots of darkness appeared in her vision. She should have reached the top by—

Mira slammed into something hard and almost dropped Ravan. She'd reached the ceiling, there was no more air.

Her lungs were on fire and her vision grew black. Mira frantically swam under the huge door, feeling for an escape, pulling Ravan with her. It had to be here, it was here before. If she could just . . .

Mira found a gap, and through the gap, she felt the chill of air on her wet hand.

She shoved herself upward, holding on to Ravan. She felt hands grab her shoulders, lift her. Her head burst through the water and the harsh afternoon sun stung her eyes.

Mira gulped in huge lungfuls of air—and then instantly coughed it back out raggedly. The hands pulled her up and through the door, and she felt her back lay flat against the warm, dusty surface.

Figures hovered over Ravan. The girl wasn't moving, she just lay lifeless in the bright sun.

In blurry slow motion, Mira watched the pirates work on her. They worked on her so long, Mira was sure she wasn't coming back. But suddenly she started coughing, expelling lungs full of water onto the ground.

She was awake. She was *alive*.

Mira sighed and lay back, letting the sun burn the chill away, feeling her mind returning, her memories, her sense of self. Mira had never felt such a strong need to simply not move in her whole life.

"Mira!" A small figure landed on top of her. "You're okay!"

It was Zoey. Mira smiled and held her. Her vision was sharpening, and she saw Max amid all the Menagerie surrounding them, running excitedly forward.

Right before he reached them he stopped short, staring at Mira, unsure. Some things never change, she figured.

"Don't worry," Zoey told her. "The Max is happy, too."

Next to them, Ravan weakly rose and sat up. Neither looked at the other, they just stared at the landscape through the chain-link fence.

"You're an idiot," Ravan said.

Mira nodded. "You could make the argument."

The storm was gone, but its effects were going to last awhile. The wheat fields that had surrounded them before had been wiped away, leaving only barren ground and rocky hills devoid of grass or trees. The wind blew around them slowly. With no trees or wheat stalks to stir anymore, it sounded almost mournful.

"Can you get us to Polestar?" Ravan asked pointedly.

"I think so."

"Once you do, all debts are paid," Ravan said. "You take the kid and the dog and you go. No one will stop you." She turned and stared at Mira, and the look was weighted. Something had passed between them in the silo. It had only been a few hours, but they had emerged very differently. Certainly not friends, but they weren't entirely enemies anymore.

"And Holt?" Mira asked.

Ravan shook her head. "Holt's off the table. He's going back to Faust, and that, my dear, is that."

Mira looked to where several of Ravan's men stood guard over a still-unconscious Holt. She studied his unmoving figure on the ground, watched his chest rise and fall. Max lay protectively at Holt's side again, glaring at the pirates. "You should keep the dog," Mira said. "He's a pain in the ass, but Holt loves him."

Ravan studied her strangely. "Okay."

After a moment, Mira stood up and made herself start walking, taking Zoey with her. It wasn't easy. She was more exhausted than she even knew.

"Mira." It was the first time Ravan had ever used her name, and the sound of it was jarring.

Mira turned and looked back. Ravan sat staring, torn, as if she wanted to say something that she simply couldn't find the words for.

Mira just nodded. "Don't mention it." Then she and Zoey moved off to gather their things. As they did, Mira glanced northeast to where they were headed. The sky there was darkening quickly.

24. HALF-FORMED IMAGES

RAVAN DROVE HER MEN hard after the silo, not just because she wanted to make up for lost time, but also, Mira guessed, because she wanted to show, in spite of her ordeal, she was still capable. As much as her men might respect her, they did so because of her strength. Mira had a feeling it wasn't a good thing to be seen as weak in the Menagerie.

They'd exited the Western Vacuum a few hours ago and pushed on down an empty highway, near what used to be the border between North and South Dakota, while the sky blackened and more dark Antimatter clouds flashed their strange, foreboding colors. Finally Mira saw what she'd been hoping for.

An old rural park, where a traveling carnival had set up before the invasion. Like most ruins in the Strange Lands's inner rings, it was aging slower than it should. Grass and weeds had grown up around its roller coasters and ferris wheels, but for the most part it looked as if it had only been abandoned a year or two.

The park was a place where Freebooters made camp on the way to Polestar, a safe zone free of Unstable Anomalies, a navigation landmark Mira had seen time and time again. Seeing it now brought a tremendous feeling of relief. It meant tomorrow they would be back on course, almost to Polestar.

Of course, what happened after that Mira wasn't sure.

They made camp in the carnival, the roller coasters twisting and towering over them as strange shadows. As Mira walked through the camp, she saw the Menagerie guards tying Holt to an old merry-go-round.

When they were done, they left him there, laughing, moving off to get their share of the camp food that was cooking at various fires.

Mira moved toward him. No one stopped her.

Up close, she could see the nasty gash on Holt's head where the Menagerie had knocked him out. It made her mad, the injury. It hadn't been necessary. He'd been through enough.

Both his legs and arms were tied, bound between two colorfully painted merry-go-round horses that immortally kicked and ran, even though the ride would never spin again. Instinctively, Mira's gaze moved to his right hand. The fingerless glove he always wore was gone. Mira remembered what Ravan said about Menagerie members taking the same tattoo. A Troth, she'd called it.

She couldn't see what was there; it was too dark. If she moved closer . . .

But did she really want to? Right now it was an unknown. And things had changed between them. But she *did* want to know. She wanted to know the truth, and if it was bad, she could learn now while he was asleep, and process it all. She wouldn't have to face him.

Mira moved forward and took Holt's hand, twisted it so she could see the wrist. Her heart sank.

A tattoo was revealed in the dim light, only half-finished, the top half had yet to be inked, but it did look like it would have been a bird, a black one. Just like Ravan's.

Mira jumped as Holt's hand closed around hers.

His eyes blinked and opened, staring around him groggily. When then they found her he smiled. Mira stared down at him a moment—and then slipped her hand out and pulled away.

His smile vanished as he remembered everything. "Oh. Right . . ."

Mira moved a few steps away, rubbing her shoulders. It felt cold suddenly.

"Where are we?" Holt asked.

Mira told him everything quickly. The loss of the Crossroads, finding the Menagerie, convincing them to help, Ravan, rescuing him in Kenmore, the missile silo. When she finished, Holt studied her, impressed, and a little guilty, maybe, that she had done so much on his behalf.

"Are you okay?" he asked.

Mira shrugged. "Ravan has been very talkative." It took a moment for what she said to sink in, but when it did, Holt looked away. "Were you ever going to tell me?"

"It's . . . not something I talk about, Mira."

"I think I deserved to know," she said. "Do you have any idea how many friends of mine have been killed by the Menagerie?"

"No. But I think, after everything I've done, I should have earned your trust."

Mira just stared at him. He was right, she knew, but that didn't make it feel any better.

"I was different back then," he said. "It was after Emily. Which meant it was a time in my life where I didn't want to feel anything. So I didn't. I only thought about survival, and the Menagerie was a really good fit for that."

"Is that all it was?" Mira asked. "Your tattoo looks a lot like Ravan's."

"You really think that's fair? Given what I had to watch at the Crossroads?"

Mira was the one to look away now. The silence that hung between them was almost tangible. "Ravan told me I could go when we get to Polestar, that I could take Zoey with me."

Holt considered her words, then nodded. "Good. You should. There's nothing you can do for me, there's too many of them. They'd kill you if you tried."

Mira felt a knot forming in her throat. In spite of what may have transpired between them, the idea of leaving him like this, with these people . . .

"Zoey needs you," he told her.

She wiped a tear away before it could fall, and looked back at Holt. Mira felt a sudden, intense desire to tell him everything, her fears of this place, her doubts about herself. But she could just make out the shape of the tattoo on his wrist. In her mind, she saw him standing over her on the plane again.

She shook her head sadly. "How did we get here?"

Holt stared back at her. "Nothing stays the same. It's just how it is."

The words were an acknowledgement of sorts. An admission that they were lost to each other, and it only made Mira feel more alone.

She headed back toward the campfires. "I . . . need to think."

"Mira." Holt's voice stopped her, but she didn't turn around. "I'm sorry about what happened."

Mira could hear the sorrow in his tone. She nodded. "I know."

And then she left him.

AS HOLT WATCHED MIRA disappear, he felt a mix of things—anger, sadness, frustration. It was his fault, this whole mess. He should have left when he had the chance. But how many times had he had that option, both before and after Midnight City? He always did the same damn thing. He always stayed. Now it had finally caught up with him.

"That girl can handle herself, I'll give her that." A figure stepped from the dark. "I see why you like her."

She was tall, lean, and athletic, as always, with a presence that was at once intimidating and magnetic. The long hair that flowed down behind her was so black it absorbed the flickering light of the campfires. She was barely anything but a shadow before him, but even so, Holt could see her blue eyes peering into his.

Ravan smiled. Like everything about her, it was an action of duality, a subtle indication of a complex, fragmented personality. The smile was warm and inviting—and at the same time predatory. At one time Holt had been closer to her than to anyone since Emily, and even he could never tell which side of the mirror was really Ravan.

Holt said nothing, just stared back. She was holding what looked like a plate of food in one hand. In the other, there was something else, and she threw it to him. His glove landed on his chest.

At the sight of it, he realized the truth. She had taken it off him, so Mira would see.

"Mira's not the kind to go and pry and find things out for herself, she wouldn't have done it on her own," Ravan told him. "So I helped her out. She wanted to know the truth, and you sure as hell weren't gonna tell her."

Holt felt anger building in him, but still he said nothing.

Ravan set the plate in front of him, maybe less than a foot away. It looked like rabbit, stewed and salted with carrots and potatoes, in some kind of thick sauce. The aroma alone almost made him pass out, it had been so long since he'd eaten a cooked meal instead of just foodstuff or MREs. But his hands and feet were still tied to the merry-go-round, and he couldn't get to it. He tried not to let his hunger show.

"I'm sorry about your head," Ravan said. "I didn't mean for them to do that. They have explicit instructions not to hurt you anymore, you have my word."

A lot of good that did him now, he thought. The pain in his head was sharp, it felt like a watermelon where the rifle butt had connected.

He watched Ravan sit on the ground in front of him and slowly pull her knees up under her chin, never taking her eyes off him. "You know you're gonna have to talk to me eventually, Holt."

Holt stared back. She was probably right. "From what I remember, you never were much for talking."

Ravan shrugged around her knees. "I talk, I just don't waste words. People never say what they really mean. It's one thing I miss about you. Always said what you felt, and you said it with as little fuss as possible."

Ravan pulled something from a pocket. "Your little friend—Zoey is her name? She had this on her." Holt saw it was his father's Swiss Army Knife. "I recognized it. I know how much it means to you. The others would have traded it away for comic books or something just as stupid."

Ravan pried open one of the knife's tools. Unlike Zoey, she found the right one immediately; its main blade, a long, gleaming knife, and Ravan gently ran her finger along its edge. "Goodness. You certainly keep it sharp, don't you?" Holt froze as he watched the knife in her hands.

"You know, you're going to have to do more than just 'talk' to me, Holt," she said slowly, twisting the knife, watching it reflect the campfires. "There are things I need to hear from you, things I need to know. I'm sure I don't have to remind you what these things are, and I'm sure you know you'll tell them to *someone* eventually. It would be better—in a lot of ways, much better—if that someone were me."

Ravan casually shifted her gaze from the knife back to him. Holt said nothing, just watched her warily. She moved toward him, holding the blade delicately. Holt watched it come toward him. There was a time when Holt was sure he was the one person Ravan would never hurt—but that was a long time ago.

She turned the knife so it pointed toward his neck, resting inches from his throat. Holt swallowed. He was helpless, unable to move, and they both knew it. Ravan stared at him a moment more—then raised the knife and cut the bonds that tied his hands to the plaster horse.

When it was done, she put the blade away and sat back down on the ground, hugging her knees again.

Holt rubbed his hands appreciatively, feeling the pins and needles of blood returning to his fingers. Then he looked at the food in front of him, steam still rising from it. He reached for it greedily, wolfing down huge portions with the spoon she'd brought.

"I see your table manners haven't improved any," Ravan said, watching with amusement. "Has it been that long since you've had real food? Must have been tough for you, out here all this time on your own. Must have been lonely."

Holt looked up as he ate. "And *you* still try to hide the questions you don't wanna ask."

Ravan smiled. "You know me pretty good, don't you?"

"If you were asking if I missed you, things are never as cut-and-dried as that."

"Some things are. It's not a hard question. Did you or didn't you?"

Holt thought about it. In many ways they had been perfect for each other. He had his walls, she had hers. The sad, ironic thing was that the parts of him that were so comfortable with Ravan were the parts he didn't particularly like about himself, but, in the end, the truth was the truth. "Yes."

Ravan hugged her knees tighter. "Do you know what it cost me when you left?"

"Do you know what it would have cost me to stay?"

"We were talented and ambitious, we had the eye of the right people—and we were *Heedless*. Once Tiberius was gone, we were in a position to run *everything*. We had it all exactly the way we wanted it."

"No, we had it exactly the way *you* wanted it. You just assumed we wanted the same things."

She studied him with a mix of frustration and confusion. "Why didn't you *talk* to me? Why did you just . . . leave? Leave and say *nothing?*"

"I tried to tell you, Ravan," Holt said, "but I knew if I did . . . that you wouldn't understand. I knew that you'd try to stop me."

Ravan lashed out in quick fury, kicked the plate of food away and sent it crashing into the merry-go-round. The pirates nearby all looked up from what they were doing. Ravan didn't care, she just glared at Holt, and he could see the pain in her eyes.

"I'm sorry," he said, and he meant it.

"Maybe I would have come with you." Ravan's voice was a whisper now. "Maybe you should have asked."

"Maybe I should have."

The pain slowly seeped out of Ravan's blue eyes, leaving only anger. She looked behind her, nodded to someone out of sight. "Somebody wants to see you."

Holt heard thundering feet, and watched a suitcase-sized shadow come barreling toward him.

Max slammed into him, rubbing his face into Holt's, and he felt the first warmth of happiness he'd had since waking. He rubbed his hands along Max's flanks, scratching him. He seemed in good shape, well taken care of.

Holt looked up at Ravan appreciatively. "Thank you."

"She said he was your dog. She said he means a lot to you."

Holt could hear the tightness in her voice. He guessed who Ravan was referring to. "Did you hurt her?"

Ravan smiled again and leaned forward. "Don't worry. She gave as good as she got."

Holt felt her take his right hand. Her hands were rougher than Mira's; harder, but no less feminine. The way her fingers slid easily through his brought back memories. Not unpleasant ones.

The half-formed image stood out prominently on his wrist. Ravan ran her fingers gently over it, tracing the broken outline.

"I would've liked to see this finished," she said.

Holt looked at Ravan's right wrist, saw the black, stoic bird tattooed there, its lower half identical to his incomplete one. Then his eyes followed the line of her arm up from the tattoo, found the scars. There were three now, he saw. There had been only one when he left. "Is one of those me?" he asked.

Ravan nodded, pointed to the second one. "I carry you everywhere," she said. He looked into her eyes. It was funny how fast you could be drawn back into old patterns, dangerous though they may be.

"It doesn't have to be this way." Ravan moved even closer. "You don't have to die, Holt. I can make Tiberius see reason. What happened wasn't your fault."

"'Examples must be made.' Wasn't that always Tiberius's philosophy?"

"Tiberius will see you're too valuable to kill," Ravan replied. "It won't be without pain, without punishment; it won't be exactly like we planned . . . but you can come back. I know you have principles, I know you have a code. I think they're weaknesses, but we can work around them."

"What if *I* can't work around them?"

"We'll find a way." She took his face in her hands, made him look up at her. Her hands were warm and firm. "I haven't gone a day without thinking about you, Holt."

She was close enough for him to take in her scent. It was different from Mira's, not the calming aroma of mint and spices, but something darker, sharper, more invigorating, like wildflowers in spring, and he felt it speed up his heart the same way it always did.

Holt knew what she wanted to hear. Her offer wasn't a bad one, and she was right, he was lucky it was her who found him. Mira and Zoey would be gone soon. He needed to start thinking about survival again, not about his heart. Besides, as before, the truth was the truth.

"I never stopped thinking about you, either," Holt said simply. The words came easily. Probably because they were true.

Ravan leaned in slowly, and the scent of her overwhelmed him. It was amazing how normal it felt, how easily her lips blended with his, how natural the heat of her felt against him in spite of all the time that had passed.

He felt Ravan's fingers in his hand, felt her move his wrist above his head, as her mouth slowly played over his . . .

Then he heard a metallic click. Sharp metal dug into his right wrist.

Holt tried to pull away, but couldn't. It was attached to the merry-go-round again. Holt saw the shiny metallic handcuff that connected him to the pole.

"Ravan, what—"

"I've been shot and stabbed, kicked and beaten, I've been burned by plasma fire, hell I even almost drowned this morning," she said softly, just inches away. "I've been hurt by professionals, I've been hurt by my family, but when *you* hurt me, Holt, it was the worst pain I've ever felt. And it never went away, you know? It just . . . festered. And remained. That kind of hurt never heals—not really—it just dulls, just blends into the background until you think about it again, and then you feel it all over, same as before." She stood up and stared down at him coldly now. "Let's make it a game, what do you say? We're going to Polestar, then farther after that. I figure there and back to Faust should take about a month. You have exactly that long to convince me you meant what you just said. If you do, I'll speak to Tiberius for you."

"Rae . . ."

"If not—well . . . why dwell on unpleasant things, yes?"

Holt angrily shook the handcuff above him, trying to pull it loose. It wouldn't budge. *"Ravan!"*

She just smiled down at him. "Welcome home, Holt." Then she moved off, disappearing into the mix of giant, twisting shadows and the firelight from the Menagerie camp.

25. LIGHTNING

THEY LEFT THE CARNIVAL at daybreak. There was no Vacuum to help them anymore. If they were going to cross into the third ring they'd have to pass through the Compactor, the Stable Anomaly that guarded the route to the other side.

Even though it was only a second-ring Anomaly, Mira hated the Compactor. It was a cube-shaped zone that generated two massive wavelike pulses of high gravity that raced forward and slammed into each other with an insane amount of force. The impact of the two waves created a thunderous, deafening sound, on par with a sonic boom, and you had to wear ear protection when you were as close as half a mile. If you were caught in the middle of it when the waves hit, well—there wasn't much left. The horrible booming always filled her dreams for days after.

Her Lexicon confirmed what she remembered: The speed of the gravity waves were identical and always consistent. It was the time in between their "launch" that varied. Fortunately, it varied in a particular pattern, according to an equation. Each subsequent pulse came at an ever-decreasing interval, until that interval was zero. Then it all started over.

You had to time the initial pulse with a stopwatch, quickly determine when the next one would fire; then, if you had enough time, race over a length of ground the size of a football field to the other side before the gravity waves fired again and slammed into each other.

Mira felt sick when she finally gave the order to go, even though she'd figured the three previous pulse times correctly. She wished Ben had been there to do it, to be the one responsible. But he wasn't. There was only her.

They all made it in one pass, dashing through in a mad scramble, Holt carrying Zoey, and Max streaming easily ahead of the Menagerie like it was all a game.

Miraculously, no one died. For the first time since the Grindhouse or the Ion Storm, no one had been killed on her watch. Again, Mira expected it to feel good or triumphant, but it still didn't. If anything, she felt more anxious, knowing they hadn't even faced the worst of what the Strange Lands had to throw at them.

Now they were in the third ring. Climbing a steep hill, northeast along a highway marked as South Dakota 20, and the line of Menagerie stretched back behind her. It was a little past noon, but the sky was as dark as dusk. Strange, bluish, swirling clouds filled the air, and the rolling landscape was like a checkerboard of overgrown vegetation and land stripped bare where Ion Storms had ravaged it over the years.

As she walked, Mira thought about Holt, and the exchange they'd had last night. At her tent with Zoey, she'd seen Ravan leaving the merry-go-round, but there was no indication what might have transpired between them. Then again, should it even matter to her, after the way they'd left things?

Mira sighed. Why couldn't she just hate Holt for carting her around like a trophy all that time, for almost hitting her, for not telling her about his past, for being in the Menagerie—for *all* of it?

For that matter, why couldn't she be content with her relationship with Ben?

The answer was, she knew, because both Holt and Ben had shown themselves to be as complicated as her feelings, to be more than they otherwise might appear.

"Why are you and Holt mad at each other?" Zoey asked. The little girl had walked beside her ever since the Compactor, but she hadn't said much.

Instinctively, the image of Holt almost hitting her on the plane filled her mind again.

Mira saw Zoey react, saw her eyes narrow in thought. She knew the little girl could see the same thing in her own mind. "That wasn't Holt," she said. "Not really."

Mira nodded. "I know. But there's more than that, sweetie. Holt was in the Menagerie."

"No, he wasn't. He *almost* was. And that's different, isn't it?"

Mira frowned in annoyance. Clearly things were much simpler for Zoey. How nice for her.

The little girl's hands went to her head and rubbed her temples.

"Your head again?" Mira asked, pulling Zoey against her hip as they walked. The headaches seemed to be getting worse, but there was still no indication why.

"Hey, you know what?" Mira said, trying to take her mind off it. "Once we get to the top of this, we'll be able to see Polestar."

Zoey's eyes followed the old highway to where it peaked atop a barren hill stripped of grass. "What does it look like? Think about it."

Mira smiled and did so. It was easy. She'd seen it a million times: the spiral of prismatic multicolored light shooting straight up from a fissure in the ruins of a lakeside small town that had once been called Mobridge.

The pillar of light marked a Gravity Well, the only one that existed inside the third ring. Gravity Wells were more common in the second, like the Asimov Maelstrom and the Mix Master, but those were different from Polestar's. They increased gravity the farther you went up, which meant they were dangerous and destructive. This one worked in the opposite way, it *diminished* gravity the higher it went. It had other useful properties, like vaporizing Ion Storms before they ever reached it.

As such, it allowed Freebooters to build a permanent outpost in the third ring, something that would otherwise be impossible, something even the White Helix had never done.

Because of the low gravity and the need to stay close to the Gravity Well's effect field, the city hadn't just been built near it, it had been built *around* it.

The Freebooters had built upward. Impossibly upward.

Spires of structures and scaffolds made of metal and thick wood foraged from the old city, or brought from outside, spiraled up and around the Gravity Well, high into the air above the ruins below.

It would have been an impossible construction without the Well—buildings balanced precariously on the superstructure, stretching far higher than they should be able to, wrapping around the massive column of light, a thousand feet into the air, balconies and towers hanging out far past the edge.

The higher you went, the less gravity there was, and at the very top sat the Orb, a spherical construction of sheet metal and glass.

Inside it there was no gravity at all, and anyone who went there could float freely around inside, as if they were in outer space, looking out through the glass, the city plummeting downward beneath them.

The light from the Well passing through the Orb lit it up like a signal tower that could be seen all the way to the Core. It was like a beacon, and it had always comforted Mira, seeing it from far away. It always pointed the way home.

Zoey smiled, the pain forgotten, seeing it all in Mira's mind. "It's beautiful."

Mira smiled, too. A few minutes later they crested the rise, expecting to see everything that Mira had just thought of.

But Mira gasped at what was there instead.

The column of light that marked the Gravity Well was still there—but nowhere near as bright. It was faded, *dim*, and most shockingly, the Orb wasn't lit. In fact . . . it was *gone*, as if a giant hand had ripped it away. Mira stopped and stared in shock as the pirates behind her began to top the rise, too.

"It doesn't look like it used to, does it?" Zoey asked.

Mira was too stunned to answer. She felt dread forming in her stomach. What could have happened here?

The rest of the city seemed to still be there. She could see the twinkling lights up and down the Spire, the buildings and the support structure, twisting and wrapping around itself in a way that should be impossible. She could see the old town that sat at its base, and the wall of steel and mortar that surrounded it.

"Polestar?" Ravan's voice asked behind Mira, unimpressed. "Kind of expected more."

Ravan and the rest of the Menagerie had piled up behind Mira on the hill, staring at the city in the distance. Holt was at the back, hands tied, his eyes on Mira. The irony of their switched roles wasn't lost on her, but it didn't give her any pleasure.

"Something's wrong," Mira told Ravan. "The Orb is . . . *gone*." It still didn't seem real, but all you had to do was look to see it was.

"I don't know what that means," Ravan said impatiently. "Should we go or not?"

Mira couldn't see any movement in the city, but then again, they were too far away for that. "I think—"

Zoey moaned and collapsed to the ground.

"Zoey!" Mira knelt down to her. Max barked behind them and ran past the Menagerie to reach Zoey. The little girl was conscious, but she was barely holding on.

Holt shoved his way past the Menagerie. They tried to stop him, until Ravan waved them off. Hands still tied, he knelt down next to her with Mira.

"What's wrong, kiddo?" he asked with concern.

"I can feel something building," she said weakly. "It hurts in my head, like it's inside and outside at the same time. I think we . . . should run . . ."

Holt and Mira looked at each other in alarm. And then Zoey's eyes rolled up into her head. She sunk into the old road and went still.

"Zoey!" Mira shook the little girl, trying to wake her, but it didn't work.

Strange thunder echoed above them suddenly. Everyone's attention moved to the sky. The dark storm clouds were swirling faster and more powerful, growing darker and darker. Flashes of color danced in between them—red, blue, green . . .

Max growled as the wind whipped up, and Ravan's black hair blew wildly behind her. "Red, what's going on?"

Mira slowly stood up from Zoey, staring into the sky. All she could do was shake her head in disbelief. "Zoey's right," was all Mira said. She could hear the shakiness in her own voice. "We have to run."

Lightning flashed out of the clouds above—but not like any normal lightning. This was a thick and vibrant bolt of blue.

It hit about a mile away, and a blast of cobalt light erupted into the air where it did. The crack of thunder that rolled over them was so loud, it almost knocked them to the ground.

"Jesus," Holt said in shock.

Mira grabbed Zoey's limp form and ran down the highway as fast as she could toward Polestar. Green lightning flashed from the clouds, and the massive blast of sound that followed it overpowered everything. She had no idea if the Menagerie were following her and she didn't care.

It was an Antimatter Storm, a big one—and it should have been impossible. This was the *third* ring. Antimatter Storms only existed in the fourth, but those types of rules had stopped applying fairly recently.

Zoey hung limp as Mira ran. She had to get her to Polestar, it was the only shelter they had. She just hoped the Gravity Well could repulse Antimatter Storms as well as Ion. It had never had to do so before.

With Zoey's weight, Mira ran slower than everyone else, and the Menagerie began passing her, heading down the hill. To her left she spotted Holt, running with tied hands.

Then more lightning flashed and he was blown to the ground as a red bolt struck just a hundred feet away. Where it hit, the ground erupted in a mound of glowing red crystals.

Ravan slid to the ground next to him and cut his bonds with a knife. "Don't guess you're going to run in the opposite direction, are you?" Mira heard Ravan say. Holt got up and started running again, followed by Max, barking and howling with each lightning hit. Thunder rolled constantly around them like cannon fire.

Mira looked ahead. Polestar was near, she could see the tall, makeshift wall encircling the old city ruins. A huge steel gate made out of the rusted remains of cars blocked their way inside. It was sealed. Hopefully, someone would see them coming and—

A lightning strike, a thick flash of green, blew Mira off her feet. She crashed down and Zoey fell from her grip, hit, and rolled limply away.

Mira screamed, then watched as Holt grabbed Zoey and kept running. Mira felt Ravan's hands yank her up, pulling her along. "Always saving your ass, Freebooter!"

More lightning flashed, more discharges of energy, more strange glowing crystals erupting from the ground all around them. More Menagerie were sent flying in the blasts, or inadvertently impaled themselves on sharp glowing crystalline masses.

Mira saw Holt and Max, with Zoey in tow, reach the massive gate ahead. In a few more frantic steps, so did she. It was painted with a giant, multicolored δ.

Mira slammed into it hard, hoping to wake up whoever was on guard duty. "Hey! Open the gate!" She banged on it furiously. "We're out here!"

What was left of the Menagerie, about twenty pirates, skidded to a stop. The lightning continued to flash down, and behind them the barren countryside was now a debris field of glowing crystals. All it would take was one hit at the edge of the wall to fry them all.

Ravan kicked at the gate. "Find handholds! Get this damn thing—"

The gate shuddered and slid open on the creaking wheels of the bottom cars.

Everyone dashed inside, and Mira looked up. The storm swirled above, but whenever it got close to the beam of the Gravity Well, it dematerialized into the air. The city was *repelling* it. Mira exhaled a relieved—

Everyone froze at the sound of gun hammers clicking into place, and stared into the barrels of more than twenty rifles.

The Menagerie responded quickly, their own weapons flashing out. Thunder rolled everywhere in the air.

"Hard as I try, I can't think of any reason why I should let armed Menagerie scumbags into my city."

Mira recognized the voice instantly. Her eyes found its owner, standing easily in the middle of a group of Polestar kids, presumably guards, all armed and ready to shoot. He was a tall boy about Mira's age, the most muscular kid in sight, black, and his name was Deckard.

No one moved. The two groups kept their rifles and shotguns pointed at each other.

Deckard calmly scanned the faces of the Menagerie in front of him, until his eyes found Mira among them—and then they widened in surprise.

"Mira Toombs," he said with disdain. "Well, that makes up my mind for me. Toss 'em all back outside."

Everyone tensed as the Polestar guards moved forward.

"Deckard, *stop!*" Mira yelled angrily. "We have a sick little girl with us!"

Deckard looked at Zoey's limp form in Holt's arms with disinterest. "Sounds like more of a 'your problem' than a 'my problem.'"

Mira glared at him. "You're *honor-bound* to accept Freebooters into Polestar."

Deckard smiled. "Don't see any Freebooters here, Toombs. All I see is a bunch of low-life pirates—and *you*."

Deckard was always an arrogant prick, but he respected obligation, more than anything else probably. Mira forced herself to speak with authority.

"You know the Librarian's edict," she told him sternly. "You were *there* when it was made. Let us inside. *Right now*."

Mira made herself hold Deckard's stare. After a moment he spat in disgust. "Fine. Already let your partner in. Distasteful as it is, might as well let you in, too."

Mira's eyes widened. "Ben's here?"

"Showed up last night after the Orb fell, him and ten Gray Devils."

Ten men? That was *half* the number he set out with.

"The Menagerie can stay until the storm passes, but they ain't coming in the city," Deckard continued. "And they'll have to do away with their weapons."

Ravan shook her head. "I don't think so. Kinda feel naked without my guns, you know?"

Deckard crossed his arms. "It ain't negotiable."

Mira turned to Ravan. "If they kick you back outside you're all dead." More distorted thunder rolled around them as if to punctuate her point. But Ravan didn't seem to care.

"How about, as an alternative, we just kill this guy and his little guards, take this place for our own?" Her tone was dangerous.

The rifles in the Polestar guards' hands all tensed. So did the Menagerie's.

"Ravan . . ." Holt said warningly. More thunder echoed from behind the gate, the sky flashing green and blue.

Ravan kept her rifle pointed at Deckard, considering. Then she relented. "Fine. Just so no one can say I can't be diplomatic. Boys . . . *disarm*." The pirates all dropped their guns to the ground. When they did, the Polestar guards started gathering the weapons up, along with all the Menagerie's gear, even the big crate they'd been carrying.

"Put everyone but Toombs and the little kid in the old sheriff's office,"

Deckard ordered. "Cram 'em into the cells if you have to. Leave 'em there 'til we get this mess sorted."

Ravan stared up at the big kid. "Such generosity." She and her men grudgingly let the Polestar guards push them down one of the old city's few streets, toward its abandoned town square.

Before they took him, Holt moved to Mira and handed her Zoey. The little girl was still out cold. Max whined underneath them, staring up at Zoey.

"Take Max, too," Holt told her. "They might kill him otherwise."

Mira nodded, studying him. Holt looked back. This was the closest they had been in a long time. "Holt . . ."

"Just go, Mira," he said quietly. "Do what you have to do now."

Holt held her gaze a moment longer, and then one of the guards yanked him away, down the street with the others. Mira stared after him until he vanished.

MIRA WATCHED HOLT AND RAVAN LED AWAY into the old city ruins. She knew where they were taking them. It used to be the Mobridge sheriff's office in the town square. It still had its jail cells, and Deckard used them when people got unruly.

But what could she do? Zoey's weight in her arms reminded her she didn't have a choice, at least not right now. So she ran until she finally caught Deckard.

"Take the kid up to the infirmary," he said. "Too busy to deal with *you* right now."

The Gravity Well flickered and pulsed in front of them, a giant column of light burning into the air, disappearing into a ceiling of swirling clouds thousands of feet above. She could hear its familiar soft hissing. Oddly, it always seemed the same volume, no matter how close you were. It was pleasant, usually, like a soft whisper, and she had always drifted off to sleep listening to it.

But now it sounded . . . wrong. It wasn't a constant tone anymore, it was fragmented, it came and went. Hearing it chilled Mira. What was happening to this place? To everything?

Polestar itself surrounded the column of light. It was made of two sections: the Mezzanine—the circular, ground-level courtyard—and the Spire, the city itself that rose up into the air around the Gravity Well.

The Mezzanine was made completely of concrete, but it was anything but plain looking. It was scored in jagged patterns, each piece either colored with some kind of metallic sheen stain, or had bits of hundreds of different shiny things set into it—glass bottles, mirrors, polished stones, even gems.

The light from the Gravity Well shimmered down and lit it all in a flickering, ever-shifting blaze of color, and the effect was dazzling.

But it wasn't all that serene anymore.

At the other end of the Mezzanine lay what was left of the huge Orb, and Mira's stomach clenched at the sight.

The massive ball had fallen and crashed violently into the ground. The bulk of it was crumbled over several ruined buildings from the old town. The rest of it was shattered into millions of shards that covered the Mezzanine like some kind of strange, otherworldly snowfall, all of it flickering and reflecting the light from the Well.

"My God," Mira said.

"Yeah," Deckard replied. He sounded exhausted.

"What happened?"

"The Well weakened last night. Gravity at the top increased and the weight of the Orb was too much. Rest of the city's fine, though."

Mira looked skeptically up at the Spire, as it wrapped and climbed a thousand feet into the sky. She could still hear the sputtering, hissing sounds from the Well.

"When the Well's back to normal we'll rebuild," Deckard continued. "Right now I gotta calm everyone down."

Mira stared at Deckard, aghast. "When it goes back to *normal?* What if it doesn't? What if it weakens even more? What if it goes *out,* Deckard?"

"The Well will be fine," Deckard replied impatiently. "Always has been, always will be."

Mira was filled with frustration. "Deckard! The Strange Lands are *changing.* For the worse. You need to evacuate everyone out of the Spire!"

Deckard spat again. "You mean like that coward at the Crossroads?"

"Do you even know what happened there? The Crossroads were overrun by *Tesla Cubes,* Deckard! Outside the first ring!"

"That don't excuse it. One kid shirks his duties and we're all supposed to? I don't think so."

"Echo's 'duty' was to the people who lived at the Crossroads. He probably saved the lives of everyone there. You need to do the same thing, and you need to do it *now*." She grabbed his shoulder with her free hand—and Deckard spun around in anger.

"You don't get to tell me what needs doing!" he yelled venomously. "I don't take advice from many people, and I definitely don't take it from pretenders and hypocrites. You don't deserve to be here, you *or* Ben. And you're welcome to 'evacuate' whenever the hell you feel like it." He started moving again, headed for a stairway onto the Spire, near where a mass of kids had gathered. "I won't abandon this place. I'll keep it breathing if it kills me!"

Mira stood staring after him. Deckard was, and always had been, the most arrogant, stubborn fool that—

Zoey stirred and moaned in her arms, and Mira decided to hold those thoughts for later. "Max! Come on," Mira called after the dog. He reluctantly pulled himself away from the smells of the city and followed after her.

They walked as fast as they could toward the same stairway as Deckard. It was the main entry onto the Spire, a grand staircase of sorts, made out of polished cherrywood from who knew where, and it sparkled as bright as the Mezzanine, wrapping upward, narrowing as it climbed, until it became a more simple walkway of metal and sanded oak. Eventually more paths branched off from the first, climbing and careening in different directions, but always upward, connecting to the hundreds of buildings and platforms that jutted out past the framework at angles that would have been impossible in normal gravity.

Mira had never ascended the Spire without stopping to marvel at the audacity it took to construct. She understood why Deckard was hesitant to leave it. Polestar was more than just a city, it was a symbol—that the Strange Lands could be tamed. That there was nothing the survivors of the Assembly couldn't accomplish if they worked together.

Mira believed in all of that, but she also knew Holt was right. Nothing stayed the same forever. So much was changing, and it felt like her entire life had been in flux for the last few months. Would it ever end?

As Mira climbed, she could see the citizens of Polestar gathered in the Mezzanine below, and they looked furious. When Deckard motioned for them to silence they only yelled louder.

He spoke to them wearily, but not weakly. "I know you're scared! We lost the Orb, it's true. But it can be rebuilt. *Anything* can be rebuilt."

"What about the Antimatter Storm?" someone shouted from below.

"The Gravity Well repelled it, just the same as it does Ion Storms," Deckard answered.

"That's not the point!" a voice yelled.

"It shouldn't be there at all, this is the *third* ring!" said another.

"How do you know the Well won't weaken any more? How do you know it's not weakening right *now?*"

The yells and jeers rose in pitch and fervor.

"Because I *do!*" Deckard shouted back, and the ferocity in his voice stifled the crowd. "Polestar has been here for years, and I'll be damned if it ain't gonna be here for years to come. Because it's our *obligation* to keep it that way. Think of everything that would be lost if this place goes—the history, the achievement. What about all the kids who died building it? You think about them at all? Huh? What's their deaths mean if we just cut and run?" Deckard gripped the stairway railing. The crowd grew quiet as they listened. The conviction in his voice almost made Mira buy into it. Almost. "No, sir. You wanna leave? You do it. Right now. No one'll stop you. But I ain't leaving. I ain't ever leaving, not 'til the Tone takes me. This place is gonna stand forever. Because it's our duty to see it *does*, no matter how hard it gets."

The crowd's loud challenges dissolved into quiet rumblings, and Mira could tell some had been convinced. She shook her head and kept climbing, taking the second pathway on the right, where it twisted up to a rounded building made from the wooden walls of an old church. Ancient stained glass windows circled around its perimeter, vibrantly reflecting more of the Well's light.

She pushed through the building's double doors, probably from the same church, and found the place empty. It wasn't a surprise, everyone was likely downstairs in the crowd.

Inside the infirmary was a circular, wooden-floored room lined with colorful windows. The ceiling was made of Plexiglas, and it let the shimmering light from the Gravity Well fill the interior. About two dozen beds lined the walls, each a different kind or shape: brass, wooden, rod iron, some with headboards, others without, canopy beds, sleigh beds.

Mira laid Zoey down on one and pulled the covers over her. Her breathing was shallow. Her hair was matted with sweat, and Mira brushed it out of the little girl's face. There was no question, she was getting worse.

But *what* was wrong with her? None of it made sense, and it only made Mira feel more helpless.

It was like she was already failing Zoey, the thing she feared the most. The little girl was sick and fading. She'd looked for Mira to get her to the Tower, and they were only at Polestar and she was almost gone.

Everything that had been building in her—the pain and the frustration and the fear, going back not just to the missile silo, or to Holt almost hitting her, or to Midnight City or Clinton Station, but all the way back—to the beginning. It all flared powerfully and Mira lashed out at a glass lantern on the steel nightstand next to the bed.

It shattered to pieces on the floor. Blood trickled down Mira's hand.

It hurt. And it felt good. For a moment. And then the false strength of anger faded—and Mira cried. Great, sobbing tears that shook her body. She desperately fought it at first, tried to stop the outpouring of emotion, but it was too strong this time, and she gave in, covering her eyes and mouth.

When it was over, Mira opened her eyes and saw Zoey again. Nothing had changed. She was still there, laying silently.

Mira wiped her face and stood up, moved to a cabinet and took out some cleaning solution and bandages. She winced as she cleaned and dressed the cuts on her hand.

The crying had been inevitable. It had even felt good. But what had it done to help? Nothing. The truth was, she may be on the road to failing, to not being strong enough or smart enough, but she wasn't there *yet*.

And she didn't have to be. She could figure this out, she told herself. She just had to think.

Zoey was getting worse. Fine. There it was. But *why?*

Mira thought back to what the Librarian had told her before he died. He said Zoey was the *Apex*. That she was the most important thing on the planet.

But what did that really mean? What was the Apex? The only person to walk out of the Strange Lands, Mira knew, that was the Librarian's theory; but even if that were true, how was it connected to what was going on?

Then a thought occurred to her. An unsettling one.

From every account they'd heard, the incidents occurring in the Strange Lands all started less than a day before Holt, Zoey, and Mira arrived.

Echo had begun abandoning the Crossroads a day before they arrived.

The Orb had fallen from the top of Polestar a *day* before they arrived.

What if Zoey was the missing link? What if she was somehow affecting the Strange Lands as she moved through it? What if the Strange Lands were changing . . . *because* of Zoey?

Or was "changing" even the right word? There was the fact that Anomalies appeared in different rings than they normally would. But— was that what was really happening? Maybe the rings were still the same as always, Mira thought. Maybe they were simply . . . *expanding*.

The realization, the connection of everything, was so stunning that the bottle of solution fell from her hand and broke on the floor. Mira stared down at it in a daze, putting more pieces together.

It explained everything they had seen so far, it even explained the Tesla Cubes at the Crossroads. The Anomalies hadn't moved beyond the first ring, the first ring had grown to encompass the Crossroads. The Strange Lands weren't changing. They were *growing!* And they seemed to be growing faster the closer Zoey got to the Core.

Mira moved for the door, leaving Zoey asleep on the bed with Max curled up next to her. She stepped outside and looked up, but what she wanted to see was blocked from this vantage. Mira moved around the walkway, climbing upward around the infirmary, until she was between it and the Cavaliers faction residence, a castle-like structure made from the wood of old highway billboards, their old images and letters fading but still visible in jumbled patterns up and down its side. The faction flag, green with a sharp yellow sword, arced outward in the breeze.

Mira saw what she was looking for. The column of light that was the Gravity Well. She could hear the strange, fragmented hissing sounds that filled the air. A horrible thought occurred to her as she studied it.

If the Orb had fallen because the Well weakened, and the Well weakened because of Zoey, then Mira had very likely brought the city's destruction right to it. And that meant—

A bag slipped forcefully over her head. A knot tied around her throat, sealing it in place.

She panicked and screamed, but it was no use. A hand covered her mouth, but there was no one to hear anyway, everyone was down in the Mezzanine. She kicked and fought, but whoever had her was too strong, and Mira felt herself dragged off and away.

27. LUCK

MIRA COULDN'T SEE ANYTHING, but she had a sense of where they were taking her. Upward. Along one of the branching stairways. She knew the sensations of climbing the Spire, the way the gravity gradually diminished. She could hear the crowd on the Mezzanine below still murmuring about Deckard's speech.

There were at least two of them, because they had her by the legs and arms, and they were strong. Big kids, she guessed by their heavy footfalls, but Mira wasn't going to make it easy on them. She struggled the whole way.

"Keep her from squirming," one said.

"I got her, don't worry. Take her in headfirst," said another.

Her captors carried her through a door, and the sounds from outside vanished as it closed. The first thing she noticed was that it was cold. Really cold. She wasn't sure what that meant, but—

Mira hit the floor and groaned. They hadn't bound her, so she quickly untied the rope holding the bag over head and ripped it off.

She was in one of the city's freezers, giant cuts of meat hanging from the ceiling. It was kept cold by Emitters, artifacts that radiated elemental forces in a similar way to the Amplifier she'd used back in the missile silo. In this case they emitted cold, and they hummed in each corner of the small, square room.

But the chill in the air was the last thing Mira was worried about.

Three boys stood in between her and the door. They were younger, big too, not as big as Deckard, but close, and she recognized them. Freebooters from Midnight City, and judging by the colors they wore, Glassmen,

207

not Gray Devils, but if they weren't Gray Devils—what did they want with *her?*

"Hey, Mira Toombs," the one in the middle said, a blond kid with rounded glasses. The fact they knew her name probably wasn't a good thing.

"What do you want?" Mira asked, trying to sound unintimidated, but failing miserably.

"Pretty simple, really," another said, the one on the left, the biggest of the three. His voice sounded like a bag of rocks. "Just have a question for you. Answer it in a way we like and you can go. Pretty much in the same shape you came in."

As they spoke, Mira's eyes scanned the locker, looking for anything that could help. The only artifacts here were the Emitters, and they weren't much use. She'd left her bags in the infirmary with Zoey.

"Last time we saw you was a few months ago, before you got that price on your head." It was the one with the glasses again. The third one so far hadn't spoken. But he did have a knife in his hand, Mira saw. Her heart beat faster. "Something interesting about that, though. Back then, me and my friends were pretty sure there was something different about you."

"That being . . . you weren't *Heedless,*" said the big kid, and Mira felt a cold tingling of fear. She had an idea what their "question" was going to be, and there was little hope she could answer it in a way they wanted. It was now official—she was in trouble.

"You're wrong," Mira lied. "I've always been Heedless. If you were Gray Devils, you'd know that."

The boy on the right, the quiet one, shook his head and finally spoke. "No. Pretty sure you weren't."

"Me, too," the glasses said. "So here's the question. How the hell did you do it?"

They started to move toward her. She took a step back.

"Tell us how you blocked the Tone," the big one said. "Tell us how *we* can do it, too, and you can go."

Mira swallowed. "What makes you think I could do it again?" She had to keep them talking.

"Heard rumors," the quiet one told her. They kept inching closer. "About an artifact you were working on, an artifact to stop the Tone."

"No," Mira said, shaking her head. "It didn't work. It won't help you, I swear."

The knife from the quiet kid flew through the air and stuck deep in the meat slab next to Mira. She jumped, barely resisted screaming.

"Lies? That makes us sad," said the glasses. He drew his own knife. So did the big one. "Really sad. We can see your damn eyes from here, Toombs. Hell, we saw 'em when you strolled through the gate. We're not idiots."

Mira stepped back again . . . and felt the cold metal of the freezer wall behind her. There was nowhere to go. She watched the kids step closer, knives at the ready, but she didn't say anything. She wouldn't tell them about Zoey. She *wouldn't*. No matter what they did.

"That's fine, though," said the big one. "You'll tell us everything in the end. Everything under the sun, I promise."

Another voice spoke over the hum of the Emitters. It wasn't soft, but it wasn't overbearing either. It was calm and certain, and something about it made the three big kids turn around. "I think the odds of that are rather low."

Mira looked past the three big kids—and felt a tremendous surge of relief. Ben stood in the doorway, his eyes on the three boys. One hand rested in a pocket, the other was balancing his brass dice cube, juggling it between his knuckles, back and forth.

In a fight, it was clear he had no real chance. They were bigger than him and they were armed. The overconfident looks on their faces dropped all the same. Probably because they knew who he was. Everyone here did. Ben was the top-rated Freebooter in Midnight City, and you didn't earn that spot without being formidable in some way.

"Fun's over," Ben told them. If he was intimidated by the three, he didn't look it. "It might not seem like it, but clearing out of here is the best option you have."

The three kids were still, their necks craned around to stare at Ben. The surprised, uncertain looks lasted a second longer—then the one with the glasses laughed out loud. The others followed.

"Brave talk for a skinny brainiac, outnumbered three-to-one. What? You hoping to outtalk us? *You're* the one that oughta leave, before you get hurt."

"It's a mathematical certainty I won't get hurt today. You three, however, are operating under a very different set of variables." Ben studied each of the three in turn, then his gaze moved around the room, as if analyzing it. "The meat. The floor. And then . . . actually, I'm not really sure."

Mira was just as confused as the three kids. Apparently, they'd had enough. "Kill this fool," the one with the glasses ordered.

They all turned and advanced on Ben. He didn't budge. But Mira saw something, something telling. As they approached, a sphere of yellow light crackled around him, then vanished.

The chains from one of the huge cuts of meat snapped apart, as if from the cold. A major coincidence, but a lucky one. The meat probably weighed several hundred pounds frozen, and when it fell, it slammed into the biggest kid, flattening him to the floor. He didn't move.

The other two boys stepped away, startled, but then the action seemed to spur them. They charged toward Ben, their knives gleaming.

Ben just watched in curiosity.

The kid with the glasses slipped on a patch of ice as he ran, went down, and there was a sickening crack as his head hit the floor. He went limp.

The quiet kid skidded to a stop, stared in shock, and then looked at Ben.

Ben stared back calmly. "Think it through."

The knife shook in the quiet kid's hand. Then he made his choice. He charged one last time.

The Emitter in the corner of the room near the door exploded in a brilliant flash of green light, spraying shrapnel in an arc. Mira ducked, then heard a scream as the debris ripped into the kid. He spun and fell, and like the others, didn't move.

Then everything was quiet. Mira opened her eyes and stared at Ben in shock. He studied the bodies of the three boys, one at a time.

"*Of course*, the Emitter. It adds up." Ben frowned, a little frustrated, and looked up at Mira for the first time. There was no hint of shame or guilt on his face. "I'm still trying to figure out the underlying algorithm. It's . . . very complex."

Mira just stared at him, still stunned by everything that had happened.

"Come on," Ben said as he moved for the door. "Let's get out of the cold."

Outside the locker, Ben leaned against a railing on the winding walkway. Mira saw that they were about a third of the way up the Spire. Above them, towers and platforms stretched and wrapped around the shimmering Gravity Well at crazy angles, but Mira just stared at Ben's back, a terrible feeling growing inside her.

"I know what you want to say." Ben stared to the north and the everdarkening sky there.

"You sure as hell should." Mira's voice quivered. "You know how dangerous it is. You know what it does to everyone who—"

"Not to me, Mira. It won't affect me like other people." He didn't look at her, just stood there with his hands in his pockets. Mira wondered which one held the Chance Generator. "I couldn't *not* use it, not with what's at stake, and I don't think it was a coincidence it came to me. I can control it. I'm probably the only one in the world who can."

"No." Mira shut her eyes. "You can't. Not even you, Ben. It makes you think that, but it's an illusion."

"You don't understand. Its power is *growing*, Mira, the farther it goes into the Strange Lands. It stays on for days at a time now. I think once I reach the Core . . . it'll be on permanently."

Mira stared at his back. Her next words were barely a whisper. "What happened to your team, Ben?"

He stiffened, hesitated . . . and said nothing.

Anger replaced the horror Mira felt seconds earlier. "They're dead, aren't they? They died because you used the Chance Generator in the Strange Lands! It killed them in order to profit *you!* That thing is the reason they're dead, and if you were thinking straight, you'd see that!"

Ben finally turned around and looked at Mira, and the sight of him up close was shocking.

He was pale, looked like he hadn't slept in days. His eyes, where the Tone wasn't crawling through them, were bloodshot and raw, and they locked onto hers. "I regret their loss. Never think I don't. But their sacrifice is anything but meaningless. If I can reach the Tower, it's worth it."

Mira shook her head firmly. "Not like this it isn't."

"You just don't see the math of it!"

"There's no math here, Ben! The math is you don't even know what the Severed Tower really is. No one does." She took a step closer, glaring at him. "Do your men know, Ben? Do they know you're using the abacus? Do they know *why* they're dying one by one in random accidents?"

Ben looked away again.

Mira's body shook with suppressed rage. She hated that artifact more than any other, more than even the horrible one she'd created all on her own. It had changed and corrupted one person she cared about, and now it was doing the same thing to another. But she would be damned if she'd let it happen.

"You have to stop, Ben. If you don't . . . I'll *tell* your men the truth. Tell them what you've done, and that the deaths of their friends are on *you*. I will, Ben, I swear to God I will, and your expedition will be *over*. Tell me you understand what I'm saying to you."

As she spoke, Ben looked back at her, and something passed over his face. A look she had never seen from him, something so foreign in Ben Aubertine's eyes it was chilling. She saw rage. Anger. Every black, vile emotion someone could feel drifted in and out of his eyes . . .

. . . and then vanished, replaced by his usual calm demeanor.

He looked at her oddly, studying her as if for the first time, as if he had woken from some sort of dream.

"Maybe you're right," he said, and she heard an audible shake in his voice. "Maybe . . . I can't control it."

Relief flooded through Mira. She moved closer to him. "You're stronger than this. Holt gave up the artifact, and he had it longer than you. You can do it, too. I'll help you."

Ben stared at her, thoughts swirling in his head. "If I do, will you go to the Tower? Tonight? Will you leave with me?"

The question startled her. She felt a rush of confusion, mainly because her reaction now was so different from before. She thought of Holt, locked in the jail below with Ravan. There was no way for her to help him now. The truth was, if she wanted to get to the Tower, Ben was her best— maybe her only chance.

"Yes," Mira told him. His face lit up in a smile filled with relief and he moved for her, but she stopped him. "Zoey has to come with us."

His smile faded. "Mira . . ."

"It's not negotiable. If you want me to come with you to the Tower, like we always talked about—Zoey has to come, too."

He studied her a long time, weighing everything, measuring the risks and advantages, doing the math. Finally he nodded. "Okay."

Mira threw her arms around him. He hugged her back.

"Meet me at the Anvil in an hour," she whispered to him. "I have to destroy my artifact. We'll destroy the Chance Generator, too, then leave."

Ben was confused. "The Chance Generator is a fourth-ring artifact. So are the components in yours. We can't destroy them here."

"I think we're *in* the fourth ring, Ben. Right now." Ben raised an eyebrow at that. "I think the Strange Lands are *growing,* and I think I know why. I also think it's going to get worse."

Mira watched the old look of curiosity appear, the one he wore when he found something new to solve, something to figure out and break down and understand. It was good to see it.

"I'll tell you at the Anvil," she said. "I'll tell you everything. Okay?"

Ben nodded. When they parted, Mira raced back down the walkway towards the infirmary to get her things. She felt light on her feet, and it wasn't just the low gravity of the Spire. Ben would lead now, she knew. Ben would shoulder the weight of the responsibility she had been carrying, he would take the fear and the worry on himself. Everything would be fine now.

She laughed as she ran, circling the massive column of light. She didn't even notice the strange, fragmented hissing sound filling the air from the Gravity Well, or that it seemed worse—*much worse,* than before.

28. SACROSANCT

THE OLD SHERIFF'S OFFICE was still in good condition, probably a result of both the Strange Lands' slowing of time and the fact that Polestar clearly used it often as a brig. The entire length of the back wall was divided into five cells, with cast-iron bars on one side and the brick wall of the building on the other.

Outside the cells, the old desks stood collecting dust. Holt could see their things lying well out of reach. Their packs and guns, including his own, and the big, wooden crate that Ravan's men had been carrying this whole time.

When they'd arrived, there had only been one other person in the cells, the rest were empty. Now each held four or five Menagerie apiece, and Holt was in the next-to-last one, along with Ravan and two of her men.

The lone figure in the cell next to them sat in a corner covered in shadows, but it didn't look like he cared much whether he had company or not. He never even looked in their direction.

Holt sat with his back against the brick wall, staring up at the skylight at the top of the ceiling, two dozen feet above them and out of reach. It flashed occasionally in different colors, and it was always followed by the rolling, fragmented thunder from outside. That crazy storm was still out there, but it sounded a little farther away now.

Ravan paced back and forth, staring past the bars. When they'd first arrived, she'd tested them, tried to find weaknesses, looked at the locks, but there was nothing she could do. They were locked up good and tight, but still she paced back and forth like a caged tiger.

"Sit down, you're making me queasy," Holt told her without taking his eyes off the flashing skylight.

"There's always a way out," she replied. *"Always."*

"You never liked being locked up. Only thing I ever saw get to you."

"Drives me crazy." She kicked the door again. It didn't budge. "Makes me want to tear my eyes out."

"I'd prefer you didn't," Holt replied pointedly. "Just try to relax. They'll let us loose once the storms break up. They just don't want you in the city."

She turned and looked at him. "They don't want *us* in the city, you mean."

She was right. He was in the same cell as them, wasn't he? He wondered what Mira was doing, wondered if Zoey was okay. She'd looked bad when he'd been taken away.

"What are you doing here, Holt?" Ravan asked. She was staring at him in genuine confusion. "It has to do with that kid, doesn't it? It's easy to figure. You don't bring a little girl to a place like this, but that's what you're doing, so it has to involve her. She's the only thing that doesn't fit."

"It's . . . complicated."

"It must be," Ravan replied. "Holt Hawkins *hates* artifacts. Going into the Strange Lands would be the last thing he'd ever do."

Holt studied her. She wanted to know the truth. But how did he tell her? "I'm just not sure it's something you would believe."

Pain flashed in Ravan's eyes again. "Never even crosses your mind, does it? That I might surprise you? If you ever took the time to try, maybe you'd find I'm more than what you think."

"Ravan, I didn't mean—"

"Just forget it," she said, and turned back around.

Watching her, it occurred to him that he had probably hurt Ravan more than anyone else he'd ever known. And he seemed to do it, over and over again. Maybe it was because in his mind, Ravan was indestructible; she could take anything the world dished out, and so he subconsciously gave himself license to disregard her feelings. Yet regardless of the image she presented, Ravan was human, she felt pain. And she deserved better.

Still, Zoey's secret was a dangerous one, and the fewer people who knew it, the better. She could stop the Tone, and he didn't like the idea of the Menagerie pirates around them learning it. Who knew what they were likely to do if they did. Then again, he'd probably never see Mira and Zoey again, or even Max. He was alone now.

Holt looked back up at Ravan. "Me being here isn't any more surprising than *you* being here. Far as I remember, Tiberius was never interested in the Strange Lands."

Ravan laughed. "Before *you*, you mean."

Holt stared at her, confused. "Me?"

"After Archer died, Tiberius had to find another way to preserve his legacy," Ravan continued, still not looking at him. "And there's only one other option, isn't there?"

The answer occurred to Holt immediately. "Avril," he said. Ravan didn't answer him, but she didn't need to. It was the only thing that made sense. "You're here to *find* her?"

"Already found her," Ravan said. "Saw her a few days ago, least I think I did. She's with the White Helix."

The White Helix? If Ravan was here for them, Tiberius had basically sent her on a suicide mission. That didn't make sense, though. Ravan was one of Tiberius's best leaders, and he was a master strategist. He'd never risk her life lightly, even if it meant getting Avril back. Then again, he was also beyond ruthless.

"From what I've heard, the White Helix don't strike me like the kind of group who hands over one of their own," Holt said. "Even if she *is* the daughter of Tiberius Marseille."

"Probably not. But they would *trade* for her."

Instinctively, Holt looked past Ravan, past the bars, to where the Polestar guards had put their gear. Sitting there among it all was the big crate Ravan's men had been lugging with them this entire time.

"Any arrangements you have with the White Helix are sacrosanct," a disapproving voice interrupted them. The figure in the other cell rose to his feet and moved toward Holt and Ravan with the controlled grace of someone used to doing far more agile things than simply walking. "They shouldn't be discussed openly."

Holt could see him clearly now—black and gray clothing, boots, cargo pants, tucked-in shirt, a vest with pockets, utility belts. A boy, eighteen maybe, the Tone creeping through his eyes.

Ravan studied the boy warily. "Him, I trust. Even if he doesn't trust me." Holt guessed he deserved that last bit. "But *you* . . . I don't know at all."

The boy leaned casually against the bars. "I was sent as your escort to Sanctum. My name is Chase."

"You're from the White Helix?" Holt asked in surprise. Chase nodded once.

Ravan frowned. "Well that's just great, isn't it? Hell of an escort, if you're gonna be locked up in the same damn jail we are."

Chase smiled. "I might be in the same jail, but I'm not locked up. When the time is right, we'll leave for Sanctum."

Holt studied the boy and his calm, dangerous demeanor. "Are you saying you got caught on purpose—to meet the Menagerie here?"

The kid shrugged. "You were told you would be met at Polestar, weren't you? Freebooters and Helix have no love for each other, and finding one alone in the landscape would be irresistible. They would capture him and bring him exactly where he needed to be. It's always easier to let the water carry you toward your goal, rather than swim against a current."

Holt looked at the bruises and cuts on his face. The guards obviously hadn't been gentle with him. If he considered that the "easy" route, Holt hated to see see a tough one.

"Fine," Ravan said in annoyance. The boy's entrance had had an effect, but she was growing less impressed now. "When will this 'right time' be?"

The Helix shrugged and moved back to his dark corner. "No way to know, but it will come." He sank down into the shadows again and blended in with them. "The Tower wills it."

Holt and Ravan looked at each other skeptically.

MIRA STOOD AT THE TOP of the Spire—or, at least what was *now* the top. Above her, the twisted, broken poles and supports that used to hold the Orb jutted outward where it had ripped loose a day ago. It didn't seem real, staring at the blank air where the massive sphere should be.

Below her the city twinkled the same as always, buildings and walkways and platforms winding downward toward the ground, around the massive column of bright, flickering energy. Look down and things appeared normal. Look up . . . and you knew the truth.

She was here for a reason, she reminded herself. She was at the city's Anvil.

An Anvil was a major artifact that facilitated the destruction of other artifacts, and could only be used in the Strange Lands. Artifacts could only be destroyed in the ring where they were created, or, in the case of a combination, only in the ring of their most powerful component. As a result, there were several Anvils in every ring, most set up along the main routes for easy access. After all, you didn't want to travel all the way to Polestar to destroy a first-ring combination.

Polestar's Anvil stood on an open-air platform of polished wood and steel, surrounded by the various buildings of the city's temporary housing—small huts built on top of each other a thousand feet above the ground, with ladders and bridges connecting them for visiting Freebooters. The platform itself stretched diagonally a hundred feet away from the main support structure, balanced on nothing more than a few thin, metal pipes, something that would have been impossible in normal gravity. The whole thing looked like it should rip loose and fall, but it didn't.

Mira looked at the artifact in front of her. An Anvil was just that, an old anvil from a blacksmith's forge. Metallic shelves sat next to this one, holding a variety of antique mallets. Any one of them would do the job. Place an artifact on the Anvil, take a mallet and slam it down. Any artifact or combination would shatter into pieces, provided they were in the right ring.

Mira set her packs and Lexicon on the platform, then pulled out her artifact combination, with the old pocket watch in the center. She set it on the black, scarred surface of the Anvil and stared at it, a complicated mix of emotions washing over her. She felt nothing but horror and regret when she looked at it now. In a way, this was the culmination of a long journey, one set in motion months ago. When she destroyed her artifact, it would be yet another turning point.

"Mira," a voice said behind her. Ben stood at the edge of the platform where the walkway connected to it. In his hand was the Chance Generator.

Ben looked even more tired than before. Pale and weak. She wondered if *he* would even recognize himself. Once he destroyed that artifact, he would be okay, she told herself. He had to be. She *needed* him to be.

"I'm glad you came," she said.

Ben stared back at her. "Are you . . . really sure about this?"

Mira nodded. "Any advantage that thing gives you is offset by what it takes. It's not worth the price. I've lost a lot to it already, and so have you, you just don't see it yet. I need you to trust me, Ben."

"I do trust you. You always see things so clearly." Ben moved toward her wearily. "It's one reason . . . why I love you, Mira."

Mira froze at the words. In all their time together, after all they had been through, he had never said those words to her.

She didn't know what to say. "Ben . . ."

He moved closer. His hands gently pulled the necklaces from her shirt. His fingers divided them, one after the other, until they found the one he was looking for. The small pair of brass dice.

"Do you remember the night I gave you this?" he asked her.

Mira nodded.

"Do you remember what I told you when I did?"

"Yes."

His eyes looked up from the necklace into hers. "I know this is going to seem like a betrayal, and like a contradiction to everything I told you then—but it isn't. I promise."

She studied him in confusion. What did he mean by—

Mira flinched as Ben snapped another necklace off her neck. The Gravity Void combination she always wore for emergencies. Before she could react, he took a step back—and threw it onto the platform at her feet.

The glass vial on the combination shattered. There was a flash and a hum—and then Mira gasped as she was yanked up into the air in a blur of ascending light particles, spinning helplessly in a sphere of zero gravity.

"Ben!" she yelled, trying to reach something, but there was nothing she could grab, she just floated helplessly. The Anvil and its shelves were out of reach. She was trapped. "What are you *doing?*" she exclaimed, but a part of her already knew.

Ben stared up at her sadly and stuffed the Chance Generator in his pocket. "The Tower is too important. I tried to explain it to you, but you wouldn't see."

"Ben, don't do this," Mira begged him. "Your entire team will die. *You* will die. This isn't—"

"I know it seems horrible to rationalize away their deaths, but the Chance Generator will guarantee I reach the Tower. And I *have* to reach it. Everything depends on it."

Mira spun helplessly in the Void. She watched Ben kneel down to her pack and remove something from it. When she saw what it was her heart sank. Her glass cylinder of plutonium, with the Dampener still attached to its surface. The one she'd been carrying all this time, the one she'd risked everything for, the one she needed if she was going to fulfill her promise to Zoey.

He put the plutonium in his own pack and looked back at her. His face was full of more emotion than she had ever seen on it. "This comes the closest of anything in my life to hurting me, knowing you will never understand why I'm doing this. Knowing you'll never forgive me. It hurts more because, once I change everything, this reality will be gone. It will be replaced with how it should have been, a world without the Assembly. And I'll never get a chance to make it up to you. Because we'll never have met."

"Ben, no!" she yelled. "I can't get Zoey inside the Tower without the plutonium!"

"That's the point, Mira. You won't have a reason to follow me now. I'm saving you this way. You can't make it to the Tower on your own, you know that. If you're honest, a part of you is relieved you no longer have to try."

"Ben, please don't!" she begged, struggling in the Void. "*Zoey* is the one who's supposed to change everything. Not *you!*"

Ben didn't answer, he just looked up to the sky above them. "I wish I could see the Scorpion, but . . . I can't. I think it's something only you can do." He looked back at her. "I meant what I said before. I love you, Mira." Then he turned and disappeared down the ramp back into the Spire.

"*Ben!*" Mira yelled mournfully, but there was nothing she could do. The plutonium was gone and so was Ben.

ZOEY STOOD AT THE top of the dam once more, staring down at the flood plain below. The shadows writhed there as before, but there were more of them this time. Thousands instead of hundreds, rising and boiling up out of the still water and reaching for her.

Why? The suggestion came, projected upward, and this time it was so strong it filled her mind with pain and darkness.

Why?

The land wasn't a still photograph anymore, it was all moving—only it moved quicker than it should, as though time were advancing faster and faster. Only the shadows seemed to move in normal time.

"Wake up, Zoey." A voice filled her mind. Her own voice, tiny and low. "Balance must be restored."

Everything sped up, faster and faster. The flood plain dried up, the trees and grass wilted to charred blackness, the dam cracked and crumbled and fell apart into dust. The world went a searing shade of white . . .

"*Wake up!*"

She did . . . and everything flashed away.

ZOEY BLINKED GROGGILY AS she awoke in a strange place that wasn't where she remembered being. She wasn't on the hill anymore, watching the frightening storm. She was in a room full of beds and cabinets and wavering opalescent light that rained down from the ceiling, and no one else was there. Except the Max. He was underneath her, staring up with worried eyes. Zoey smiled and rubbed his ears.

The movement caused her head to hurt, and she winced. "Ouch . . ." she said.

Zoey slowly rolled over and sat up, and the pain blossomed in her head as she did. It wasn't as bad as before, when she had gone to sleep, but it was still painful.

Then Zoey noticed something. Sensations. All around her. Filling the air. It was connected to the pain in her head, just like when those strange cubes had appeared at the junkyard city. It was like energy flowing everywhere, but it gave off no heat or feeling, she just knew it was there, and whenever she felt it pulse and blossom, the same happened in her head.

Zoey stood up and moved for the exit. Max whined and followed her outside.

An amazing city was all around them, stretching high above on an impossible collection of scaffolding and supports. Buildings, much bigger than they should be, jutted precariously out from the support system that wound and wrapped upward into the sky.

It was Polestar, Zoey knew, because she had seen it all in Mira's mind, and it was beautiful. But it was also different. Zoey saw what was left of the Orb shattered on the ground below. A hundred or so kids moved over it, like worker ants, disassembling what could be salvaged and laboriously cleaning up the rest. At the very top of the city, Zoey could see where the thing had once rested, as well as the twisted metallic supports that had ripped loose when it came crashing down.

The ground below was ablaze in prismatic, reflected color, which must be from the Gravity Well, but she couldn't see the Anomaly. The twisting spiral of buildings and walkways was blocking her view, so she started downward, following the path as it wrapped around and in between the city's multisurfaced buildings. She moved through throngs of kids, none of them really paying her much mind, they were too busy talking about the Orb and the Antimatter Storm and whether or not they should leave while they had the chance. Even so, very few were headed down to the exits—they were all climbing back to their homes and lofts and workshops.

Zoey realized they were all wearing the same colors as the kids in Midnight City. Looking upward, she could see banners fluttering out from some of the buildings, each with different symbols and colors. The factions from that place were represented here, apparently, which made sense. Freebooters came from Midnight City, and this was a Freebooter outpost.

She stepped onto a colorful stairway that curved to the ground, and when she reached the concrete-covered Mezzanine, Zoey followed the light reflected from it back up into the air, and finally saw it.

A giant, massive column of pure bright, flickering energy that streamed upward into the sky. The Spire of Polestar wrapped around it in a dizzying corkscrew. It was strange to look at. It felt like the entire thing should come immediately tumbling down, but somehow it didn't. It just hung precariously in the air, and she could see a thousand kids climbing up and down its ladders and twisting paths.

But mainly she looked at the Gravity Well.

She could tell it was the source of the sensations she was feeling. The pain in her head ebbed and flowed to its rhythmic pulsing. And there was something else, something probably only she could really see. It was growing dimmer, the time between its flashes was lengthening. As it did, the pain in her head seemed to lessen.

Zoey saw a brick wall erected in a circle around the base of the Gravity Well, where the energy exploded out of the ground. But it wasn't sealed. An archway allowed entrance inside, and Zoey moved for and passed under it.

On the other side was a circular courtyard with benches and tables for people to watch the Well as it pulsed upward. Zoey could see why; from this close, it was staggeringly beautiful.

Max whined as she moved toward it and stood at the very edge of the concrete, the Well itself just a foot or two away. Oddly, it didn't give off any heat, Zoey noted, and barely emitted any sound, just a strange, fragmented hissing that wasn't at all unpleasant.

Instinctively, Zoey closed her eyes and concentrated on the Anomaly—and when she did the pain in her head lessened.

She sighed in relief, grateful for the reprieve, even though she didn't know why it happened. She could feel the giant column of energy, feel it streaming upward, feel it gathering the weight of the world and absorbing it into itself.

It felt amazing. It felt like—

Zoey opened her eyes. Something was wrong.

The Gravity Well flickered in front of her, and not like before. It flashed violently, the hissing intensifying, cut off and then returned. Next to her she heard Max growl, but she was too focused on the Anomaly.

It flickered again—and this time it didn't come back as bright.

Zoey took a step back, realizing the truth. The Well was about to die. She could tell, because the sensations around her were slowing and becoming fainter. It had been weakening before, but now it was doing it much faster. Somehow the Well was the source of the pain in her head, and that pain was lessening. In horror, she realized it had all started when she moved *close* to it.

The Well flickered again, seemed to fade, the hissing dimmed, it was almost indiscernible now. She heard the city above groan deeply as more weight settled onto its supports.

Zoey's eyes widened in fear. "No . . ." she moaned. The idea of what she might be responsible for chilled her like nothing else in her life. If the Gravity Well went out the city would fall, and everyone on it would die, including Mira and Holt, and it would all be her fault. *All* of it.

"Please, no . . ." Zoey closed her eyes again. Maybe she could save it somehow, maybe she could stop it. She reached out with her mind and the Gravity Well was there, she could feel it like before, but it was noticeably weaker.

Zoey called out for the Feelings—and they rose from the recesses, filling her with confidence and strength, almost enough to forget what was about to happen. The Feelings blended and merged with the Well through her mind, and she saw what they intended, what they suggested. She knew what she had to do.

Zoey concentrated on the Anomaly, pouring her own energy *into* it.

Golden light flared and blossomed like fire all over her and streamed into the Well, filling it back up, replacing the color and light that was bleeding out of it. The pain in her head returned as the Well grew stronger again.

But it wasn't going to be enough, she could tell. All she could do was delay the inevitable.

"Please . . ." she moaned again. She had to slow it down, give Holt and Mira and everyone else above time to escape.

The supports of the Spire groaned again. Max barked wildly in alarm, trying to get Zoey's attention.

But Zoey didn't move, as much as she might want to. She could run and escape, maybe, but she didn't. Tears streamed out of her closed eyes as the pain slowly increased in her head.

Please let them escape, she thought. *Please.*

All around her the world began to fall apart.

30. THE FALL

HOLT WASN'T SURE WHAT HE'D HEARD, but whatever it was woke him from a deep, dreamless sleep that he would have much preferred to remain in. He glanced around, looking for any sign of—

It came again, the sound. A deep, mournful groan that filled the air outside the sheriff's office. It sounded like metal bending and shifting under stress. A *lot* of stress.

"You hear that?" Ravan asked next to him. Her men were all stirring in their cells. "I think—"

A new sound, this one from hundreds of sources, and one Holt recognized immediately. Screams.

Everyone got to their feet instinctively, trying to peer through the windows at the other end of the building, but all they could see was the flickering, prismatic light from the Gravity Well outside.

The groaning again, but stronger, a deep, violent rumbling that shook the building. The Menagerie murmured nervously.

"The time is now." Everyone turned to the lone White Helix in his cell. He rolled his shoulders, stretching his arms, preparing for something. As he did, he looked up.

Holt, Ravan, and the pirates followed his gaze. There was only the skylight and the old exposed air-conditioning ductwork along the ceiling—and it was almost thirty feet above their heads.

"You're kidding. Right?" Ravan asked skeptically.

Chase didn't answer. His eyes moved from the ceiling down to the cell bars, studying them, planning, then he grabbed two and scaled them like a spider, straight upward. Even without their rings, it seemed the White Helix were still very agile.

"Um. Yeah." Holt's eyes widened at how effortless he made it look.

When Chase reached the top there was no hesitation, he lunged backward into the air, spun and grabbed hold of the exposed ductwork at the top. It creaked badly, but it held. The Helix's legs flew outward, swinging him back and forth on the ductwork, gaining momentum and speed. When he had enough, Chase swung one last time, flew upward . . .

. . . and crashed straight through the skylight, feetfirst, shattering it to pieces.

Seconds later another skylight broke apart, and Chase fell through it, landing outside their cells in a crouch that absorbed his weight.

Everyone stared, dumbstruck, as the Helix moved to the lockers at the far end of the office. He opened one and grabbed his things—his goggles, his mask, various pieces of equipment, the three glowing crystal rings, and finally his double-pronged weapon.

It was the first time Holt had seen a Lancet. It looked pretty much like how the stories described it, but it was still a hell of a sight. He could see the two glowing crystals on either end, one red and one blue, and the dual triggers on the shaft.

More rumbling echoed outside, and a violent crash filled the air. Screams followed.

Holt felt a desperation build in him. Whatever was happening out there, it was bad. And Mira and Zoey were right in the middle of it.

"Stand back," Chase said as he approached, the double-pronged spear spinning in his hands in blurs of blue and red.

No one argued or questioned him, they just backed up. The weapon spun faster—and then gracefully struck outward straight through the lock on one of the cell doors in a shower of sparks.

The lock mechanism exploded. The door opened. The pirates inside were free.

Holt was impressed. Those doors were solid steel, and whatever those spear points were, they passed through it like it wasn't even there.

Chase repeated the move for each cell in the office, plunging his weapon into them, blowing them apart. But when he reached Ravan and Holt he stopped. "We have to move fast, there isn't much time."

"Why?" Holt quickly asked.

"I can feel the Gravity Well fading outside. It's going to die, and this place is going to die with it." He stared pointedly at Ravan. "If you want to live, your men must do exactly as I say." Ravan and Holt nodded without hesitation.

Chase punctured the lock to their door, freeing them. Ravan and the last of the Menagerie exited and moved for their things.

So did Holt. He slipped his pack over his shoulder, and it felt good there. He hadn't had his things in a long time. Holt grabbed his shotgun and rifle, slipped them over his back, and reached for the Beretta.

From around the room came the clicking of a dozen guns being primed.

"What do you think *you're* doing?" Ravan asked. Holt slowly turned to look at her, carefully slipping the Beretta into its holster as he did. Ravan's gun wasn't raised, but six or seven others were.

"Mira and Zoey are out there," Holt said.

"Don't be an idiot, it's suicide," Ravan replied. "It's all about to come down, and you'll be buried with everyone else. It's *survival*. You *know* that."

"It's more important than you think." Holt stood his ground, neither moving for the door nor surrendering his guns.

"No." Ravan drew her sidearm, a Beretta 9 like his own, and aimed it at his chest. "We had an agreement. You're not going anywhere."

Holt didn't move or react, he just stared at her evenly. "Zoey can heal the Tone, Ravan. She can stop it from spreading, reverse it." The Menagerie all around him hesitated, unsure they'd heard him correctly. "And she has other powers, amazing ones, powers the Assembly are hunting her for."

"The Prime . . ." The soft, musing voice behind everyone grabbed their attention. It was Chase, leaning against a wall and staring at Holt. "The Prime . . . is with *you?*"

Holt stared back in confusion. "You mean Zoey? The Librarian called her the Apex, is that what you mean?"

Chase stood up straight, studying Holt in a new way. "Avril's Arc has been searching for her for days. When Gideon said she was here, I didn't believe it. It seemed so . . . impossible. We have waited for her return a very long time."

Holt was even more confused, but Ravan interrupted them both.

"This is insane. The Prime? Magical powers? *This* is why you're here?" Ravan looked disgusted. He wasn't surprised. If he hadn't seen everything he had with his own eyes, he doubted he'd believe it either.

"What *happened* to you, Holt?" Ravan continued. "You never would have gotten involved in anything as hopeless as this. Never would put something intangible above survival. It isn't you."

"It's *not* intangible," Holt said. More groaning from outside. He had to get out there. "I've *seen* it."

Ravan stared back at him like a stranger. "So the little girl has powers, so what? She's one little kid. What can she possibly do, *save the world?* Is that what this is all about? I mean, *really?* Look *around you*, Holt." She stared at him intently. "There's nothing *left* to save!"

Holt held her gaze. "I used to believe that, but not anymore. If you'd seen what I've seen, you wouldn't either. I have to go, Rae. If you need to kill me—then that's what you should do." Holt took a step toward the door. The guns tensed all around him. "But I'm going after them."

"After *her*," Ravan said. Her voice was ice.

"After *both* of them." Holt took another step. The Menagerie looked between Holt and their Captain, unsure. Holt, for his part, just stared at Ravan. He could see the pain there, but there was nothing he could do. Things were the way they were, regardless of what he felt for her. "You wanted me to trust you, to think you might be more than I believed. That's what I'm doing right now."

She stared back silently. The gun shook in her hand. Holt took another step. The building shook again, there were more screams outside.

Ravan lowered her gun. So did her men. "Go," she told him, her voice a ragged whisper. "Just go."

Holt felt relief flood through him, and at the same time guilt. He had hurt her again, the latest transgression in an unending cycle.

"Go!" she yelled at him in fury, and Holt spun and dashed outside, leaving her and the pirates behind. The relief he felt was quickly replaced by shock and fear.

Everything was chaos.

People fled and tripped and shoved each other as they raced down the stairways of Polestar, trying to escape the city. Others were bypassing the line altogether, leaping from the lower buildings onto the ground. Whoever made it ran in a mad scramble as fast as they could away from the Spire.

The once beautiful Mezzanine was buried in the remnants of several buildings that had fallen from the top of the city, and Holt was in time to see another one slam into the ground in an explosion of steel and wood, spraying debris everywhere.

Holt stared up at Polestar in stunned silence. Ravan was right, it was suicide. But it didn't matter. *They* were up there somewhere, and they needed him.

Holt shoved his way through the panicking crowd, the only figure in a sea of people trying to get *into* the city. He saw what looked like a giant stairway on the ground, climbing upward and dividing into different walkways and bridges that went in every direction.

He kept pushing and shoving, and when he reached it he saw someone he recognized. The overseer, Deckard. He stood at the entrance to the city, staring around in a daze.

"Where's Mira?" Holt shouted as he ran toward him. Deckard said nothing, just stared into the distance mutely. Holt grabbed him and slammed him against the stairway in spite of the kid's size. *"Where's Mira?"*

"I . . . don't know . . ." the big kid spoke. "Don't matter anymore, anyway."

In desperation, Holt craned his neck to look upward at the city. Where would she go? Where would she be? A thought occurred to him. He gripped Deckard harder. "Where would she go if she wanted to destroy an artifact?"

"The . . . Anvil." Deckard said. He looked like he was in shock, but Holt didn't particularly care.

"Where the hell's *that?*"

"At the . . . top. Very top."

Holt sighed. "Of course it is." He let Deckard go and started pushing his way through the crowd again, climbing up the stairs.

"It's all coming down, you know?" Deckard's voice was laced with horror. "All of it. It's all through."

Holt ignored him and pushed on. He had to get to them. He *had* to.

————

ZOEY STOOD WHERE THE giant, hissing Gravity Well erupted into the air. In the background she could hear the sounds of screams and metallic shudderings and violent crashes and even the Max's barking, but she tried not to think about any of it.

She only had one thing to worry about now, trying to keep the Gravity Well alive. Tears streamed down her face as golden, wavering luminescence poured off her. She was pumping all her energy into the Anomaly. Even so, she was still only stalling it. The pain in her head was almost unbearable.

But she held on, and she would keep holding on until the strain was too much and she collapsed and was buried under the fallen city, but at least she might be able to buy time for Holt and Mira and everyone else to escape. Maybe she could make up for all the damage she had done. Maybe they would all forgive her, then . . .

Zoey held on. The pain continued to build.

MIRA HUNG HELPLESSLY IN the air, spinning in slow, lazy circles in the zero gravity, while Polestar collapsed all around her. She felt sick watching it, the death of a place that had meant so much to her, and, fittingly, she had the best seat in the house. She would sit in her perch while it all horribly fell in on itself, and then have the next few hours to think about it before the Gravity Void finally lost its power and she plummeted to the ground more than a thousand feet below.

Mira shook herself out of her funk. She wasn't dead yet, so she should stop acting like it. If she could just find a way out of this Void she could escape.

She looked around for anything, but just like before, there was nothing to grab. However, as she looked, she saw something unexpected. It took a moment for her to figure out what it was.

Far beneath her, on the ground outside the city, a dozen figures dressed in black and gray ran toward the walls. Bright points of color followed after them—red, green, and blue. They were Antimatter Crystals, and it meant the figures were White Helix.

She watched as they leaped over the wall in flashes of yellow light, easily dodging all the falling debris, jumping and spinning through the air onto the city's various levels, fanning out, as if searching for something—but *what?*

"Mira!" Holt charged onto the Anvil platform.

"Holt!" She had never been happier to see anyone.

He ground to a stop suddenly, staring at her spinning in the Void.

"What?" she asked.

"Sorry, it's just . . . it's a little ironic, is all."

"Shut up and get me out!" The platform they were on shifted dangerously. It wasn't going to stay up long.

Holt grabbed his pack, unhooked one of the straps, and threw it into the Gravity Void at Mira, holding onto the length of fiber.

Mira grabbed it. Holt pulled. She fell out of the Void onto the platform and looked at him. Her emotions were a jumbled mix, but she pushed them away. There wasn't time right now.

"Zoey's in the infirmary," she told him.

The platform shuddered violently under their feet, almost throwing them to the ground. "Then let's go!" Holt shouted, starting to move.

"Wait!" Mira shouted, grabbing her wretched artifact off the Anvil. She wasn't leaving it for someone else to find. It was still her responsibility. She scooped up her packs and Lexicon and ran after Holt.

Together they dashed for the bridge, and they could feel the platform shaking and weakening under them. Halfway there, Mira screamed as it ripped completely apart, shattering into chunks of wood and plaster, falling downward behind them.

"Jump!" Holt shouted, and they both leaped off as the platform fell away into the abyss. They slammed onto one of the main stairways and rolled, barely stopping from sliding off the edge.

Holt looked at Mira, breathing hard. "Hands down, my favorite city in the whole world."

Mira frowned and yanked him to his feet, pulled him down the stairway. The Gravity Well hissed and sparked. All around them, the supports of Polestar moaned and shuddered as more and more weight was placed on them.

Just below, two of the city's cold storage buildings ripped free of their supports, crashing into a garden platform and carrying it with them as they fell heavily toward the ground. As it did, Mira saw figures flipping and spinning out of the way in flashes of color, moving over what was left of the various buildings, jumping into the air right as they began to fall.

The White Helix again, but what were they doing here?

Holt pulled Mira back as a fragment of their stairway broke loose and disappeared into nothing, barely keeping him from falling.

"This way!" Holt leaped onto the roof of some kind of workshop, grabbing its blackened chimney for support as he slid down.

Mira followed, right before the bridge they were just on came loose, falling and crashing away.

"There!" Mira pointed out the infirmary below. It was still there. As long as Zoey was inside, there was still a chance to save her.

"We're going to have to jump between the platforms," Holt told her. "The bridges are almost all out."

He was right, Mira saw, the walkways and bridges were like an incomplete jigsaw puzzle now, the gaps in between what was left of them were too much to jump over.

Mira followed Holt as he jumped down and hit the steep, metallic roof of the badly leaning Cavaliers residence hall.

As they slid, Holt dragged his feet, slowed himself, and caught Mira as she flew past. Her eyes widened as she dangled on the edge. There was nothing below her but open air, hundreds of feet to the ground.

The building shook under them, its supports creaking badly. Holt strained as he pulled her up, and they crawled to the top. They stared at the infirmary, one building across and below them. They had to jump. It was going to be close.

"Still your favorite city?" Mira asked, studying the gap warily.

"Feels like a second home to me."

Together they ran and leaped into the air, legs kicking underneath them as they free-fell out and then down. They slammed onto the flat roof of the infirmary, barely keeping their balance.

There was a thunderous roar behind them as the Cavaliers residence hall tipped over, disintegrating in a massive cloud of wood and plastic and metal that fell in a torrent toward the ground. Screams echoed from below as the fleeing people tried to get out of the way, and a lot didn't make it. Mira closed her eyes as it slammed into the ground in a massive crash.

Holt dashed for the center of the roof where the big skylight rested. He stomped down on it hard with his foot once, twice, three times, and it shattered apart. They both jumped through into the infirmary.

Inside, Mira looked around quickly—but there was no sign of Zoey. Screams and crashes filled the air outside.

"Where is she?" Holt asked.

"She . . . she was here," Mira replied, dread beginning to fill her.

"Where is she *now?*"

"I don't know!" Mira ran to the door, but stopped short. Beyond it was a dead drop, all the way to the ground. The stairway outside was gone. She turned and stared at Holt fearfully.

"We'll find her," he said. "But we have to get to the ground. If she went anywhere, it's—"

The infirmary shook horribly—and then Mira and Holt fell, sliding down the floor into the far wall as the structure began to lean. Mira gasped and closed her eyes, her heart racing, waiting for the whole thing to fall.

But it didn't. She could heard the supports crumple and snap, but they held. For now.

Holt got to his feet, stood with one foot on the wall and the other on the floor, and jumped diagonally up to where the skylight used to be, pulling himself up and out. Then he spun around and reached for Mira and pulled her up with him.

When she was out, Mira's heart sank at what she saw. There was nowhere else to go. What was left of the walkways and bridges were too far away. So were any other buildings. They were trapped. All around them the city was crumbling. Buildings crashed and fell, people screamed. It was a nightmare.

Holt turned to Mira. She looked back. They both knew.

"You shouldn't have come for me," Mira simply said, and she meant it. Now he was going to die, too, just like she'd feared all along, and it was her fault. "Why didn't you just leave?"

Holt looked at her as if the answer should be obvious. "I couldn't not come."

Mira sighed and looked away. Ben had left her at the top of the Spire. He couldn't have known the city would fall, but he hadn't come back for her either. Holt had been the one to do that. She could still see him on that airplane, could still see the tattoo on his wrist, but she slowly reached out and took his hand anyway. It was the first time she had touched him since the Crossroads.

"I'm . . . sorry," she said. "For the dam, for getting you into this."

"Don't ever apologize for the dam," Holt said. "It meant something to me. All I needed was to know . . . was that it meant something to you, too."

Mira looked back at him as the cataclysm continued around them. The infirmary shook again, crumbling where it stood, about to fall.

"Holt . . ." Mira whispered.

His arms wrapped around her and she shut her eyes. It was all about to be—

Five figures landed on the infirmary in flashes of orange and purple light, black goggles, masks over their noses and mouths.

Holt tried to rise, but the White Helix were too fast. A kick sent Holt slamming back down, a glowing red crystal stopped just inches from his throat, humming loudly. He went still, glaring up at the Helix.

Mira didn't even bother to resist. One of them stepped forward and raised the goggles off her eyes. She was small, black, with dark hair tied behind her head. It was the same girl Mira and Ravan had encountered in the Grindhouse.

"Where is the Prime?" the girl demanded. She seemed angry and frustrated.

"The . . . *what?*" Mira asked in confusion.

More buildings fell from the air and crashed. The Gravity Well flickered. What was left of the superstructure of Polestar groaned pitifully.

"She means Zoey," Holt said.

The girl looked at him now. *"Where?"*

"We don't know!" Holt told her. "She might be at the bottom, but we're—"

"She's *not* at the bottom!" the girl yelled in exasperation. "We would have felt her, but we felt nothing!"

"If she's near the Well, it might block her connection to—" Another Helix started, but cut off as the building shook violently, pulling free of its supports. It was about to take them all with it.

"Damn it!" the girl yelled in frustration, lowering her goggles back over her eyes.

"What do we do with *them?*" one of her men asked.

"Let them die," spat another. "Let them die here with this place."

"No," the girl said sternly. "Bring them. They can answer to Gideon for the loss of the Prime. *Go!*"

With that, she turned, ran . . . and leaped straight off the edge of the building. Mira stared in shock as the girl fell through the air and disappeared.

Polestar shuddered its last death throe. All around them the Helix leaped off the infirmary into the air with excited yells. Mira felt hands yank her up, saw two others grabbing Holt.

Then they were both being shoved toward the drop.

"Wait!" Mira gasped, trying to pull away.

A Helix whispered in her ear, "Hold on or die, Freebooter."

Mira screamed as the building disappeared under her feet and she was falling through the air faster and faster, the ground hurdling up at her. There was a sudden flash of orange, and their descent slowed violently, as though they had used a parachute.

The effect floated them downward, and as they did Mira saw more White Helix, flipping and spinning in flashes of color, leaping between the various buildings as they fell to pieces, shouting gleefully as they tumbled through the air a thousand feet above the ground. They were actually enjoying this.

The Helix landed gracefully on what was left of the Mezzanine, but Mira hit the ground and collapsed. So did Holt right next to her. They looked at each other, wide-eyed. One minute they were on the infirmary, hundreds of feet in the air, the next—

"Get up, Outlanders!" one of the Helix yelled as he ran by. There was excitement in his voice. "*Run!* Run for all you're worth!"

Above them the massive column of energy flashed and flickered once, twice . . . and then it died. Fading to black. Mira gasped in shock, she couldn't believe it. The Gravity Well was gone, after all this time . . .

The Spire of Polestar groaned mournfully, what was left of the main supports buckling and crumbling under its own weight. Screams echoed up and down its length, the final sounds of those still trapped there.

Holt yanked Mira up, dashing away from the city as fast as they could, dodging through the refuse of the once-beautiful buildings and bridges that had spiraled high into the air.

As they ran, Mira saw a lone figure sitting where the grand stairway once was, staring off into space.

"Deckard!" she shouted. She thought he looked up as she ran, but she couldn't be sure. Either way, he didn't move. He just sat there calmly, alone, waiting for it all to end.

Then Polestar, the pride of the Freebooters, the great beacon of the third ring, came crashing down in a thunderous symphony of destruction that was unlike anything Mira had ever imagined.

"Zoey!" she yelled in anguish—but there was nothing anyone could do.

ZOEY'S ENTIRE BODY SHOOK, her knees buckling, the throbbing in her head unbearable. But still she held on.

She felt Max grab her pants in his teeth, try to pull her away, but she fought him off, too. "The Max has to go!" she yelled over the rumblings and crashings and screams in the air. *"Go!"*

The dog just growled, kept trying to drag her away.

Tears streamed from her eyes. This was all her fault, it was all—

She sensed something suddenly. A suggestion, like those from the Royal and the Mas'Erinhah. But it wasn't them. It was something else.

Scion, it said. *Let go.*

Zoey hesitated. She was confused, didn't understand.

It ends, the suggestion came again. *It falls. Let go.*

The sensations were growing stronger, their source was coming closer, racing toward her. Zoey opened her eyes and looked up.

Max howled as a five-legged, silver Assembly walker exploded through the stone wall that surrounded the courtyard. The same walker that had appeared twice before.

Zoey stared at it wide-eyed as it landed in front of them, barely able to keep control, barely able to hold on as the walker rushed toward her and Max.

We are here. Let go.

Zoey had little choice. The pain in her head was too much, her energy was spent. The golden light vanished around her, the connection with the Well severed, and she collapsed painfully to the ground.

Everything was a haze now. She could hear Max barking wildly next to her, could feel the giant, silver walker above her, and she could see the Gravity Well in front of her.

It flickered again—and then died, snuffed out like some massive candle wick. Snuffed out by *her*, Zoey thought with guilt.

The city roared above as it began to collapse straight down toward them.

The energy shield of the colorless Assembly walker flashed on, sealing them away in a wavering, powerful cocoon of light, as the world thundered apart around them and everything went black.

PART TWO

THE SEVERED TOWER

31. CONSTELLATIONS

BEN AND MIRA MADE CAMP in what was left of an old country church in the second ring, three days' journey from where the Time Shift had almost killed them at the antique shop. The building's roof had fallen in long ago, revealing the night sky, and where the ceiling used to be the stars burst apart in prismatic color, over and over again, like tiny fireworks forever in the distance. Something about the atmosphere over the second ring filtered and changed the light from the stars, and gave them this mesmerizing effect.

Mira and Ben were wrapped together under their blankets, her head on his chest, and it felt like they had lain there for weeks instead of hours. The photograph of her father was propped up on one of the church's old pews, and Mira stared at him, studying the lines around his eyes, the curve of his smile. They were things she never wanted to forget or lose, and she almost had.

"Is it just me," Ben asked, "or is it a little weird that we've been doing what we've been doing with him there?"

"No." Mira smiled. "He'd be happy, I think. Happy I was happy."

"You miss him a lot." Ben's fingers moved through her hair.

Mira nodded. "This picture's a good memory."

"Tell me another."

Mira thought a moment, then rolled over so she could stare up at the flashing sky through the ceiling.

"So, okay. That's Libra," Mira told him, pointing upward. "The big triangle, see it?"

"Yeah," Ben answered.

"East is Andromeda, and Scorpio is in between them."

"It's supposed to be a scorpion?" Ben asked skeptically.

"You have to use your imagination to see it," Mira replied softly. "It took my dad a million years to point out all the different stars to me before I saw the shape—but the whole time I never felt like he wanted to be anywhere else. And when I saw it, he was just as excited as I was. Every time I see it I think of him."

Ben stared up at the constellation thoughtfully. "It just looks like a bunch of dots to me. But I've never been very good with imagination."

Mira turned and studied him. "What do you know. Something Ben Aubertine isn't good at."

They lay there, watching each other in the firelight. "What would you do," Ben asked, "if you could do anything?"

Mira's answer came so easily, it surprised her. "Stop the Tone."

Ben nodded. "Why?"

"Because . . ." Mira felt a sting of pain at what she was about to say. The truth was it was always at the back of her mind, the one thing that drove her and kept her going. The possibility that not everything was lost. She looked at the photograph again. "Because maybe I could have my dad back."

"Me, too," he said. "That's why I wanted to be a Freebooter. To change things."

"Change them how?"

"There are ways. One way, really. If you found it, you could make it so the Assembly never came here. You could reset everything. Start it all over," he said, studying her. "You could see your dad again."

Mira stared back silently. She knew what he must mean.

In a land full of myths, the Severed Tower was the biggest one, the most glamorous and exciting. Supposedly, if you could reach and enter it, the Tower would make one wish come true. For Mira, it had always sounded too amazing to be real.

"It might not be a good idea to think like that, Ben," Mira said carefully.

"Why?"

"What if the Tower's not real? What if it's just something someone made up? What if you believe in it and you get there and it isn't what you think?"

"It's *real*," Ben said with conviction, "and I think I might be the only person in the world capable of making the right decision inside. I think it's what I'm supposed to do." His gaze refocused on her, turning serious. Or, at least, more serious than usual. "I don't know why I told you that. I've never told *anyone* that."

Mira smiled again. She liked knowing there were parts of him that were only accessible to her. "I've never met anyone like you, Ben. I don't know what the Tower is, or what happens when you're inside it, but if someone were supposed to go there . . . I think it would be you."

The barest glimpse of a smile formed in Ben's eyes. He leaned over and dug through his pack, pulling something out. It was a necklace, a gold chain with two small pendants. Mira recognized them instantly. They were brass dice, the same kind Ben juggled between his knuckles when he was thinking.

He slowly slid it around her neck and she took it in her fingers, watching the firelight reflect on the tiny brass surfaces.

"Now we each have something of the other," Ben said.

She looked up at him, confused. "What do you have of mine?"

"The best thing you could give me." Ben looked back up at the stars, at the constellation Scorpius. "Something to figure out."

Mira smiled and moved closer to him. "We'll work on that."

"You were wrong, you know," Ben said, serious again. "It's not me that's supposed to go to the Tower. It's *us*. In here we're one person. We can't survive alone, I know that now. I need you, and you need me."

Something about that statement, as sweet as it was, seemed . . . off. But Mira felt warmth spread through her nonetheless, pushing away the doubt. A warmth she hadn't felt in years. It was the feeling of belonging, of being home.

"I'll always protect you, Mira. Always keep you safe." Ben's fingers gently slid along the length of her jaw. "I *promise*."

They lay there holding each other, staring up at the sky where the stars shattered apart in bright, streaming flashes, over and over.

32. AI-KATANA

MIRA WOKE FROM EXPLODING STARS to the sounds of strange, fragmented thunder. The light around her was dim, and what little there was had been filtered to a sickly shade of yellow. It meant she was deeper into the Strange Lands. Soon there would be no light at all.

She blinked groggily, trying to push through the gloom. The horribly mournful sound of snapping metal and wood of Polestar as it fell was something she would hear the rest of her life. Platforms and buildings and memories, all of it cascading down in slow motion.

Mira closed her eyes, trying to seal it away, but it did no good.

"You were dreaming," someone said.

Mira opened her eyes. Holt sat with his back against what looked like the bottom rung of a set of bleachers.

They were in what was left of an old basketball arena, a high school one, judging by the banners and posters still clinging to some of the walls. ELECT WAYNE LEONARD CLASS VP one read. EMILY BRANDT FOR FIFTH GRADE TREASURER said another. The school had apparently been in the middle of student council elections when the Strange Lands had formed. More in a long list of decisions and choices that now would never be made.

Most of the gym had been blown apart by Antimatter lightning, and its walls were full of gaping holes that gave glimpses of the dark landscape outside, and the occasional flashing of red, green, or blue. The court rested in tattered pieces, about half of it consumed by glowing upsurges of Antimatter crystals.

The White Helix were there, too. A dozen of them, broken into three groups of four. Each group stood equidistant from the others in a triangle, practicing different skills. One group sparred against itself, their Lancets whizzing and humming through the air. Another worked agility drills, tumbling and balancing in handstands. The third practiced with their Antimatter rings, leaping high into the air, floating back to the ground, dashing from one point to another in blurs of motion, all while wrapped in flashes of different colors.

Every few minutes their small, fiery leader would clap her hands loudly. When she did, the Helix stopped what they were doing, moved clockwise to the next point of the triangle, and began training again, this time in a new skill.

Watching the White Helix train was something Mira never thought she would ever do, the kind of thing that would have thrilled her not that long ago. Now the sight failed to move her at all.

"You okay?" Holt asked.

Mira's answer came instantly. "No."

"We don't know she's dead."

"She might as well be." Mira didn't want to, but it was all she could think of now. Zoey alone in the Strange Lands, lost, helpless. If she wasn't crushed under the ruins of Polestar . . .

"That kid comes with a lot of surprises," Holt said. "I can't think we came all this way just to be stopped here."

"I can. She came with *me*." She felt Holt look at her.

"It wasn't your fault," he told her.

Mira's smile was full of irony. "Yes it was. It wouldn't have happened if she'd been with Ben."

"Ben left you to die, Mira," Holt said. "Took your plutonium, trapped you and ran. You really think *he's* who we should have trusted? I'd put her in your hands all over again."

Mira didn't say anything. Holt was biased, his feelings for her clouded his thoughts—and besides that, he didn't understand. Not really. No one did. No one except her and Ben and Echo and Deckard. Now she and Ben were the only ones left—and even Ben wasn't Ben anymore. Her eyes stung, started to glisten, and it made her angry. Just another sign of her weakness. Just more proof she didn't belong here.

The flashing of Antimatter lightning flared outside through the broken remains of the gymnasium walls. Everything beyond them seemed barren and lifeless.

"What happened here, Mira?" Holt asked softly.

Mira exhaled a long breath. Why not tell him? He deserved to know who he was traveling with. "To be a Freebooter you have to pass a trial. Mine was to go to a place called the Mix Master, in the second ring. It's a Gravity Well, but different than Polestar's."

Of course, Polestar and its Gravity Well no longer existed, did they? Mira tried to ignore the thoughts, kept talking.

"Ben was there, too," she said. "So were Echo and Deckard, and others. I had this plan to beat the Anomaly. I was only ten then, but still really impressed with myself." She paused, the memories and the guilt all coming back. "A group of people decided to follow my plan. And . . ."

"They died," Holt finished for her.

"Most of them. Not all. Echo survived. So did Ben. But not the rest. And it was my fault. They followed me, and they're not here anymore, same as Zoey."

Holt studied her. "These people. You made them come with you?"

Mira sighed. "It's not that simple."

"It was their choice, sounds like, and whatever your plan was, it couldn't have been all that bad. *You* survived it, didn't you? Maybe they just weren't as good as you. That's not your fault, either."

"I survived because of Ben," Mira whispered. "I couldn't have been a Freebooter without him. Hell, far as Deckard and a few others were concerned, I never should have been."

"But you made it this far *without* any of them. Didn't you?" Holt asked. "Why do you keep discounting everything you've done? It's like all you can see is the negative."

Mira turned to him, unable to find an argument, but also unable to bring herself to agree. He was right. Why *was* it so hard for her?

"The Arc is entering meditation." A sharp voice made them jump. The small girl, the White Helix leader, stood almost on top of them, still sweating from the morning training. Behind her the other Helix had disbanded. Neither Holt nor Mira had noticed her approach. It was disconcerting.

"Well," Holt replied, "thanks for the update."

The girl's stare didn't waver. "After meditation we leave for Sanctum. We'll get there tonight, if they haven't resettled."

"Who *are* you?" Mira asked.

"My name's Avril," the girl said, and Mira remembered the Forlorn Passage, how Ravan seemed to recognize the girl. "I am the Doyen of the twenty-seventh Arc of the White Helix. And I *had* been given the honor of returning the Prime to Sanctum, but that . . . isn't going to happen anymore, is it?" Her voice was bitter. That "honor," it seemed, was something she valued, but Mira felt no sympathy for her.

Avril balanced on one end of her Lancet. Where the sharpened, red spear point touched the tattered wooden floorboards, a thin trail of smoke began to rise. The crystal was burning through it, a testament to its power, and Holt studied the effect curiously.

"Can you . . . shoot those things?" he asked.

Mira's eyes moved to the Lancet. The weapons were infamous, even outside the Strange Lands. In a world of high alien technology and low-rent firearms from the World Before, the Lancet was an enigma. Ornate and well crafted, no two were exactly alike, but they were all the same in design. Long, close to five feet in length, with their colorful spear points of glowing Antimatter crystals. Avril's was made of dark cherrywood bound together with silver metal casings that contrasted each other like ice and fire. The spear point on the floor was red, while the one at the other end glowed green. A double helix was etched in white on either end of the weapon, both worn smooth from use.

Holt's question was spurred by one of the Lancet's most unique features, the dual hand grips and triggers on either side.

In answer, Avril spun and raised the Lancet in a blur, sighting down it like a rifle. There was a click as she pulled the trigger closest to her—and the crystal exploded from the end with a loud, strangely harmonic ping.

It ripped the air like a missile, and punched straight through the faded, black eye of a huge yellow jacket—the old school's mascot, most likely—on the far wall in a burst of red sparks, leaving nothing but a smoking hole.

"Huh." Holt studied the hole in the wall with a mix of fascination and skepticism. "Nice, but, seems to me, not all that practical. I mean, with only two shots, you'd better make them count, right?"

Avril pressed the glowing red Antimatter ring on her middle finger against a similar glowing crystal on the weapon's shaft. There was a spark and a rumbling from the distance. Then the same wall from before exploded outward in a shower of debris as the spear point burst *back through* it.

Avril's eyes found the projectile, raising her Lancet up and around. Another strange, harmonic ping ripped the air as the crystal slammed back into the end of the Lancet. Avril dispersed the inertia from the impact in a spin that landed her in low, agile crouch.

When it was done, she looked up at Holt and Mira.

"I . . . stand corrected," Holt remarked.

But while the show was definitely impressive, it only reinforced Mira's confusion about something. "It's never made sense to me," she said. "Why train for that? Why train so hard, way back in the deepest parts of the Strange Lands, where the only thing you run into is the occasional Freebooter?"

"I've asked the same question." Avril slowly stood back up. "We all have. Gideon says we will know when we are 'strong' enough—and we grow stronger every day."

Mira could hear the frustration in Avril's voice, and she understood. All that training, the development of skills, without any outlet to really use them. She saw the fall of Polestar again, remembered the White Helix leaping and riding the wreckage to the ground in bursts of color, yelling in excitement. At the time it had felt insane, but now she saw it was a release. The White Helix were caged panthers, Mira realized, eager to expend their formidable energy. It made them even more dangerous than they already were.

"But you can ask Gideon himself," Avril continued. "You'll meet him soon enough. Though I can't say you're all that important anymore. The Prime will reach Sanctum some other way, I suppose."

Mira sat up. "You know she's alive?"

"I can feel her. Everywhere. The Pattern moves whenever she moves."

"What does that mean?" Holt asked.

"Everything here is tied together," Avril said. "The Anomalies, the artifacts, the earth. The Strange Lands is all one thing now, blended together into something we call the Pattern; but we are separate from it, you and I, because we do not belong. We can sense it, we can avoid it, even dance and spin through it, but that's all. The Prime, though . . . *belongs*. When she moves, the Pattern ripples around her like water after a stone's throw. I've . . . never felt anything like it." Avril's voice was full of wonder—and something else. Fear, it sounded like. Mira wondered just what kind of mythology the White Helix had built up around Zoey, and why.

Holt jumped in surprise as someone grabbed him by the wrist. A tall White Helix, handsome, powerful but lean, with long, wavy hair. Like Avril before, no one had seen him coming. Holt struggled, but the Helix simply twisted his arm and pinned him facefirst onto the floor.

"Hey!" Mira shouted as she moved to get up, but more hands shoved her back down and kept her in place. The rest of the White Helix had surrounded them.

"Dane!" Avril yelled in anger.

Holt groaned as Dane pushed him harder against the floor, holding his right wrist, twisting it painfully so Avril could see what was there. The half-finished tattoo of a black bird, an image that marked him as something many people didn't like very much. Mira stared at the image and felt cold. She remembered Ravan's words. *We were much more than friends . . .*

"He's Menagerie!" Dane told Avril. *"Look!"*

Dane had lowered himself to a crouch, instead of centering his balance on his knees. It was a mistake. Holt had been in enough fight-or-die situations to develop his own instincts, and he lashed out and swept Dane's left foot completely off the floor. The Helix lost his balance and tumbled backward with wide eyes.

Holt twisted around, and when he did his fist connected hard with Dane's jaw and sent him crashing down. The Lancet burst from Dane's hands and skittered toward Mira. She grabbed and aimed it at the boy. She might not know how to fire it, but she could definitely thrust it forward.

The other Lancets around them all pointed at her and Holt, but it didn't matter now, and she and Dane both knew it. They might kill them—but Dane would die first. She kept the blue glowing spear point at his throat.

"You think that's the first time someone's pinned my arm?" Holt asked sourly, staring back at Dane. "You guys really *have* been out here too long."

Out the corner of her eye, past all the humming spear points, Mira noticed one odd thing. Avril's Lancet wasn't raised. She just stared at the charged situation around her.

"Stand down. Everyone," she said with slow, pointed words that dripped with anger.

"But—" one of them started. Avril kicked outward in a blur of motion, her body covered in bright white light. The boy towered over the small girl, but he went flying backward as if he weighed nothing, and slammed to the ground. The others stared at her warily.

"I am Doyen," Avril's voice was ice, "and it displeases me to repeat myself. Stand down. *Now.*"

The others immediately lowered their Lancets and took two steps back, but their eyes stayed on Holt and Mira. So did Dane's.

"Dane," Avril said slowly. "Apologize for your actions."

"What?" The boy's eyes shifted to Avril's. There was shock in them. "Avril—"

At the use of her first name, Avril's stare turned to pure heat. Her voice was barely audible. "*What* did you call me?"

The anger in Dane's face dropped away immediately. He looked down, clearly aware of some grievous transgression. "Forgive me, Doyen. I . . . forget myself."

Calling Avril by her first name apparently was a violation of some rule, and her reaction showed it was a bad one to break. But he hadn't just used her name, Mira noticed. He'd used it with *familiarity*. He was used to calling her that, it was obvious, and it made her wonder about the relationship between Dane and Avril when they were alone, and whether or not *that* was against the rules, too.

"You have dishonored this Arc," Avril spoke with venom. "You have attacked a helpless enemy without provocation, and, more importantly, you have lost your weapon to the hands of that enemy. You will apologize to both of them and when you are done, you will spend your meditation period and the *entire* trek to Sanctum practicing walking Spearflow. Maybe that will help you learn to hold your Lancet with a tighter grip. Do you understand?"

Dane forced himself to look at Holt and Mira, the glowing, pointed end of his own Lancet still aimed at his throat. "I . . . apologize for attacking you. It was dishonorable, and shameful to myself, my Arc, and my Doyen."

Holt and Mira glanced at one another, unsure.

"Ask the Freebooter if she will give you your weapon back," Avril told him.

Dane looked sharply up again. Avril stared back coldly. "You look surprised. Have you forgotten *all* your oaths, or just this one? You have committed *ai-Katana*. Your weapon now belongs to your enemy. She can keep it if she wishes. It is her right, but that will be the end of your honor."

There was a slight hint of pain in Avril's words. A glimpse of feeling that only another girl would notice. Mira's suspicions about her and Dane were all but confirmed. It hurt Avril to punish him this way, but she had no choice. She was a leader. She had responsibilities beyond her own feelings, and the revelation stirred something in Mira. Images of the Mix Master flashed in her mind.

Perhaps she and Avril weren't all that different.

Dane's gaze slowly shifted back to Mira. She saw a mixture of emotions there. Shame, anger, fear. "Freebooter, my weapon is yours," he said slowly. "May I . . . have it back?" The words, it was clear, were incredibly painful for him to say.

Mira looked at Holt. He just shrugged. Her choice.

She held the Lancet against Dane's throat a moment longer—then handed it to him. Dane slowly took it and stood up. The tension in the gymnasium began to release.

"Spearflow," Avril said tightly. "Now. The rest of you will do double meditation to ponder and learn from Dane's mistakes."

Dane turned and moved away without argument. So did the others. Avril, however, stared at Mira and Holt. "I apologize for Dane. He is . . . passionate. It's his weakness," she told them. "We have that in common, Gideon says."

"Passionate's . . . definitely a good word for it," Holt replied, rubbing his wrist.

Mira saw the girl's eyes drift downward to the unfinished tattoo. "Do you know who I am?"

"Yes," Holt said.

Avril nodded, her stare hardened. "Archer's dead. Isn't he?"

At the words, Holt stiffened. "Yes."

Avril's eyes never left the tattoo on Holt's wrist, but they filled with some kind of deep, complicated emotion. Mira had no idea who Archer was, but Avril had certainly known him, and her feelings on the matter were conflicted. "Did he . . . die well?"

"I wish I could say he did," Holt answered, and there was something dark in his voice.

Avril's grip on her Lancet tightened. "It doesn't matter. The Menagerie will *not* have me. My place is here."

"You have my word," Holt said back carefully, "I am not here for you, and I am *not* Menagerie."

Avril held his stare a moment more, then turned and moved off toward the others. Mira watched the girl walk away, finally feeling her pulse starting to calm. "What was that all about?"

"Avril is the reason Ravan and her men are here," Holt answered. "They're trading whatever they're carrying in that crate for her."

"Trading . . . For a specific White Helix?" It didn't make sense.

"She's not just a White Helix. She's Tiberius's *daughter.*"

Mira's eyes widened in shock. "As in Tiberius *Marseilles?*"

Holt just nodded. Mira looked back to Avril, at the other end of the gym, with new curiosity. Tiberius Marseilles was a famous figure and for all the wrong reasons. He was powerful—the founder and leader of the Menagerie pirate guild. And frightening. She knew, she had dealt with him once, long ago, made a deal and almost gotten killed for it. Her reward, her only reward, had been the Solid she'd used to make Ravan help her rescue Zoey, and it was no small thing to get, that Solid.

"Did you know her?" Mira asked, eyes still on the girl.

"No. She left long before I showed up. Didn't exactly see eye to eye with her dad. Not like her brother, anyway."

"Archer?" The pieces were starting to fit.

Holt nodded. "He's dead now. It's why Ravan's here."

"I still don't understand."

"Archer and Avril aren't Tiberius's natural children," Holt said. "He traded for them, at great expense. Twins, Heedless like himself, a girl and a boy. He wanted a legacy, something to last once he was gone. Archer and Avril would have carried on the Marseilles leadership of the Menagerie into the future, but Avril didn't stick around. She came here."

Across the distance, Avril caught Mira's gaze for a split second before she sat down with her men, crossed her legs, rested her palms on her knees, and closed her eyes. Silence fell over the gym as the White Helix's meditation began.

Something occurred to Mira. Something dark. "How did Archer die, Holt?"

His voice was low. "That's not something I like talking about."

"If things are going to be anything like what they used to be between us, I think you have to."

Holt didn't look at her, just stared at the ground, thinking. Whatever he had to say, whatever the truth was, it wasn't something he liked dredging up. Mira felt trepidation, waiting for him to respond. It was what she had wanted to know, of course, but she hoped whatever it was didn't shatter the rest of her feelings for him.

"Like I said, I never knew Avril. She left before I got to Faust," Holt finally said, and Mira had to slide closer to hear. "But Archer I knew. For a while he was a friend. He was . . . Volatile isn't the right word. He swung one way or another, and you never knew what he might do or when. Lavished his friends one second, then threatened to have them executed. When he was good, he was very good. When he wasn't, he . . . wasn't."

Holt kept staring at the wooden floor, slowly tracing patterns in the dust with his finger while he talked. Mira had only heard his voice this conflicted when he'd told her about his sister, about how he felt responsible for her loss.

"Archer was in love with a girl at Faust," Holt continued. "Her name was Evelyn. Pretty girl, hair almost as dark as Ravan's. She was a cook, had a food stall in the Commerce Segment, made these really great puffed pastries. Always reminded me of Pop-Tarts, you remember those?"

Mira did, and smiled in spite of herself. She liked the strawberry ones best.

"Archer loved Evelyn, but it wasn't mutual. She loved someone else. She told Archer, told him nicely even, and that was not a smart thing to do." Holt stared at the patterns he'd made in the dust on the floor. "Sometimes I wonder how obsessed he would have been if she'd just given in to him once or twice. He would have moved on, found something else, it was his way. He couldn't hold onto any one desire very long.

"But she didn't. She refused him. Pointedly. And Archer Marseilles was definitely not used to that. He went to his father. Tiberius rarely denied him anything, especially things he thought were trivial, like some little girl who made pastries in the market. He decreed they were to be married. The next day. So Evelyn and the other boy did the only thing they could."

Mira could guess what it was. "They ran."

Holt nodded. "Tiberius was furious. Now it was serious—someone had defied the Menagerie leader, and that was something he couldn't let stand. So he sent Ravan and me to find them. It was what we were good at, after all," Holt said with a note of bitterness. "Pastry cook and a blacksmith, both about fifteen? Yeah, they didn't make it very far. Didn't know how to move fast or cover their tracks, and they certainly didn't know how to handle someone like Ravan. It wasn't much of a chase, is what I'm saying. We brought them back, and when we did, they dragged the boy off to the gallows and Evelyn up to Archer's room.

"They started my tattoo that night," Holt said, his voice growing more animated with repressed feeling, and Mira felt a chill build in her. "It was my reward. Was going to start with a star point, a rare thing, but Tiberius was grateful, and generous when it came to Archer. I didn't even feel the needle, I just stared up the Pinnacle to Archer's room. I could see the lights there, flickering, candles or a lantern. I knew what was going to happen there. I could hear the crowd roaring at the gallows. I knew what was going to happen there, too."

Holt studied his half-finished tattoo. "I looked down at the thing forming on my wrist, and . . . it was hideous to me. Bigger it got, the more dread I felt. I told them I needed a break, told Ravan I'd be back. She gave me this odd look, I remember, like a part of her knew or guessed, but, still, she didn't follow me. At the time I didn't think she would have understood. I'm still not sure she would have."

The statement was an admission of just how close Holt and Ravan had been, but Mira's views on everything now were so conflicted, she wasn't sure what she felt about it.

"I moved fast as I could, knew I could only save one of them, there wasn't time for both. I chose Evelyn. I don't know why, maybe because I knew her better, the girl with the Pop-Tarts. Maybe because I thought her fate was going to be worse than the boy's. Who knows." Holt looked out through one of the gaping holes in the gymnasium, watching the lightning flash outside. "I went to Archer's room, I burst inside—and I'd gotten there before it happened. He'd pinned her on his bed, he had a knife. I told him to stop, to get off her. Archer just stared at me. Then he laughed. He didn't really believe I'd do anything to stop him. After all, I'd always stood by before, everyone had—stood by and let him do whatever he wanted—but . . . not this time. I told him I'd shoot him between the eyes if I had to. Told him he had to let her go. He didn't listen, he just laughed again, told me I could stay and watch if I wanted, and then moved back towards her with the knife. So I shot him."

Mira exhaled her tension. She wasn't sure what she felt.

"It was clean, one bullet," Holt said, his voice a whisper once more. "The girl screamed, I remember that. I grabbed her and pulled her out of there, got my things and left. We barely made it out before they sealed the city. Worst part was, coming back down—we heard the cheers at the gallows, we knew what had happened. I saved that girl's life, but there wasn't any gratitude. She didn't look at me with any less revulsion than she had Archer. I remember that, too. Maybe if I'd saved them both, but . . . I didn't."

"What happened to her?" Mira asked.

"Covered our tracks for three days, laid false trails. I knew Tiberius would send Ravan, and that he would want me dead, but she never found me. Not sure if that was because I knew her so well—or if she let me go. Either way, I set the girl loose, got her on a Landship for Winterbay. Never heard from her again."

Holt kept his stare on the floor. Mira watched him sit there, reliving everything, torturing himself all over again. She knew how he felt, she suddenly realized. All this time she felt distant from him, even looked down on him for just *almost* being in the Menagerie, but the truth was, she was no better. She'd made similar mistakes. She'd tried to fix them in similar ways, and she lived with the consequences, just like him.

Mira reached out and pulled Holt to her. He rested his head on her shoulder as she ran her fingers through his crazy, unkempt hair.

"Why do we . . . make our decisions after it's too late?" Holt asked quietly. "Even when they seem obvious. Why don't we make them right there and then, instead?"

It was a question Mira had asked herself many times. "I don't know."

They both sat there staring out at the ever-darkening landscape beyond the walls of the crumbled gym.

33. AMBASSADOR

EVERYTHING WAS DARK AND SILENT. Peaceful even. But within all the blankness, Zoey sensed something like movement. Wavering bands of light floating in the emptiness, but not of any specific color. It seemed, instead, like a mix of all of them, blended into a spinning shape that was there and not there, always just out of view.

Zoey had seen colors like this before. When she was with the Royal and his Hunters. It was how their presences manifested in her head. Which meant, wherever she was, a similar presence was close to her now.

Scion. You are safe.

It was a projection of pure sensation shoved into her mind, and the words were the closest Zoey could get to its most intrinsic meaning. It was exactly how the Royal communicated with her, but this was not that presence. It was different. It wavered at a different speed.

Zoey stirred and opened her eyes, and was surprised to find the real world just as black.

As she did, another "presence" made itself known, this one of a more physical variety. It was hairy and warm. It whined and pressed against her. Zoey smiled in spite of everything, as it licked her face.

"The Max . . ."

The dog was just a dark, squirming shadow in all the black, and when Zoey tried to pet him she found she couldn't. Something hard and cold surrounded her on all sides, like a metallic coffin, and she couldn't move.

The realization brought with it a surge of memories. She remembered the Gravity Well flickering and fading to nothing, and the sound of the giant city above her collapsing.

Zoey's smile vanished. Panic sunk in. She was trapped. Buried alive surely, in some dark hole, crushed underneath all the weight of Polestar's remains, and she would never be found. She would lay there, imprisoned, unable to move, until the darkness finally faded. The thought was terrifying. Zoey screamed and squirmed in the tiny, metallic space that was her tomb, trying to—

The walls of the coffin lifted powerfully and slowly up and off her. Gears and actuators twisted, mechanics hummed. It was a machine of some kind, held aloft by five giant legs. The world around her groaned and rumbled as the thing somehow displaced the impossible weight of the ruined city which had buried it.

Max barked wildly, and Zoey pulled him close against her. She knew now what had been resting on top of her, and it was more than just the ruins of Polestar.

It was an Assembly walker. The one without any colors, the one that had been following her, the one that appeared right before everything came crashing down and covered her at the fall.

Scion. Be still.

The flickering light from the thing's energy shield pushed the darkness away and surrounded them in a curving sphere that stretched about ten feet in every direction. Beyond that, Zoey could see the remains of Polestar, a now solid, crumpled mass of wood and metal and pipes and shattered glass, all of it pressed heavily against the walker's shield, the only thing protecting them from being crushed.

There was an electronic, distorted rumbling, and Max growled at the sound. Zoey's first impulse was to push away from the machine, but there was nowhere to go. Not here.

Scion. You are safe. Be still.

Zoey didn't feel reassured. What was she going to do? The shield around them seemed to flicker more and more, like it was weakening. With all the weight pressing on it, she wasn't surprised. How long until it finally gave out? Her panic rose, she felt tears forming.

Scion. Be still. We are here.

But we're trapped. She instinctually projected her thoughts, just like the Royal had shown her. *Are we . . . going to die?*

There was a pause before the walker responded. *Die. Cease to be.*

It seemed unsure, as if having difficulty understanding the concept. She wasn't sure why, but the idea of death to the Assembly was not something well understood. Somehow, death, while possible, was not a forgone conclusion for the aliens, and the concept carried a tremendous weight.

No, Scion, the walker projected back, *we can remain. But you must understand.*

The shield outside flickered brightly, the weight of all the metal and wood and debris pressing down on it groaned. The ruins were winning, it looked like. The shield would fall soon.

We can shift. But you must touch us.

Zoey couldn't make sense of that. Maybe she had translated it wrong, or maybe there was simply no real translation.

I don't understand, she thought.

We can shift. Somewhere else.

Zoey thought back to the first time she saw the walker, how it appeared from thin air in a flash of light. It had done something similar at the Crossroads. Maybe "shifting" meant . . . teleporting? Could it get them out of this place and back into the open air?

Yes. The machine sensed her thoughts. *Touch us and we will shift.*

The shield flickered again, the city's corpse rumbling. Zoey didn't hesitate. She held onto the Max with one hand and thrust her other up, touching the undershell of the armored walker.

No. Touch us.

The ruins groaned horribly. The Max barked wildly. Zoey felt her panic begin to rise again. *I am!*

No. Touch us.

Her hand was firmly pressed into the walker's metallic plating, she *was* touching it. But . . . was the machine really who she was communicating with? Or was it the complex crystalline shape inside? If so, then how did it expect her to touch it?

The shield flickered violently suddenly . . . and *shrank* inward! The ruins outside thundered as they shook, falling just a little bit. There wasn't much time.

Zoey couldn't reach inside and touch the entity with her hands, but there was one way she knew she could. She wrapped her arms around the Max and shut her eyes. Zoey reached out with her mind, concentrating on the swirling mass of color in the darkness, pressing her consciousness towards it. When she did, the colors exploded in prismatic brilliance, and she felt energy wash through her.

Then there was a sound. Like a powerful blast of static and noise, and a quick wave of heat washed over her. The Max howled. Zoey's stomach clenched, her ears rang—and then it was over.

A new silence was broken by the whine of gears as the walker slowly stepped off of Zoey and Max. The little girl opened her eyes and gasped.

The infinite, crushing mass of debris that had buried them was gone. Instead there was *daylight*. Not the sickly, muted light from the Strange Land's interior, this was *full* sunlight, bright and strong, and Zoey sighed at the feel of it. What was more, the pain in her head was mercifully gone. One possibility occurred to her. The walker had teleported them some-where *outside* the Strange Lands.

Just like that.

Zoey peered up at the machine. Like all Assembly, it had the same red, green, and blue three-optic eye, and the sensor whirred and rotated as it studied her, then shifted to Max as the dog let out a single, defensive bark. Zoey quieted him, pulling him back. "It's okay. I don't think it saved us just to hurt us." The Max seem unconvinced.

Zoey stared up at the powerful machine. She was closer to it this time, and, for once, she wasn't running for her life. It meant she could study it in detail. Its five legs were spaced equally around its body, and were the thickest and most powerful of any she'd seen. Its fuselage was blockier and somehow looked more solid, too. Zoey remembered she had never seen it fire weapons. It had always barreled into opponents. Is that what it was designed for? Just as the Hunters were designed for stealth and speed?

Scion. A new projection entered her mind. *You remain*.

Remain. It was hard, translating the Assembly's images and feelings, but that was as close as she could get. The entity inside the machine had used that expression earlier. Then, it had meant "alive." Maybe it meant the same now.

Thank you, Zoey projected back at the walker. *Are we out of the Strange Lands?*

A simple thought entered her mind in answer. *Yes.*

How?

We shifted.

Can you . . . "shift" anywhere you want? Zoey was curious. If so, it was an amazing ability.

Only where we have been. The machine stood motionless, its multicolored optic eye the only point of movement, whirring and rotating. The eye never seemed to keep still, shifting just bare inches, up and down, left and right, as if analyzing her inch by inch. Zoey chuckled. It was funny-looking, that eye, like some kind of big, spasming bug caught in a jar.

Have you been following me? Zoey asked.

We are few, but we are not one.

Zoey's eyes thinned. *There are more of you?*

Zoey's head filled with images. She saw more walkers, some she had seen before, like Spiders and Mantises, and others, a dozen or more, all painted various colors. She saw several like the one in front of her, big, stocky, five-legged brutes, each painted a dark shade of purple.

Laser light streamed over them, sizzling away their colors, stripping them down to bare metal. When it was over, their silver bodies flashed in the sun.

You . . . removed your colors, Zoey thought up at the walker.

We do not believe, it projected back.

In what?

In you.

Zoey blinked, staring at the machine. Something about that simple statement had a hint of menace in it. *I don't understand. Why are you helping me?*

You are the Scion. You are the first.

The first of what?

Many.

At the projection, she felt a sudden, strong outpouring of emotion from the machine, and it wasn't what she expected. She had never felt anything like this from the Royal, its emotions had all been exactly how she would have predicted. Strong, menacing, and arrogant. These were altogether different.

Why are you sad? Zoey projected.

New, vivid imagery filled her mind. She saw a crystalline shape, beautiful as always, but it wasn't golden. This one was a distinct shade of indigo, and it fluctuated like purple silk made into light.

A million sensations and feelings and presences, all in the background, all fighting to be heard and felt, throbbed in her consciousness. She sensed the severing of some connection. The loss of those millions of voices. Then . . . nothing but silence.

These were its memories, Zoey somehow knew. It had made a choice. And she thought she knew what that choice was.

You're alone now, she thought. *Without the others' thoughts.*

Zoey understood. Whatever the Assembly were, whatever their nature, they were all connected together. Their thoughts and feelings and emotions all swirled in one giant storm that each was always touching, and this one, the silver one, had made a choice to cut itself free from that connection. As powerful as it was, as strong and bold, it was sad at the loss. Even a little frightened. For the first time in probably eons . . . it was alone.

Zoey couldn't help but think about her own abilities, the way she could read people, how their thoughts and feelings came crashing into her mind without warning. The more that ability had developed, the more she disliked it. It was never quiet when others were around, even others she loved, like Holt and Mira. Ironically, the being in front of her had lived with far more voices in its "head" for far longer—and seemed to *prefer* it that way.

I have something to ask. Indeed she did. Maybe the most important question in her entire world. One that the Royal had refused to answer, and punished her for even asking. One no one seemed able or willing to explain. *What do the Assembly want with me?*

The walker's eye spun as it considered her. *It is dangerous.*

What is?

The truth.

What did that mean? Answering the question would be dangerous?

Your memories, the machine continued. *They were removed.*

Yes. It was true. Zoey had no memories from before Holt found her, even though the Oracle had shown her evidence that she should. *You took them away.*

For good reason, the entity replied. *It is dangerous.*

Zoey sighed. Clearly, this one wasn't going to tell her any more than the others. It only made her desire to reach the Tower that much stronger.

Do you have a name? Zoey asked now.

No, the machine projected in reply. *Names are of you. Not of us.*

I have to call you something. Zoey thought about it, studying the machine curiously. *What do you do?*

Our function?

Yes.

There was long pause before the walker answered. *Ambassador.*

Ambassador? Zoey thought back, confused.

From those with no colors. Ambassador to the Scion.

Zoey smiled, said the name out loud. "Ambassador." It did have a nice ring to it. "I like it. It's your name. Okay?"

We have . . . a name? the walker projected.

Zoey nodded.

Ambassador. The machine's multicolored eye whirred and spun. *It is agreeable.*

Something else occurred to Zoey. *The others don't want me to reach the Tower, do they?*

No.

But they can't get through the Strange Lands.

Few have the electives.

Electives?

Attributes chosen by color, Ambassador projected. *Few have the electives to pass through this place. It was never anticipated.*

"The Mas'Erinhah," Zoey said out loud. "They can pass through."

Yes. Apparently, Ambassador could understand her spoken words as well as her thoughts. *They have proper electives. They are coming. We will take you.*

"Take me where?"

The broken place, it projected. *You say, the Severed Tower.*

Max barked as Ambassador took a powerful step forward. Clearly, it meant to take her there on its own.

"Wait!" Zoey held up a hand in alarm, took a step back—and the giant machine stopped. Its eye whirred and focused on her.

Zoey stared at the walker curiously, something occurring to her. "Take a step backward," she commanded.

Instantly, the walker stepped back with its powerful legs.

Zoey smiled. "Turn right."

Max barked again as the walker rotated where it stood, facing to the right.

"Turn left."

The machine obeyed.

"Turn all the way around back to me."

The silver machine revolved in place until it stood facing her again. Max barked even louder, watching the huge machine do Zoey's bidding.

You have to do what I say? Zoey projected.

You are the Scion, came the response. *You have named us.*

Then you aren't taking me to the Tower, Zoey thought firmly.

Where, then?

Zoey knew what she wanted, but was it the best thing? Were they any safer without her? Maybe. But the Oracle had shown her things, and it had indicated Holt and Mira were a part of them. Zoey had a feeling she needed them, and, just maybe, that they needed her, too.

"I want to find my friends," Zoey said. "I want you to take me to them." Ambassador's eye studied her in a way that somehow seemed disapproving.

SUNLIGHT WAS A FORGOTTEN thing. The world was dark, the sky full of obsidian clouds that let loose dangerous flashes of color. Strange thunder rolled everywhere.

But the one the Scion named the Royal paid none of it any mind. Its concentration was on the remains of the large human encampment, now nothing but a smoking, charred pile of broken debris, flames still licking along its edges. Eventually it would only be ash, and just as forgotten as the sunlight.

But ruined cities did not interest the Royal. Only the Scion did.

She had been here, it knew. She and the wretched Mas'Shinra that festered inside her. Certainly it had been helping her all this time. It would need to be removed, and there were ways to accomplish that. Then the Royal would have the honor of inhabiting the Scion, of being the first of many. The Mas'Erinhah would take their rightful place as Those Blended with White.

But first it had to find her.

Above it, from the south, came the sudden roaring of engines.

A mass of aircraft decloaked, two different types, all painted bright green and orange. One kind was smaller, more lithe, with two gleaming cannons, their armored shells like half circles set on their end, the curved part facing behind. The second type was bigger, with two powerful, rotating engines on either wing, and two or three walkers dangled underneath each one. Dropships. Reinforcements.

The airships floated and bounced, trying to regain control in the chaotic turbulence. It was difficult. A flash of green lightning lanced downward in a shower of sparks into one of the smaller ships. It spun in a crazy descent and slammed into a dropship. Both ships listed badly and tumbled down, crashing into the ground in a giant blossom of flame.

The Royal trumpeted angrily. The Mas'Erinhah were one of the few clans whose Electives allowed them to pass through this land, but, still, it would not be easy. It would lose half its forces hunting the Scion, but that was why it had summoned so many. In the end, it would all be worth it.

From the burning wreckage of the crashed airships came a burst of light. The Ephemera were leaving their Hosts, forming into their golden, fluctuating, crystalline shapes. They had no choice, their machines were burning, but it was clear something was wrong.

The shapes, bright as they were, flickered weakly, the energy that encompassed them losing cohesion. It couldn't form, couldn't solidify. The Royal, and every other Mas'Erinhah, felt the sensations that bled off the Ephemera and colored the Whole with their light.

Pain, dread—and fear.

The light of the Ephemera dimmed as the Royal and his Hunters watched. The energy stored within those shapes dissipated into nothing, vanishing into the air like gold liquid thrown into the sea. At their loss, even of just a few, the Whole grew less colorful, less bright.

The Royal trumpeted in frustration. It was this place. Its kind could not survive here, not out of their Hosts, and it sensed more fear stirring the Whole. But it would not tolerate weakness.

It projected its anger and resolution, and its forces responded. The fear vanished, the doubt, too. They would follow, even to their destruction. They had no choice.

Behind them the dropships began to unload their cargo, depositing new walkers onto the torn, fragmented ground, amid the glowing crystals that dotted it. One after the other, hundreds of them, filling the darkened landscape with their numbers.

34. NEW FRIENDS

HOLT AND MIRA FOLLOWED THE WHITE HELIX north in a seemingly unending march through what was once North Dakota. Now it was a nightmarish world: oppressive, dark, absent of life. The foliage had all died long ago without sunlight, and the spidery, unsettling remains of dead trees were the only indication it had ever been anything else. Green lightning flashed, and the strange, everpresent aurora field wavered in the black sky.

They had been following an old train track the last few miles, and now they had come to an obstacle. Holt took another precarious step across the top of the old train, trying to balance in the dark. Its roof was wide and solid, but that wasn't the issue. The problem was the sheer drops on either side that streaked down to a shadowy river hundreds of feet below. The remainder of the train, dozens of cars, had broken loose of their tracks and tumbled over the edge, and if Holt looked behind him he would see all of them, *hanging in the air*, paused in time as they fell, the bridge breaking into pieces.

They were in what Mira called a Time Loop. Where the semitruck from a few days ago came unstuck if you touched it, this train and the disintegrating bridge entered back into real time at fixed intervals. They had less than eleven minutes before that happened, according to Avril. The train would unstick in time and the entire thing would come crashing down—and then it would all go back to how it was—frozen, waiting to repeat again.

Holt tried not to think about it. He hated this place.

Mira was behind him, moving between two White Helix escorts. The others were already across.

During the entire journey so far, Dane had practiced what Avril called the "Spearflow." It was intense weapon practice coordinated with his movement. Each step he took resulted in a different form or swing of the Lancet. After watching it awhile, Holt could see a pattern. It took about seven minutes to go through one entire repetition of the Spearflow.

Dane suffered his punishment quietly, sweating profusely, but he never faltered, never slowed, and he never took a break. There was always a moment near the middle of the exercise where he spun and walked backward, and each time he did, he glared directly at Holt. And every time Holt held the stare. He had no animosity toward Dane, but the feeling clearly wasn't mutual.

That was a problem for later. Right now, Holt's concern was crossing over the top of this train without plummeting to the river below. He carefully moved his feet one step at a time.

"Is it possible for you to go any slower?" Mira asked from behind. "I only ask because the White Helix and I have a bet."

"You ever hear 'measure twice, cut once'?" Holt retorted without taking his eyes off his feet. "I'm applying a similar principle."

"Slower isn't always better. We need to get clear of this thing, and we have, like, three minutes to do it."

"And the Outlander plans on using all three," the Helix behind them observed. "Never seen anyone make putting one foot in front of the other look tough." The boy was a little shorter than Holt, but a little bigger, too, with short brown hair and the same easy gait that all White Helix possessed. His name was Castor. The Helix girl in front of them was Masyn. She was taller than Avril but just as lithe, with long, blond hair tied in a braid that hung down her back and brushed the top of her Lancet.

"Works for me," Masyn said. "Always wanted to ride this thing down, anyway."

"I'd prefer we didn't," Holt said testily. The entire time they'd been moving across the train, Masyn had been entertaining herself with somersaults, skipping backward, or doing handsprings. Right now she was walking on her hands, and it was unsettling to watch, with the dropoffs on either side, but it didn't seem to bother her. That only made Holt like her even less.

"Then move, Outlander," Castor said from behind.

Holt sighed and took another step, staring down warily.

"We have names, you know," Mira said. They'd been called Freebooter or Outlander since they'd left Polestar, and it was starting to get old. "I'm Mira. He's Holt."

"And I don't care," Castor replied. "Walk."

Holt took another step. Masyn was maybe only a year younger than Mira, but, oddly, the creep of the Tone in her eyes was much less prevalent than it should be. Castor's eyes were more solidly filled in, but he was old enough that he should have Succumbed already. Holt had seen the same thing in the eyes of the other Helix. For them, the Tone seemed to advance slower, probably because of the Strange Lands's effect on time. If more people knew about that particular advantage to being White Helix, Holt wondered how many more would make the journey every year.

Ahead of them, Avril stood impatiently with her arms crossed, watching them move over the train. Dane was behind them, still stepping back and forth, practicing with his Lancet. He was drenched, but showed no signs of weakening. The rest of the White Helix waited there as well.

"What's Avril going to do with us?" Mira asked.

"Avril isn't going to do anything with you," Masyn said, gently lowering her feet back down and walking again. "It's not her place. It's Gideon's."

"Gideon's your leader?" Mira asked.

"Our teacher. A great man."

"Because he makes you strong?" Holt asked back carefully. It was a phrase he'd heard the White Helix use a number of times. It must mean something. Masyn turned around and studied him curiously.

"No," she said. "The Pattern does that. Not Gideon."

"You mean the Strange Lands," Mira said. "How do *they* make you strong?"

"By weeding out the weak," Castor answered. "When one of us falls, the rest grow stronger."

"How Darwinian of you," Holt observed.

"Gideon says it's the way of all things," Masyn continued, slowly somersaulting backward. "Here most of all. It's making us ready."

Ready for *what?* Holt wondered. He started to ask more, then froze, looking past the train to the end of the bridge. "Where'd your pals go?" he asked. There was no sign of the White Helix now. All ten of them were simply gone, as though they had vanished. Everyone turned and followed Holt's gaze, staring at the empty space at the end of the bridge where Avril and her Arc had been.

"That's . . . never a good sign," Masyn stated, alarmed.

"Well, that makes me feel much better," Holt replied.

"If they're gone, they have a reason." Castor unslung the Lancet from his back. Masyn did the same. "Keep going."

Holt didn't argue. He started moving again, faster than before. One step, another—and then something flashed ahead of them, near where the others had been. Something big—reflective enough that it amplified what little light there was in the darkened landscape.

"Outlander!" Castor exclaimed behind them.

"Holt—" Mira started in exasperation.

"Wait," Holt said, staring ahead.

"There's nothing there but—" The air around them fizzled suddenly. Little sparkles of light materialized and floated like fireflies. Holt studied them in confusion, and then looked at Mira. Her eyes were wide with alarm.

"It's syncing back!" she shouted, and shoved him forward.

Holt darted forward across the metal roof with abandon now. The static hiss in the air grew louder and he could feel the train underneath him begin to vibrate through his shoes. Things were about to get unpleasant.

They kept running. The end of the train was in sight, they were—

The sparkles in the air doubled, tripled, became so many that Holt's vision turned white. The hiss of static drowned out everything. Then a jarring roar filled the air as the train and the bridge violently reconnected with the timeline.

Holt heard Mira scream, thought he saw Castor and Masyn leap clear in flashes of purple. The world upended, the aurora in the sky rolled past over and over, as the sounds of grinding metal and snapping wood filled the air, Holt free-fell down toward—

Everything went pure white.

Within the white he saw something. Something familiar. Holt saw *Zoey*. Standing still, staring at him, all around her a strange, vibrating flux of colored light that was both a part of her and separate at the same time.

There was a sound like a powerful, punctuated blast of distorted noise, and a quick wave of heat. Holt gasped, his stomach clenched, his ears rang . . .

He rolled over onto his back and opened his eyes.

Through the eerie, twisted fingers of dead trees, the strange aurora wavered. He wasn't in the middle of a raging river or crushed beneath tons of train cars. He was alive in the woods, and everything was quiet.

Mira stared at him, also on her back, her eyes full of confusion. "I saw . . ." she started slowly.

"Zoey," Holt said, holding her look.

A strange, electronic rumble sounded above them. They both looked up . . .

. . . right into the red, green, and blue three-optic eye of an Assembly combat walker. Five legs, a powerful, blocky body, armor bereft of color. It was the same one that had appeared twice before, and now it stood almost on top of them.

It was so surprisingly surreal that neither really reacted. They just looked at it, stunned, watching the strange eye whir and spin, left and right, studying them back.

"Hi, Holt," a tiny voice said behind them. Both Mira and Holt turned. Zoey stood there, smiling. "Hi, Mira."

Each of them stared at the little girl with the same blank look.

"Zoey . . ." Mira whispered, still unsure. It only took a few more seconds before it all clicked. *"Zoey!"* Mira lunged toward the little girl and pulled her close. Zoey giggled at the attention.

Before Holt could move, something big and furry slammed into him and knocked him back to the ground. Max wiggled on top of him, licking his face. Holt laughed and petted the dog, rubbing his head and ears. He felt just as much relief seeing Max as he did Zoey. He hadn't really been sure if he would ever see either again.

Holt looked past Max at Zoey. The little girl stared through Mira's red hair and smiled at him. "I get a hug, too?"

Mira let Zoey go and watched her run to Holt. He looked at Mira as he held her, and they shared the same emotion.

"You okay?" Holt asked Zoey.

"Yeah," Zoey said. "Ambassador brought me here. I asked him to." Behind them came the same strange, distorted rumbling. Slowly, both Holt and Mira turned back to the huge, silver walker. It just sat there silently, watching and hulking over them. Holt felt the first stirrings of apprehension.

"Don't worry, Ambassador's nice," Zoey said. "He's my friend. I think."

"Is that right?" Holt asked, not entirely convinced.

"Well, he's not really a 'he,'" Zoey continued. "The Assembly don't have boys and girls, but that's how I think of him."

"It has a name?" Mira asked, studying the thing warily.

"I gave it to him. He was going to take me to the Tower, but I wanted to go with you instead. He has to do what I tell him. It's pretty cool, actually."

"If that's the case," Holt said, "have you thought about . . . maybe telling your new friend to disappear back wherever he came from?"

Zoey shook her head. "That's the only thing he won't do."

"Of course." This was getting more confusing by the second. Holt wasn't sure, but it seemed like, somehow, this thing had not only saved Zoey's and Max's lives, but his and Mira's as well. That still didn't make his feelings for the thing all warm and fuzzy. It was an Assembly walker, a big, weird one, and every instinct told him to get as far away from it as he could.

"He has a connection with someone again," Zoey explained. "He doesn't like being without other voices. It bothers him."

"Great." Holt sighed. "World full of killer alien robots, and we get the nervous one."

The thing's three-optic eye shifted to ponder Holt. It rumbled its strange sound.

Holt studied their surroundings. It looked like they were in the dead trees that had been flanking the train tracks, but the tracks themselves and the bridge and the White Helix were nowhere to be seen. "Zoey, did your friend . . . *teleport* us away from that bridge?"

"Yeah," Zoey replied, rubbing her temples. "Ambassador calls it 'shifting.' But he can only do it if you touch him. The pretty shape inside the machine, I mean. So . . . I had to help."

"That's why we saw you," Mira said.

"I touched all of us at once. And the lights, did you *see* them, Mira? Like strings that blossom out like flowers in all kinds of colors?"

"Yes." Mira nodded. "They were pretty."

"That's Ambassador," Zoey told them. "That's what he looks like. In my mind, anyway. He—" The little girl cut off with a groan, clutching her head. Holt reached out for her, and Mira moved closer, alarmed.

"Max, get back," Holt said, pushing the dog clear. "Zoey, are you okay?"

She didn't respond, just moaned and shut her eyes tightly. Mira and Holt both held her, trying to talk through the girl's pain, to get her to answer, but she didn't.

Above them, the big silver walker rumbled. A stream of green laser light shot from a diode on its body and enveloped Zoey.

"Hey!" Mira shouted at the machine. Ambassador didn't move, though his multicolored eye flickered toward Mira. "Leave her alone! You hear me? Leave her—"

"Wait," Holt said, watching as the green light pulsed around Zoey's head. There was something familiar about it.

"Get her *away* from it!" Mira yelled at him.

"I think it's helping her," Holt said.

Mira spun, clearly intent on ripping Zoey out of his arms and away from the—

"Look!" Holt exclaimed and Mira stopped. Zoey had relaxed. Her eyes were still shut, but she was peaceful, not in pain, her breathing soft. "They did the same thing to me."

Mira looked at him questioningly.

"After they took us, the Hunters, after the Crossroads. I was hurt. They healed me somehow. I remember this laser light, this *green* light." The energy continued to stream from Ambassador, massaging and coating Zoey's head, taking away her pain. "It's *helping* her."

They stared down at Zoey hopefully. After a few seconds, she opened her eyes and looked up. "Sorry, Holt," she said sincerely.

Holt brushed the blond hair out of her face. "Okay, but how about we don't do that anymore?"

"I can't help it," Zoey replied weakly. "It happens more, the farther we go. But I have Ambassador now. He helps me. He stops the pain. Not all of it, but some. Enough so I can still be me."

Mira breathed and looked away. It bothered her seeing Zoey like this. It bothered Holt, too. It was all the more reason to finish what they'd come here for. The green laser light flickered off, and when it did Mira looked back up at the silver walker. Its eye shifted to her.

"Thank you," she said. The walker studied her with its optics. If it understood, it gave no indication.

"The Max," Zoey said softly. The dog had pushed his nose under her hands, and she was petting him.

Movement appeared in Holt's peripheral vision. He looked up and just managed to see a blur of blue-and-red light silently leap between two of the dead trees. He knew what it meant. "Oh no."

Before Mira could ask, Ambassador stomped toward them. There was a flash, as a sphere of flickering energy blossomed to life, a protective shell around not just the walker but all of them.

It came just in time. Figures landed all around the walker in flashes of cyan, each holding their glowing Lancets. Their masks were over their mouths, their goggles covered their eyes, a dozen of them. Through the light of the crackling shield, Holt could make out Avril, Dane, Masyn, Castor, all of them.

Holt didn't know what those crystal spear points would do when they hit Ambassador's shield, but he was pretty sure he didn't want to find out.

"Wait! Avril! *Avril!*" Holt yelled. The White Helix leader was right on the other side of the shield, but she didn't turn to look. Of course she couldn't *see* them anyway, with those goggles. She was using other senses now. "Avril, listen! He—*it* isn't an enemy. It's with *us*."

"It's *Assembly*," Avril said with disdain, and Holt felt a little relief. At least she could hear him through the shield.

"Yeah, it is. Which means, unless you want to die, attacking it probably isn't the best idea."

"We will grow stronger," Avril replied automatically.

"Damn it!" Mira yelled through the shield. "I'm sick of this samurai crap. It's not helping!"

Avril did nothing. The Helix all around them tensed. Ambassador rumbled in anticipation.

"Avril," a small voice said. Zoey's voice. And, soft as it was, her voice carried. *"Avril."*

The sound of it changed everything. In spite of her goggles, Avril turned toward Zoey.

"Ambassador is my friend," Zoey said, still lying in Holt's lap. "He won't hurt you. You can trust me. Like you trust Dane."

Avril slowly pulled the goggles from her eyes, and her stare locked on Zoey. She gazed at the little girl with what seemed like awe—and then slowly lowered her Lancet.

"Stand down," the Doyen said. The others looked at her, unsure. *"Do it."* Slowly, her Arc lowered their weapons and backed up.

Zoey looked away from Avril to Ambassador. The walker's eye moved to the little girl and it rumbled. Holt guessed they were "talking," that Zoey was suggesting similar things to the machine—and it must have worked. A few seconds later its shield flashed off, returning the landscape back to shadow.

No one moved. Everything was silent.

Avril slowly lowered herself to one knee. The rest of the White Helix did, too, removing their goggles.

"The Prime . . ." some murmured.

"We grow stronger," said others.

Zoey studied the White Helix, and then looked back up at Holt and Mira. "You made new friends, too."

"I'm . . ." Holt said carefully, "not sure I'd go that far."

Zoey turned back to the figures in black and gray. She studied them one at a time, until she got to the Doyen. Her little eyes narrowed. "Can I call you Avril?"

Avril looked up at Zoey with surprise. "It . . . would honor me."

"Avril," Zoey continued. "We have somewhere we need to go. Don't we?"

At the question, the other White Helix looked up as well, and Holt saw their anticipation begin to grow.

Avril nodded. "If you will permit it."

Zoey smiled and scratched Max's ears. "Okay."

Holt and Mira shared a look. Things just kept getting better and better.

35. SANCTUM

THE GROUP QUICKLY BACKTRACKED to the train tracks and followed them through the dark. They made good time, all things considered: a dozen White Helix escorting two prisoners, an honored guest—and a giant Assembly walker that could barely fit between the rows of dead trees. Everyone kept their eyes on the silver machine, and Avril even ordered Dane to stop his grueling Spearflow march. If things went south with Ambassador, she wanted him ready. Holt could relate.

The machine was Assembly, after all. A conquerer that had helped lay waste to this planet, and it had taken Holt's sister and his family from him. Every hardship he had ever faced had been because of the Assembly, and now he was being asked to walk next to one. Holt might be able to do that—but he would never *trust* it. No matter what Zoey said.

Max followed next to Holt, dividing his attention between Zoey and the silver walker. When he looked at the latter, the dog made a low growl. He didn't like the thing any more than Holt, but it was clearly hard for Max to know how to react. It had saved his life, too.

Ambassador, for his part, seemed only interested in Zoey. She walked maybe a mile before she had to stop, the pain in her head flaring again. Holt pulled her onto his back, and she hung there weakly while Ambassador bathed her in the green laser light, easing her pain.

Wrong as it felt, in this regard, Holt was grateful for the walker's presence. It was the only thing that could make Zoey feel better, and if he had to walk next to it for that to happen—then he'd walk next to it. Forever, if need be.

As they marched, the husks of dead trees began to dwindle, thinning out until they were gone altogether. What they could see of the dark land-scape gradually shifted to something more rocky, and just as lifeless. The White Helix were split in two, one group in front of them, and the other behind. Holt could see Castor had taken point. Masyn was gone, scout-ing ahead, and Avril and Dane walked nearby.

"If your home is always moving, how do you ever find it?" Zoey asked from Holt's back. Avril looked back at the little girl with a strange look. She almost seemed nervous.

"Everything in the Strange Lands . . . *echoes*," Avril said. "That's the best word I've got; but when you're in tune with the vibrations, with the way it hums, those echoes become easier to feel. And they all feel unique. The numbers of White Helix at Sanctum make a very powerful echo."

"How do you *sense* the land?" Mira walked next to Holt, her hand holding Zoey against him, worried the little girl's grip might weaken. "I don't get it."

"Sure you do. You already sense it," Avril replied. "You call it the Charge."

Holt rubbed his arms, flattening the hairs back down where they had lifted up. Avril was right, the Charge had become a very noticeable thing since Polestar, like constant static electricity all over him. He didn't much care for it.

"That's the hum," Avril continued. "It's all around us. You've just never looked without your eyes. Your eyes . . . confuse things. Give you too much information. You have to get rid of them in order to truly sense the Pattern."

If that's what the Helix believed, then it explained their black goggles. They were clearly too dark to see through.

"You don't . . . run into things?" Zoey asked curiously.

Avril smiled. "No. We don't run into anything. The Charge tells you more than your eyes ever could."

Something flared into the sky ahead of them. A streaking line of red light, followed by two more bursts of color, flashing upward after it. Both blue.

Holt recognized what they must be instantly: the spear points at the end of a Lancet, fired by lookouts. Avril yelled for Castor at the front to stop, and the entire line halted. She looked slightly perplexed.

Ahead, the grassy hills of rock yielded to reddish bluffs and ridges. A river cut straight through one of the rocky mesas, into a canyon of high walls. It was from the top of either end of the canyon entrance that the shots had gone up. Looking now, Holt couldn't see anyone standing there. Not that that was surprising. He studied the flatlands around him warily, wondering just how many hidden eyes were out there.

"What is it?" Mira asked.

"Sanctum advance guard. They know we have the Assembly with us. They're alarmed, and I don't blame them." The statement implied a communication in those fired crystals, probably tied to the colors they shot up, Holt guessed.

Avril pulled her Lancet from her back and called for Castor again. When he looked back, she held up two fingers. He nodded, then unstrapped his own weapon. She fired the green end of her Lancet into the air with the same jarring, harmonic ping. The crystal projectile streaked upward like a missile—and was quickly followed by both of Castor's spear points, both glowing in red light.

"You're telling them everything's okay?" Mira asked.

"I'm telling them we have enemies with us, entering Sanctum peacefully," Avril replied. Whether she meant Ambassador or Mira and himself, Holt wasn't sure.

"How do they know you're not the walker's prisoner, or that it's using you?"

"We have a different signal for that."

Of course they did, Holt thought.

Everyone waited, seconds seemed like minutes, and then there was another volley from the distance. Three new flickering streams of color shot into the air. All of them were green. The sight seemed to relax Avril, and she recalled her spear point, whizzing through the air and connecting with the end of her Lancet in a pulse. Castor did the same.

"Keep Ambassador slow and calm, if you can," Holt whispered to Zoey as they started marching again. "No sudden movements. Okay?"

Zoey nodded weakly. "Okay. I'll try." Holt and Mira shared a nervous look.

They entered the canyon, and the walls rose up high, stretching a hundred feet or more on either side. In the dark, the colorful walls of painted rock were muted but still visible.

The group wound their way through the rocky gorge, on either side of its small river, for almost a mile without any sign that indicated there were others here. There weren't even tracks on the ground, Holt noted. The White Helix were very good at hiding their presence.

Around the next bend he finally saw what he'd been waiting for. Signs of life—and of strategic planning. The ground was covered in boulders, clearly broken loose from the walls on either side of them. It was a smart decision. The boulders and the river made it so any group, even the Assembly, would have to divide and stagger their approach to avoid the impediments, making them easier targets. Six White Helix guards stood behind the field of rubble, waiting for them.

They zigzagged through the debris field until they finally reached the guards, Lancets drawn, held at the ready, staring warily at Ambassador. The machine rumbled uncertainly.

"Where is everyone?" Avril asked. Clearly, she expected more of a welcoming party. But the guards just kept staring at the big silver walker. *"Roderick,"* Avril said with more emphasis, and one of the guards, the one in front of the others, looked at her.

When he did his look was ominous. "Gideon's called a Gathering, Avril. You . . . should be there. Masyn already went ahead."

"Why? What's wrong?"

"Just . . . come with us." Roderick forced himself to look away from the silver walker and start moving. Everyone followed, and Holt could tell Avril was worried. Something was wrong.

They moved through the canyon, following the river around another bend—and Holt's eyes widened at what was there. So did Mira's. Even Zoey, clinging to his back weakly, perked up for a moment. "Wow," she whispered.

Ahead, the canyon rolled northward in a near-straight line, and resting along its length was Sanctum. It was nothing like Holt expected. Tents of all sizes and colors, made of a mashup of fabric and materials—leather, bright silks, cotton, parachutes, flags, clothing, some of them even used wood or metal to create walls—stretched into the distance. They weren't just on the canyon floor, the walls of the gorge were lined with smaller, brightly colored tents, somehow attached up and down the rocky embankments, hundreds of them, stretching out of sight. There were no ladders or bridges between the tents, and Holt figured they weren't needed. The White Helix could probably leap from the canyon floor all the way to the top if they wanted.

In the dark, the glowing tents and structures made a field of glimmering amber all along the canyon walls, and reflecting in the river as it flowed past, making it a wavering strip of light that drifted southward. It was beautiful, Holt thought, but it looked more like a proper city than a caravan. How did they *move* all this?

Holt felt Mira's hand touch his—but when he reached to take it, it disappeared, as if she reached out instinctively at the amazing sight, and then thought better of it. Holt sighed, but he didn't look at her. It was what it was.

The group kept walking, Ambassador's footfalls echoing in the canyon, and as they moved, Holt noticed something else. The colored, glowing tents were all empty. There was no one around but the six guards who had been on sentry duty. He understood why Avril had been confused now. With this many tents, the place should be flooded with people.

The answer became apparent after another hundred feet of winding through the glowing tent city, where the canyon widened into a rounded, egglike shape. There were no tents there, but Holt could see that they continued on the other side of the clearing. It had been purposefully kept open, and it was obvious why.

It was a meeting place. A crowd had gathered, though "crowd" was an understatement. The sheer numbers of them almost made Holt trip. They stood on the rocky floor where the river raced past, or hung from the walls, each flanked by two points of color from their Lancets—red, green or blue—and the combined light was even brighter than the tents. One or two thousand of them, if Holt had to guess, and it was stunning to look at.

"My God," Mira said beside him.

"Did you have any idea?" Holt asked.

"No." She hadn't guessed the White Helix had such numbers. The realization was sobering. Simply imagining the skill Holt had already seen Avril and her Arc display, and magnifying it to the potential in front of him, it equaled an army of enormous size. Yet here it was in the Strange Lands, alone and isolated. Holt wondered again what the point of it all was.

The Gathering didn't seem all that aware of their group, they were circled around something, peering down at it or straining to see over each other on the ground. Whatever it was, it was enough to hold their attention.

At least until the sound of Ambassador's heavy footfalls reached them. The mass of kids, a sea of black and gray and glowing points of color, turned and stared, watching as a five-legged Assembly walker strode through their camp, green laser light streaming from it around a small child. The reaction was similar to that of the advance guards. Lancets yanked from their backs, some leaped into the air in flashes of yellow to claim elevated positions.

Ambassador rumbled. Mira looked at Holt. All it would take was one Lancet to fire, and thousands more would follow.

"Hold!" a voice yelled. Something was odd about the voice. It was old for starters, from a man probably in his seventies. That was unusual enough, but there was something else. It was accented. It sounded . . . Asian. At the voice, the White Helix hesitated and a stillness swept through their ranks. They were clearly used to obeying it.

"The invader is not to be harmed," the voice commanded, the source still unseen. "It is not a guest, but it does not come as an enemy. At least not today. It will pass."

Ahead the crowd parted—and Holt saw what the Helix had been interested in. On the ground, in the center of the clearing, spanning the river, was a simple, flat wooden bridge, barely wide enough to hold one person. Which was good, because there was only one person on it. Sitting cross-legged on a rug, the river flowing past below. Four White Helix guards stood on either side, holding two identical flags. Vertical, and each black with a white symbol on the front: the double helix that Holt had seen over and over again since encountering these strange people.

Next to the bridge was something very out of place: a telephone booth. The kind you would see in the streets of any city ruin, but this one was different. Long metal poles were attached to either side, lengthwise, as if it were meant to be tipped over and carried; and the outside of it was scrawled with shades of black and gray and dozens of double helix symbols, but that wasn't the strangest thing. The telephone booth's glass doors were closed, and inside it, visible through them, was a swirling mass of sparkling, gray energy, like the contained swell of a tempest. Holt knew what it must be, and he frowned. An artifact. A major one, certainly. And probably powerful.

In front of that phone booth stood a group of people decidedly out of place. Two dozen strong, each hefting combat rifles, colorful tattoos on their right wrists, all standing protectively around a central figure that stood unintimidated in spite of being vastly outnumbered. Black hair trailed like an obsidian waterfall down her back.

She turned, and when she did, her eyes found Holt. He smiled in spite of himself, relieved. Ravan had made it after all.

But not everyone was as happy. Avril glared at the Menagerie, standing before the bridge that had some sort of ceremonial meaning. Emotions flashed across her face—anger, trepidation, and shame. Holt understood. This was probably a moment Avril had never imagined coming, but here it was. The Menagerie, the followers of her father, had come for her. After all this time.

A figure leaped in a flash of yellow and landed protectively next to Avril. Holt didn't have to look to see it was Dane.

"Greetings, Avril," the voice echoed through the air again, and the man on the bridge slowly but gracefully rose to his feet. He wore the same black-and-gray outfit as his followers, carried the same Lancet. Even from this distance, Holt could see he was old, but he held himself with a bearing that was still powerful. There was only one person it could be. "How do you return?" Gideon asked.

It took a moment for Avril to even realize she was being addressed, so intense was her stare on Ravan, but finally she answered. "*Stronger*, Master." Her words were laced with bitterness, and she looked forward with stern emotion.

Holt and Mira jumped as the thousands of figures around them all shouted one word in unison that shook the canyon walls. "*Strength!*"

Gideon let the sound of his disciples' voices fade away, and then smiled with a strange mix of sadness and resolution. "Then welcome. You are honored. And . . . we were just speaking of you."

ZOEY PEERED OVER HOLT'S SHOULDER through the green laser light. Her head throbbed, but it wasn't overwhelming. Ambassador kept the pain at bay, but he couldn't stop it entirely. They were too far inside the Strange Lands now. But she could be strong. She had to.

There were so many emotions flying around in front of her that she could barely make sense of them. From Holt she felt a confused mix of relief and apprehension, as he stared across the way at Ravan. It was funny, she sensed almost the same thing from both her and Mira. It was a strange triangle that had formed between them. None of them seemed able to either completely love or hate any of the others.

"How can you do this? How can you make deals with *them?*" Dane shouted, pointing to Ravan and the Menagerie. Heated anger poured from him, and bits of fear, too. He was scared of losing Avril, Zoey sensed, and it only fed his outburst. "You can't trust them!"

"Can I not?" the old man asked, and from him, Zoey sensed nothing. He was blank to her. Like the Librarian, Gideon must have a strong grip on his emotions and thoughts. His focus was razor sharp. "The world is a reflection of ourselves, Dane. The untrustworthy are, by their nature, *untrusting*. But here the Menagerie are. They have braved a dangerous land they do not understand. They bear their most valuable possession. Outnumbered. Defenseless. This implies . . . a great deal of trust."

"Would it be too much for me to know," Avril's voice was hoarse, "what I'm being traded away for like some trophy?" Avril's emotions bled off her unchecked, a thick mix of anger and pain. She felt betrayed,

Zoey could tell. Betrayed by Gideon, someone she trusted. And there was fear, too. Zoey saw flashes, remnants from Avril's memories. Heat waves rising from some desolate landscape. A massive city built between huge, rusted metal spires that spat giant flames into the air. Wherever this place was, it was one she hated. A place she had run from, and Avril would rather die than go back there.

"If I said you were being 'traded' for a grain of salt, would that change anything?" Gideon asked her back. "Would such insult give you reason to dishonor your vows?"

Avril looked down at the admonishment. "No. Master." The words were difficult to say but she believed them.

Gideon turned to Ravan now, but his gaze seemed to drift slightly in the wrong direction. Zoey couldn't tell why. "Show her."

At the words, Ravan nodded to one of her men. Nearby lay the heavy wooden crate the Menagerie had carried all this way. A pirate nearby drew a key from a pocket and slipped it into each of the crate's three locks, snapping them open one at a time.

When he opened the case, a collective gasp filled the air from the thousands of White Helix.

Inside was a large, long, black box, with two heavy doors, side-by-side, that served as its lid. It was painted with faded colors of red, green, and gold leaf that twisted around its edges. A faded white rabbit was on one end, wearing a gray top hat and grinning evilly, holding a wand that shot sparks in an arc of old, cracked, silver paint. Large, flamboyant letters spelled out a flowing script of words:

**THE MYSTERIOUS, MAGNIFICENT MOLOTOV—PREPARE
FOR AMAZEMENT!**

In spite of the pain in her head, Zoey perked up at the sight of the strange, wondrous box. It was beautiful in its own way. It reminded her of the Oracle, somehow, the faded and ornately decorated fortune-telling machine from Midnight City. They both looked like they could have come from the same old circus.

Silence hung for a few seconds. Then, from somewhere, a cheer went up, and it was echoed all throughout the canyon. Colorful plumes of sparks burst into the air as the White Helix thumped their Lancets to the rhythm of a single, repeated word.

"*Strength! Strength!*" they chanted, over and over. "*Strength! Strength! Strength!*"

"Oh, my . . . God," Mira breathed, as the chant continued.

Holt looked at her. "You know what that is?"

"The Reflection Box." Mira whispered in awe. "It's a major artifact."

Zoey wanted to know what the thing did, what could cause such a jubilant reaction from the Helix. Or, at least, from most. Dane's and Avril's reactions were not so enthralled. The girl's shoulders slumped in defeat. Dane stared at her, at a loss for words, and she felt the fear inside him overpower the anger from before. Whatever the box was, it was apparently worth the trade.

"Now do you see?" Gideon asked. As he spoke, the chanting died down. "Time is a shuffling of events. Cycles upon cycles. Each with a beginning and an end." The old man paused and looked at the thousands of youths surrounding him. "There are nine keystones. What is the *third?*"

Zoey flinched as the Helix all shouted as one again, filling the canyon with their voices. "*The Tower's will is hard!*"

"The Tower's will is hard," Gideon repeated, looking back at Avril. "And we all, each of us, bear it the best we can. You may take the worst of it, Avril Marseilles, but make no mistake, we all share in it with you. You make us stronger."

But Avril wasn't flattered. She stared at her teacher, and Zoey could feel the hopelessness starting to overtake her. "How do you know it's real? How do you know it isn't just some look-alike?"

Gideon turned slightly toward Ravan. The pirate just shrugged. "Thing's yours now, do what you want with it."

Gideon spoke some words Zoey couldn't hear, and one of the Helix near him unslung his Lancet. He grabbed the glowing, green spear point on one of its ends by the brass casing and twisted. There was a spark as the glowing crystal disconnected.

Another Helix, a small redheaded girl, bent down and gingerly opened both ends of the mysterious black box. Zoey could see it was lined with soft red-felt cushions and nothing else.

The first Helix, the boy, placed the glowing, humming spear point into one end of the box and shut the first lid. The girl shut the other, letting the white rabbit rest back in its original position. Both of them quickly moved away, and a hushed anticipation filled the canyon.

The black box sat unassumingly on the ground. At least for a second. Then it was as if what little light there was in the canyon all drained just a little bit—before the box shook violently and flashed. A loud boom, like a thunderclap, rocked the ground, and Zoey felt Holt jump under her.

When the sound faded, the two same Helix, with trepidation, opened the double doors and reached inside. They each lifted out the exact same thing.

A green, crystalline spear point for a Lancet. Where there had been one inside the box before, now there were *two*.

Shocked intakes of breath came from the White Helix. They stared in silence at the two glowing spear points. Then they erupted into cheers again. Sparks of color flashed everywhere. *"Strength! Strength! Strength! Strength!"* they chanted once more.

Zoey felt despair wash out from Avril. The box, whatever it was, apparently was the real thing.

"You are honor-bound to serve me." Gideon started walking toward Avril, and as he spoke the chanting died down once more. "*This* is how you will do it. It is not what you wanted or intended. In fact, it is the opposite. But, the Tower's will is hard."

"The Tower's will is hard," the crowd repeated softly.

Avril glared at Gideon when he stopped before her. "Is honor so important?" Her voice was barely a whisper.

"Honor is not about our choices," he answered. "Honor is about how we live with the consequences."

Avril held Gideon's gaze a second longer—then nodded. Dane looked away. Apparently it was decided, and there was nothing either could do to change it. Back near the tiny bridge and the river, Ravan smiled.

"Did you find what we have all been waiting for?" Gideon asked.

Avril looked toward Zoey, clinging weakly to Holt's back, the air around her fluctuating with Ambassador's green laser light. As Gideon's attention shifted to her, she saw something strange. His eyes were free of the Tone, but they were also clouded milky white. It was . . . odd.

"Do your . . . eyes not work right?" the little girl asked.

The White Helix close enough to hear turned in shock.

"Zoey . . ." Mira said cautiously.

But Gideon only smiled. He moved toward Holt and Zoey felt him tense slightly. Ambassador rumbled behind her.

"No," Gideon said. She still couldn't feel anything from him, but his voice was soft and comforting. "But they once did."

"What happened to them?" Zoey asked, studying them up close when he stopped in front of her. It was like they were full of fog, but it didn't look scary or painful.

"What is your name, little one?"

"Zoey."

Gideon paused, considering the name, and right then there was a slight sense of feeling from him. Like the release of some long-held tension. But it lasted only a moment, and the old man was unreadable again. "I lost my sight when the invaders came but as it turned out, the loss was—auspicious." He spoke without any hint of bitterness or regret. "My name is Gideon, and we are very humbled by you, Zoey."

Zoey's eyes narrowed. "What does humbled mean?"

Gideon smiled once more, his gaze drifting off to the left. "It means . . . it makes us happy that you are finally here. We have waited for you a long time."

"Why?"

For once, Gideon seemed surprised. "You don't remember?"

Zoey shook her head. "I don't have many memories. Not since Holt found me. I think . . . *they* did something to block them."

"Interesting." Gideon's blank stare lifted up to the huge silver walker, as if studying it curiously. Ambassador rumbled back. "The Tower's will is complex."

"Why does everyone believe this Severed Tower place can control things?" Holt asked. "It's just another Anomaly, isn't it?"

The White Helix, Avril and Dane included, stared at Holt as if he had uttered something unspeakable.

"Comparing the Severed Tower to an Anomaly is like comparing the light from our tents to their reflection in the river," Gideon answered with patience. The water flowed past, headed south, a wavering, shuttering band of muted color. "Anomalies exist *because* of the Tower."

"But what the hell *is* it?"

"It is where everything began." Gideon's gaze shifted to Zoey again, or at least as much as it could. "And where it will end. The Tower is special. Unique, perhaps in all the universe, and it shapes the Pattern to its will. It has been doing so since the beginning. Orchestrating a symphony of events and choices all leading to this moment. To the return of the Reflection Box—and the return of the Prime."

"Why?" Mira asked.

"I do not know," Gideon admitted. "The Tower has a will, it is clear; I've seen too much to doubt it. But that will is mysterious. And unknowable."

"A friend of mine believes, like you," Mira said, "that the Tower is conscious; that it makes things happen."

Gideon's gaze shifted toward Mira but never settled on her. "The one who stole your Offering. The one who uses the relic of luck. He is right. And astute. He sees things in a different way. Perhaps he knows more than even I, who is to say?"

Mira stared back at Gideon with alarm and wonder. "How did you . . . ?"

"Like everything, he and it pass through the Pattern and leave a wake behind them. That wake, those vibrations, show much to those trained to sense. If your friend manages to reach the Tower . . . then it is as designed."

"You're saying the Tower wants Ben to make it inside?"

"I'm saying that nothing happens by chance, where the Tower is concerned. If he lives and enters it, he has some role yet to play. And if he has your plutonium, then our path is clear. We must find him before he does so, otherwise the Prime will lose her chance. Which means . . . the Tower will have provided a way." Gideon's gaze, such as it was, moved back to the hulking silver walker behind Zoey. "Which brings us back . . . to this. Something else out of place. It cannot be coincidence."

"His name is Ambassador," Zoey informed Gideon. "He helps me feel better."

"Then I am grateful. Tell me, what abilities does this machine have?"

"It doesn't have any weapons," Holt said. "Seems built for ramming. It's got an energy shield of some kind, too."

"And it can *teleport*," Mira said pointedly. Gideon raised an eyebrow at that.

"That's right," Holt agreed. "It teleported *us*."

"Ambassador calls it 'shifting,'" Zoey clarified.

"And can it 'shift' anywhere?" Gideon asked.

Zoey started to shake her head, then stopped. It hurt when she did that. "No. Only to places he's been before."

Gideon thought another moment. "Zoey, can you ask Ambassador if it can shift to a location that *someone else* has visited?"

Zoey closed her eyes and reached out to Ambassador. His presence blossomed in her mind, a shimmering field of colors that was there and not there.

He responded instantly. *Scion. These . . . are friends?*

The walker was worried for her safety, and she didn't blame him. They were surrounded by thousands of warriors, each bearing powerful weapons and the skill to use them.

Yes, Zoey thought, though it was more complicated than that. *They want to know if you can shift to a place where someone else has been, even if you haven't?*

Ambassador did not reply immediately, the answer must have required thought. *If they touch us, yes.*

Zoey looked back to Gideon. "He can do it, but whoever does has to touch him. Holt and Mira couldn't do that, so I did it for them. I touched their minds to his."

"What are you thinking?" Holt asked, staring at Gideon suspiciously.

"I have been to the Tower, or at least as close as one might get without an Offering. If the Prime can touch our minds to the invader's, it can teleport us there. We will make up the time that has been lost, and we will be able to catch your friend." Gideon's gaze hovered a few inches to the side of Zoey. "Girl, you must listen to me and answer honestly. How many do you think you can 'touch' at the same time?"

Everyone looked at Zoey and her face reddened at the attention. "I . . . don't know. I'd never done it before."

"How difficult was it?" Gideon asked her. "How difficult was touching two minds, including your own, to the invader's?"

That one she could answer. "It was easy. It only hurt a little."

"Good," Gideon nodded, as if that was the answer he was hoping for. "Avril, prepare two Arcs, you and another will lead them, and I will accompany you. The rest of the Helix will disband Sanctum and make speed after us."

"Wait a damn second," a new voice yelled behind them. It was Ravan, and she and her men were advancing forward. "Avril's not going anywhere but with me. That was the deal."

"When we are assured the Prime has reached the Tower, then she will be yours. As is her duty, as is her obligation."

Avril looked down, trying with difficulty to contain her frustration.

"You're a damned liar and a crazy old man," Ravan said.

"Rae . . ." Holt started, but she waved him off.

"I don't believe in any of this, I don't believe in fate or destiny, and I sure as hell don't believe in some magical tower that pulls everyone's strings. I make my *own* choices. I believe in my wits and my men and that's it, and anyone who believes in anything more is an idiot."

"No one has asked you to believe anything, nor do I proclaim to know anything. I simply observe. It is all anyone can truly do." Gideon did not turn to Ravan as he spoke. "You are *here*. And the Prime would not have reached me without you. Perhaps the Tower is done with you now, who is to say? But Avril will not be yours until we reach it. If you want her, then you must come with us. This is why I feel you still have some role left to play."

At the words, Ravan stared uncomfortably at Holt. He looked back with an equal level of discomfort. Neither of them liked the fantastical or the idea of fate, but both had come here anyway, out of obligation. They had a lot in common, Zoey knew. It was the source of all their feelings—and all their problems.

"Fine," Ravan said, "but my men come with us, and that's not negotiable."

"That's insane!" Mira exclaimed. "You're talking about *four dozen* people at once!"

"I believe Zoey has the ability," Gideon said simply.

"You don't even *know* her," Holt shot back, and Zoey could feel the anger in him. "She's hurting, *look* at her! Every mile we go, the weaker she gets. What you're talking about might kill her!"

"You underestimate the Tower's influence. Look what it has done." Gideon gestured to the silver walker. "Arranged events so that this machine would be here, at this moment, with its unique abilities. Only by doing so could we catch the one who has your Offering in time. The Tower *wants* Zoey to reach it, and so she will."

"And who the hell says that's a good thing?" Holt asked pointedly.

"I assume," Gideon answered, "that *Zoey* does."

Everything stopped. The people all looked at her again. Zoey knew she had to answer, and that she was making a choice by doing so. She wondered, though, given what Gideon thought of the Tower, if she had any real choice at all.

"I want to try," Zoey said. "I think it's important."

At the words, Holt and Mira's anger faded, but their trepidation remained.

Gideon turned and studied his disciples. His voice was loud enough for all to hear. "The Assembly are here, in force. They move slowly, but they *are* coming. Concentrate and you will feel them shift the Pattern, as I do."

Murmurs echoed from the thousands of White Helix around them. Zoey knew Gideon was right. She could feel them, too. It was the Royal, and it would do exactly what it had told her. Find her, no matter what. The thought chilled her.

"These Assembly are not like the one here now." Gideon pointed toward Ambassador. "Their goals do not align with ours. They know the Prime is close to the Tower. They will try and stop her from entering, they will try to claim her for their own, but they will *not* succeed." Gideon's sightless stare swept over the multitude one last time. "Break camp. Form the caravan. Prepare yourselves. The cycle we have waited for begins this day."

Cheers erupted again, Lancets pounding and spraying hosts of multicolored sparks that lit up the darkened landscape. Even Avril and Dane looked at each other with anticipation and eagerness.

"Strength! Strength! Strength! Strength!" The chant filled the air.

Holt, Mira, and Ravan stared at each other with uncertainty. Zoey buried her head in Holt's back and shut her eyes, trying to drown out the loud chants and the world, as it shook all around her.

HOLT WATCHED THE CITY break down around him, and it wasn't a delicate process. Tents broke loose from the walls and fell to the canyon floor below, in heaps of fabric. The effort continued on the ground, the Helix swarming over the tents and structures like ants, methodically and efficiently disassembling everything at once. It looked like it would be done within hours, but one question still remained. How did they *transport* it? It would be a monumental feat to carry everything that made up this place.

The small bridge Gideon sat on earlier was broken into three separate pieces near the flowing river, stacked in front of the strange phone booth from before, the only thing in the entire camp that, so far, had yet to be touched.

Seconds later Holt saw why. There was a loud groaning as someone opened the rusted, glass door. The gray, sparkling storm that had been swirling inside the thing erupted outward, but it didn't dissipate in the air or explode or even expand. Instead, there was a deep, muted thump of sound as the energy rearranged itself into a perfect circle of dim light that swirled like a pinwheel, around and around in the air.

The pieces of the bridge began to move forward, pulled by some unseen force. As Holt watched, they lifted up into the air and flew straight into the wavering energy field, disappearing in flashes and loud thumps that filled the canyon and then were gone.

Holt's eyes widened.

A line of White Helix began to march toward the phone booth, carrying the tents and structures, and, one by one, threw them into the spinning gray field. They must be able to place the pieces and parts of their city inside that energy, reseal it all back in the phone booth, then transport it. It was an ingenious system—and a frightening one. What would happen if a person were sucked inside that thing?

"Does it make you nervous?" a low, intense voice asked. Dane stood next to him, staring at the strange, spinning circle of energy.

"Everything in this place makes me nervous," Holt said back.

Dane didn't reply with the dripping sarcasm Holt expected. Instead, he merely nodded. "It's not like it is for Freebooters, coming here. There's no training before you step into the Strange Lands. You have to find the White Helix on your own. It's a test, and many don't survive it."

Holt studied Dane. He wasn't sure what the point of this conversation was, but he listened anyway. He didn't have any desire to antagonize the guy.

"I made it halfway through the first ring before I saw anything out of place," Dane continued. "Two Landships, crashed and burning next to each other. Wind Traders never come into the Strange Lands. Must have gone off-course or tried to lose some Assembly gunships, but, either way, it was a bad idea. They ran right into a Phase Field. You know what that is?"

Holt shook his head.

"Neither did I then." Dane still didn't look at him, his words slow and thoughtful. "Nastiest Anomaly in the first ring. Make anything passing through them intangible for a second or two. Sounds harmless enough, until you figure that being intangible means you sink *straight into* whatever you're standing on. Roof of a building, hood of a car, even the ground. And then, when the field vanishes—you reform inside solid matter."

Holt winced at that last part.

"Ships were all merged and blended together, it didn't even look real," Dane recalled. "Dumb kid that I was, I went inside, slipped in where one of the hulls had split, but I only took a few steps before I saw the legs. Hanging down from the ceiling where their owners had fallen through the top deck and reformed. Just legs. Still in jeans, still wearing shoes. Torsos were up top, no doubt, on the other side, but I wasn't about to go check. My curiosity was kind of gone at that point. Never felt fear like that before. *Real* fear. Like ice in your veins. I almost turned around, headed back to Freezone, but I didn't. I kept going, not sure how. For years, you know, I saw those legs hanging from that ceiling. Every time I slept. Every time I didn't have anything else to think about. It's why I drove myself so hard. Kept myself so occupied I didn't have time for nightmares. Then I met Avril. Somehow, I don't know, she took it away. She made it stop. I think it was because she gave me something else to focus on. I'm probably not making much sense."

"Actually, you are." Holt thought of his sister, Emily, the weight he'd carried for so long, and how Mira and Zoey had helped take it away. It was as Dane had said, they'd given him something else to focus on, too.

"Good," Dane replied. "Then you understand what she means to me. Why . . . I reacted the way I did. With you."

Dane had already apologized to him for what occurred back at the gym, but that had been at Avril's command. What he'd just said now was probably the closest thing to a real apology Holt would ever get, which was fine. He didn't need one to begin with. "I get it."

The two of them stood there silently, watching the line of Helix tossing pieces of Sanctum into the swirling energy field, and then Dane turned and left as silently as he'd come.

"Just making friends all over the place, aren't you?" Ravan studied him from behind with a dry look.

Holt studied her back. His feelings, where she was concerned, were a conflicted batch now, but he was still glad she was safe. "You're the one here to take Avril away. If he's looking to put the hurt on anyone, it's you."

"That places him at the end of a very long line," Ravan said, "and if I were you, I'd be more worried about Avril finding out who pulled the trigger on her brother."

"Well, I don't intend to tell her. Do you?"

"Don't know," Ravan said with a smile. "Depends on how nice you are to me on the way back to Faust."

Holt frowned, started walking instead of continuing the conversation. But, of course, he sensed Ravan next to him. "That deal was made when you had me tied up," he said.

"A deal's a deal, and I always have more rope. Found inventive uses for it before, I'm sure you remember."

Holt, in fact, did recall. Vividly. His face reddened. "Ravan . . ."

"Oh no, look at that," she said with mock concern. "I've embarrassed him . . . and I wasn't even trying." She liked getting under his skin, making him squirm. Sometimes it had been attractive. Other times not.

Holt tried to shift the conversation. "What do you think of this place?"

"I think it's all silly. More silly even than that crazy Freebooter city in the sky. Bunch of kids, holed up back here for no reason I can see."

"The Tone doesn't affect them as much. You notice that? That's probably one reason," Holt said.

"Just because you don't Succumb, don't mean you're living. You have to do that on your own, and you can't live back here. All you can really do is survive."

"So what's *your* theory, then?"

"I don't care enough to have one, but Tiberius thinks Gideon's building something."

"Building *what?*"

"No clue, but it makes sense. Only reason you live in a place like this, a place the Assembly won't even go, is to avoid prying eyes."

"Some of the Helix told me Gideon was using the Strange Lands to make his people 'stronger.' Some kind of weird natural selection thing."

Ravan shrugged. "Maybe so. But there's more going on here, I guarantee. I don't know what it is, and, with luck, I'll *never* find out."

Holt couldn't agree more. The only problem was, he had a feeling Gideon's agenda was directly tied to Zoey. Which meant he might have no choice but to participate in it.

"I'm . . . glad you got out of Polestar," Ravan said, her voice softening just slightly. "I saw that place come down. Even from a distance it was scary. Thought you might be . . . you know."

Holt looked at her. "Well, I'm not."

Ravan looked back. "Good."

They held each other's gaze a few more steps, conflicted thoughts hanging in the air. "And you saved the Freebooter in the process," Ravan said. "Her knight in shining armor."

"She has a name."

"I know," Ravan replied. "Used it once, and that was enough for me."

"Mira told me what happened in the silo. Sounds like you owe her your life."

Ravan seemed unmoved. "Owe lots of people all kinds of things. So does everyone else these days."

The words resonated, because Holt knew he owed her in similar ways. He wished he could express it to her, but he didn't know what to say, or what she even wanted to hear anymore. In the end he opted for his usual response. Changing the subject. "What was up with that thing you brought? The artifact that replicates things?"

"Menagerie stole it off a Landship in Freezone years ago. Some kind of really valuable artifact. Tiberius kept it, even though he never cared much for artifacts. He knew it was a big bargaining chip with the right people, if he ever needed it."

"Turns out he did," Holt observed. "Tiberius must be making it worth your while."

Ravan nodded. "Two star points."

Holt instinctively looked at her left hand. The star tattoo was there, with four of its eight points filled in. Two more would make her someone with real power in the Menagerie. "A Commandant," he said, impressed. "Still, with Archer out of the way, that really does just leave Avril. And . . . we both know what you really have your eye on."

"Who knows *what* Avril will do. She hates the Menagerie *and* Tiberius. Convincing her to be her father's heir apparent is going to take work, but that's Tiberius's problem. If by some weird occurrence she does take over, it doesn't change anything. I get myself as high a ranking as I can before Tiberius dies. Then . . . well, I was always gonna have to fight for his place, wasn't I? If it's Avril I fight, so be it. The sooner we can grab her and get out of here, the better, far as I'm concerned."

Holt didn't particularly like her use of "we." "I'm not going back to Faust, Ravan."

Ravan studied him dubiously. "Of course you are. Going back's your only real option. This place is crazy. These *people* are crazy. What *you're* involved in is *beyond* crazy. You have to know that, we're too much alike."

He couldn't argue. Even so, he was different than she remembered.

He had changed that night, when he fled Faust. He'd changed again at Midnight City; but a part of him, a big part, agreed with her. It *was* crazy, and it was getting worse.

"If I were you," Ravan went on, "I'd take my chances with Tiberius. Otherwise, the Menagerie will just keep hunting you. You should end things with him, in person, one way or another, not spend your life running."

"And you'd still vouch for me?" Holt asked, though he was skeptical it would help much. He knew Tiberius too well.

Ravan nodded. "We play the angle, somehow, that you were in the Strange Lands looking for Avril. I'll say you wanted to set things right, that you were integral to finding her, that it wouldn't have happened without you, so on and so forth."

"And Archer? How do you explain that away?"

"We don't. You killed him. He was a son of a bitch and he was going to do something inhuman right in front of you. You gave him a chance to not be a monster and he didn't take it. Tiberius won't like that answer, there's no answer he would, really, but he'll sure as hell respect it."

Holt looked at her doubtfully.

"I said it's your best shot," Ravan told him. "Not a sure shot."

"Why help me?" Holt asked. It was an obvious question. "After everything?"

She looked at him intently. "If you're anything, Holt, you're sincere. Wearing masks isn't something you do very well. Back at the merry-go-round—that was *you*." Ravan held his stare. "You'd come back, in time."

As much as he might want to deny it, it would be easy for him to slip back into the way things were. Still, he had his obligations. He'd made promises and broken them. He didn't want to break them again.

"We'll see," he said noncommittally.

Ravan nodded. "Yes, we will."

MIRA WATCHED FROM A distance as Holt and Ravan moved through the ever-shrinking camp. They never touched, but they walked close. And it bothered her. Which, in itself, bothered her more. She remembered what he'd done on the wing of the plane, the keeping of his past from her—but those things were starting to carry less weight than they used to. Zoey was right, Holt hadn't been himself at the Crossroads, and his explanation of the Menagerie connection, the choices he made and lived with . . .

Well, it wasn't as easy to hate him for any of it now.

She sighed and shut her eyes. Why couldn't anything be simple?

"Hello." Mira jumped at a gentle yet gravelly voice behind her. When she turned, she saw the last person she expected. Gideon studied her, or, at least, as much as he could. His white-clouded gaze seemed to drift just a little bit to the right. It was disconcerting, but also disarming in a way. There was something about the fact that he couldn't see her that made him less imposing.

"Hi," she answered, studying him with uncertainty.

"May I ask your name?"

Mira hesitated. The question itself wasn't odd, but she wondered about his interest. "Mira."

"It is agreeable to meet you, Mira." Gideon bowed as he spoke, but he did it with such familiarity that it seemed genuine, instead of some out-of-place custom. Gideon was Asian, obviously, born in some Eastern country. The idea made Mira's thoughts turn to the rest of the world. What was happening in Japan? Or China? What struggles and adventures were their children having? It made her feel guilty realizing, in all her time since the invasion, she had never once thought about the rest of the planet. There had just never been time.

"The Prime is resting, I hope?" Gideon asked as he rose back upright.

"She's trying. Ambassador helps with the pain, but I don't know how much longer that will last. It just keeps getting worse."

"Yes," Gideon nodded. "And will continue to, I'm afraid."

"Why?" Mira asked pointedly. "Don't sidestep the question like everyone else does."

Gideon cocked his head to the left slightly, like some interesting concept had just presented itself. "Walk with me," he said after a moment, and then moved off without waiting to see if she would. Mira shook her head and stepped into pace beside him.

It was always strange and slightly sad when Mira encountered an older Heedless, someone for whom the Tone had no effect. Adults were as much

relics these days as automobiles and computers, and it was always difficult being reminded of it, of how things once were.

Gideon wore the same pattern of black and gray as his students, the
same white double helix symbol around his neck, and a similar combination of belts and gear, with only one exception. Attached to a clip on one
of the straps on his chest hung a small, old, leather book, with its own
ballpoint pen. His Lancet hung from his back, and surprisingly, of all the
ones Mira had seen, Gideon's was the most basic. Made of just a simple
winding tree branch, the bark removed and the wood sanded and oiled,
and little else. In fact, the only thing ornate about it were the two blue
crystal spear points on either end, wrapped in their flowing, brass casings.

"Your Lancet," she said. "It's very simple."

"What need do I have of decoration?" Gideon asked. "Who would
appreciate it? My enemies?"

Mira instantly regretted her words. He was right, what did a blind
man need with an ornate weapon? "I'm sorry," she said.

Gideon smiled. "I have found that seeing isn't as critical as you might
think. We place too much value on what our eyes tell us. Ironically, they
often assign importance to things that do not deserve it. In this place, I
do not need to see. I can sense everything. So can my students. It is my
hope *you* will be able to sense as well."

Mira looked at him in surprise. "Why would you want that?"

"Because I can see the Pattern forming, and I feel the task of guiding the
Prime to the Tower may fall to you. If that is the case—you must be ready."

Mira felt a sense of dread. "But . . . *you'll* be there. You understand
this place better than anyone, *you* should take her. Or one of your students. Any of them would be—"

"As I said, Mira, I can see the Pattern forming. I fear our destinies lie
in different directions," Gideon replied in a low, unsettled voice. Whatever that direction was, he was conflicted about it. "Besides, the Offering
you will use to enter the Vortex will only be enough to shield the Prime
and one other."

Mira felt her heart sink. Every time she thought she'd found a way to
hand off the responsibility for Zoey to someone more capable, it just
came right back to her. "I . . . I don't think I can do it."

"Why?"

"Because I'm scared."

"Fear is an emotion and little else. It only has the power we grant it."

"I wish it were that simple, but it isn't. I'm scared because I know I'm not good enough."

"And why do you think this?"

"Because the first time I was ever here, I failed," Mira said tightly. "In a big way. I'll fail again, I know it. I can't do it alone. There *has* to be a better choice than *me*."

"No." Gideon's pace gently slowed until he came to a stop. "There is no better choice. And you must come to *believe* that."

Mira looked around at where they were. A dozen or more White Helix were filling hundreds of canteens with water from a series of large plastic vats connected to the river by mini aqueducts made from PVC pipe and funneled by an ingenious system of paddles and wheels. All of it, like everything else, was being disassembled and carried toward the phone booth at the other end of the camp.

Gideon unclipped the small leather-bound book from the strap, and Mira saw it in more detail. It was old, more than a hundred years probably, and its black leather cover had been inscribed with the white double helix symbol that all of Gideon's followers wore. "Would you believe me if I told you this was the most powerful artifact in all the Strange Lands?"

Mira looked at the notebook skeptically. It didn't seem likely, but then again, the Chance Generator was unassuming to look at, and she knew the horrible power it wielded. "What is it?" she asked.

"I will show you," Gideon replied, pulling the pen free from the binding. She watched as he opened the notebook, and to her surprise it was *empty*. The pages were yellowed with age, their lines barely visible, and they were all blank. Gideon wrote only a few words inside—and then abruptly ripped out the page.

As it yanked free, a slight flickering line of flame burst to life down the seam where it had been ripped loose. Almost instantly, another page rematerialized in its place, flashing to life in a similar brief flicker of fire.

Before Mira could see more, Gideon shut the notebook, replaced the pen, and reattached all of it to the clip on his chest.

As he spoke, he began folding the piece of paper. Small, specific folds, over and over, blending the corners into seams in the middle, working them with his hands. "Once long ago, there was a demon named Asegai. He was vile and terrible, and there was none more feared. One day, Asegai was traveling through the villages of the countryside with his attendants. In one of these villages, they witnessed a man performing walking meditation. Nothing uncommon on its own, but as they watched, the man's face suddenly lighted up in wonder. For he had just discovered something amazing on the ground."

Mira watched the old man's hands move over the piece of paper, folding and blending it into some complex shape.

"Asegai's attendants asked what the man had found," Gideon continued, "and Asegai simply replied, 'A piece of truth.'"

"'Doesn't this bother you when someone finds a piece of truth, Evil One?' his attendants asked. 'No,' answered Asegai. 'Right after this they often make a *belief* out of it.'"

Mira tried not to roll her eyes at the parable. "If something's true, it's true," she retorted.

"Yes, but it is *we* who determine what is *true*," Gideon countered, still folding the paper. With each fold it became smaller as a whole, and more complex. "We are what we *think* we are. You—you think you are afraid . . . and incapable. And so that is what you are."

Mira sighed. "Okay. Fine. I think you're probably right, and my rational self believes it, too, but, for whatever reason . . . the rest of me doesn't."

"You have spent much energy running from your fear. What has it gotten you?"

"Nothing," Mira said in exasperation, "but what do I do?"

"Understand that fear is a part of your experience, yet something separate from who you *are*. See that having fear is irrelevant. It simply *is*." His hands stopped moving, but Mira couldn't see the final result. It was now clutched mysteriously within a double fist.

Mira looked at him in frustration. "And how the hell do I do all that?"

"Normally? With years of study and meditation."

Mira sighed and looked away.

"But there are alternatives, assuming you are willing to accept a small amount of pain." His fists uncurled, he held the paper out to her. It had been folded into the shape of what looked like a dragon.

"Origami?" Mira asked skeptically.

Gideon smiled almost sheepishly. "A childhood skill, one I never enjoyed then, but the folds are more beautiful to me now that I can only *feel* them. I'm not sure why that is." The last part he said musingly, as if examining a riddle; but it only distracted him a moment. "The energy of the 'idea' must be stored on the paper of the notebook, and folded before it releases. It need only be folded once, but . . . I indulge myself."

Mira smiled. She liked Gideon, and understood now why his followers were so devoted. He was another reminder of what the world had lost. There were no great teachers anymore.

Something occurred to her about what he had just said. "An . . . idea?"

Gideon nodded. "A single idea. One I believe will help you, if only you can recognize it."

"Why not just tell me, then? Why use the artifact at all?"

"Learning an idea is just as difficult as learning a skill," Gideon answered. "Hearing me explain how to use a Lancet is not the same as practicing it with discipline. In the same way, *hearing* an idea is not the same as *accepting* it. Simply telling you to believe in yourself . . . will not make you believe."

Mira said nothing. She couldn't argue the point.

"You will accept it this way, it will take root," Gideon continued, "but it is not without its price."

Mira looked down at the folded dragon in her hands. "How?"

"Unfold it and read. The power of the artifact will do the rest."

Mira studied the paper dragon. What if Gideon could do what he said? What if she could overcome her fears by simply unfolding a piece of paper? But she was still unsure. "There's . . . pain?"

Gideon nodded. "Nothing of value is ever without pain, Mira."

Mira stared down at the folded dragon a second longer, then made up her mind. She began pulling it apart, undoing the shape Gideon had meticulously crafted. More and more it unfolded, an unending series of bends and twists, unwinding back to its original shape, until there was only one fold left. The initial one, the fold that had cut it in half.

Mira's fingers trembled. She steeled herself—and then opened the final fold.

Inside the paper was writing, and Mira stared at it, confused. It was written in Asian characters, each a blocky mass of jagged lines. Japanese, she assumed. Whatever it was, it made no sense to her.

Angry and frustrated, she looked away from the paper . . .

. . . and gasped as a searing, burning agony flooded every nerve in her body. It was like being set ablaze.

"Release the note and the pain will end," Gideon's voice echoed in her head, "but you will learn *nothing*."

Mira almost did exactly that—the pain was too much, too horrible— she felt her fingers loosen, about to drop the terrible piece of—

An image flared to life in her mind. It did nothing to cloud or obstruct the pain, but it did give her something to focus on.

The image was a mirror. In the mirror she saw herself, and she didn't look as she expected. She didn't look frightened. Or weak. She looked—

The pain continued to build and Mira groaned, crushing the unfolded dragon in her fists; but she had to hold on, had to see what it was showing her.

The mirror again, the image of her in it. She looked confident and strong, capable, resourceful. She looked like the person she wanted to be.

And with that realization, the pain ended. The world rushed back and Mira fell to her knees.

A slight tingling in her hand made her look down, and she saw the paper burning into cinders, drifting away in the breeze. The dragon was gone, the experience was over. Mira swallowed. Her clothes were damp from sweat. A chill ran through her at the memory of the pain, but had she really learned anything from it?

"What did you see?" Gideon's voice brought her the rest of the way back. He had kneeled down before her, his empty gaze glancing just to the left.

"A . . . reflection," Mira said, her voice raspy.

"A reflection of what?"

"Myself."

"And what did your reflection look like?"

Mira shook her head. "Strong. Confident. But I don't *feel* that way!"

"I never said you would *feel* any differently," Gideon replied, and offered his hand to her. Mira took it and stood up. "I only gave you an idea. You must now make sense of it."

"How?" Mira asked in frustration. "It was just me in a mirror. That's *it.*"

Gideon studied her patiently. "Perhaps you are focusing on the wrong thing. Perhaps the reflection is irrelevant. Perhaps what you should truly be considering, is the *mirror.*"

"The mirror?" He was making less and less sense.

"We all have mirrors," he answered. "Things that reflect ourselves so that we can see. Some show what we really are. But some produce only distorted images. Yet, sadly—we accept them. Blindly."

"I don't understand."

Gideon nodded. "I believe you will. When the time is right."

Mira shook her head and looked away. At least *he* was optimistic. Then something occurred to her.

"The notebook," she said. "Is it how you teach the *Helix?*" It made sense, actually. If the White Helix learned what they knew from Gideon, the only way they could become so skilled so quickly would be the use of something like the notebook. If it could really do what Gideon claimed, then the Helix, Avril, Dane, all of them, would be able to learn directly from Gideon's knowledge, absorbing it like memories.

"Yes," Gideon answered, "but it is no easy road. You felt the pain yourself, and that was for one simple idea, now growing in your subconscious. Imagine the pain involved for the *mastery* of a skill. Then consider all the skills my pupils possess."

Mira shuddered. If she'd had to learn how to be a Freebooter that way, she wasn't sure she could have done it. She suddenly had a new respect for the White Helix.

"Many do not survive the learning," Gideon continued in a low voice, "but the Strange Lands is like a forge. It hones and shapes us, makes us *strong.* In that way, we use it against itself."

Mira shook her head. Gideon was an enigma, but a fascinating one. "Gideon doesn't sound like a very Asian name."

"No." He chuckled lightly. "I was once called something different, but that is a story for another day. A long one. I have done many things in my life I would prefer not to think on." The mirth in his voice slowly dissipated. "I have always thought it odd. It was not until the Assembly came that I lost my sight; and it was not until I found this place that I truly learned to *see*. I would not be who I am now, in that other world—but none of us would, I suppose."

"I guess not." Something else occurred to her. Something she had been curious about. "The Reflection Box. It's a powerful artifact, I get it, but—why is it so important to you?"

"It is important, not for this moment, but for others," Gideon answered. "If what I fear does come to pass, then it will be an integral part of what follows. It is my hope that you will not need it, but, if you do, you will know why when the time comes." Gideon and Mira considered each other a moment more, and then Gideon began to walk back toward where they had started. "Come. You are as prepared as you can be."

Mira followed after him. "Prepared for what?"

"For all that is left."

They walked the rest of the way of in silence.

38. SHIFT

ZOEY WALKED IN BETWEEN MIRA AND HOLT, holding their hands. Max was in front and Ambassador stomped behind them, its green laser light taking away as much pain as it could. Together, they slowly moved into the canyon, and as they did, Zoey saw that Sanctum had been completely disbanded. The infinite stretch of glowing tents was gone, leaving only darkness—but it was by no means abandoned. When they reached where the meeting had taken place earlier, the multitudes of the White Helix were there, filling the canyon walls in flickering spots of color, awaiting her arrival. The old phone booth was closed, the strange, swirling storm of gray light once again trapped inside, and everything was eerily silent.

"Kiddo," Holt said, glancing down at her. "You don't have to do any of this, you know. Not if you don't want to."

She could sense his sincerity, his concern, and she smiled through the pain. "I know."

The strange group, human, canine, and machine, moved into the center of the canyon, and as they did cheers erupted, drowning out everything. Colored sparks shot from the walls and the ground, flashing in the air like lightning.

"*Strength! Strength! Strength!*" the Helix chanted as Zoey moved, and she pushed against Holt instinctively.

In the middle, another group waited. Zoey could see White Helix and Menagerie, two dozen of each, glaring with distrust at one another. Avril, Dane, Masyn, and Castor were among them, while Ravan stood with her men impatiently. Out in front, by himself, was Gideon.

308

When they reached the center, Zoey and the others stopped, waiting, unsure, listening to the chants. Then Gideon held his hands up—and everything went silent again. He turned slowly where he stood, as if looking at the thousands of students that filled the canyons, waiting eagerly for his words. But, of course, he wasn't "looking" at anything.

"The Pattern has honed us. Made us sharp. Forced us to grow strong." His voice echoed against the dark, painted walls. "I have asked much of you, I know, and you have never questioned it, but in your hearts you wonder what the intent of all this is. You wonder why we have made ourselves the way we have. You wonder about your purpose, about who you really are. I promise you that soon, all too soon . . . you will have your answers. For the dawn we have waited for is approaching, and it will wipe away *everything*."

Max whined underneath Zoey. She reached out and scratched his head.

"What is the first Keystone?" Gideon asked.

The Helix instantly responded, filling the canyon with their voice. *"We are what we think we are!"*

"We are what we think we are," Gideon responded, and it seemed, just for a moment, that his blind eyes looked toward Mira. Zoey felt a sudden sense of trepidation from her. Those words had some meaning to Mira, though Zoey was unsure what. "When the day comes that I am no longer with you, whenever you question yourself or what you must do, remember the first Keystone. Remembering *it* . . . is remembering *me*. You are all my children. You are all my equals—and you each give me great pride."

From the thousands of White Helix that surrounded them, Zoey sensed a flood of overwhelming emotion. Excitement, anticipation—and love. They *loved* Gideon. He had made them something special. He had taught and nurtured them. He had been a father, something that the vast majority in the world now never experienced or knew.

"Form the caravan," he continued. "Make all speed to the Tower. When you reach it—you will know then *who* you are." His sightless gaze passed over the multitude one last time, then he spoke his final command. "Go."

Immediately, the White Helix began to move, leaping from the walls, either to the ground, or to the top of the canyon—droves of them, a massive wave of sparkling color and gray shadows that blended into the darkened landscape. Half a dozen tipped over the phone booth and grabbed the lengths of metallic poles on either side, carrying it between them, blending into the crowd. Zoey watched as they became strobic silhouettes against the flashing Antimatter Lightning in the distance, heading north toward where she and the others, hopefully, would be very soon.

The remaining White Helix and the Menagerie moved close. Holt and Mira, Ravan, Avril, Dane, they all stared at Zoey expectantly.

"I still think it's too many people," Mira said. "It should be cut in half."

"We can reduce the strain on the Prime, if it proves necessary," Gideon said, as he slowly knelt in front of Zoey, "but I don't believe it will."

Zoey studied Gideon as he lowered himself, his foggy eyes never looking completely at her. "You are scared," he observed without judgment.

Zoey nodded. She was. She didn't know if she could do what he wanted, and she desperately didn't want to fail Mira or Holt.

"Can you sense my emotions," Gideon asked, "in the way you do others?"

Zoey shook her head no. It was true. Even now, with him this close, he was unreadable to her.

"Try again," he instructed.

Zoey reached out toward him—and this time, Gideon's feelings were *open*. Whatever walls or self-control he normally maintained were gone, and she could sense everything he felt, a wide array of complicated emotion that stretched out before her, and amid all that mix of sensation was a confidence so radiantly bright that it overpowered everything else.

A confidence in *her*. That she had the ability and the will to do exactly what he thought she could. Gideon's confidence in her gave her strength, pushed the pain in her head even more into the background than Ambassador's laser light could, and she smiled as she felt it.

"You are everything I hoped you would be, Zoey." Gideon smiled at her. "Are you ready?"

Zoey nodded and moved closer to Ambassador. His flickering eye stared down at her.

Holt and Mira each took one of her hands. Holt's was shaking. Mira's eyes were glistening. Zoey didn't need her powers to know what each of them felt.

"We love you very much," Mira told her.

"I know," Zoey replied.

"Oh, God, please, if we're doing this thing, let's get it over with," Ravan said impatiently. Mira glared at her, but the pirate didn't seem to care.

"What do you need us to do, kiddo?" Holt asked. His voice was tense.

"Just . . . close your eyes, I guess," Zoey said. "When you touch Ambassador, you'll see his colors. Gideon will imagine where we need to go, and then, you know—hold on."

"Right," Holt said with very little enthusiasm.

Zoey breathed in slow and deep—and then closed her eyes. She reached out and instantly found Ambassador, his colors bursting to life in her mind. That was the easy part. Now came the hard one. She reached out again, but this time toward the minds of the people around her. One by one, their thoughts and memories merged with her own. Holt, Mira, Ravan, even Gideon, and with each new presence she touched, the pain in her head flared hotter.

She kept building the connection, trying to merge all of them, one after the other, but she—

Zoey broke the link and fell to her knees. It was just too much.

Ambassador rumbled above her. Max whined and she felt Holt's hands wrap around her.

"This is insane!" Mira cried. "She shouldn't be doing this!"

"Zoey," said Gideon softly. "It hurt?"

Zoey nodded. The pain subsided enough that she could open her eyes and look at him.

"Pain is seldom the end of a path," he told her. "More likely, it is just an obstacle to the other side."

"What's on the other side?" Zoey asked weakly.

"All the answers you have ever sought. Is it not worth a little more pain . . . so that you might be free of it forever?"

"Don't manipulate her like that!" Mira's voice had an edge to it that Zoey didn't like. She could feel Holt start to lift her up and away.

"Wait," she said. "Let me try one more time."

"Zoey—" Mira started, desperate.

"I *want* to try one more time," she reiterated, and Holt and Mira went silent. Even Ravan stared at her with a look that bordered on respect.

Before anyone else could argue, Zoey closed her eyes again and reached out for Ambassador. When she touched him this time she tried something else. She called on the Feelings, bringing them to the surface, and they heeded her call, rising up and filling her.

Once more she reached out toward the people around her, touching each one at a time, their memories and thoughts flowing through her. As she did, the Feelings expanded, showed her other ways, ways that could more efficiently connect her mind to the others, and Zoey followed their suggestion.

The pain grew in her head as she connected each mind, flaring up, growing stronger and stronger; but Zoey held on to the Feelings, let them aid her and give her strength. One mind after another she added to the string, and each one brought new flashes of pain and dizziness—but she kept going, fighting through it, each presence she touched was one more closer to her goal.

Then it was done. Zoey touched each of them, more than fifty minds in all, and there was a moment, a brief moment, where she marveled at what she had done. But then the pain threatened to overtake everything, and she shoved forward toward the wavering, bands of color that were Ambassador.

The world flashed and upended. She felt a wave of nausea and pain, but she held on.

There was a sound. Like a powerful, punctuated blast of distorted noise, and a quick wave of heat. Zoey gasped, her stomach clenched, her ears rang—and then the pain in her head exploded. She cried out, but she wasn't sure anyone could hear.

Everything went black. She thought she felt a blast of cold wind, thought she heard screams and explosions.

Then, from the distance, a projection entered her mind. Thoughts, pure emotion. Ones she recognized. They were not Ambassador. They were from another source. A terrifying, dark one.

Scion! We are here!

The last thing she remembered before she gave in to the pain and the darkness, was that the Royal had found her, just as it had promised.

MIRA SAW AN IMAGE of Zoey, like before on the train bridge, but this time the girl wasn't smiling. She was grimacing in pain. Then there was a burst of sound, a wave of heat . . . and everything around her was suddenly windswept chaos.

A cracked and fragmented road ripped forward. Frightening, twisted shadows stretched into a pitch-black sky of swirling clouds that glowed with eerie yellow light. It was a city, or at least its ruins, and Mira had a good idea what it was.

Bismarck, the center of the Strange Lands. It meant Ambassador and Zoey had done what they intended. They had teleported them deep into the Core, deeper than most Freebooters ever dreamed of going, and one look around showed her why.

Her hair blew wildly from the intense winds that roared around them, so strong, it was hard to keep her balance. Antimatter Lightning flashed almost constantly in the sky. There were other things, huge things, moving in the distance. Giant funnels of swirling black that roared powerfully through the landscape.

Dark Matter Tornadoes, one of the most powerful Anomalies in all the Strange Lands, and here Mira was watching half a dozen of them.

As they moved, Dark Matter Tornadoes displaced physical space. Whatever they touched remained solid, but its atomic structure was stretched and bent, and the effects of their continued passage through the ruins was plainly visible. The broken streets were filled with a mishmash of cars and vehicles that were still solid, but twisted into impossible shapes, like some kind of abstract painting. The buildings, if they still stood, were just as haphazard, stretched and blended into one another. It was painful to look at.

Mira watched one of them move, rumbling in the distant east, and following it brought her eye to something that made a chill sweep over her. The others, two dozen Menagerie, two dozen White Helix, were all staring at the same thing.

To the north, less than a mile away, a giant mass of tiny, flashing particles swirled like some huge alien sandstorm stretching out of sight. It was called the Vortex, and behind it, just visible through the veil, rose a massive black elongated shape that stretched into the sky. It didn't touch the ground, just hovered over everything. Even more amazingly, it was broken in half about two-thirds up its length, the top piece having separated and tilted outward as though it was falling . . . but it never did. It just hung there suspended in place, unmoving behind the Vortex.

It was the Severed Tower.

The center of the Strange Lands. The very thing she had been laboring so hard to reach, and it was right there, maybe three miles away. A giant shaft of darkness that seemed to stare down at her with menace. She had wondered whether or not it was even real, so few people had seen it. If she was honest, a part of her had hoped it wasn't—but it was. And it hovered there like some impossible monolith, waiting for her, stretching thousands of feet into the air.

She felt a surge of dread. How did Gideon or anyone else think she could get them to that? How did—

"Zoey!" It was Holt's voice, and Mira instantly hated herself. Her attention had been on the Tower and not on the little girl who had sacrificed everything to bring them here.

Holt ran toward Ambassador, the only one of the group immune to the fierce winds. Underneath the walker lay Zoey. She wasn't moving, she didn't even look like she was alive.

"Oh, God . . ." Mira slid onto the rough pavement. Holt pushed a whining Max out of the way and knelt down, too. Ambassador rumbled above them, bathing her in the green light, but it no longer seemed to have an effect.

"She's breathing," Holt said, and Mira sighed in relief. At least there was a—

The healing laser shut off. Mira stared up at Ambassador. "What are you doing?" she yelled at the machine. "Help her!"

The walker's eye shifted to Mira for a moment—and then it took two loud, powerful steps backward.

"*Help her!*" Mira shouted again in fury.

Ambassador considered them a moment more, then there was a flash, the same violent burst of sound . . . and the machine was *gone*.

"No!" Mira shouted.

"I knew we shouldn't have trusted that rusted piece of—" Holt began, and then was cut off as explosions rocked the ground. He shoved Mira down, covering both her and Zoey.

Behind them, the Menagerie and the White Helix ran for cover wherever they could find it—Dumpsters, the sides of walls, the twisted shapes of cars and trucks, all while the explosions continued.

Mira saw the source. The sky behind them, to the south, away from the Tower, was *full of ships,* dozens of them. She could see their burning engines and flashing plasma cannons, raining down yellow bolts of light. It was the Assembly. They were already here.

Even so, the winds were so strong, the gunships were struggling to stay in formation, spinning and drifting out of place—but still they fired, unleashing volleys of heated death at the group. Mira could just make out the colors on the ships. Green and orange.

"Yeah," Holt said. "Not good."

"Avril, Dane," Gideon shouted nearby. He was crouched behind the shattered shell of an ice-cream truck, which looked like it had been melted. "Divide your Arcs, we *must* distract them from the Prime. Use the Pattern, the invaders are weak against it."

Avril and Dane yelled orders to their groups, and the White Helix raised their masks, lowered their goggles, and bolted from their positions, each in a random direction, and leaping into the air in flashes of orange and purple. The gunships tried to target them, their cannons blazing, but the Helix's accelerated movement was too fast for even them to track. And the gale-force winds weren't helping. Two of the gunships slammed into each other and exploded, crashing to the ground in a fireball on the other side of an old post office.

Ravan wasn't sitting idly by either. "I want six men each in those top floors," she yelled, signaling the two tallest buildings near them. "The rest of you take up spots in the intersections on either side, there's plenty of cover. If we catch them in a crossfire while the Helix are jumping all over the place, the winds might knock them out."

Ravan's men didn't hesitate, instantly dividing and moving. Ravan looked at Holt, and then nodded to something on the ground. It was his pack and guns. The pirate had brought them.

"Mira." Gideon approached them, ignoring the explosions. "It is time."

Holt got up and studied the little girl underneath him. "What about Zoey? She's not even conscious!"

"Mira can carry her. The Prime does not need to be awake to enter the Tower."

Mira shivered in fear. Gideon was right, the time had come, and she wasn't even close to ready. Holt seemed to sense it.

"I'll go with her," Holt offered.

Gideon shook his head. "Mira's Offering is only enough to protect two people."

"But I don't have the plutonium!" Mira cried. "And . . . I'm not . . ."

"Trust in the Tower, girl. It will provide. And remember the dragon. Remember the mirror." Gideon held her gaze meaningfully another moment, then turned and ran, leaped into the air in a flash of yellow and disappeared after his students.

"Holt!" Ravan shouted. Yellow bolts sizzled through the air.

Mira stared at Holt desperately. He studied her back. "I can't do this," she told him pitifully.

"Mira—"

"I can't! Everything is depending on me, and I'm not good enough. I'm not good enough to—"

Mira cut off as Holt's hands circled her face and drew her to him. He kissed her deeply, the trepidation and fear and explosions forgotten for one merciful moment. Her heart raced. When he pulled away, she stared into his eyes.

"I know what happened to you here, but it doesn't matter," Holt said. "You're not that little girl anymore. I wish you could see yourself the way I do. You're the most amazing person in my life, and I try to live up to your example every day."

As he spoke, new sensations and feelings filled her, fighting with her doubts and fears. In spite of the chill of the wind and the danger, she felt warm.

"You've always had it in you, you just never looked for it because you didn't believe it was there," he continued, forcing her to look back into his eyes when she tried to look away. "I've never believed in much, but I believe in *you*, Mira, and if you have any faith or trust left in me, if I haven't completely destroyed it all and burned it away, then trust me now. I *believe* in you. You can do this, and I know you will. I know it . . . because I know *you*."

Mira was stunned, overcome. Words wouldn't form. "Holt . . ."

"Take Zoey, get to the Tower." He held her look and said the next part with as much emphasis as he could. "I'll see you when you get back."

Then he was gone, running toward Ravan, grabbing his things and hefting his rifle, both of them dodging out of the way of more plasma fire and blooming fireballs.

Mira stared after him a second more, her heart thundering. Then she did what she had to do. She reached down and grabbed Zoey, lifted her up, and ran as fast as she could toward the black, hulking shape that hung suspended in the air to the north. The sounds of explosions chased after her.

HOLT GRABBED HIS PACK AND GUNS off the ground at a full sprint and ran with Ravan, slipping his equipment on as he did. Out of the corner of his eye, he saw Max bolting after him.

"You sure about this?" he asked the dog wryly. Max made no answer. "Yeah, me neither."

Another explosion blossomed to life about twenty yards to his right, and Holt slammed down behind a crumpled delivery truck next to Ravan.

She looked at him. "You sure can show a girl a good time."

More explosions thundered and shook the truck. Engines roared above them as the gunships struggled in the raging winds. The Hunters had brought air power. A lot of it. Looking closer, Holt could see they weren't Raptors, they were smaller, shaped like a half circle, with the curved part at their rear, and the flat edge at the front. He could make out their engines and cannons.

Holt and Ravan peered over the hood and watched the gunships fire in a chaotic stream of directions, shooting everywhere at once, and one look let Holt see why. Two dozen White Helix flipped and darted between the vehicles on the street or the rooftops of buildings. The blasting wind drowned out most of the sound, but Holt had a feeling if it didn't, he would hear them shouting with excitement.

"Those guys really are crazy," Ravan observed, though there was a note of respect in her voice.

"Yeah, but they're still human. They'll run out of gas eventually, and when they do they'll start making mistakes."

Gunfire rang out, and Holt saw sparks explode from some of the ships. Menagerie muzzle flashes lit up the intersections on either side of the two buildings. From the top floors, glass exploded outward as more gunfire strobed. It was a valiant effort, but Holt knew it was probably useless.

"Give them something else to shoot at, anyway," Ravan said.

Max howled as a gunship roared above them, struggling to right itself in all the turbulence. Before it could, a green flash of lightning arced into it in a shower of emerald sparks.

The gunship fell straight downward in flames—right toward their truck.

"Well, of course," Ravan said, yanking Holt up. Max darted out in front of them as they ran, and the gunship crashed in a fireball where they just were.

They reached a group of Menagerie behind an old street trolley, firing up at the gunships. Holt ducked down next to them and pulled Max close. More plasma screamed through the air, and the side of a building nearby exploded outward.

"Cruz!" Ravan shouted at one of her men, his gun blazing automatic fire. He stopped and looked at her. "Since you're not hitting anything, at least quit wasting bullets and switch to semiauto."

"Skipper, how long we supposed to hunker down like this?" another pirate asked.

"What, you bored? Maybe you oughta go run around with the tribesmen out there."

The Menagerie laughed—and then ducked as a blast of debris rained down on their heads.

In spite of the jokes, everyone knew it was serious. They were surrounded by dozens of Assembly gunships, and if that weren't bad enough, they were now lost in the deepest part of the Strange Lands with no way home.

"They're pulling back!" someone shouted, and Holt and Ravan peered out past the trolley. Sure enough, the sounds of engines whined as the gunships started to pull away from the buildings, struggling to stay aloft in the winds—and then each one flickered and vanished, cloaking shields covering them, just like the walkers.

Cheers went up from everywhere, but Holt didn't feel as jubilant. If they pulled back, they'd done it for a reason. The look on Ravan's face showed she agreed.

Everyone jumped as the White Helix landed near them, one after the other, up and down the street in flashes of cyan, and, for all their strength, they were exhausted. Holt saw Masyn almost lose her balance before Castor caught her.

Avril leaned against the twisted remains of a taxi, breathing hard, and she and Dane shared apprehensive looks. They were tired, Holt thought, unsettled. But they weren't running.

"Doyen!" one of Avril's Arc shouted in alarm.

In the distance, maybe two miles away, illuminated by flashes of colored lightning, shapes moved. A lot of them, and they were big.

Holt ripped the binoculars from his pack and peered through them. Ravan did the same. The optics magnified the view, but it was still hard to make out detail. It was dark as night here, and the powerful winds stirred up a lot of dust. What he could see was only revealed in intermittent flashes of red and blue, but it was enough.

Holt watched each shape shamble forward in the same fluid, mechanical way, stomping toward the city with power. "Walkers," Holt groaned.

"I'm seeing two lines of them, one behind the other," Ravan said. "Probably fifty, I'd guess, and that's just the ones I can see."

"There are many more than fifty," a voice said behind her. Gideon stared sightlessly to the south. "There are hundreds. Two different types, small and large."

Looking around, Holt could see the looks on the rest of the White Helix's faces. They didn't need binoculars. They could sense the Assembly moving through the Pattern, and they didn't like what they felt.

"*Hundreds* of walkers, plus air support?" Ravan was aghast. "We can't hold out against that."

"Yet we must," Gideon replied calmly. More lightning flashed, the winds raging. "The Tower wills it."

"I don't believe in your stupid Tower, old man!" Ravan shot back and stood up. "I'm taking Avril and I'm getting my men the hell—"

Everything stopped at a blast of distorted trumpet sounds. Five Hunters decloaked about two hundred yards down the street to their right.

No one moved until the plasma bolts started flying, sparking all around them, then everyone darted for cover in different directions, Menagerie scrambling over the vehicles and the Helix leaping into the air.

Only Gideon kept his composure.

He loosed the simple Lancet from his back, and in one smooth, quick motion, fired a spear point. It hummed through the air like an arrow—and punched straight through one of the Hunters in a shower of fire and blue sparks.

The plasma fire from the other walkers cut off. They trumpeted in surprise, watching their compatriot crumple to the ground. Even Assembly armor, it seemed, could not withstand an Antimatter crystal borne of the Strange Lands.

Gideon didn't hesitate. He touched his index and ring fingers together and dashed toward the remaining tripods in a blur of purple. Holt watched the old man cover the distance and leap up and over the surprised Hunters, the other end of his Lancet striking downward into a second machine. More blue sparks, more flame, and another walker fell.

"That's—not unimpressive," Ravan said next to Holt. Everyone, Helix and Menagerie, watched as the walkers finally recovered their senses. Their cannons twisted toward Gideon and spun, priming, unleashing volleys of plasma.

Gideon zigzagged gracefully backward, dodging the sparkling bolts, leaping into the air and landing behind another tripod. There was a hum and he caught the spear point on the end of his Lancet and jabbed outward, puncturing a third walker, felling it in a spray of blue fire.

More plasma bolts shattered the debris and ruined vehicles around him, but Gideon dodged left, ducking and weaving in a blur of purple energy. He spun and fired again. The fourth walker shuddered as the projectile hit home, blowing it to—

Gideon groaned as the last walker rammed into him, sending him crashing violently into the brick wall of a crumpled church and falling to the ground.

He struggled to his feet—then dodged another stream of yellow bolts. As fast as the old man was, the walker had the advantage now. One bolt caught him in the arm. Two more hit his leg. Another sent him crashing to the ground.

The Hunter landed above Gideon, its three-optic eye burning. It raised one of its razor-sharp pointed legs, ready to strike.

Another hum, as Gideon's spear point exploded straight through the last walker on its way back to his Lancet. The machine shook uncontrollably, collapsed in a shower of fire and didn't move.

"Gideon!" Avril shouted as the White Helix raced forward. Holt and Ravan did the same.

As they ran, the darkness was wiped away by golden, shimmering fields of energy lifting up and out of the fallen walkers on the ground. In the surrounding darkness, they were blinding to look at.

But they didn't form as Holt had always seen. Their brightness faded almost immediately, the energy seeming to lack cohesion. Another few seconds, and they dimmed, flickering in and out, merging and vanishing into the air.

It must be this place, Holt thought. Something about the Strange Lands disrupted those shapes, whatever they were, just like the water had done at Midnight City. Before he could think it through, he reached the White Helix ringed around their fallen leader.

Holt stared down at the old man—and instantly wished he hadn't.

Plasma bolts weren't kind to human flesh. Gideon was still alive, breathing weakly and staring up at his students. Avril held his head in her arms while the rest watched on, stunned.

"Gideon . . ." Masyn whispered, staring down in disbelief. It was the first time Holt had ever seen anything approaching fear on their faces. Gideon was larger than life. To them, he could never fall, never die, and yet here it was. If *he* could be killed . . . certainly any of them could.

"You must . . . hold the line . . ." When Gideon spoke, his voice was raspy and cracked. His blind gaze stared straight up to where the colored lightning flashed. "The Prime . . . must reach the Tower."

"How can we do that?" Castor asked nervously. It was a good question, there was an Assembly army coming for them.

"Fight them," was Gideon's response.

"Fight?" Ravan asked. "There's hundreds of walkers out there, you said so yourself!"

"Now . . . there are five less," Gideon answered.

Ravan wasn't impressed. "You gotta be kidding me."

"You saw them fall. Five of them, defeated . . . by an old blind man." Gideon coughed and struggled for air, his eyes drifted to his students around him. "This . . . is what you were *made* for. What *I* made you for. I told you, before we left, you would know who you are, and you *are* the invaders' reckoning."

Dane looked at Avril and she back at him. The other Helix all stared at each other in the same way. Confused and scared and uncertain.

"What is . . . the first Keystone?" Gideon asked.

"We are what we think we are," the Helix intoned automatically. In the distance, Holt heard the stomping of mechanical legs, the roar of engines in the air.

"Say it *again*," Gideon commanded.

"We are what we think we are!" the Helix said, this time with strength.

Gideon nodded. "You must . . . see the truth. You must see yourselves as you are." His voice was growing weaker; he was fading. "If you have ever believed me, believe me now. After today . . . your enemies will fear you."

His foggy eyes came to rest on Avril. She stared down at him with emotion. "Avril. When this is over, honor your obligation. It may seem . . . a waste, but it has . . . purpose. If you honor me, you will do this."

Tears formed in Avril's eyes. The old man's hand reached up and gently felt her face.

"I can see you, Avril," he said, his voice fading. "I can . . . see you . . ."

Then he was gone, his body went limp, the life drained away.

The White Helix were frozen in place, staring at Gideon's body. Avril softly rested his head on the ground, then looked up at Dane. Something passed between them, part fury, part resolution.

Avril stood up, walking purposefully, followed by Dane and the others. Whatever they were thinking, it seemed they were of one mind.

The White Helix fanned out, forming into a long line that stretched twenty-four strong. Each unslung the Lancet from their backs, the glowing crystals humming, as they stared to the south, toward the walking death that was approaching them.

The machines there were clearer now. Two lines, one, the bulk of the army, made up of the smaller, fast tripods. The other . . . was something else. Something much bigger and still unseen. The smaller walkers darted forward, leaving the bigger ones behind, rushing toward what was left of downtown Bismarck.

"They're coming, but they're lined up nice and straight," Avril yelled. "Fire both volleys."

"We'll recall before we reach them," Dane shouted next to her. "With luck, we'll drop a few more before we take them one-on-one."

"One-on-one, huh?" another Helix asked skeptically.

"We're faster than they are," Masyn told him, smiling, one of the few. "Just keep moving. Try to lead them into a crossfire."

Avril lifted her mask up over her nose and mouth. The others did the same. "Ignore the wind, listen for my voice, remember the Spearflow. It's taught you everything you need."

Holt stopped behind the line of warriors, staring past them at the rushing onslaught. So did Ravan and her men.

"*Fighting* the Assembly is suicide," Ravan told Avril. Holt was inclined to agree. It looked insane, impossible. Every experience he had ever had with the Assembly said it was.

"Not if what Gideon said is true," Avril answered. The others were lowering their blackened goggles over their eyes. "And he's never lied to me before."

"Avril, there's too many," Holt said next, trying to get through to her. "Every one of you is going to die."

"Then we will grow stronger," Dane said, next to Avril. The two looked at each other and smiled. Then they lowered their goggles and looked south again. The line of tripods, countless numbers rushing forward, less than a mile away. Holt felt nothing but dread and horror now. He had no love for the White Helix, but he didn't want to see them slaughtered.

"Fire as one!" Avril yelled.

Holt flinched as twenty-four glowing spear points launched forward with loud pings, streaking through the air like torpedoes.

"Again!"

Another flash, another burst of sound as the second volley launched and arced ahead in flickering green, red, and blue.

"*Move as one!*" Dane shouted next—and two Arcs of the White Helix, led by their Doyens, charged forward in flashes of purple, rushing toward their enemies almost as fast as the streaking crystals.

The Hunters never even slowed. They were Assembly. No military in the universe had ever come close to defeating them and they raced forward without fear.

Explosions burst upward into the sky, as the first line of crystals hit. So packed tight were the machines in their line, that nearly every one found a mark, some of them even two.

The walkers saw their mistake too late, tried to spread out, but the second volley ripped through their ranks before they could, spraying fire and debris into the dark. In seconds they had lost almost fifty of their front line, and all the while the White Helix charged forward, leaping between buildings and old vehicles.

The walkers finally returned fire, flinging a massive wave of plasma bolts toward something they hadn't seen since the initial invasion years ago. Humans that weren't running. Humans that actually dared to *engage* them.

Holt just barely heard a shout from Avril in the distance. "Recall!"

The spear points hummed to life and ripped from the ground, streaking backward toward their owners. Explosions flared again as the crystals punched back through the Assembly lines, and more walkers fell in colorful bursts of flame.

Then something stunning happened. Something Holt never would have imagined seeing in his lifetime. The line of Assembly Hunters, hundreds of them, all ground to a halt, trumpeting uncertainly, watching the small line of jumping, darting warriors bearing down on them. The machines were confused, disoriented and, Holt guessed, stunned.

The White Helix were none of those things.

They caught their spear points from the air and charged into the walkers fearlessly, spinning and flipping between them, their Lancets colorful blurs of death that struck into the machines and blew them apart from the inside out. Holt and Ravan stared in shock as the tripods returned fire in a way that actually seemed desperate.

"Tiberius was right," Ravan said with a note of awe. "Gideon *was* building something here, he was building an army. An army to fight the *Assembly*."

Impossible as it seemed to Holt, it looked like that was exactly what the crazy old man had done. As he had told them, the White Helix now knew who they were, and they relished in that revelation, yelling with excitement as they fought in the distance.

There were flashes above them suddenly as the green-and-orange gunships uncloaked, filling the sky. Plasma bolts rained down, and Holt and Max barely lunged out of the way.

"Into the buildings! Move!" Ravan shouted, and the Menagerie dashed toward whatever edifice was closest. Not all made it, some were cut down, but the rest kept moving and firing upward.

As he and Max reached and lunged through the door of a ruined post office, Holt risked a quick glance to the south. Past the White Helix and the Hunters, he could see the other walkers now, the bigger ones. They just sat there waiting, but waiting for what?

40. VORTEX

MIRA STUMBLED FORWARD IN THE RAGING WINDS, moving through the fragmented street between the cars, all of them blended and morphed into each other. Only a few hundred yards ahead of her, red lightning revealed the Vortex, a wall of spinning, glowing particles that stretched out of sight and supposedly tore anything inside it to pieces. It was what the plutonium was supposed to somehow shield her from, but looking at the massive energy storm, that idea seemed ludicrous.

She didn't even have any plutonium, and the Vortex was probably the most rawly powerful Stable Anomaly in the Strange Lands. How could anyone possibly expect—

Mira stopped herself.

She couldn't think like that anymore. She didn't have a choice—she *had* to do this. She remembered Holt's words. Even if they weren't true, Mira wanted to be the person he saw. She just had to think and figure out how.

Mira lowered Zoey down onto the ruined street, catching her breath, leaning against the remains of a crashed helicopter. Zoey was still breathing, but she was cold and limp, and the sight of her stung. Mira had to get her to the Tower. If anything could save her, maybe *it* could. She had to *think*.

She couldn't carry the girl in her arms the whole way. The Vortex promised to be a daunting experience, and she was already exhausted. Mira needed to attach the little girl to her body somehow.

Quickly, she unslung her pack and removed the straps. When she was done with that, she set them on the ground and opened the bag, digging through what little was left inside. A strand of rope, her roll of duct tape, and the Aleve she always carried.

She stuck the Aleve in Zoey's pocket. It would make the girl much lighter, but that was only half of what she needed. Mira took the straps from her pack and circled them, one apiece, around Zoey's thighs, and then hefted the girl into her lap and arranged her legs around her waist. The wind howled around her as she ran the two straps through one another and pulled them tight, feeling Zoey's legs circle her torso. Mira ripped loose long lengths of duct tape and wrapped them around the strap edges, securing them.

Next she took the rope, and holding Zoey's chest against her own, started circling it around them both. When she was done, Mira tied off the rope and stood up.

The Aleve did its job. Zoey weighed next to nothing now, and the straps and rope kept her secured. Mira let herself smile. That was one problem solved. Now she just needed to—

A deep, concussive roar drowned out the furious winds. Mira looked in time to see a Dark Matter Tornado descend from the swirling, black clouds and touch down on the street.

As it moved, it changed everything, twisting objects into impossible shapes, warping buildings, and blending cars and trucks into singular chunks of metal, like blown glass.

At first Mira stared in fascination, her natural Freebooter curiosity overriding her fear, but then she darted around the side of the helicopter, away from the advancing funnel of darkness. Everything shuddered as it approached.

She ducked around the side of a building just as the Tornado rumbled by, twisting and morphing everything. Seconds later the Anomaly dissipated, rising back up into the dark clouds as they flashed green and blue.

Mira closed her eyes and leaned against the wall. She was still here. She wasn't dead yet. The Vortex was just ahead of her, less than a block away, a giant swirling wall of death. She could have been the best Freebooter in the world, but without plutonium, there was no—

Mira noticed something in front of her.

Leaning against the flattened wheel of a tow truck sat a backpack.

One she recognized. Old and faded and gray, with black leather straps and a white δ etched into it. She had seen that pack countless times, carried it more than once herself. It was Ben's pack, and Mira's eyes widened at the realization.

Zoey stirred in her sling as the wind cut into them. It brought Mira back to reality. "Hold on, sweetie," she said, moving for the pack at a run. "Hold on."

Mira reached it, her heart thundering in her chest, not from exertion, but from apprehension. It couldn't work out so easily. Could it?

With shaking hands, Mira opened the pack. It was full, much fuller than her own, with artifact components and supplies, and she dug through it all frantically, desperately searching for what she—

Mira's hands closed around the cool, smooth, glass canister of plutonium.

She almost cried in relief as she pulled it free. It wasn't unlikely that Ben would have left it behind, he wouldn't want to carry two batches of plutonium, who knew how the Vortex would react. What *was* unlikely, what seemed nearly impossible, was that Mira would have chosen the exact same route to the Vortex as *he* did.

She heard Gideon's words and a chill ran over her. *The Tower will provide.*

Mira stared down at the plutonium. It was the same one she had gotten herself all that time ago in Clinton Station. She remembered that night—almost dying from the Fallout Swarm, rescued by Holt and promptly bound. When she analyzed all the decisions she had made, all the seemingly disconnected events that had to happen to bring her here . . .

Mira looked up again, to the giant, black tower-like shape that hovered in the air over everything. Something about the sight of it made her feel powerless, and she was running right toward it.

Zoey moaned on her chest. In the end it didn't matter, did it? She knew what she had to do.

Mira swallowed, tucked the plutonium under her arm and dashed toward the Vortex, where it rose straight into the air. As she approached, she could see it more clearly, see that it was made up of billions of tiny flickering particles. She heard a static-like hiss that hinted at something powerful. She closed her eyes . . . and rushed inside.

The Vortex immediately encircled her, and the force of it almost ripped her from the ground. It wasn't like the wind before, this was like stepping into a fast-flowing river. It took everything she had to keep her balance.

Regardless—she wasn't dead, and that was something.

The plutonium in her hand flared brightly, a superheated pinprick of light. There was no real indication it was working, only the billions of swirling particles of the Vortex never reached her. They just dissolved, their light dying out before they hit, and as she moved through the Anomaly she was surrounded in a sphere of blank air.

Yet she still felt the Anomaly's force. It knocked her sideways, and it took a Herculean effort to just move forward. There was nothing to grab onto either. No buildings or vehicles, all of it had been stripped clean, but still she could see where she needed to get: the black, hulking tower, less than a mile away.

Of course, a mile in this insanity might as well have been—

Mira screamed as the Vortex yanked her off her feet. She tumbled in the air, then hit the ground hard on her left arm, barely avoiding crushing Zoey or losing the plutonium.

She felt the bone snap. It was more of a shock that jarred through her than pain. That came later, when she tried to push herself up—a burning, electrical agony that shot through her arm.

Mira gasped outloud. Her vision went dark. Thick nausea overtook her.

Then the fear set in. Her arm was broken, badly, but she had to get up. She had to do it *now,* or she would succumb to the pain and exhaustion, and then it would all be over.

"Get up!" she screamed, pushing to her feet, struggling forward through the powerful stream of particles. The Severed Tower was there, she could see it, everything she was supposed to do, what she had *promised* to do. It was within her grasp. She forced herself to move, ignoring everything that—

Mira lost her footing again, was lifted up a second time and thrown down hard. The wind gushed from her lungs. Pain flared and blackness threatened to overtake her. She struggled to get to her feet—but then she was rolling over the ground, backward, away from the Tower, tossed like a leaf in a hurricane, the pain blossoming with each hit.

When she came to a stop her mind was fading. There was nothing she could do. She was too weak. She had been an idiot to think she could accomplish this. The Severed Tower was even farther away now. She would never reach it, no matter what anyone thought.

"I'm sorry, Holt . . ." she said, and then the Vortex yanked her and Zoey violently back into the air.

41. GROW STRONGER

HOLT AND MAX DASHED THROUGH the ruined post office as plasma bolts shredded the walls, the windows, the ceiling, all of it, the half-circle gunships trying to mow them both down from outside.

The end of the building was coming up, a brick wall lined with windows. There was nowhere else to go. Holt yelled, and burst through the glass, spiraling down and crashing into an old Dumpster in an alley. A pile of decade's-old trash in a cloud of dust and worse exploded around him.

He coughed, started to rise—and Max dropped on him from above, driving him back down.

"You always have to land where I do?" Holt asked testily, grabbing and dropping the dog over the edge before rolling out himself.

In the sky, the gunships circled, firing everywhere, and Holt could see muzzle flashes at the top of the buildings from the Menagerie positions, shooting back.

Colored lightning flashed. One of the impossibly huge Dark Matter Tornadoes materialized from the clouds and drifted downward, and behind him, at the other end of the alley, flashes of light strobed, as six green-and-orange Hunters decloaked.

One of them was different. Its markings bolder, more commanding. Holt knew that walker—and it knew him. Its three-optic eye whirred as it focused in his direction.

"I really hate this place," Holt reiterated. He and Max ran the opposite direction.

Yellow bolts shredded the alley, spraying mortar and brick everywhere, and Holt ducked. A piece of debris caught him on the side of the head and he stumbled, crashing into the street outside.

Pain flared, making him dizzy, and there was blood on his scalp. Hands grabbed and yanked him up, and he stumbled after a figure, eventually slamming down behind a twisted city bus. About seven Menagerie pirates were there, dirty and bleeding, reloading their guns.

"This belong to you?" one of them asked.

Through his blurred vision, Ravan crouched down next to him. "A prized possession."

Holt stared up at her through the pain. "Hi."

"What the hell happened to you?" she asked, studying not just the blood, but the dirt and grime all over him.

"Just . . . give it a second."

The tripods burst around the corner, trumpeting angrily, led by the Royal, and Ravan ducked out of sight. "Well, okay then." She motioned to one of her men, and he tossed her a shotgun. Holt had the same idea, switching out the Sig for his Ithaca. They both started loading shells.

"You know, I've killed these things before," Holt informed her.

Ravan was unimpressed. "Me, too." Behind them the Hunters trumpeted, searching. Explosions flared in the distance.

"I was being chased by, like, a thousand Forsaken at the time," Holt retorted.

Ravan shrugged. "I was dodging a time-locked semitruck exploding through a wall."

Holt kept loading shells. "Killed mine with shotgun blasts, close range."

"That's funny. So did I."

Holt pumped the final shell into the chamber. "Guess we have a plan, then." Ravan smiled back at him.

Holt whistled four short notes, and Max bolted right and out into the open. The tripods tracked the dog, opening fire, but Max dodged and weaved in his best White Helix imitation.

While the Hunters were distracted, Holt and Ravan rolled out from cover. Their shotguns thundered. Sparks exploded from two walkers, staggering them back, one blast after another, until flame exploded out their exhaust ports and the machines crumpled to the ground.

Holt and Ravan slid back into cover, just in time to see two Hunters land on top of the bus, staring down at the Menagerie.

"Maybe that wasn't the smartest idea," Holt said.

Plasma cannons opened up. Two of Ravan's men fell, instantly dead.

"Run!" Ravan ordered, but more Hunters appeared on either side, blocking them. One was the Royal. Holt looked around for any escape as the thing's cannons began to prime. There wasn't any.

Then a stream of new plasma bolts slammed into the walker and flung it backward, clearing out the threatening tripods.

Everyone turned and looked. Two other machines stood a hundred yards away. One had five legs, a powerful blocky frame, and an energy shield crackling around it. The other one was a Mantis. Ten feet tall, raised off the ground by four legs, and heavily armored with twin mounted plasma cannons and a missile battery. Like the five-legged walker, its colors were gone, leaving only the bright silver of bare metal.

"Ambassador . . ." Holt breathed, feeling hope.

The street filled with bright, wavering flashes, and multiple bursts of distorted sound, as more five-legged walkers, half a dozen, teleported into the battle zone—each bringing reinforcements. More Mantises, and something else, too. Something that towered over the ruined buildings, something huge.

A Spider. The largest, most powerful walker in the Assembly arsenal. Thirty feet tall, almost as wide as the street, with eight large legs holding its huge fuselage. Spiders were the most feared sight on the planet, and this one, for the moment, was on *their* side.

A frightening sound bellowed from the huge machine, like electronic whale song, and it stepped forward, its footfalls shaking the ground. The Hunters trumpeted uncertainly, and then scrambled as plasma fire sizzled toward them. Two of them crashed to the ground, their armor disintegrating in flame.

The remainder, including the Royal, withdrew—and Holt caught a glimpse of a gray blur chasing after them, growling evilly.

"That dog's even dumber than you are," Ravan observed, "but I'm kinda starting to like him."

Holt whistled and Max skidded to a stop and ran back, tongue lapping out of his mouth.

All three of them, with what was left of the Menagerie, ran toward the silver walkers. The gunships arced in the sky. Plasma bolts streaked everywhere, raining down into Ambassador's small but imposing force. The shields flared to life around each of the five-legged walkers, and they charged forward.

It was total war, and Holt and Ravan ran through the middle of it.

AVRIL GROANED AS SHE burst through the cloud of fire that erupted from the fallen Hunter. She landed on the ground and recalled her missing spear point, catching it with a jerk back onto her Lancet.

Each of her Arc, one-on-one against these small Assembly walkers, were more than a match for them. She could see Gideon's vision, even his strategy for individual encounters. Two Helix for a Mantis, six to take down a Spider, it was all so clear to her now. Gideon hadn't lied. They *were* made for this.

The problem was, right now it *wasn't* a one-on-one fight. There were only a little more than twenty White Helix facing hundreds of Hunters plus airships, and whatever those larger walkers did. The grim reality was clear. For all their skill and strength, they would be overtaken soon.

But it didn't matter. They were never in this fight to win. They simply needed to hold off the Assembly long enough for the Prime to reach the Tower. Then, whatever was going to happen would happen.

In the distance, bright flashes of light sparked to life up and down the line of larger walkers. Seconds later, the popping sounds of ordnance being fired echoed through the air.

Avril's eyes widened. She had a sense of what was coming. "Heads up!"

There were explosions in the air, and Avril saw streaks of light raining down, as if something large had burst into dozens of smaller pieces.

A second later she knew what they were.

The small buildings and old cars filling the streets rocked as hundreds of explosions blanketed the area, and Avril leaped up and away in a flash of yellow.

She saw two of her Arc, and one of Dane's, consumed in the fireballs and disappear. Avril grimaced, but kept moving.

She knew what the larger walkers were now: artillery. She also noticed something else. The flurry of cluster bombs exploding all around never once struck one of the green-and-orange walkers. It couldn't be a coincidence. It meant the ordnance had the ability to differentiate targets. It was brilliant, given the Hunters' propensity for stealth and speed. It allowed them to lunge into a fight they might be outclassed in, with devastating support from behind.

Two more of Avril's Arc fell, caught by plasma bolts, unable to avoid all the flying death in the air, even with their skills. They would be cut to pieces in this storm.

New plasma bolts suddenly flared around her, and she saw, back near the center of the ruins, something amazing. Mantis walkers and a giant Spider firing *back* at the Hunters near them. In front, charging forward, was a line of five-legged walkers, like the one that had befriended the Prime.

Each was silver, their bodies bereft of color.

"Pull back!" Avril yelled. "Pull back to the buildings!" She heard Dane shout the same order, saw the Helix dashing away as one, covered in purple or yellow light. If they could get back to the buildings and those silver walkers, they might actually have a chance.

Avril leaped into the air after her Arc. The onslaught of Hunters fired after them and gave chase, renewed by the Helix's retreat.

MIRA'S VISION WENT BLACK as she slammed back to the ground, the Vortex tossing her like a rag doll, in a flurry of flashing particles. She had a feeling her leg was broken now, too, but the pain had yet to register. Somehow, she managed to hold onto the plutonium that kept the Anomaly at bay, and Zoey had avoided being hurt as well. It was Mira's final wish to protect the child as long as she could.

She moaned and looked up. Above her, the Severed Tower loomed, a shadow that stood massive out amid the glowing haze of the Vortex, two giant shapes broken apart in the air.

There had been a time when she dreamed of seeing the Tower, the deepest part of the Strange Lands. She and Ben had talked late into the night about it, imagining what it looked like, what it might actually do.

Now she felt nothing for it but revulsion. This thing that, if what Gideon and Ben believed was true, had arranged every little detail of her life to bring her to this point. And for what? To die? To be beaten and in pain? What was the point of that? She hated the thing now, whatever it was.

As the Vortex roared around her, she thought of Gideon's idea, of the paper dragon, the pain that came from opening it, the image it had seared in her mind. She saw the mirror, her own reflection, but it hadn't been her. It had been everything she wasn't—strong, confident, and assured.

She remembered what Gideon told her, that maybe the mirror was the important thing. Not the reflection. But what did that mean? She was supposed to find something that reflected a true image. Something—or maybe, the idea occurred to her—*someone*.

Holt's last words rang in her head. *I believe in you.*

They had stirred something. It wasn't just the words, it was how he had said them. Forceful and pointed. He wasn't just telling her what she needed to hear. He was telling her something he *felt*, and it had moved her. She wanted it to be true.

Mira realized something then. Looking back, she knew why Holt was different from Ben. He gave her strength. Since her father had disappeared, he was maybe the only one who ever had. Not Lenore, not even the Librarian—and definitely not Ben. Ben took her strength, intentionally or unintentionally made her rely on him. Holt made her feel like she could do anything all by herself.

If he made her feel that way . . . maybe it was because it was true.

It was him, she suddenly knew. It was Holt. *Holt* was her mirror. It had been there the whole time, but she had never seen it.

The realization filled her with renewed strength. The world snapped back into focus; and with it came pain. Horrible, lancing pain in her broken arm and leg. The pain helped focus her as much as the thoughts of Holt.

She stared with anger back up at the Tower looming over her. "Let's see what you know," Mira said in a cracked voice. *"Let's just see!"* She couldn't walk, not with her leg, but maybe that was for the best. Every time she stood up the Vortex ripped her off her feet.

Instead, this time, Mira rolled onto her back, keeping her arm around Zoey and the plutonium, and pushed back with her good leg across the empty ground, toward the Tower. One leg length at a time—and each push was agony.

Mira's vision blackened, but she kept at it. Kept pushing, over and over, through the raging Vortex. She was doing it somehow, and she kept pushing until she hit something and stopped.

She opened her eyes. A figure stood over her, wrapped in a similar cocoon of blankness that repelled the Vortex, holding a brightly flaring glass cylinder.

"Mira?"

It was Ben.

HOLT WATCHED TWO OF the Menagerie in front of him spin and fall as he ran. Ravan cursed next to him, but kept moving. Holt had a feeling she was going to lose a lot more men before this was over.

There was no way to tell how many Hunters the Menagerie and White Helix had killed, but there didn't seem to be any end to them. They kept dashing into the streets from the south, and Holt knew the bulk of their force was still to come.

Ahead of them were two Mantises, their colors stripped bare, firing at the tripods chasing after Holt and Ravan.

"Get behind the silvers!" Ravan shouted to her men.

She didn't have to answer Holt twice. He and Max lunged behind them as more plasma screamed by. Giant footfalls came from a few blocks away, and Holt saw the hulking form of the lone silver Spider, its huge cannons flashing and booming, sending bolts screaming toward the green-and-oranges.

Any other time, being relieved at the sight of an Assembly Spider walker would have seemed ludicrous, but Holt didn't have time to ponder the irony.

The rapid-fire pops of automatic gunfire echoed down from above. Ravan's men were still at the top of one building, holding their position, and they'd even managed to drop one of the gunships, sending it spiraling to the ground and exploding.

"Get those guys out of—" Ravan started.

The top of the building exploded, as four gunships targeted the shooters inside, blasting it with plasma until it was just a burning skeleton. Ravan glared up at the building with silent fury.

"I'm sorry," Holt said, shouldering the Ithaca and pulling loose his Sig, ramming in another clip of ammo.

Ravan did the same thing with her own rifle, peeking back out behind the Mantis. "Don't be. We got bigger problems."

Holt followed her gaze. Several blocks away the White Helix reappeared, jumping toward them and flipping in flashes of color between the rooftops. There weren't as many as they had started with, but that wasn't what bothered Holt. If *they* were falling back, it wasn't a good sign.

Seconds later it was confirmed. A swarming mass of movement appeared. Hunters, hundreds of them, pouring into the city, plasma cannons firing up at the Helix. Holt watched one of the warriors take a hit and slam into a wall, tumbling downward a hundred feet and out of sight.

Holt and Ravan looked at each other somberly. They could both do the math. They weren't getting out of this one. None of them were. Even so, it didn't mean they were about to give up. They would make as many Assembly pay as possible.

"We need a choke point," she said.

Holt nodded, looking around. He saw something that might work a block away, and darted out from cover, whistling for Max. He felt Ravan, and what was left of her men, on his heels.

He led them to where two semitrucks had jackknifed into each other years ago, their trailers arcing out in a V shape. Dark Matter Tornadoes had warped and blended the vehicles together in a strange, disturbing mix of melted metal. If they got in between the trailers, any Hunters that followed would have to bunch up. They could take them one at a time.

"Get to those Dumpsters!" Ravan shouted, and her men dashed toward two big rusted metal trash containers at the end of the street. Holt saw what she intended. They'd make nice cover—at least until they got shredded.

Holt helped the Menagerie push the Dumpsters into position between the trailers. Another irony, he and the Menagerie working together.

"Get behind!" Ravan yelled. The onslaught of Hunters rushed forward. The silver walkers stood in between them, but they wouldn't last long. "Fire in turns. You run out, you get at the back, reload."

No one said anything, they just leaped over the Dumpsters as plasma bolts sizzled past them.

Holt saw two of the Mantises explode and fall, saw the five-legged ones charging and ramming the tripods back, but it wasn't enough. The

Hunters swarmed past like a tidal wave, their cannons firing—and then they were on them.

The trailers did their job. The walkers had to enter one at a time, and when they did the Menagerie opened fire, dropping each one in turn, creating a pile at the entrance that the walkers had to leap over to get past. But it took a *lot* of shells to hurt the Hunters. The first line ran out of ammo, cycled back, and Holt and Ravan moved up, opened fire, dropping more in bursts of sparks and fire.

The strange, glowing fields of energy rose out of the machines, lighting up the dark and bleeding into the air, unable to form.

Holt's rifle clicked empty, and he grabbed Max and dashed back, started reloading with Ravan.

The trailers on either side shook as two Hunters landed on top. Holt fired up at them—and then shoved Ravan to the ground as one returned fire. It got one of her men instead.

They both stared up at the machines, their targeting system tracking them, guns about to fire . . .

. . . and then one exploded in a burst of green sparks. So did the other.

When the smoke cleared, Dane crouched where the walkers had been. The tall Helix smiled at Holt, then leaped away in a flash of yellow light. Holt frowned. Great. Now he owed his life to the cocky bastard.

All around them, in the air, Holt saw the White Helix flipping and darting, their spear points firing like missiles into the swarm of Hunters, trying to turn the tide; but there were just too many. The green-and-orange swarm continued to advance.

The Menagerie at the front fell as bolts shredded them.

"Pull back!" Ravan shouted. "Under the trucks!"

She darted underneath one and Holt scampered after her. Max just watched, staring around nervously at all the chaos.

"Max! *Move!*" he shouted, and the dog tore loose and dashed after him.

They all crawled out, the sounds of battle everywhere. Ravan looked at him. "I don't know about you, but—"

The air above them exploded. Streaks of light rained down like shotgun blasts. The ground flashed in fire as the projectiles hit—except where a green-and-orange walker happened to be.

"Guided artillery," Ravan said wearily.

"Stop admiring it and go!" Holt ran in the only direction open to them—away from the horde of green and orange. Explosions followed after them, a hell of flame and heat and shrapnel.

THE STREETS WERE A battleground. Droves of Hunters poured in from the south. The silvers returned fire, holding their ground, but artillery was raining down on everything that wasn't green and orange. Right then, though, Avril had other things to worry about.

She twirled her Lancet and fired both projectiles straight downward, backflipping between two ruined city buses. Both shots were hits, punching through Hunters and incinerating them.

She landed and moved to recall her crystals, but two more leaped up after her, their cannons spinning.

Avril reacted instantly, using the empty shaft of her Lancet to vault out of the way of lines of sizzling plasma bolts, landing on the ground in a crouch.

More Hunters charged after her, and she realized she was defenseless. She tensed, ready for—

One of the tripods shuddered as the glowing blue end of a Lancet punctured it in a stream of fire. Masyn flipped up and over, plasma fire following her, and it gave Avril the time she needed. She spun and caught both of her spear points from the air, then ducked down and let her weapon flare outward in an arc, slicing through the legs of another walker, crashing it to the ground.

Masyn landed next to her and the two moved back-to-back.

"They're a lot dumber than I expected," Masyn said.

"With numbers like this, they don't need strategy," Avril replied. "Spearflow, movement Seventeen—then adapt."

"Yes, Doyen," Masyn said. She was winded, but there was still a note of excitement in her voice.

Both girls broke in opposite directions, performing the movements the Spearflow had prepared them for, touching all three glowing crystals on their fingers in a flash of bright white light. Their Lancets struck forward blindingly fast, then flipped into reverse thrusts with the opposite ends. Each attack found a different target, and four walkers fell in flames.

Then they were leaping away and dodging through a sky full of plasma. The girls landed a block apart, Masyn on top of an old gas station, Avril on a taxicab that had been warped together with a limousine.

Masyn smiled—and then saw something. To the south, Castor flipped and dodged through volleys of plasma bolts. Avril could see his weapon was empty. He needed to land to recall his crystals, but that was harder than it—

A bolt sparked and sent him crashing to the ground. He tried to rise—and three more cut him down where he stood.

Masyn howled in anger and leaped toward the fallen boy.

"Masyn!" Avril shouted, but it did no good. She charged forward in a blur of purple and waded into the Hunters around Castor, her Lancet cutting them down one at a time—but there were too many, and they were closing in.

Avril moved to leap for her—then saw movement out of the corner of her eye. Dane jumped between two buildings, chased by three gunships, and then wheeled as a blast of artillery exploded on the rooftop next to him. He fell and vanished, the gunships firing after him.

A chill ran through her. It was bound to happen. To both of them, but the sight of it, knowing he was hurt, maybe dead—was beyond anything she expected.

Behind her, Masyn fired a spear at two Hunters lined up one behind the other, blowing through both. Avril could only reach one in time, and even then, in the end, it would still be too late.

"Go, Doyen!" Masyn shouted, striking and jumping, surrounded by Hunters.

Avril made her choice. She touched her index and middle rings together and leaped straight into the air. Behind her, she heard the plasma cannons around Masyn, but she didn't need to look back to know the girl had fallen. She could sense it in the Pattern, could feel her echo weaken and vanish.

Avril landed on the roof, saw Dane on top of the building's water tower. He'd dispatched two gunships, but his Lancet was empty. The third opened fire, peppering the tower with plasma bolts and shredding Dane, knocking him down.

Avril felt her insides turn to ice.

She flipped forward. The gunship spun where it hovered, targeting systems realigning—but it wasn't fast enough.

Avril's Lancet punctured it once, then twice, as she flew up and over, and it exploded and crashed in a fireball.

She landed on the tower, grabbing Dane before he slid off. He was bloodied, torn, and barely conscious.

All around her the chaos continued. The green-and-oranges poured into the city, plasma seared through the air and fire streaked downward from the sky. There was no one left. It was all but over now. Avril looked down at Dane . . . and managed to smile. They would face the end together at least.

THE ONE THE SCION named Ambassador slammed into two more Mas'Erinhah and sent them flying and crashing in crumpled heaps to the ground. Plasma bolts sparked against its shield, and it could tell it was about to fail. The colors of its kin, the Mas'Asrana, had all faded. The Mas'Shinra defectors were all gone now, too, except for the largest, and even it would fall soon.

Ambassador spun its blocky frame—and saw the object of its obsession.

The one the Scion named the Royal stood at the end of the street, four guardians on either side of it. Ambassador knew these would be its end. They would fade its colors.

But . . . this was what had been chosen.

The walker rumbled and charged powerfully forward. Streams of plasma flared from the Royal's guardians, slamming into Ambassador's shield. The barrier flickered once, twice, then *died*.

The ordnance seared into Ambassador's armor as he charged, ripping into the machine. It sensed its hydraulics begin to flame, a short in a servo hub, but it didn't matter now.

The Hunters tried to bound out of the way at the last moment. Three of them didn't make it, and Ambassador drove them hard through a building wall. It whirled around as more plasma bolts found it. So did a stream of missiles, slamming into the walker in violent explosions that sent it stumbling back.

It tried to jump forward again, but two of its legs were severed, it could only pathetically shamble.

More plasma bolts cut into it, bursting through its armor, tearing into its electronics and mechanics. The machine took two more steps . . . then crashed to the ground, fire shooting from its exhausts.

Still, the walker tried to pull itself forward. It would not let the Mas'Erinhah see it give in. It would push toward them until the Void claimed it.

The Royal trumpeted with disdain—and then leaped into the air and angled its razor-pointed legs toward Ambassador's fuselage. There was a violent shudder. Sparks. Its sensors died, its vision went dark, and without its connection to the Whole, it was utterly, ultimately alone.

HOLT AND MAX RAN after Ravan, and what was left of the Menagerie, toward the nearest building, trying desperately to avoid the guided artillery that was falling everywhere.

"You really think a building's the best place to be?" he shouted after them.

"What do you wanna do?" Ravan yelled back as she ran. "Stay out here in the rain?"

To his right, he saw the last silver Mantises explode and crumble. The huge Spider was ahead of them, blasting everything, but the gunships were focused on it now, concentrating their fire, and its armor sparked and buckled.

And everywhere the Hunters poured into the city. It was the worst battle Holt had ever been in, and it was only getting worse. He just hoped he could buy Mira enough—

A Hunter landed just to the left of Holt and Max, plasma cannons screaming. The bolts caught and spun him to the ground in burning pain. The pirates kept running, unaware.

Holt fired the last three shells from his Ithaca, but it wasn't enough. The walker advanced on him, its plasma cannon priming . . .

. . . and then something leaped onto it, snarling, jaws sinking into the hoses jutting from its actuators. It was Max. He was defending his master. Holt reached for his Glock, ripped it free, aimed . . .

"Max, let go!"

It was too late. The machine whirled and twisted, shook the dog off and sent it crashing to the ground. Holt, eyes wide, desperately fired every round he had, trying to distract the thing from Max if nothing else, but the bullets just sparked off the walker's armor uselessly.

Max yelped horribly as the tripod impaled him with one razor-sharp leg.

Holt screamed in anguish, frantically started to rise and—

An artillery explosion rocked the ground, sending him flying away . . . and the world morphed into an unreal, slow-motion haze.

He didn't hear anything anymore, could barely see through the blood. There were blurs of movement that could have been walkers or explosions or White Helix. He didn't know.

The world shifted. He thought he heard someone yelling, and then he was being dragged, pulled into a strange white place with broken tables and counters that used to be shiny. An old ice-cream parlor, Holt's mind barely put together.

His vision focused a little. His body was searing pain. He wondered absently if he was dying.

He saw Menagerie firing frantically out the windows of the old shop, saw them take hits and fall. Ravan appeared, hands on his face, yelling something he couldn't make out. She pulled him close and kissed him. He wished he could feel her, he really wished he—

A stream of plasma bolts threw Ravan violently away. Holt weakly turned, saw her lying still, blackened and bent. Still he felt nothing but pain, and even that was fading, mercifully.

Past the door of the shop, in the streets, there was chaos, death, and destruction, but it all seemed like a dream. Just vague, blurry images. Hunters in the streets like ants. White Helix leaping and striking in colorful movements, then falling to the ground. The giant Spider walker overwhelmed, burning, collapsing downward, right toward him, in a strange, slow-motion fall he wasn't sure would ever reach him.

"Mira . . ." Holt breathed, though he couldn't hear his voice. He saw her one last time—around a campfire in some forgotten forest, dancing with him. Smiling.

The Spider crashed. The world went white. The pain ended.

AVRIL CLUNG ONTO THE water tower at the top of the building, overlooking the destruction below. Dane was barely conscious, and she held him in place so he wouldn't slip away.

They were the last left. She had watched the rest of her Arc fall one at a time, their deaths burned into her memory. It hurt more than plasma burns ever could.

Below her the Hunters advanced into the city. She saw the Spider fall in flames and crash. She watched the five-legged walker, the one who had come with the Prime, valiantly charge into the swarm. It took on eight Hunters by itself before they overwhelmed it.

It was all very heroic, and in the end all very futile—but that's how it was always going to be. She only hoped the Freebooter had gotten the Prime to the Tower. In the distance she saw it, looming over the city, and Avril stared at it with hatred. She would tear the thing down if she could.

"Avril . . ."

Dane's eyes were open. He was still handsome, she thought, still strong. She could hear the roar of approaching engines.

"Go," he said. The bulk of the Assembly were past them now, headed north, unimpeded, toward the Tower. She could escape, but she knew she wouldn't. "*Go.*"

"Ssshhh . . ." she told him, stroking the hair out of his eyes. "Quiet now."

She pulled Dane close as the gunships rose into the air around them, and his familiar shape and warmth was comforting, even then.

"We grow stronger," she whispered into his ear. The plasma bolts unleashed from all directions, searing heat overtook everything, and they were falling, falling into nothing . . .

MIRA STARED THROUGH THE pain up at Ben. He looked worse than he had at Polestar. His face was ashen, his eyes dark and hollow. He clutched two things, one in each hand. A glowing cylinder of plutonium, and the Chance Generator.

"Ben . . ." she said weakly. He made no move toward her.

"Are you . . . real?" he asked, his voice haunted. "I'm . . . seeing things now."

"It's *me*, Ben," she assured him. Even now, being close to him had its comforts. He was a missing piece of her in this place. "I almost made it," she said with guilt, feeling Zoey's fading warmth against her.

Something about the statement seemed to get through to him. Ben's eyes focused, and he looked to the side. "No. You *did* make it."

The Vortex swirled around them, but Mira noticed it was weaker now. Ben was standing easily, not having to fight so he wouldn't be swept away. Looking closer, she could see why. A few feet away the Anomaly ended. There was nothing beyond it but a bright field of white, almost bright enough to block out the sight of the Tower, hulking directly above her now, so close.

The realization hit her, and flooded her with something like happiness. She *had* made it, after all. By herself. As Holt told her she could.

"It's beautiful," she said.

"It's everything," Ben replied.

Mira set her plutonium on the ground next to her, and then, with her good arm, started slowly untying Zoey, trying to do it as carefully as possible.

"When I saw the Tower, for the first time," Ben said, "it . . . felt wrong. I always thought you would be there."

"If I had, I would be dead now, wouldn't I, Ben?" Mira asked. The Chance Generator seemed to waver with heat in his hand. "Like the ones who followed you?" Mira kept untying Zoey, loosening her legs from the straps, pulling her free.

Ben looked back to her, confused but blank, as if he hadn't heard. "You should have been there. I . . . promised you . . ."

"You can still keep that promise, Ben," she told him, and she meant it. "You don't have to do this. You can help get me back. You can help Zoey get into the Tower." She finished untying the little girl.

"You don't understand," he told her, and she saw the strange, foreign flash of anger in his eyes. "After everything that's happened, you *still* don't understand. I'm *supposed* to do this!"

Mira shook her head sadly. "No, Ben. You're not, but someone is."

With the last of her strength, she grabbed Zoey and the plutonium with both hands. Pain lashed through her broken arm, but she fought through it . . . and heaved the little girl and the cylinder into the bright white light on the other side of the Vortex.

Zoey flew past the swirling particles and then, what Mira could see of her, flashed and slowed down, moving in slower and slower motion before flaring in bright, fragmented color and vanishing.

Pain, horrible and sharp, covered Mira's body. She screamed, her cocoon of protection gone, and even though the Vortex was weaker, it was still active. The charged particles raked over her.

"Ben!" Mira cried. She felt no shame at begging now. The pain was beyond anything she could have imagined, and the process was slow enough that she could feel it all happening. *"Ben, please!"*

Ben stared at Mira, frozen in horror, watching the Vortex slowly tear her apart. "Mira . . ." he moaned in anguish.

Mira tried to speak but the pain was too much now. She curled into a ball and screamed.

"I'm sorry . . ." Ben said so low she could barely hear him. The look on his face was wretched. "I'll fix it. I'll fix *all* of it, I promise!" Then he leaped into the white light after Zoey—and vanished in the same prismatic flash, leaving her there alone.

The last thing Mira saw was the Severed Tower stretching up into the sky, just on the other side of the white barrier. There was something familiar about it now. She had seen it before—or, rather, something like it. Somewhere else.

For one brief, merciful second, the pain was forgotten as she made the connection. She knew what the Tower really was . . . and it made perfect—

Mira's consciousness disintegrated as what was left of her body shattered into billions of pieces and merged with the Vortex, like ash thrown into a hurricane.

THE WORLD WAS BLACK. A complete absence of color or light, of any world at all. It was silent, too. Still, Zoey was aware of it. In fact, it felt like she was standing on something.

Under her feet a platform materialized, like a bridge of bright white energy that stretched between nothing. It glowed powerfully, but the illumination revealed only more black. Wherever she was, it was massive in scope, stretching farther than even the light could reach.

In the far distance, very far, another sliver of white blazed to life. A second platform. And Zoey thought she could see a figure standing on it as well.

Where *was* she?

You are separate from space, disconnected from time, a voice said from somewhere, and the sound was jarring. Zoey took a step back, frightened. *You are everywhere and nowhere. Both at once. Yet neither.*

Zoey looked for the voice, but it had no source she could find. "Hello?" she quietly spoke. Her voice sounded strange and disconnected. It just . . . ended in nothing, like the platform under her. *"Hello?"* she shouted.

She looked back to the slit of light in the far distance—and saw something surprising. Now there were a dozen more shining platforms, each with a single, solitary person. There was something familiar about those figures, but from this far away she couldn't tell what. As she watched, they became a hundred more, multiplying in the dark.

"Zoey," said a tiny voice.

She spun and saw something impossible.

Herself.

A perfect replica, calmly staring back with her own eyes, speaking with her own voice. She instinctively took another step back . . . and her twin figure did the same, in an exact echo. It was like looking into a mirror, a three-dimensional one.

Experimentally, Zoey raised her left hand. So did the replica. Zoey balanced on one leg. So did the replica. She slowly lowered her foot back to the platform, watching her twin do the same. Zoey stared in wonder. "Are you . . . *me?*"

"No." The replica's mouth moved, Zoey noticed. It seemed to be the only thing that wasn't tied to what Zoey herself did. It still didn't make any sense. "Regardless of Deviation, Zoey, there is only one you."

Zoey's eyes narrowed. "Who . . . are you?"

"It would be more efficient to exchange the idea of 'who' for the idea of 'what.'"

"*What* are you, then?"

"The combined manifestation of six million, four hundred thousand and sixty-seven entities and their Deviations." Zoey didn't understand any of that, and the look on her face, the one she saw reflected in the replica's, made it very clear. "We are what you refer to as . . . the Severed Tower," her twin clarified.

Zoey saw her own eyes widen, and a host of memories came flooding back. "Am . . . I *inside* the Tower?"

"It is inefficient to think in geographic terms. The Severed Tower has no inside or out. It simply *is*."

It didn't sound simple at all. In the distance, there were thousands of platforms now, each with *two* figures standing on them. A few were close enough to see detail. On every one stood two versions of *Zoey* facing each other, just as she stood facing her own mirror image.

The effect was startling. "Why does everyone look like me?"

"Because they *are* you, Zoey. They are you in other Deviations." Zoey looked back at the mirror image in confusion. "A Deviation is a break in time."

"I don't understand."

"You come to a fork in a path. You can go left or right. You choose right. That is a Deviation. You easily could have chosen left. Another Deviation exists for that possibility. Deviations exist for every possibility in all the universe, Zoey. They are infinite, and each connects here at the Severed Tower."

Zoey swallowed. "What *is* the Severed Tower?"

"To understand that, you must understand the Strange Lands, and to understand the Strange Lands, you must first understand some truths about the invasion of this planet. Are you aware that the alien race you know as the Assembly uses massive base ships to transport its people through space?"

Zoey nodded. She had been inside one of them, the Oracle had shown her the memories. There were hundreds of them, called Presidiums, scattered throughout the world, stuck like giant daggers into the hearts of the planet's largest cities. But what did that have to do with anything?

"Presidiums are powered by singularities," the image continued. "Contained, miniature black holes that produce tremendous amounts of energy and grant them faster-than-light travel. One of these Presidiums intended to land here, in this city, but, as it began its descent, something went wrong. The vessel's drive core failed, and the energy of the singularity was unleashed in the Earth's atmosphere. The resulting discharge violently ruptured space and time in an initial wave of two hundred square miles."

"It formed the Strange Lands," Zoey whispered.

"Correct. More so, everyday objects that were caught in the disturbance were altered at the quantum level, the effects of which gave them unique properties based on their original functions."

"Artifacts . . ."

"Ruptures in space-time throughout the blast radius created pockets of chaos that manifested in various dangerous ways. The farther one moves from the center of the blast, however, the less powerful these pockets are."

"Anomalies . . ."

"Lastly, every entity, human and Assembly, millions of them, the energy and experience and consciousness of each, was compressed into a single force."

"You," Zoey stated.

"Correct. Though, it is more efficient to think of us as a 'we,' or multitude. Our intelligence is infinite, albeit . . . temporary."

Before Zoey could ask more, bright light flashed in the distance. There were hundreds of thousands of lighted platforms now, some much closer, with both figures staring right back at her.

She saw the source of the flashing. Some of the platforms had been replaced with a field of white light, as if they, and the darkness around them, had simply been wiped away. It happened to several hundred more while she watched. Something about it was . . . ominous.

"What's happening?"

"In those Deviations, balance has been restored," her doppelgänger replied.

Zoey had heard that statement before, in her dreams. She didn't like it. "What does that mean?" More and more platforms flashed and disappeared, thousands of them, but there were millions more left, stretching everywhere, as if into infinity, like stars.

"The answer is—complex. You are of the Tower, but your intellect is limited to the age of your human form. You may not be able to understand."

"I want to try," Zoey said, watching more and more of the platforms and figures being wiped away.

"Ninety-two-point-one-percent of all Deviations answered similarly," the mirror image stated, as if making an observation. "The universe is a structured thing, Zoey. It naturally attempts to replace any aberrant form of chaos with an ordered system. Planets naturally align themselves around the pull of a sun. Moons around planets. Electrons around nuclei. Even in biology, the pattern continues. Separate, singular pieces of organic information naturally evolve into ordered strands. It is why the one you knew as Gideon chose the human symbol for DNA to represent his White Helix. He understood this concept. He knew that the Severed Tower and the Strange Lands, by their nature, were unordered and chaotic. He and the Librarian both knew the time would come when the natural chaos of the Strange Lands would be replaced with order."

Zoey watched as more and more platforms, thousands at a time, were wiped away and replaced with empty white light. Zoey didn't like watching it.

"Why is the balance coming back now?" she asked.

"Because you have returned to the Tower. You are its final piece, and all pieces of an unordered whole must be present before they can be ordered."

"But . . . what happens then?"

"When the Presidium suffered its containment failure, the explosion ripped the ship into two pieces. The impact never occurred, however. Time, in its ruptured state, halted at the epicenter of the quantum disturbance and throughout the expanding blast of energy."

"That's why they're growing," Zoey said, thinking about what Mira had believed. "It's . . . an *explosion*. The Strange Lands is a weird kind of explosion. It was frozen in time and now it isn't."

"Correct. The closer you, Zoey, move to the epicenter, the more energy of the blast is released. Now that you are here, the energy in its entirety can be released, and when it is gone, balance will be restored. The Strange Lands will be no more, the quantum disturbances will normalize, and the Severed Tower will cease to exist."

Something occurred to Zoey then. "What will happen to all the people in the Strange Lands?"

"They will die," the mirror image stated.

Zoey stared in disbelief. "The White Helix? All of Mira's friends?"

"As well as the denizens of Midnight City. The quantum blast will expand and engulf it as well."

Zoey's hands shook at the idea, one part of her mind trying to imagine the devastation, another part picturing images of other people. Ones she knew. Holt. Mira. The Max. Gideon. Even Ambassador. They would die, too. Because of *her*.

"Concern for your friends is inefficient," her twin said, sensing Zoey's thoughts somehow. Around them, the flashes continued violently, wiping away tens of thousands of Deviations at a time.

"Why?" Zoey asked.

"Because they are already dead."

Zoey felt the tingling of fear. The thing in front of her couldn't have meant what it just said.

"They died fighting a large Assembly force in an attempt to ensure you reached this point. They succeeded," the mirror image said, as if it should be some sort of consolation, but it wasn't.

Pain and sadness erupted inside Zoey with an intensity she had never known. Tears welled in her eyes, she forgot to breathe. It couldn't be true. It couldn't . . .

"If it provides you comfort," her twin continued, the flashes strobing everywhere in the distance, "in ninety-seven-point-three-percent of all Deviations, your friends perish. There is nothing you could have done to save them. You have not failed them in any way. You have merely fulfilled your purpose."

"And they died because of it!" Zoey shouted in despair and stepped forward. So did the mirror image. "*Everyone's* going to die because of it! Because of *me!*"

In her mind she saw Holt carrying her on his back; Mira showing her how artifacts worked; the Max pushing his nose under her hand. Zoey's vision blurred, her body wracked with sobs. She collapsed to the platform and felt her twin do the same.

Please, don't let it be true, she thought. *Please . . .*

"We do not understand your grief," the mirror image stated with genuine confusion.

The words instilled a foreign emotion in her. White, hot anger. It flared through her, and she wiped the tears away and stared into the twisted version of herself. "When I got here, something *good* was supposed to happen!"

"Something good *will* happen, Zoey. Balance will be restored."

"How is that *good?* How is it good if everyone dies?! *This* is what I was supposed to do? This is why the Librarian and Gideon and the White Helix and Mira and Holt and Ambassador and everyone else tried to get me here? *This?*"

Around them, hundreds of thousands of platforms vanished in flashes of bright light. There were few left now, she noticed. In a few more moments they would all be gone.

Zoey breathed in and out heavily, shaking, the tears staining her cheeks. She asked her next question almost in desperation. It was the one thing she had wanted to know, the one absolute, the thing that, in the end, drove her need to be here, to find this horrible, unfair place. It was the reason for everything. "Who . . . *am* I?"

"Who do you think you are?"

"I don't know," Zoey admitted. She felt nothing but sadness now, the rage was gone. "I don't remember. The Librarian called me the Apex. The White Helix call me the Prime—but I don't know what any of that means."

"Different terms for the same thing. While the mathematical equations that underlie the Strange Lands and the absorption of its entities are immense and complicated, they are not efficient. They resulted in a remainder."

Zoey was still confused. "I don't—"

"If you take ten numbers from eleven numbers, what do you have left?"

"One," Zoey answered, wiping away the tears. She had to concentrate, had to listen. Maybe there was a solution in what the Tower was telling her, maybe there was something she could still do.

"Precisely. The reality is far more complicated than eleven minus ten, but the concept is the same. In the end, there was a mathematical remainder—and that remainder was you, Zoey."

Zoey remembered what the Oracle had shown her. She remembered being on the hillside, watching the falling stars that turned out to be something much worse. She remembered her mother, and the explosion in the air, and the panic that swept through the crowd. She also remembered the rushing wave of energy that washed over her.

"Did I . . . die?" she asked, though she wasn't sure she wanted to know the answer.

"Not entirely. Your original physical form was wiped away with everyone else, but your essence, your consciousness, remained, as did theirs. Instead of being absorbed into the mass that became us, however, you were reborn."

"Am I human?"

"You are human and more. Your body was re-formed from the energy of the Strange Lands. As such, you inherited the same chaotic, improbable nature. You are the person you were—and you are something else. A life-form of pure quantum distinguishability. Your biological structure is beyond unique, adaptive in ways that defy even the power of evolution. You are still mortal. Left alone, you would age and grow and eventually die, just as anyone else. You are human in every sense. Yet you are not human at all. You are of the Strange Lands, yet independent of it. You are both an Anomaly *and* an artifact. You are the final piece of the Tower, the remainder of a vast equation, and now you have returned."

"And you . . . brought me here? All this way?"

"Without you, the chaos cannot be ordered. We have repeated the effort among millions of Deviations. Arranged countless seemingly irrelevant events, altered probabilities, all to bring you home. Holt, Mira, the Librarian, the Oracle, Ravan, the White Helix, Gideon, and hundreds of other small decisions or actions that led directly, one after the other, to your return. And you must return in every Deviation."

Zoey looked back into the space around her. The millions of Deviations were all gone, wiped away, and the world was full of only bright white light now. But something was wrong about that. It took Zoey a moment to figure out what.

"Why haven't *we* been wiped away?" Zoey asked, looking at all the brightness.

"Because in this Deviation there is an aberration."

Zoey looked back at herself. "What's an aberration?"

"Something unplanned for or paradoxical. Something that should not be," her twin said. "You know him as Benjamin Aubertine."

It took a moment for Zoey to connect the name in her mind, and when she did it didn't seem possible. "*Ben?* Mira's friend? He's . . . *here?*"

"Correct. Which should be impossible."

"Why? He had plutonium, didn't he?"

"A radioactive substance is necessary to pass through the Vortex, but it will not aid in entering the Severed Tower. Attempting to do so always results in the individual's energy being absorbed into our own."

Zoey thought about that a moment. It was contrary to what Mira had said. "I thought . . . people had made it inside the Tower before."

"Correct. In this Deviation, seven in total, but none have ever returned from doing so. Their energy and consciousness are now a part of us. Anyone who has ever claimed otherwise speaks falsehoods. There is no exit from the Tower."

"Then . . . Ben is part of you, too?"

"No. He is an aberration. Like you, he remains. It is a paradox."

"Why?" Zoey asked. Something about this seemed important.

"He has with him an artifact, the one artifact in all the universe whose power supersedes our own. It has the power to shift probabilities in the favor of whomever possesses it, and currently it is shifting probabilities to keep him alive. It is preventing him from being absorbed into our essence."

The Tower must have meant the Chance Generator. The bad artifact that had almost turned Holt into someone else. Another question occurred to her, a possibility, a glimmer of hope.

"Why is he here?" Zoey asked, wiping the rest of her tears away, looking at all the white around her where the various platforms had been erased. Her Deviation, for the moment, still existed.

"We do not understand the question," the mirror image stated.

"*Why* is he here? There must be a reason."

"Why must there be a reason, Zoey?"

"Because it's different! It can't be a coincidence!"

"Where the Tower is not concerned, there are *only* coincidences, Zoey."

"But out of all these realities," Zoey stood up and motioned to all the white, "all these possibilities, he's here in just *this* one!"

"It is irrelevant."

"No! *Stop!* You're supposed to be smart!"

"Our intelligence is infinite, Zoey."

"Then stop thinking in straight lines!" Zoey shouted in anguish. She had to find a way to save them, to make everything okay again. She *had* to.

Her twin hesitated, remaining quiet a second or two—and for something as intelligent as it was, two seconds was an eternity.

"You . . . theorize that we think *linearly*," the mirror image finally said. "Interesting. No other Deviation has ever made this analysis. It is . . . wholly unique."

Zoey pressed on, her excitement building. "Don't you see!? This one is different than all the others! Which makes it *important!*"

"What are you proposing, Zoey?"

Now it was Zoey's turn to hesitate. It was a good question. What *was* she proposing? There was a solution there, she knew it. She just had to figure out what might be different in her Deviation that she could use. There seemed to be only one thing.

"The . . . Chance Generator," she said. "It's keeping Ben alive?"

"Correct. Though, even here, its power will wane. The artifact will expend its energy, and when that happens, balance will be restored."

The excitement she felt a moment ago faltered. If what the Tower was saying was true, it meant time was running out. If the Chance Generator died, then everything would continue as it was. Her Deviation would be wiped away like all the others, and Mira and Holt and Max would be truly gone.

Again, everything seemed to point to one thing. "What if . . . what would happen if I took it? What would happen if Ben gave *me* the Chance Generator?"

Again her mirror image hesitated. "An . . . intriguing proposition. The restoration of balance would still only be delayed, but, as the remainder, you would . . . inhabit a unique opportunity."

"What opportunity?" Zoey felt the hope building again.

"You are part of the Tower. Its singular piece. Balance would still be restored, the energy of the singularity would still be released, but the Probability Influencer would . . . shield you from the discharge. You would not be swept away with everything else. You would, again, remain, and, more so, you could direct the energy as it was released."

"Direct it how?"

"For a brief, limited amount of time, thirty-nine seconds to be precise, you could use it to shape time and space, though only in how it relates directly to your experience in this Deviation."

"I could save them!"

"Understand, Zoey, that balance must be restored. It is a mathematical necessity, and you are part of the same equation. Though the Probability Influencer will shield you from the initial realignment, you are still an aberration to this Deviation. Where you are concerned, things must be balanced as well. Making this choice does not remove that requirement."

Zoey thought she understood. It was a grim solution, but, without question, a much better one than the alternative. Everyone she loved would still be alive. She could undo all the damage she had done.

"I understand," she said.

In the distance, amid all the white, a rectangle of pure blackness opened, like some kind of shadowy door. It began to grow, as if racing toward her. Zoey watched it warily.

"There is one variable that remains," her twin said. "The aberration. He has become reliant on the Probability Influencer. He will not give it up willingly, and you do not have the physical strength to take it from him."

Zoey nodded, seeing the problem, but there had to be a way. "I have to try."

"Are you sure this is what you want?" her twin asked pointedly. "If you somehow take the artifact from the aberration, the energy of the singularity will be released and the Tower will be yours to control. You can shape the timeline how you see fit, to an extent. But . . . you do know where this path leads, don't you, Zoey?"

Zoey stayed silent a long time, watching the black doorway rushing toward her. Much of what the Tower had told her was beyond her ability to grasp, but she still thought she understood what this decision meant. How would she ever explain it to Holt or Mira? Of course, those would be wonderful problems to have. It would mean they were alive and she was with them. "It's the right thing to do."

"We find this interesting," her replica stated. "This choice was . . . unpredicted. Perhaps you are right. Perhaps this Deviation is singularly important. We wish we could observe the end result, but . . . balance must be restored. This will be the last time we speak, Zoey. From here until the inevitable end, we can no longer help you."

"I understand." The door was almost there, rushing toward her. "And . . . thank you."

"An inefficient sentiment," her twin responded. "Good-bye, Zoey."

Her mirror image faded. The door roared toward her. Zoey closed her eyes—and was swept away.

"ARE YOU . . . REAL?" BEN asked.

It had been an instant transition, without pain or sensation. One moment Zoey was in all that empty, bright whiteness. Then she was here. An old, ruined church, most of its ceiling missing, the stars visible outside. A campfire lit the interior in flickering orange.

Ben sat on one of the ruined pews, staring up at the night sky. At the sound of her approach, the boy calmly turned and considered her. He seemed slightly dazed, as if he were waking from a dream. Zoey saw the Chance Generator, and the hand that held it shook slightly.

Zoey nodded. "Do you remember me?"

Ben pushed his glasses up the rim of his nose and blinked. "Your name is Zoey. You were with Mira."

"I was?"

"In the Vortex." Ben's voice sounded haunted. "Where I . . . left her."

Zoey wasn't sure what that meant. She had been unconscious at the time, but whatever had happened with Mira clearly bothered Ben a great deal. For the first time since she had known him, she could see things were wearing on him. He looked exhausted, confused, not entirely present, but whether that had to do with the Chance Generator or something about this place, she wasn't sure. All she knew was that she had to find a way to get him to listen to her.

"I did it because I was supposed to come here," he continued, "but nothing has happened. The only thing that's been different is you. You're the first thing that's changed. I don't . . . feel right."

"It *isn't* right, Ben," Zoey said. "You aren't supposed to be here."

"Yes, I am!" he yelled with a pained stare. "I *know* it! But . . . nothing's *happening*. Why won't something happen?"

"Ben, I need you to listen," Zoey said, trying to stay calm. Who knew how much time they had before the Chance Generator was used up? "Everyone outside is gone. They're dead."

Ben barely reacted, he just nodded. "I know. I watched her . . ." He trailed off without finishing. "Why is nothing *happening?*"

"It doesn't have to be this way. We can change it."

"How?"

"I'm a part of the Tower. It . . . made me. Long ago. It's why I can enter and everyone else just gets absorbed and becomes a part of it and disappears."

For the first time Ben's stare focused. She guessed it was because what she was saying was intriguing. From what she understood, that was a big part of who Ben was. "Absorbed?"

Zoey retold the Tower's explanation as best she could, but she wasn't sure she got it right. It had been horribly confusing. Ben, however, listened to what she said, processed it, and the look in his eyes suggested he not only understood it, but that it made sense to him somehow. He looked down at the old abacus in his hand. "It's this, isn't it? I'm alive because I have *this*."

"Yes," Zoey answered.

The realization set off a chain reaction of other realizations in Ben's mind, which Zoey knew could only point in one inevitable direction, and for him it was a horrible one. "I was . . . wrong," he whispered, barely loud enough to hear. He seemed dazed. "All along, I was *wrong*. I wasn't *supposed* to be here."

"Ben, I think—"

"But, I . . ." His eyes lost their focus again, they blurred and moistened, both his hands shook. "Oh, God . . ."

"Ben . . ."

"She died because of *me*. I stood there . . . and I thought . . . I thought I could fix it. I . . ."

"Ben, you have to *listen* to me." Zoey was unable to keep the note of urgency out of her voice. They were running out of time. "Mira doesn't *have* to die. None of them do."

"What have I done?" he whispered painfully, ignoring her.

"Ben!" she yelled with as much force as she could. It got through. He looked at her. "We can still *save* her."

"I *saw* her die!" he yelled back in a raw voice.

She looked at the abacus in his hand, saw how white his knuckles were from gripping it. "You have to give me the artifact. The one in your hand."

Ben looked at the Chance Generator. "Why?"

"If I have it, I can control the Tower. I can fix things. For a little bit, but there isn't much time."

"You can fix it?" He looked at her with hope. "You can make it so the Assembly never came?"

"No." Zoey shook her head sadly. "The Tower doesn't work that way, Ben, but I think I *can* fix it. It won't be like you hoped, but I can save them, if you help me."

A dark hint of suspicion passed over Ben's face. "You . . . you're *lying* to me. You *want* it. You want the abacus for yourself."

Zoey tried to stay calm. "Why would I want that, Ben?"

"You're like everyone else," he snarled. "You want to take it from me, but I won't give it up. Why would I ever give it up?"

Zoey hesitated. This wasn't working. She had to think of something different. She looked around them, at the church, the flickering fire, the exploding stars above. "This place—it's important, isn't it?"

The change of subject seemed to jar Ben out of his hostility. "It doesn't exist anymore. It fell down not long after she and I were here."

"You and Mira?"

Ben nodded. "Why is *this* what the Tower looks like? Why show me this place?"

"Maybe . . . you see what you want to see here," Zoey answered.

Ben's stare moved all around the church. "I guess, if there was one place I'd want to be for eternity, it would be here, but it would be with her. Not alone." Ben looked back up at the stars bitterly. "I was . . . I was *supposed* to be here."

Zoey almost argued with him again, but then something occurred to her. Something profound. "I believe you."

He looked at her hopefully. "You do?"

She nodded, thinking it all through. "Don't you see? If you *hadn't* been here, if you hadn't come—I couldn't fix any of it. We would already be gone, all of us, but . . . because of you I can." She and Ben stared at one another as the impact of what she was saying sunk in. "I think you *were* supposed to be here, and in spite of everything, you found a way to do it."

Ben's gaze softened at her words and he slowly deflated back into the pew, thoughts running through his mind. Zoey couldn't read Ben in this place, for some reason his emotions were closed to her, but just by looking at his face and the barest expressions which formed there, she knew what he was feeling all the same. Relief. Contentment. Resolution.

"If I give you the abacus," he quietly said, "I'll die. Won't I?"

Zoey stared back at him. "I don't know what happens when someone is absorbed into the Tower, Ben, but I don't think it's the same thing as dying."

Ben was quiet a moment longer, then he looked back down to the artifact. His hand was no longer shaking, Zoey noticed. "It was so hard to give up before . . ."

"You can do it. Holt gave it up. You're just as strong as he is—only in different ways."

Ben looked up again. "If what you said is true, that we see what we want to see here, then . . ."

As he spoke, what was left of the ceiling was wiped away and the breadth of the night sky opened itself. The stars burst apart in prismatic color, over and over again. It was beautiful. In spite of the situation, Zoey stared up in wonder.

"The problem was always too much interference," Ben said. "Too much data. I always wondered . . ."

Above them the stars flashed out, one by one, one after the other, until nothing was left but a single, strange-looking constellation.

"There." A smile spread across Ben's face. From what Zoey knew of him, that was a rare thing. *"There."*

"What is it?" Zoey asked.

"A scorpion." He almost laughed as he spoke the words. "I can *see* it."

Zoey stared up at the cluster of stars in the black sky, but it looked nothing like a scorpion to her. After a few moments Ben turned to her. He pulled something from a pocket and placed it in Zoey's palm. It was a single brass cube of dice.

"Will you . . . tell her I meant what I said?" Ben seemed calm now, at peace. "At the Anvil."

"She knows, Ben," Zoey answered, "but yes, I will."

He nodded . . . and then his hand slowly raised and held out the Chance Generator. Zoey stared at it hesitantly, as if the old, innocent-looking abacus were a coiled viper. If she wanted to make everything alright, she would have to take it. Slowly, she forced her hand around it, and she and Ben held it at the same time. He stared down at it intensely—and then finally, slowly . . . he let it go.

At first there was no indication anything had changed. Then a crimson sphere flashed around Zoey. She saw Ben's form begin to lighten and glow. Streaks of light drifted off him, rising into the night sky, each streak reducing his luminosity by a fraction.

Whatever was happening to him, it didn't seem painful. He was smiling again. "It's . . . like pure knowledge," he said.

Zoey watched as he faded, bits of light drifting up from him into the sky, until his entire body gently broke apart and blended into the air. When she looked up, the stars had been repopulated with those streaks, and their light rained down on her . . . and then he was gone.

Zoey looked at the abacus. She knew what she had to do. She knew the sacrifices involved, but she'd promised Ben. She'd promised them all.

The last thing Zoey felt before the world exploded in white, was the brass dice cube in her tightly squeezed fist.

43. BALANCE

TIME STREAMED BACKWARD PAST AVRIL in painful blurs of light, and it felt like her mind was being split apart.

Then it abruptly ended.

She barely recovered fast enough to avoid a burst of plasma bolts from an Assembly Hunter, flipping up and back and just catching the edge of a crushed Volkswagen. Instantly, she fired her remaining crystal and watched the walker fall in a burst of flame.

What had just happened? The last she remembered, she was holding Dane on the water tower, both of them bleeding and clinging to each other.

Dane.

Instinctively, she searched the battle raging around her—and found him. Crouched on a rooftop, staring right back at her. Avril breathed in stunned relief. So did he. But it was clear neither knew how it was possible.

All around her, Avril saw her Arc—Masyn, Castor. Most of the others. Flipping and darting through the air as yellow bolts sizzled past them, firing their spears, continuing (or repeating, she wasn't sure) the same fight.

In the distance, bright flashes of light sparked to life up and down the line of larger walkers. Seconds later, the popping sounds of ordnance being fired echoed through the air.

Avril remembered this. She *remembered*. "Heads up!" she yelled to the jumping Helix around her. She saw the streaks of light rain down just like before . . . but they never fell.

The sky flashed. The projectiles slowed . . . and then burst harmlessly apart above the White Helix.

Two massive Dark Matter Tornadoes suddenly descended from the clouds right on top of the artillery walkers. The huge machines sparked and burst into flames as the black funnel clouds moved over them, warping and ripping them to pieces. In just seconds the huge walkers disintegrated into flaming, twisted metal.

Lightning—red, blue, and green—fired down from the sky. Explosions flared everywhere as the lightning targeted the Hunters, one by one, blowing them apart in showers of colored flame, leaving craters of glowing crystals.

Avril watched, stunned, as the lightning ripped through the Assembly ranks, saw them turn and run, confused, unable to defend themselves as the land itself turned against them. More Tornadoes descended from the clouds, barreling down on the army.

Toward the north, in the far distance, Avril saw something even more incredible.

The Vortex was gone, as if it had never existed, and without it, the truth of the Severed Tower was fully revealed.

The black shape of an Assembly Presidium base ship hung over the city ruins, broken into two giant pieces, one falling away from the other in a rupture that was, somehow, stuck in time.

The winds ripped through Avril's hair. All around her she could hear explosions and streaking missiles, but her eyes were on the Severed Tower . . . and a single speck of glowing brightness hovering in front of it, a thousand feet off the ground, wrapped in shimmering golden light.

"Zoey . . ." Avril breathed in awe.

THE ONE THE SCION named Ambassador felt the world rip backward and resume at the most opportune moment. It was surrounded by seven Hunters and the one the Scion named the Royal.

Each opponent hesitated, confused, dazed, unsure what had happened.

But Ambassador hesitated the least.

It plowed through three of the Royal's guardians, driving them into the ground in bursts of flame.

As before, the others twisted, trying to target the five-legged walker—

but this time they had no chance. Red and green lightning streaked down and blew them to pieces, one at a time.

The Royal trumpeted in shock, suddenly facing its adversary one-on-one, its advantage lost.

The tripod barely lunged out of the way of Ambassador's charge, its cannons whining and firing.

Ambassador's shield collapsed, like before, but it didn't care. This was the opportunity it had waited for. It would vanquish an ancient enemy. Or that enemy would vanquish it. There was no middle ground.

It spun around and charged. The powerful walker connected with the Royal in a horribly violent impact, sending it crashing through what was left of a drugstore. As it did, bright, glowing things formed in the air. Each the shape of a cube.

The cubes drifted toward the tripod as it tried to stand and right itself. One of them made contact with the Hunter's armor and a great plume of sparks shot from it. The Royal stood up, tried to move . . .

And another cube sank into it. Then another, and another. More and more, piling on top of the machine. The Royal trumpeted, and if Ambassador had still been connected to the Whole, it was sure it would have felt its enemy's fear.

The desperate machine burst through a window, crashing outside, but it was too late. Its armor disintegrated as dozens of the glowing cubes burrowed into it, driving it to the ground. Flames shot everywhere. The green-and-orange Ephemera of the Royal drifted into the air, glittering and flashing, frantically trying to form, but it couldn't. It broke into a billion pieces and dissolved into nothing, while Ambassador watched in satisfaction.

HOLT GASPED OUT LOUD as he unwound from time.

The first thing he noticed was Max licking his face. The second was that he was lying on the ground between two jackknifed semitruck trailers that were warped and merged together. Ravan and her men were there, too, staring at each other with odd, disturbed looks.

Holt shuddered as he remembered Max dying, Ravan's limp form against a wall, the huge Spider walker crashing down on top of them. What the hell just *happened*?

Explosions shook the trailers violently. Plasma bolts sizzled through the air. Holt could hear the trumpetings from a hundred Hunters in the air.

"Get your asses up!" Ravan yelled, grabbing her rifle.

Everyone got to their feet as two Hunters leaped onto the roofs of the tractor trailers on either side of them, their cannons priming to fire. The Menagerie's rifles opened up, spraying bullets upward, and the tripods shuddered and fell away.

More were coming, thundering toward them in a stampede, threatening to overwhelm what was left of the silver reinforcements that were firing desperately in all directions.

Holt and Ravan braced themselves, her men tensed . . .

And the air was suddenly full of flashing bright shapes that Holt recognized. Tesla Cubes, Mira had called them, the things that had destroyed the Crossroads. They appeared from nowhere, thousands of them, flashing to life right in front of the charging Hunters.

The walkers skidded to a stop, trying to avoid the Anomalies, but there was nowhere to go.

Sparks flew everywhere as the cubes covered and burrowed into the machines, dissolving them where they stood. Lightning flashed down from the swirling clouds, striking in pulses of color. Thunder shook the ground.

The Menagerie watched as the Assembly was torn to pieces by the environment.

A huge, triumphant bellow emitted from behind them, and Holt saw the silver Spider walker stomping forward, its massive cannons firing, sending plasma hurdling into the crowd of dying Hunters.

"Oh, my God . . ." Ravan said, and Holt turned. They stared above them, past the trailers and the flashing lightning and the fields of glowing cubes, toward the north.

There in the distance, the Severed Tower hung, but the swirling mass of the Vortex was gone, and he and Ravan could see it clearly now. It was . . . a *Presidium?* It didn't seem possible, but that was exactly what he saw: a massive Presidium base ship, broken in half, hovering in the air. Standing out against its huge black shape was a small dot of glowing, golden whiteness. It was a figure, Holt could tell. A small one.

"Is . . . that your girl?" Ravan asked.

"Yeah," Holt said, smiling. "That's my girl."

ZOEY HUNG SUSPENDED JUST in front of where the Presidium had broken apart all those years ago. She could feel the energy streaming out from it, growing and building. Soon it would be too much for her to control, but it didn't matter. She would be done by then.

Everything stretched out into infinity. Not just the Strange Lands below, but everything. Pasts. Futures. Presents. Every possible combination of every potential possibility relating to her converged at that exact moment—and every other moment—and they were hers to shape.

For one brief period, she *was* the Tower.

Time yielded to her, and she forced it back, rewinding it all in a blur. Below she saw Mira disintegrate and then re-form. Saw the White Helix cut down, then rise up. Watched the giant silver Spider walker crush Holt's building and then stand back onto its giant legs.

But she had to do more than that, and she could.

She reached out to the Strange Lands, felt its chaotic power.

Dark Matter Tornadoes dropped from the swirling, black clouds. Antimatter Lightning rained down. She summoned Tesla Cubes, Quark Spheres, and Daisy Chains; she made Time Sinks and Landmines and Pulsars and she flung all of it, the full force of the Strange Lands itself, at the massive Assembly army below, and it stumbled and faltered under the onslaught.

From some of the Assembly, she sensed a new intention. They already hated this place, were terrified of it, and the sight of Zoey, the Scion, controlling all of it, holding their fate in her hands, was enough to break their resolve.

But only for some. Those she spared, directing the energy of the Strange Lands away from them. She did the same for Ambassador and the silver reinforcements it had brought. That was all. She watched as the Tower's energy tore into the rest and scattered them like leaves in a furious wind.

The air below was covered in flickering, golden energy fields, hundreds of them, lighting up the darkness, but only briefly. They never took shape, it was impossible here. Their energy bled away into the air. Their colors faded.

Scion, a sudden mass of projections reached her, from hundreds of sources. She could sense their shock, their fear, bleeding off of them. *Why?*

The energy of the Tower kept building. It was getting too strong, and the Chance Generator's influence was fading. She had to redirect it, let it release before it was too late, but still she hesitated. She remembered what the Tower had told her.

Balance must be restored. It is a mathematical necessity. And you are part of the same equation.

Only, she wanted to see Holt again. Wanted to see Mira and the Max. She wanted it all so badly.

The Feelings stirred, rising up eagerly, filling her with strength. Zoey listened, sensing their intentions, their idea. Could it work, she wondered? Was it cheating? She thought the process through, the chain of events she would set in motion. She knew where it led.

But was it the right thing to do? Is it what Holt or Mira would do? Maybe not. Maybe it was selfish, but didn't she deserve it this once? After all she had done?

The Feelings swirled pleasantly, agreeing, encouraging.

Zoey made her choice. She unleashed the full, impending blast from the singularity, the one that had been building all this time, and used all that chaotic power to shape one final set of events. Events that would still lead to true balance. Only later.

She hoped it would be enough, she hoped fate accepted her bargain.

Behind her, the Assembly Presidium, once known as the Severed Tower, shuddered and flashed blindingly, unsticking in time.

There was a violent, gut-wrenching explosion as it disintegrated into the ground, shaking the earth in a massive fireball that bellowed outward. Zoey closed her eyes and focused. Concentrating the energy, directing it, sending it away from everyone she loved.

Finally, moments later, for the first time in more than nine years— balance was restored.

44. SUNLIGHT

"MIRA . . ."

The voice was far away. It wasn't what she expected. She never expected to hear anything ever again.

"Mira . . ."

It was a girl's voice, she could tell. A little girl, and it sounded worried.

She heard and felt other things in her hazy delirium—the sound of a gentle wind, the warmth of the sun—and for some reason, those sensations seemed very out of place.

"Mira."

The insistent tiny voice pulled her out of the dark. Light poured in as her eyes blinked open—and what she saw didn't make sense.

The sky was directly above her. It was midafternoon, bright and sunny.

Pieces of buildings and other things hovered over her—windows, gutters, old billboards she couldn't read, the top of a rusted ambulance, all of it warped in twisted shapes. The wind stirred her red hair gently.

A little girl was next to her. Someone she recognized. Someone she never thought she would see again. Staring down at her with a slight, wondering smile.

"Zoey . . ." Mira whispered.

"Mira, look," the little girl urged. "It's not like it used to be."

Mira was stunned by what she saw. She remembered the Vortex, tearing her apart in unbelievable pain. She remembered Ben, too. Then she woke here, with Zoey. But where was *here?*

It took a moment for her mind to connect the dots.

She was exactly where she had been. In Bismarck. The heart of the

371

Strange Lands. Only the Strange Lands were gone. No oppressing darkness. No black, swirling clouds or furious winds. Even the Charge was missing.

Instead, the sun shown down. *The sun.* Shining through white clouds that only partially covered a brilliant blue sky. Where the Tower had been there was nothing now. Just a massive blackened scar, as if from some epic blast of fire, stretching northward. Everything there was flattened and charred, but to the south it was all untouched.

"What happened?" Mira asked.

"Everything's like it's supposed to be," Zoey told her. "Well. Almost everything."

Mira wasn't sure what Zoey meant, but she was too shocked to ask. She couldn't believe what she was looking at.

"Thank you, Mira," Zoey said.

"For what?"

"I couldn't have gotten here without you. You were the only one who could do it."

The words eclipsed whatever awe Mira felt at the landscape. They were words, just yesterday, she would have thought impossible to hear. It reminded her of Holt. Which reminded her of many other things.

"Did we . . . die?" she asked. "Did you save us, Zoey?"

"No." Zoey reached forward and put something in Mira's hand. "Someone else did."

It was Ben's brass dice cube. The sight of it, without him holding it, was jarring. She had never not seen him with the object. Mira felt her emotions begin to build.

"He wanted you to know he meant what he—"

"I know." Mira nodded and wiped away the first of the tears. "I know."

She looked to the south. There was destruction there, too—burning buildings, the wrecks of Assembly walkers—but it also had life. There was movement, figures slowly wandering the streets and gathering together.

In the far distance there was even more motion, just becoming visible. A mass of thousands of figures marching toward them, moving through the now-quiet battle zone. Each was flanked by two shining points of color.

The White Helix were arriving.

"Come with me," Zoey said, holding out her hand. Mira took it and slowly rose. There was no pain, her limbs were no longer shattered.

"Where are we going?" she asked.

"To *them*. I have something I need to do, before . . . before everything else."

They walked through the ruins, all of it warped and twisted by Dark Matter Tornadoes that, already, in the sunlight, seemed like a foreign concept. "What does that mean, Zoey? Everything else?"

Zoey squeezed Mira's hand tightly. "It means it isn't over."

45. EVERYTHING

HOLT EYED HIS COT and sleeping bag wantonly. He would sleep for a week if no one stopped him. The way his luck had been going, though, that didn't seem likely.

He was inside one of the offices where the Menagerie had set up camp. They were small offices, still filled with the ruined possessions of their owners, all of them fused to one another and immoveable. The Strange Lands were gone, but the Artifacts remained. They still had their powers, even now. Holt wasn't sure if that was a good thing or not.

The office's windows looked out on the streets of Bismarck, and for once they were empty. The White Helix had gone to bury Gideon. Holt wasn't sure why Zoey couldn't save him like the others. Maybe his death happened too far back in time to influence. Maybe she had her own reasons for not helping him. Either way, he was gone, and though the White Helix mourned, they were resolved. For what exactly, Holt couldn't say.

Ambassador and the silver Assembly set up to the south, including several dozen green-and-orange Hunters and their artillery walkers. Holt wasn't sure why they hadn't been wiped away with the others, but they seemed cooperative at any rate. Still, everyone gave them a wide berth. They were Assembly, after all.

The office had a door, which was good. It made it private. Holt moved to shut it, wincing as he unbuttoned his shirt. Every part of him ached.

Ravan leaned against the door, smiling conspiratorially. Holt sighed. All he wanted to do was shut his eyes. "Ravan . . ."

"Just pretend I'm not here," she said, studying his shirt.

"Not sure I'd sleep all that well with you staring at me," Holt retorted.

She hid it well, but Ravan was tired, too. Holt knew her well enough to see the signs. He knew when something was bothering her as well. It was the same as always. She wouldn't talk about whatever it was unless he asked. "You okay?"

Ravan held his stare. "Not as good as you, surprisingly."

"I think I'm too tired to be worried about much right now."

"We were *dead*, Holt. Dead and gone, and that little girl of yours brought us back."

Holt leaned against the door frame across from her. "You don't sound all that thrilled. Would you prefer she hadn't?"

"No," Ravan said. "I'm just saying . . . it's a pretty scary power to be able to tap into. There's gotta be a price, messing with the order of things like that. Repercussions."

Holt rubbed his eyes tiredly. "What's your point, Ravan?"

"You care about her, I get it, but a power like that sets off red flags, and it should. If I were you, I'd be asking myself just what it is I'm traveling with."

"She's a 'who,' Ravan, not a 'what,'" Holt said with intensity. "And I don't just care about her, I trust her. She *saved* us."

"Just pointing out something you might be too close to see," she told him. "You used to value that."

Holt frowned and looked away. Ravan wasn't totally wrong. What Zoey had done . . . It didn't seem possible. Controlling machines was one thing. Reversing time was quite another. If Zoey could do that, what else could she do? And did he want to find out?

"Thought anymore about Faust?" Ravan asked.

He shook his head. "I have to help Zoey, Ravan."

"You'll help her a lot better without the Menagerie hunting you down, and with Avril, it's your best bet of changing things."

"Yeah," Holt replied. "Also my best bet for getting shot between the eyes."

Ravan smiled. "It's still better odds than you had two weeks ago, and you won't get near that good again. Besides, we had a deal, you and I." Her stare drifted downward, to the half-finished image on his wrist.

"I break deals all the time," Holt said half seriously.

She looked back up at him with her sapphire eyes. "No, you don't."

A shuffling outside the door broke their attention. Mira stood in the hall. The sight of her, watching him and Ravan, caused a twinge of unease.

"Sorry," Mira said. "I can come back . . ."

"That's okay, Red. I'm done," Ravan replied. She looked back at Holt as she turned and stepped into the hall. "Think about it."

Holt watched her disappear, waited until the sound of her footsteps faded, and then looked at Mira. She wore her feelings much more on her sleeve than Ravan did. "Hi," he said.

Mira smiled a little. "What was that about?"

Holt turned and stepped back into the room. "The usual. Old debts."

"She wants you to go back with her?"

"Yeah," he replied.

"Is that what you want?"

"Not particularly, I like my head where it is."

"But she thinks you can fix things. With the Menagerie. Wouldn't that be worth it?"

"There's no fixing anything with Tiberius." He reached the end of his room, near the window overlooking the strange, twisted streets, all of it eerily contrasted by the bright sunshine. Those two things didn't belong with each other. Like a lot of things in his life, now that he thought about it.

Mira stepped into the room and closed the door behind her. In spite of everything, the silence between them was still thick. Holt hated it. The apprehension that existed whenever they were close now, but it was what it was.

"Where's Zoey?" he asked.

"At the burial. No one except her and the White Helix were allowed, but I watched from a roof. After they were done . . . she started cleansing them."

"From the Tone?"

Mira nodded. "All of them, one at a time. There were thousands, Holt, waiting their turn, and more are still coming in. I just wish I knew what we're supposed to do *now*."

"I don't have the first idea," Holt admitted. "I guess we just keep following Zoey's lead." Holt hesitated, looking at Mira. She was unkempt but still beautiful. Her hair had grown even longer now, stretching past the back of her shoulders. He liked her with longer hair, he decided. "I wanted to tell you I . . . don't want it to be weird between us. We don't have to try to be what we were. Or . . . almost were. You know what I mean. But we shouldn't go our separate ways. Not now. Zoey needs us—maybe more than ever—and we need her."

Mira just stood there silently. He hadn't expected anything else, really. After all, what was there to say? She didn't owe him anything, not anymore. God, he was tired. "Look, I need to close my eyes, and I'm sure—"

"You believed in me," she interrupted him softly.

Holt blinked. "What?"

"When no one else did," Mira continued, staring at him. "I would have quit without you. It's what got me through the Vortex. It's what's gotten me through everything that came before, I just never saw it."

Holt stared back, unsure what to say or think. All the same, he felt his heart beating faster. He watched her move to him, slowly reach down and take his left hand, running her fingers across the unfinished tattoo there.

"This used to be something that bothered me," she said, "but it doesn't now. Now it's proof you really are who I thought you were, and I don't think you should cover it up anymore."

The words had more impact on him than he expected. Slowly, Holt ran his fingers through hers. He half-expected her to pull away, but she didn't.

"You asked me something and I never answered," Mira said, looking up from their hands and back into his eyes. "You asked if what happened at the dam meant something. If it mattered to me like it did to you. I should have answered, but I was . . . scared then. I'm not anymore. It *did* matter, Holt. It meant more than something. It meant *everything*, and it still does."

Something about the way her voice gently broke at those last words pulled Holt forward like a magnet, his exhaustion forgotten. He wrapped his arms around Mira and pulled her to him, and their lips found and moved over one another. It was a release more intense than any he had ever known, and he could feel in the way Mira desperately clung against him that it was just as intense for her.

She gasped as he lifted her up and off the floor, their mouths and hands roaming wildly, carrying her to his cot and laying her on top of it, the heat from their bodies melding together and slowly intensifying until the world melted away and there was nothing left but them.

ZOEY STARED AT THE RUINS below from her perch at the top of the tall building. The White Helix had buried Gideon and now they filled the streets. The brightness of the world, now drenched in sunlight, startled them. The dark oppression of the Strange Lands was normal, and all this light and warmth was unsettling.

She had cleansed all of them—so many, one after the other, that time lost its meaning. She didn't know how long it took, but she stayed until every White Helix was free of the Tone. Whatever else they felt for her, there was gratitude now, loyalty.

Mira sat next to her, feet dangling over the edge. From her, Zoey sensed old emotions. Ones that had been lost in recent days. Mira's mind shifted occasionally to images of her and Holt, intertwined and lost, and it made Zoey smile in spite of everything. She hoped they could hold on to that through what was to come.

Zoey told Mira almost everything she had learned in the Tower. Only the details about her final choice, about the bargain she struck with fate, she left out. She would learn that soon enough.

"I still don't get one thing," Mira said when Zoey finished. "Why are you so important to the Assembly? Why do they keep chasing you?"

It was a question Zoey had asked herself, the biggest question really, the only one that remained, and she had her theories. In their conversation, the Tower had never *once* mentioned her abilities, how she could control machines or feel the emotions and memories of other people. It confirmed for her that those things didn't come from the Tower at all.

She remembered the vision the Oracle had shown her, that horrible, black room and the blue-and-white shape that buried itself inside her and the pain that followed. It wasn't until then that she had first felt the Feelings. The ones that rose whenever she called, and gave her aid.

If the Feelings really were what she now suspected, then her path was clear. It was why she had used the Tower to arrange things the way she had. In the back of her mind, she wondered again if she had done the right thing. Would it have been better to die with the Tower, to not cheat destiny? What she had risked by making her choice, she didn't know yet, but she *did* know what she had gained.

Zoey looked at Mira, felt her emotions for Holt all over again. They were both alive. They could go on and be happy. All it meant was Zoey had to find a way, in whatever was to come, to make sure it stayed that way, and there was only one place she could do that now. She was starting to feel the weight of her choices.

"I haven't thanked you, you know," Mira said softly, staring at the world ticking by below, "for saving us."

Zoey could feel her gratitude. That and something else. Guilt. She realized it came from Mira's belief that Zoey had done something she could never repay, and she desperately wanted to. Not because she didn't like owing people, but because Zoey meant so much to her.

Zoey reached out and rested her tiny hand on Mira's.

Mira's hand squeezed hers. "I love you."

"I love you, too, Mira." She meant it. It made everything that was to come that much harder. "I need to share something with you." Mira looked at her, unsure. "It's something you'll need, and you'll know why when you do." Her grip on Mira's hand tightened. "Close your eyes." Zoey felt Mira's uncertainty, but she did as Zoey said.

Zoey closed her own eyes, then reached for the Feelings and they responded, rising up from the depths. They saw what she intended, and for the first time since they had been a part of her, she felt dismay from them. Revulsion even, but she didn't care. It was the price the Feelings would have to pay if they wanted what was to come. And she had a feeling they desperately did.

Golden energy formed and flickered like flames, slowly spreading up Zoey's and Mira's arms, leaving a trail of tingling warmth as it moved. She could feel Mira's trepidation growing.

"It's okay, Mira," she assured her. "It's going to hurt, but only a little."

Mira's mind opened to hers. Zoey saw the infinity that it and all minds represented, stretching out in an unending field of memories. She pushed forward into it, wading through thoughts of herself and of Holt and Ben, drifting past memories of her father, finding a very specific part. Zoey reached for that part and wrapped herself around it. Mira shuddered. The pain seared Zoey's mind the same as hers. She hated hurting Mira, but there was no other choice.

That piece of Mira's mind unlocked, and when it did Zoey sharpened it, made it stronger, more resilient. It would never be anything like her own abilities, Zoey knew, but it would be enough.

Then Zoey pulled back and out. The golden energy faded. The Feelings receded into the dark, and Mira and Zoey both opened their eyes.

"What . . . what was *that?*" Mira stared at her.

Zoey squeezed her hand one last time, then pulled it away. "Now you're ready, Mira."

"Zoey, what did you just *do?*"

"Can you feel them yet? They're close now."

A new emotion formed within Mira. It started small but grew fast, fueled by instinct. Mira was starting to guess the truth. That Zoey had set something in motion, something horrible, and it was quickly approaching . . .

"Zoey . . . what did you—"

In the distance, a series of rapid-fire pops and bangs echoed through the air. Mira turned to look, but Zoey didn't need to. The silver walkers were firing to the south, outside the ruins, flinging streams of plasma bolts into the air.

"I'm sorry, Mira," Zoey said. "I . . . made a deal, kind of. A trade. It was the only way to make things right."

Mira's eyes widened. Just visible to the south was a flight of Assembly ships, two dozen maybe, and these were not silver or green-and-orange. They were *blue-and-white,* and streaming toward them.

Zoey could feel the fear from Mira then. Not just fear of those ships—but fear because she could *feel* them. Just as Zoey did. The sensations bleeding off them. Horrible feelings of victory and elation, of long roads finally traversed.

"Zoey, what have you done?" Her voice was horrified. The roar of engines filled the sky now. The White Helix stirred nervously below. "Tell me what you did so we can *stop* it!"

Zoey shook her head sadly. "We can't, Mira. Not this time."

Plasma cannons flashed above them, and flames blossomed on the ground and out the sides of buildings as the blue-and-white ships advanced. The White Helix below flipped and dodged. Crystal spear points streaked into the air, a few punching through the ships in bursts of colored flame, but it wouldn't be enough. Things were set now.

"Pet the Max for me, okay?" Zoey asked Mira. She was almost out of time. "Scratch behind his ears, he likes that the best."

"Zoey!" Mira moved for her—and then they were both blown in separate directions as explosions rocked the roof. Zoey hit and rolled and stared up at the ships, their engines drowning out everything.

From one of them came a flash. Zoey flinched.

There was a violent crunching as the Vulture's claw slammed down around her. She had just enough time to look through the blades at Mira, vainly struggling to get to her feet, to reach the little girl, to stop this from happening, but it was too late.

"Good-bye, Mira," Zoey whispered.

Then she screamed as the claw yanked her up into the sky and the flight of airships powered away, leaving Bismarck and Mira and Holt and Max and everyone and everything behind.

Scion, the chilling projections came. Zoey shut her eyes tightly. *You are home.*

MIRA LUNGED OUT THE DOOR and into the street. Her head was still dazed and foggy, and it wasn't from the attack. What had Zoey *done* to her? She had *felt* those ships approach. It had been like sharp, cutting whispers in her mind, but without language, just sensation. It felt like she had heard them *thinking* . . .

Mira shoved through the crowd, ignoring the flames and the yells of pain and shock. The gunships were gone, but they had left their mark. A burning building collapsed nearby. White Helix carried injured friends to hurriedly erected aid stations. The Menagerie were trying to lift a crumpled, warped sedan off where it had trapped someone.

"Mira!" Holt shouted, and she spotted him pushing through the crowd. Max was with him, staring with anxiety at all the chaos. They met next to a bent station wagon, and she could see the look of worry on Holt's face. "Where's Zoey?"

The question hit her like a hammer. She hadn't let herself think about it, had only concentrated on the immediate. Focusing, grabbing her things, getting down to the street, putting one foot in front of the other.

Now she saw it all over again. Zoey's last words. The explosion that divided them. The sight of her being ripped away, her screams. Zoey had been there one second, then gone the next. It had all happened so fast.

But that was no excuse. It was *her* fault.

Holt took a surprised step back as Mira swung her pack and shattered what was left of the car's rear window. Everyone nearby stopped what they were doing and stared.

It only made her feel worse.

She raised the pack again to—

"Mira," Holt's hand stopped her. She looked at him—and then she felt the tears form. Hot, angry ones. She leaned against the car and brought her shaking hands to her face, trying to hide what was obvious to anyone who looked.

Holt's arms wrapped around her. She sunk into his chest and time seemed to slow. Zoey was *gone*.

She sensed the crowd moving in, heard figures land on top of the station wagon. "Where's the Prime?" a voice she recognized demanded.

Mira held on to Holt and looked up at Dane and two other White Helix. It was clear they had already guessed the answer. "You *lost* her!"

The words cut like a knife.

"Back off!" Holt yelled up at Dane. "You saw those gunships, what was she supposed to do?"

"She shouldn't have had her on the *roof!* She lost her!" As he spoke the Lancet twirled from his back and aimed down. In the same instant Holt drew his Ithaca and pulled Mira behind him. Max growled low and vicious.

"Dane!" A strong voice stopped him cold. Maybe the only voice that could. Avril stood a few feet away, out front of what was left of the Menagerie. Her hands were bound, Mira saw. Her Lancet was gone. Ravan stood next to her, and in spite of everything the daughter of Tiberius Marseilles seemed calm.

"The Tower's gone now," Avril said, wincing in the sunlight. "It can't help Zoey anymore, there's nothing anyone could have done."

Dane didn't seem to hear the words. His fury at Mira was quickly replaced with fury at the lengths of rope that bound Avril's hands. His eyes found Ravan and he spoke with barely contained menace. "Set her free—or you will all die."

Ravan just smiled. She didn't even reach for the rifle on her back. "Well, that wouldn't be very . . . *honorable* of you. Would it?"

"It's *my* choice, Dane," Avril said, though it was clear she wasn't completely resolved. "It's what Gideon wanted."

"Gideon's *dead!*" Dane spat. "And with the Prime gone, so is everything he believed in. What was the point of *any* of this? Can anyone tell me?"

Mira heard Zoey's last words in her mind. *I . . . made a deal, kind of. A trade.*

Thoughts swirled in her head, trying to form into something solid. "I think she may have planned this," Mira said, and everyone looked at her. "It sounded like . . . she used the Tower to set all this in motion."

"You mean she *wanted* the Assembly to take her?" Ravan asked dubiously.

"How convenient for you, Frebooter," Dane said with a sneer.

"Mira," Holt said, tilting her face up with her hands. "If she told you that, then she had something figured out. You *have* to know what it is; she would have told you somehow."

Mira thought back desperately, running through the conversation again, but only one thing really stuck out. "Zoey did something to me. She . . . touched me. Went inside my mind, changed something."

"Changed *what?*" Avril asked.

She shook her head. "When the airships got close, I could . . . feel them. *Hear* them. Their thoughts. I could—"

Mira cut off suddenly as similar "thoughts" pushed into her mind. They were like projections of sensation, forced to the forefront, and while they didn't hurt, it wasn't pleasant having her own thoughts overwritten. They weren't words. It was more like the inherent meanings *behind* words, the intent, the emotion, and they stood out in her mind, whether she wanted them to or not.

Guardian, they said. *We come.*

Mira stood up and away from the car and peered to the south. A five-legged walker charged toward them, flanked on either side by two Hunters. The sight of them was striking. Their distinctive green and orange was gone. Now there was only bare metal, shining in the sun.

The White Helix tensed as the walkers approached. So did the Menagerie. But the walkers stopped several blocks away, keeping distance between them. "Ambassador . . ." Mira said.

Guardian, the projection came. It was clear who she was communicating with, and the realization sent a chill down her back.

"Why call me that?" she asked out loud. She could see everyone staring back and forth between her and the walkers in the distance. The idea that she could suddenly talk to the Assembly, the great enemy of humanity, was an unsettling one, but Mira didn't care.

You are the Guardian of the Scion, Ambassador projected into her mind.

Mira felt her shame intensify. Whether the title was meant as an insult, given what had just occurred, she couldn't tell, but she didn't like it much, regardless.

"Do you know what's happened?" Maybe she could use her mind to talk to the aliens, but she'd be damned if she would. She wasn't one of them, and they weren't her friends. She felt Holt's hand slip into hers and she took strength from it.

Mas'Shinra has the Scion, came the reply. *They fly west.*

"What's west?"

The Collective. Mira stared back in confusion, and her frustration must have been discernible. *You say the Citadel.*

Mira's eyes widened. The Citadel was something she knew. Everyone in North America probably did. She had never seen it, but it was supposedly a giant Assembly structure that rose over city ruins far to the west, so big it dwarfed even the Presidiums. Unlike those base ships, the Citadel had been built by the Assembly where it stood, fabricated from tons of harvested resources from all over the continent. Most survivors considered it the Assembly's seat of power, and everyone gave it a wide berth.

"They're taking her to the Citadel," Mira said, and stunned murmurs swept through the crowd.

"If that's the case, your little friend's good and gone," Ravan declared. "The Citadel's in San Francisco. It'll take weeks to get there, and you have to go through the Barren to do it. Whatever the Assembly plan to do with her, they'll have done it long before you ever make it."

Mira wanted to feel anger at Ravan, but she couldn't. She was right, and Mira only felt anger at herself. The Assembly might as well have been taking her across the sea.

"Landships," Holt said next to her. "In Freezone. Currency is . . . what? Two days' hard walk from here? We can take Landships from there, be at the Citadel in less than a week."

"Even if you somehow got the Wind Traders to help you, that's still too long," Ravan said. "Those ships'll be there in a *few hours.*"

"Well, we have to do *something!*" Holt yelled back. "We have to try!"

"This is ludicrous," Dane said above them.

"Your eyes are clear, Dane," Avril said. "She healed us, and brought us back from the dead."

Dane looked at Avril with intensity. He didn't say anything else.

Ravan, however, wasn't convinced. "She saved my men from the Tone, too. I'm grateful, don't get me wrong, but I'm not marching off to the ocean on some fool's errand. I got things that need finishing." Mira saw her stare settle on Holt, and he returned it.

More murmurs passed through the crowd, doubtful ones, and it broke apart around Holt and Mira into hundreds of groups, all debating and yelling. Mira ignored it all. There was only one person whose opinion mattered to her, and she looked at him now.

"Ravan's right," Holt told her. "Even if we got there in a week, even if we somehow wrangled enough Landships to carry all the White Helix— it's suicide. Have you ever seen the Citadel? Because I have. You think the army we saw yesterday was big? It's nothing compared to what's *there.*"

Mira stared at him in genuine dismay. "So you're saying . . . what? We just . . . let her go? We let them have her?"

"No." Holt shook his head. His next few words he said as soberly and as pointedly as he could. "I'm saying . . . if we do this . . . it's going to be a one-way trip."

Mira stared back at him, his meaning sinking in. There was no real chance of success. They would die trying to free Zoey—but they would still have tried.

Mira stared at Holt a few more seconds, then simply nodded.

Holt grabbed his Ithaca from the ground and tightened his pack in place. Mira did the same with her things, and they both started walking, pushing past the angry, yelling crowd, ignoring all of it. Holt whistled and Max chased after them.

Mira motioned for Holt's shotgun. He handed it to her, along with a fistful of shells. "You know how to do that?"

"I can build six-tiered artifact combinations," she said and shoved a shell into the chamber, then rammed the pump, priming the shell. "I can handle loading a shotgun."

"I like you more every day," Holt said and grabbed a magazine for his rifle, loading it as they walked.

As they moved through the crowd the arguments silenced, and everyone turned and watched the two figures heading south purposefully.

Ravan leaned casually against a warped sedan, staring at them. After a moment, she sighed and rolled her eyes. "Boys, mount up," she said forcefully. "I believe we are done here." Her men obeyed, securing their packs and guns. Ravan stood away from the car and pushed Avril forward. "That means you, too, dear heart." The small Doyen stared daggers, but started moving all the same.

As the Menagerie stepped into line next to them, Holt and Mira glanced at Ravan. The pirate shook her head with contempt. To Ravan, what they were doing was a bad idea, it was foolish to put other people's needs before your own, but Mira didn't care. It was what she had to do.

Something fell to the ground in front of them. A pair of black goggles, the kind the White Helix wore. Two more pairs fell. Four more. A dozen more. Everyone looked up as they walked. There, high above, figures leaped in between the ruined buildings in flashes of yellow and cyan.

"Well, well," Ravan said with amusement, watching the White Helix jump rooftop to rooftop. "Aren't *we* a motley crew?"

Avril looked up with everyone else—and smiled at the sight of her brothers, dozens at first, but growing, gradually becoming a wave of color that followed after them. Dozens turned to hundreds. Hundreds became thousands, blocking out the sky, dropping their goggles to the ground as they did in a shower of black. They no longer needed them, Mira guessed. There was no more Pattern to *see*.

Guardian, a projection cut through everything. Ambassador and the silver Hunters waited just a block away, their three optic eyes flickering back and forth. Mira stared at them.

We are . . . of you, it projected.

It was cryptic. Had it been just words, Mira might not have understood, but it was more. It was emotion, and intent. For reasons still uncertain, Ambassador and the others had come here to keep Zoey from falling into Assembly hands. They had failed—and now there was only one course open to them. The same as Mira's and Holt's.

Mira nodded to the machine as they approached, and answered with a single word. "Okay."

Ambassador turned and stomped southward, followed by the Hunters. Light flickered brightly off the armor of the rest of the silver Assembly in the distance. Engines roared to life. Walkers began to move. Dropships lifted off, gathering up machines for transport.

Bright flashes and pulses of sound accompanied dozens of other walkers like Ambassador, teleporting in with yet more forces. Mantises, even three or four Spiders, all of them beginning to move, joining the others, their footfalls echoing like thunder.

All around them the White Helix were landing on the ground, thousands, stretching in every direction, following after Holt and Mira, chanting a single word, over and over. *"Strength! Strength! Strength!"*

For once, she and Holt weren't alone. On the contrary, as strange as it was, it appeared they had an *army*.

"Go find her, boy," Holt told Max, and whistled three loud notes.

Max darted forward, eagerly tearing ahead of everyone, blowing past three of the silver Hunters. They trumpeted in surprise, racing after the dog, but even they couldn't keep up with him.

Holt took Mira's hand. She gripped it tightly. They walked south; down one last, unseeable road. Together.

Don't miss the third book in the

THE CONQUERED EARTH SERIES

VALLEY

OF
FIRES

AVAILABLE FALL 2014